IMPECCABLE

THE PHOENIX CLUB
BOOK SEVEN

DARCY BURKE

Zealous Quill Press

IMPECCABLE

Society's most exclusive invitation...

Welcome to the Phoenix Club, where London's most audacious, disreputable, and intriguing ladies and gentlemen find scandal, redemption, and second chances.

Former courtesan and pretend widow Evangeline Renshaw is happy with her reinvented life as a patroness of the Phoenix Club. She doesn't need or want a husband or a lover...until she meets the devastatingly charming and surprisingly virtuous Lord Gregory Blakemore. He'd like to court her, but he'll have to settle for a short, thrilling affair instead.

After the death of his father and the marriage of his older brother, Lord Gregory can finally focus on what he wants: a government appointment. However, the enchanting Evie makes him desire intimacy for the first time, and now he wants her most of all. Their entanglement is supposed to be temporary, but he can't let her go.

As Gregory reveals himself to Evie, she wonders if she might finally share the truth of her past. Unfortunately, there are those who seek to ruin her carefully crafted second chance. To protect Gregory's dreams, she must sacrifice the only love she's ever known.

Don't miss the rest of *The Phoenix Club* series!

Do you want to hear all the latest about me and my books? Sign up at <u>Reader Club newsletter</u> for members-only bonus content, advance notice of pre-orders, insider scoop, as well as contests and giveaways!

Care to share your love for my books with like-minded readers? Want to hang with me and see pictures of my cats (who doesn't!)? Then don't miss my exclusive Facebook groups!

Darcy's Duchesses for historical readers
Burke's Book Lovers for contemporary readers

Want more historical romance? Do you like your historical romance filled with passion and red hot chemistry? Join me and my author friends in the Facebook group, Historical Harlots, for exclusive giveaways, chat with amazing HistRom authors, and more!

CHAPTER 1

Oxfordshire, December 1815

*E*vangeline Renshaw could almost imagine she was strolling in the park, as she liked to do at home in London. She was, however, at her brother-in-law's sprawling new estate. Did her sister Heloise actually live here? Evie could hardly believe it. Or that Heloise was a mother. Or that she was happier than either of them ever dreamed they could be.

And that made Evie happy.

A soft whimper sounded from the hedgerow not far from the dirt track where Evie was walking. She held very still and listened, wondering if she was hearing things that weren't there. But the sound came again, prompting her to venture onto the damp grass and make her way to the hedgerow.

Crouching down, Evie peered into the shrubbery. "Is someone there?"

A white head poked out, its dark brown eyes fixing on

Evie. The animal surveyed her a moment before letting out another gentle whimper.

"Are you caught?" Evie moved closer.

The dog jerked back into the hedgerow, surprising Evie. She lost her balance and fell back on her rump. "Blast," she muttered.

"Is someone over there?" A low masculine voice called from the other side of the hedgerow.

Evie stared at the shrubbery as if she could see through the thick greenery. "Yes. There is a dog in the hedgerow. I think he—or she—may be stuck."

"I thought I heard a whimper," the man said.

"I seem to have frightened it," Evie said. "It showed me its face, but when I moved too close, it retreated."

"Let's see if I can coax him out. Here, doggy," he cajoled. "Let us help."

He received another whimper in response.

"Do you see him?" Evie asked, pushing up to her knees and leaning forward.

"I do. He's very sweet."

"Or she."

"Or she," he said. "How are you, then, little doggy?" the man asked in a surprisingly tender voice. "He—or she—looks young."

Evie hadn't noticed, but then her experience with dogs was limited to the ones she'd fed scraps to on the streets of Soho in her youth. "You are familiar with dogs, then?" she asked.

"Somewhat." His voice changed to that softer lilt. "Can you come out? Or are you stuck in there, poor thing? Let me help," the man coaxed.

This was met with a yelp and considerable rustling in the hedgerow. The dog's white face peeked forth once more on Evie's side, along with the upper half of its body. Evie grabbed its shoulders and held fast, despite the animal's wriggling. "I've got you," she said softly.

"Don't let go!" the man called. "I'm coming!"

He was? Rather than look up and down the hedgerow for an opening, Evie kept her gaze fixed on the small dog who was still trying to get loose of her grip. She attempted to pull the animal free, but this was met with a louder whimper than the rest. It seemed he—or she—*was* stuck.

"Do hurry!" she yelled to the man, wherever he was.

"We're only trying to help," she said to the dog. "Will you let us? You're awfully cute." Evie brought her face even with the animal's, perhaps unwisely. What if it tried to bite her? "You won't nip at me, will you?" she said with a confidence she didn't quite feel. "We're going to be friends. In fact, I think we are already."

The dog stopped struggling so much. Its gaze held hers, then he—or she—let out another whimper. Where was the gentleman?

Evie turned her head to the right and saw him bearing down on them. She didn't have time to assess him before he was down on his knees in the grass beside her. "It seems stuck," she told him. "I can't pull it free."

"Hold on, and I'll reach in." The man tucked his hands into the hedgerow around the dog. "Ah, yes, there. Its foot is stuck in the branches. I can work it free..." He pressed himself against the hedgerow as he worked, allowing Evie a view of his profile. He was white, with pale, narrow brows that drew together over his rich brown eyes as he worked. His strong jaw clenched, pressing his lips together. He was very attractive. And he looked familiar.

Suddenly, the dog vaulted forward, straight into Evie's chest, sending her off-balance. Because she was on her knees, she fell to the side. She managed, however, to hold the dog close. "I've got you," she murmured.

The dog squirmed, and Evie feared it would run away. "Don't go," she pleaded, not yet ready for this unexpected adventure to end.

Was that because of the dog or the gentleman?

The dog! She had no interest in gentlemen, even if they were handsome and vaguely familiar.

"Are you all right?" the man asked.

"Yes, just give us a moment. I think he—or she—is settling down." Evie kept her gaze locked with the animal's. "Aren't you? This isn't a bad place to be, is it? Certainly better than that nasty old hedgerow."

"I would say so," the man responded.

She resisted the urge to look toward him, thinking it was best if she maintained her attention on the dog. Doing so seemed to calm it.

"You're doing wonderfully," the man said. "You must have a great deal of experience with dogs. Or animals in general."

It depended on the type of animal, but she was fairly certain he didn't mean those of his own species. Those, she knew quite well. "Actually, no. I've never had a pet." Or known anyone with a pet.

"Extraordinary. Well, I'd say you're naturally inclined. I think you may have a pet now."

"I can't have a pet." She said the words without thinking and immediately hoped the dog didn't somehow understand and take offense. "But if I did, I would choose you," she said, smiling at the dog.

The dog tipped its head, then nuzzled her chin. Oh, dear.

"I don't think the dog agrees that you can't have a pet." The man chuckled softly. "Can I help you up?"

She couldn't lie about in the damp grass. "What do I do with the dog?"

The man edged forward slowly and spoke softly to the dog, whispering encouragement and endearments. It really was quite sweet. Then he stroked the animal and gradually transferred it into his arms. Moving the dog, which did appear to be an older puppy, perhaps, to one arm, he rose, then gave his hand to Evie.

She clasped him, and her gaze immediately riveted to his. He helped her to stand, all while keeping the animal in his grip.

"Well done," Evie said. "You are quite the hero."

"No more than you. I am Gregory Blakemore." He inclined his head, still holding her hand.

Now she knew him—they'd met last Season in London. "Don't you mean *Lord* Gregory?"

The man's father was a marquess. Or had been. Evie recalled that he'd passed away in the spring. Which meant Lord Gregory's older brother was now the marquess.

"I suppose," he responded. "Seems unnecessary here, in this moment," he added. His brows knitted. "Have we met?"

Evie released him. Somewhat reluctantly, which she refused to credit. "Last Season. You were nearly courting a friend of mine—she is now Lady Overton."

"Ah. Forgive me for not recalling you, Miss…"

"Mrs. Renshaw," she said. "I am widowed." Why had she felt the need to add that detail?

"So young," he murmured. Not terribly young. Evie was twenty-five. "I'm sorry for your loss."

"Thank you." She always felt a small sting of discomfort when people said this. Because she wasn't actually a widow. Evangeline Renshaw was a fabrication. Or, more accurately, a reinvention. "I'm sorry for yours—your father, I mean."

"Thank you."

She saw the flash of sorrow in his warm brown eyes. "Were you close?"

He nodded. "I miss him a great deal."

Evie wondered if he still had a mother—she'd lost her

parents long ago. It was just her and her older sister, Heloise. "At least you have your brother," she said kindly.

This time a shadow passed over his features. "I do."

There was an undeniable tension in his response, but Evie wasn't going to pry. "What are we going to do about the dog?" He—that was no longer in question now that he was free and fully visible—was happily snuggled in Lord Gregory's embrace. Evie fancied that was a rather nice place to be. She wondered what he smelled like.

No, she did *not. Would* not.

"You should take him home. And feed him immediately. He feels rather skinny." He scratched the pup's head. "Aren't you, boy?"

"Didn't you hear me?" Evie tried not to sound aghast. "I can't have a pet."

Lord Gregory appeared bemused. "Why not?"

"Because…I've never had one, and I don't know how. Please, you must keep him."

He looked down at the dog. "I suppose we should try to see if he has an owner. Perhaps one of the tenants had a litter in recent months. I'd say he's a few months old at least."

"I will tell Alfred—that is, Mr. Creighton—about it." Alfred was Evie's brother-in-law, but since she'd reinvented herself two years ago as Mrs. Renshaw, she couldn't claim Heloise as her sister. Not without exposing herself and her disreputable past.

Lord Gregory's eyes lit. "How is it you are associated with our new neighbors?"

"The Creightons are dear friends of mine." She sought to quickly change the subject to avoid further questions. "Does this hedgerow divide your estate from theirs?"

"It does. Though, it isn't my estate. It's my brother's."

"Then I suppose you'll have to ask his tenants as well. There's no telling which side he came from."

"You make a good point," Lord Gregory said. "I will keep him while we search for a potential owner."

Evie looked at the sweet puppy and stroked his head. "You will be well looked after."

"He will indeed, and if we are unable to find whoever owns him, I shall endeavor to change your mind about taking him. Everyone needs a pet at least once."

She kept her mouth closed, not wishing to debate him. "I'll walk with you back to wherever you came through." Why? She should take her leave immediately. She didn't need or want a pet or a gentleman friend. She had plenty of gentlemen friends in London. None of whom made her heart pick up speed or her flesh tingle.

"I squeezed between the shrubbery and that ash tree." He nodded in the direction from which he'd come.

"Ash," Evie murmured, looking at the pup. Perhaps she could try having a pet. And what if it didn't work or she was terrible at it? She couldn't abandon the poor thing. She would never do that. "We should call him Ash," she suggested.

"It goes with his coloring for certain," Lord Gregory said with a faint smile. "Ash it is. Remember, I am only keeping him for you until you're ready to claim ownership."

"I won't, but I would appreciate the opportunity to visit."

No, you would not. You should run away from both these creatures.

They started toward the tree.

"I'll see about having my brother invite you and the Creightons to Witney Court. I should like to meet them."

Evie wondered if that would actually happen. Not Lord Gregory speaking with them—she believed he would do what he said. She just didn't think the invitation would be forthcoming. Alfred had purchased Threadbury Hall six months ago, and they'd moved into the house in July. At no point had their neighbors at Witney Court made any invitation or overture of any kind, which Alfred and Heloise attributed to the fact that the household was in mourning. However, the marquess had married nearly two months ago, so Evie supposed it was *possible* an invitation or visit might occur.

Or not.

Cynicism about members of Society was something Evie doubted she'd ever be able to shed. It was ironic since she had so many friends who moved in that upper echelon. But those people were different. They were the members of Society who didn't feel as though they entirely belonged or who had been ignored or disdained for one reason or another. These were the people whom her close friend Lord Lucien Westbrook invited to join the Phoenix Club, a membership club for men—and women—that Evie managed. She was also one of four patronesses of the club, which was as close to that most revered sector of Society as she ever wanted to get.

That Society had refused to welcome Heloise after her marriage to Alfred was perhaps the primary reason Evie couldn't ever embrace it fully. Heloise had been Alfred's mistress, and though they'd fallen in love, the ton couldn't forgive or forget Heloise's past. What would they think if they knew the truth—that she and Evie were the daughters of a French chevalier who'd been killed during the Terror? Evie wasn't naïve enough to think that would matter. Many in Society liked to think they were better than others. It was the basis of their self-worth.

"Did I lose you?" Lord Gregory asked as they approached the tree.

Evie shook her head gently. "Not at all. I'm certain the Creightons would be delighted to meet their neighbors."

Heloise, in the interest of being friendly, might even try to invite them to Threadbury Hall.

Lord Gregory turned to face her, his lips turning up slightly. "This is where we leave you, I'm afraid. What will I do if Ash despairs in your absence?"

Evie knew that was nonsense. Was Lord Gregory flirting with her? It didn't seem like it—he was refreshingly genuine. "He won't."

"I suppose not. You did say you wished to visit, and I shall ensure your parting is short, if not temporary."

"Your persistence is unwavering. Anyway, I suspect you'll find where he belongs. A child is perhaps missing him even now." That pulled at Evie's heartstrings, both because she hated to think of a child saddened by the loss of their pet and because she didn't want Ash to belong to anyone.

Except perhaps to her.

No! She didn't have time for a dog.

"That may be true," Lord Gregory said. "I'll keep you informed." He started to turn toward the opening between the hedge and tree, but Evie stopped him.

"One last nuzzle," she said softly, cupping Ash's sweet face. His round brown eyes met hers, and she nearly succumbed. The pup didn't need Lord Gregory's help in trying to persuade her to keep him.

Evie kissed the dog's head and quickly backed away. "Thank you for taking care of him."

Lord Gregory inclined his head, then disappeared through the hedgerow. She watched him turn to the left, which was the direction she would go. Indeed, she could just make out the top of his hat over the shrubbery. He couldn't see her, however.

"Are you still there?" he asked a moment later.

Evie smiled to herself. "For a while. Until I need to turn toward the house."

"I see. There is an assembly in town day after tomorrow. Will you be there?"

"I don't know." Evie didn't really want to go, but Heloise would continue trying to convince her that it would be engaging. In the end, Evie would likely attend in order to please her sister.

"It will be my first social event since my father died," he said in a lower tone that made her have to strain a bit to hear him. "Except for my brother's engagement ball in London and his wedding breakfast at Witney Court. Those don't count, however, as I wasn't actually looking forward to attending them."

She wasn't sure if she ought to encourage him or not. "Only go if you're ready."

"I appreciate you saying that." Indeed, she heard the warmth in his voice even though the hedgerow separated them.

Evie heard a horse's hooves from the other side of the hedgerow and looked over to see a white female rider approach Lord Gregory.

"What do you have there, Gregory?" The voice belonged to a young woman and carried the cultured tone of London High Society.

"We found a puppy in the hedgerow. I'm going to determine if he belongs to anyone. Poor thing needs food and water, I think."

"Who is 'we'?" The question was haughty, almost accusatory.

"I met your new neighbor. Well, their guest anyway. Are you there, Mrs. Renshaw?"

Evie froze. She didn't want to be part of that conversation. It was nearly time for her to turn toward the house anyway. Except she didn't go. Instead, she edged closer to the hedgerow so she wouldn't be seen over the top by the rider.

"Where is she?" the young woman asked.

"She was on the other side of the hedgerow, but she must have continued on her way to the house. I told her we'd invite the Creightons—and her—for…something. Dinner, perhaps?"

"I'm not sure Cliff is ready to do that." The young woman, who must be Lord Gregory's sister-in-law, sniffed.

"He seems ready to attend the assembly in a few days." Lord Gregory sounded strained, almost…irritated.

"Yes, well, that's different from entertaining. Honestly, Gregory, don't you know anything about these new neighbors? His father was *in trade*, and she was his mistress before they wed."

"How would you know that?" Now he definitely sounded annoyed.

"My mother told me in a letter after I informed her who our new neighbors were."

"I don't know why any of that matters. I'm sure they're lovely people."

"Oh, Gregory." She laughed. "Your fervent kindness and understanding are so quaint. You are going to make an excellent bishop one day."

Bishop? Evie now vaguely remembered that he was rumored to perhaps be looking for a living—surely his marquess father or now brother could have provided one. She also recalled that he'd taught at Oxford.

"I'm going to talk to Clifford about this." Lord Gregory sounded farther away, as if he'd started walking.

"Go right ahead. In the meantime, do not bring that mongrel into my house. He'll have to stay in the stables." Hooves sounded against the ground once more, and Evie determined the busybody had ridden away.

Frowning, Evie cut across the damp grass toward the track that led back to Threadbury Hall. She regretted not taking Ash with her. He wouldn't be happy in the stables all by himself.

But he wouldn't be, of course. Certainly, the stable lads would be delighted to have him. Indeed, he'd likely be more pampered there.

Or perhaps Lord Gregory would ignore his sister-in-law's edict. That house had been his home for far longer than hers, after all. Yes, that was what Evie wished to believe, that Lord Gregory would keep Ash safe and warm.

By the time she reached the house, she'd convinced herself that Lord Gregory would find Ash's home quickly and she'd never see the puppy again. That was for the best, just as it would be that she didn't see Lord Gregory again. He was far too charming. Too handsome. Too…kind and understanding, to borrow his horrid sister-in-law's description.

Heloise was seated in the small drawing room, which Evie entered from the rear patio. "How was your walk?"

"Chilly." Evie said nothing about finding Ash or encountering Lord Gregory. She especially wasn't going to mention the nasty neighbor. She'd tell Alfred about the dog and ask if he could investigate the matter with his tenants.

"I've news to share." Heloise's blue eyes, so similar to Evie's own, sparkled with excitement. "We've decided to host a dinner party for some of the neighbors. It will be a couple of nights after the assembly."

Evie paused in removing her hat. "Which neighbors?"

"Several people, notably the vicar and his wife, and Lord and Lady Witney. The vicar said they are receiving invitations and will attend the assembly."

"Did you already invite everyone?" Evie asked, hoping these were plans that had not yet been executed.

"Yes. Alfred went to distribute the invitations. I would have gone with him, but Henry was fussing." Henry, named for their father, was Evie's year-old nephew.

Suppressing a groan, Evie tried to summon a smile and failed. She didn't want to tell Heloise what she'd overheard earlier, but then she ought to prepare her sister for Lady Witney's meanness. Except Heloise looked so happy. She deserved a nice evening. Perhaps Evie could ensure the Witneys didn't come. It wasn't as if they wanted to.

"I've decided to attend the assembly after all," Evie said, sweeping her hat from her head and removing her gloves.

"Splendid!" Heloise's joyful response was cut short when her eyes narrowed slightly. "Why the sudden change of heart? I thought I was going to have to drag you."

"Because I know how much it means to you," Evie said warmly. That, and she'd use the opportunity to encourage Lord Gregory to keep his brother and sister-in-law at home.

"I'm so pleased, thank you. I know you worry you'll be recognized someday." Heloise's gaze filled with sympathy. She didn't like that Evie had chosen to hide her identity, to pretend to be someone she wasn't. And sometimes Evie agreed with her. Sometimes, she wanted everyone to know that she and Heloise were sisters, that they'd been visited by tragic circumstance and had risen from the ashes—like phoenixes—to not only survive, but thrive.

However, Evie wasn't like Heloise. She didn't have her sister's strength and confidence. Everyone thought Evie possessed those traits, but they didn't *really* know her. She didn't want them to. It was easier to hide herself, particularly her past as a courtesan, than face scrutiny and certain rejection.

"I'll just keep my eyes open for who is in attendance. It's unlikely any of the gentlemen who might recognize me from my Cyprian days will be at a rural assembly in Oxfordshire." Most of those men were either her friends, or they wouldn't want to reveal her past for fear of implicating their own scandalous behavior. Evie smiled at her sister to ease her concern.

Heloise nodded. "I'm sure you're right about that."

Evie had preferred when her sister and Alfred had lived farther north, in Nottinghamshire. There'd been little chance of running into anyone from London there. But they'd wanted a larger house, more land, and to be closer to Evie in London.

"I'm going to take a warm bath," Evie said, crossing the drawing room.

"Wonderful," Heloise murmured.

Evie paused at the doorway and looked back at her sister. Her head was bent over her needlework. She looked the consummate country squire's wife—exactly what she should be. No, she should be a countess or a duchess. That had been their station. Before war and chance had torn it away.

Stiffening, Evie turned and pushed the bitterness from her mind.

CHAPTER 2

*G*regory Blakemore hadn't been terribly enthused about attending the assembly in Witney until he'd met Mrs. Renshaw. He only hoped she actually came, for she hadn't responded to his query on the matter.

He'd sent a note the afternoon before, letting her know he'd found the tenant whose dog had birthed Ash and several other puppies. They'd been happy to let Gregory keep him. He'd also asked if she would be at the assembly. Her response had only said she was delighted he would get to keep Ash.

"You coming?" Clifford Blakemore, Marquess of Witney and Gregory's older brother by eighteen months, peered up into the coach.

"Yes." Gregory stepped down outside the small assembly rooms. They were rustic compared to what they were used to in London, but Gregory liked their simplicity. They also reminded him of his youth, of dancing with young ladies when he was home from Oxford. And of preventing and saving Clifford from bad behavior ranging from drinking too much brandy and falling unconscious next to the reflecting pool in the garden to nearly being caught kissing the innkeeper's wife near the retiring room.

Susan, Gregory's sister-in-law, pursed her lips, her thin, sharp brows drawing together over her deep brown eyes. "It's so...lacking."

"You haven't even been inside yet," Gregory said, trying not to let her agitate him. He found her arrogance most tiresome. It was also a shame, because when he'd first met her last spring before their father had died, she'd seemed rather pleasant. Her demeanor had changed entirely after she'd become betrothed to Clifford.

"They aren't so bad," Clifford said. "They're no Almack's, of course."

Thank goodness, Gregory thought.

"The gardens in the rear are quite lovely," Clifford continued. A faint, somewhat lascivious smile passed over his features, and Gregory wondered which misbehavior he was recalling. Perhaps it was one about which Gregory wasn't even aware, though hopefully there were few of those. Gregory had taken care to keep his older brother from causing trouble or embarrassment given their family's position in the community. "My father funded their maintenance. I suppose that's my responsibility now."

"Shouldn't everyone in the area contribute?" Susan asked. "It isn't just for *our* enjoyment."

"That's not very charitable of you," Gregory noted, working to keep the irritation from his tone. "The town of Witney has been our family's seat for generations. It is the marquessate's duty, indeed its honor, to provide such support." He turned toward the doors. "Now, let us join the festivities." Where he would do everything possible to avoid her for the rest of the evening. He was glad Witney Court was so large. With the exception of dinner, he was able to mostly keep himself from her path.

Before Clifford offered his arm to his wife, he leaned toward Gregory and whispered, "Please be kind to Susan."

Gregory gritted his teeth, summoned a bland smile, and followed them inside. Immediately, he looked for Mrs. Renshaw. It was possible, if not probable, that she wasn't present, but Gregory would hope. She would stand out, for she was a stunning beauty. Indeed, he couldn't understand why he didn't recall meeting her last Season, especially since she remembered him.

Ah well, he'd set out—rather nervously and at his father's behest—to find a bride last Season. He'd thought Miss Wingate, now Lady Overton, might be the one, but she'd apparently been falling for her guardian, who was now her husband. In any case, the sudden death of his father from apoplexy had cut the Season short.

There she was. Standing near the rear doors dressed in a vibrant, coral-hued gown, Mrs. Renshaw exuded confidence and grace. Gregory made his way toward her, purposely keeping his gaze from connecting with anyone else's. First and foremost, he wanted to greet Mrs. Renshaw.

He slowed his gait as his brain took charge for a moment. Why Mrs. Renshaw? He'd never paid particular attention to any woman, the former Miss Wingate notwithstanding. She had been a recommended means to an end, and while he'd liked her, he hadn't been *drawn* to her. Not like he was to Mrs. Renshaw. Why her?

He wasn't shallow enough to credit her beauty alone. She'd heard the puppy in distress and stopped to investigate. Not every woman would have done so. He was fairly certain his new sister-in-law wouldn't have. Perhaps it was the way Mrs. Renshaw had looked at Ash, as if she'd already fallen in love, but didn't dare succumb to the emotion. He found that reaction intriguing. He found everything about her intriguing. He was eager, almost desperate, to know more.

Quickening his pace, he made his way to her. Her enchanting blue eyes, round and turned up at the corners, sparked as she saw him. She was white, but her skin wasn't ivory like so many women in Society. Her complexion glowed with a rich color that looked as if she'd been kissed by the sun. Her brown hair possessed the same quality, as occasional golden strands seemed to shimmer in the candle-light. Her full lips pursed slightly as he stopped before her.

He bowed. "Good evening, Mrs. Renshaw. I am delighted to see you decided to come."

"Good evening, Lord Gregory."

Gregory realized the woman standing next to her was watching them. Mrs. Renshaw turned slightly toward her. "Heloise, this is Lord Gregory Blakemore, one of your neighbors at Witney Court."

The white woman's blue eyes were remarkably like Mrs. Renshaw's. Indeed, Gregory might have thought they were related. She smiled at Gregory and the white man beside her also gave his attention.

Mrs. Renshaw continued. "Lord Gregory, allow me to present my dear friends Mr. and Mrs. Alfred Creighton of Threadbury Hall."

Gregory bowed to Mrs. Creighton and offered his hand to her husband. "It's my pleasure to make your acquaintance. I do apologize for not calling on you. You will likely know we have been in mourning."

"Yes, of course," Creighton said, inclining his head. His thinning brown hair was compensated by rather long side-burns. It reminded Gregory of something his father said, that if a gentleman found the hair on his head to be lacking, he could be assured of it growing excessively well somewhere else. "My condolences on the loss of your father."

"Thank you. It was a shock, but we're adjusting. Finally." The months following his death had been awful, at least for

Gregory. He'd been very close to their father. Far closer than Clifford had been.

Gregory realized it had been just two days ago, when he'd met Mrs. Renshaw and found Ash, that he'd at last felt somewhat like his old self.

"I take it you and Evie know each other from London?" Mrs. Creighton asked.

Evie. A charming, buoyant name that suited her perfectly. Her parents must have seen her spirit the moment she was born.

Blast it all, he was beginning to think like a romantic.

"Yes," Mrs. Renshaw answered, since he was too busy generating silly thoughts. "We also encountered each other a few days ago—when I was out for a walk."

"Oh?" Mrs. Creighton's light-brown brows shot up as she glanced toward Mrs. Renshaw. Mrs. Creighton was clearly surprised, and Gregory found himself wondering why Mrs. Renshaw hadn't told her about meeting him.

"Yes, they found the puppy together," Creighton said to his wife. "Did I not mention that part?"

"You did not," Mrs. Creighton murmured, appearing slightly perturbed. Recovering, she gave Gregory a pleasant smile. "I take it you are caring for the dog?"

"I am." Since Mrs. Renshaw didn't want to. Belatedly, he realized why she hadn't wanted to take Ash with her—she was a guest in someone's home.

"How lovely of you," Mrs. Creighton responded.

Creighton clasped his hands behind his back. "I hope you heard about the dinner invitation I delivered to Witney Court. I spoke with Lady Witney briefly. I didn't know you were in residence. I do hope you'll come too."

Gregory wasn't entirely surprised that Susan hadn't told him about it. Given her haughty attitude and condescension about their new neighbors, he wondered if she would even deign to go. He'd bloody well make her—and his brother—attend. "I'd be delighted. Remind me when it is?" He didn't want to make it known that Susan hadn't shared the invitation with him.

"Day after tomorrow. We wanted to welcome everyone into Threadbury Hall as we've made some refurbishments."

"Splendid. I haven't been inside the house since I was a child. I shall be delighted to see what you've done. As it happens, I have a special interest in architecture and considered a career in it, but my father steered me toward the church."

Why had he told them that last part? Because it had been so much a part of his life the past several years that he'd done so without thinking. His father had wanted him to be a bishop, and Gregory had worked—if unenthusiastically—to achieve that end. And now that his father was gone, he could change course.

Creighton's sherry-colored eyes lit with interest. "I've more plans and would be keen to discuss them with you."

"It would be my pleasure." Gregory looked especially forward to the dinner. Spending the evening with Mrs. Renshaw was enticing enough. Now he had even more reason to anticipate the occasion.

He turned his attention to her. "I wondered if you might partner me—"

Mrs. Renshaw held up her hand, cutting him off before he could finish. "If you're going to ask me to dance, please don't. I did not come to dance."

Why had she come, then? He wanted to ask the question—and would—but not in front of her hosts. "A promenade, then? The gardens are lovely, and it's not too cold out if you have a wrap."

She hesitated before answering, and in that moment, Mrs.

Creighton shot her a puzzled look. "I can fetch it," Mrs. Renshaw said. "A promenade would be pleasant."

Gregory offered her his arm and inclined his head toward the Creightons.

"My pelisse is in the cloak room," Mrs. Renshaw indicated as they circuited the ballroom.

He'd assumed as much, which was why he hadn't steered them outside. "Do you not care for dancing?"

"I did before I wed," she said. "But I haven't done so in years."

"You can't have forgotten how," he suggested with a smile.

"No, but I don't find it as engaging as I once did."

"A promenade gives us more chance to talk anyway, so I can't say I'm disappointed. I thought you might like to hear how Ash is doing."

"Yes, please. I was wondering…does he sleep in your chamber?" She looked up at him—for she was a good seven or eight inches shorter than his six feet—expectantly.

"He does, in fact. My brother tried to persuade me to lodge him in the stables, but then he would interrupt the lads' slumber and perhaps their duties. I'm afraid he enjoys a jaunt somewhere between four and five in the morning. To relieve himself," he added in a whisper.

"I see. You are kind to care for him personally."

"I confess, when I am out with him at that hour, I completely understand why you preferred not to take him with you."

She laughed softly as they reached the cloak room. "I hadn't considered that, but I shall be grateful to my past self."

After they retrieved her pelisse, he helped her don it. She buttoned the front over her bodice, covering the flesh above it up to her neck.

Gregory offered his arm once more. "You don't regret not

taking him? I thought I might still persuade you. He's awfully sweet."

"I'm certain he is. However, I have not changed my mind about caring for a pet. I also had an agenda for seeing you this evening," she said, sparking his curiosity. And making his heart beat a trifle faster.

"I can hardly wait to hear it," he murmured, quickening their pace so they would get outside faster.

Suddenly, his brother blocked their path. "Care to introduce us?" Clifford asked, his gaze landing on Mrs. Renshaw, and his nostrils flaring almost imperceptibly.

Gregory recognized his brother's reaction. He'd never disguised his interest in attractive women. Indeed, his passion for them had frustrated their father no end. Clifford was married now only because he'd promised his father on his deathbed that he'd do so before the end of the year. That he'd kept that promise had impressed Gregory—and surprised him more than a little.

"Allow me to present Mrs. Renshaw. She's a guest at Threadbury Hall. Mrs. Renshaw, this is my brother, the Marquess of Witney and his wife, Lady Witney."

Susan hadn't stepped in front of them as Clifford had. She surveyed them from beneath hooded lids, her lips pursing slightly as she looked at Mrs. Renshaw.

The widow offered a curtsey to Clifford. "Good evening. I'm pleased to meet you, Lord and Lady Witney."

"The pleasure is mine," Clifford said, smiling broadly. "How do you know my brother?" He gave Gregory a look that seemed to ask why he hadn't been made aware of her.

"We know each other from the Phoenix Club in London," Mrs. Renshaw responded.

How Gregory hadn't put that together was astonishing. But then he'd only visited a few times. He'd been there the night his father had suffered his fit.

"Ah yes, I've heard of that. Vaguely." Clifford waved his hand as if the club were inconsequential. Of course, he would think so—he hadn't been invited to join.

"I'm a patroness there," Mrs. Renshaw said with a touch of ice. "I'm not surprised you aren't familiar with it, since you are not a member." Now she flashed a smile, but it was as cool as her tone.

"I wonder why that is?" Lady Witney asked. "He's a marquess after all."

Mrs. Renshaw lifted a shoulder, then looked to Gregory. "Shall we continue?"

"Yes. Pardon us, Clifford." Gregory guided her around his brother, who finally stepped aside.

They remained silent until they walked outside. Once on the terrace, he felt her relax slightly. "They made you tense," he observed.

"They are why I wanted to see you tonight." She glanced over her shoulder toward the doorway. "I was hoping you might ensure they don't attend the dinner at Threadbury Hall."

"Won't your hosts be disappointed?"

"Perhaps. However…" Her mouth tightened in consternation. "I overheard what Lady Witney said the other day on the other side of the hedgerow. I don't want to subject the Creightons to her."

Damn. He should have considered that she might have heard Susan's nonsense. "My apologies for my brother and sister-in-law. They…" What could he say to excuse them? "I would like to offer a reasonable explanation for her behavior, but I fear I cannot. I can ask them not to come, but it may be best if I say nothing." Susan didn't even want to go, which he wouldn't reveal to Mrs. Renshaw. In fact, it might be best if he didn't go either—perhaps Clifford and Susan would forget all about it.

Selfishly, Gregory didn't want to do that. He wanted to go.

"I see." She kept her gaze directed to the path in front of them, and he couldn't tell from her profile what she might be thinking.

Gregory chose his words carefully. "I could try speaking to Clifford, but I'm afraid my brother does what he likes. In some instances, my preferences will only ensure he does the opposite."

"He's spiteful, then?"

"On occasion." When they were children, Clifford had liked to laugh at others' expense. He still did, but had finally matured enough to realize neither Gregory nor their father appreciated such humor. That didn't stop him from laughing with his friends or perhaps even his wife, however.

"Then I suppose we must suffer their presence." Her tone was one of resigned distaste.

"I can promise to intervene if they cause any upset. Would that help?"

"Have you had to do that before?" She arched an elegant brow at him, and the expression stirred him in ways he found almost shocking. They were having a conversation about his irritating brother, and Gregory was moved to passion?

"Not them, no, but they've been married less than two months. I've sometimes had to usher my brother out of a situation—for his own good, mostly."

"You sound as if you should be the older brother."

Her words hit him straight in the heart. His father had said something similar as he lay dying. He'd told Gregory that he wished he'd been the heir. And he'd asked Gregory to look after his brother, to try to ensure the marquessate didn't suffer under his custody.

Gregory would try, but he doubted he'd be much help.

Clifford had made it clear since their father's death that he was glad to be free of his management, that he was eager to establish himself as the marquess.

"I am not the older brother, however," he responded. "Do you have siblings?"

"Yes. A sister."

He was reminded of how she and Mrs. Creighton looked as though they could be related. But if they were, Mrs. Renshaw surely would have said so. "I hope you are closer than my brother and me."

"Based on what you've said, I would say so. I admire her very much. This garden is beautifully laid out," she said, effectively changing the subject. He didn't mind.

"My family has supported it for generations. It is far more stunning in the summer, as you can imagine."

"I'm sure. What a wonderful thing for your family to do."

Gregory only hoped it would continue. Alas, regardless of what his father wanted, Gregory couldn't control what Clifford would do. In the end, if he wanted to cease the marquessate's support of the garden, he could. Very soon, Gregory was going to have to get back to his own life and pursue a career. For the first time in months, he was eager to do so—and he credited meeting Mrs. Renshaw.

"I didn't realize you were a patroness at the Phoenix Club," he said, impressed. "That is where we met?"

"Yes."

"I apologize for not remembering you. Indeed, I can't understand how that is possible. I must have lost my wits just before making your acquaintance."

She let out a soft, short laugh. "I am not offended to be found unremarkable. On the contrary, there is peace in anonymity, I think."

"It is statements like that one that make you utterly *remarkable*." Feeling inexplicably bold, he added, "I find myself captivated by you, and that has never happened before."

Color flamed her cheeks, and he was sorry to have caused her any discomfort. He rushed to say, "I didn't mean to embarrass you."

"It isn't that," she said. "It's just… You aren't like any gentleman I've met. They don't typically reveal what they are thinking in such a direct manner. It also seems as if you genuinely mean it, that you aren't offering an empty platitude."

"I *do* mean it. Flirtation and subtlety are somewhat beyond me." He shook his head, smiling faintly.

"I should be equally frank. While I am flattered, I am quite happy in my widowhood, and I've no plans to change my status. *Ever.*" She spoke kindly but firmly, leaving no question as to her intentions.

Now he *was* embarrassed. "I didn't mean to suggest anything. I like you. Perhaps we can be friends." Unless she preferred not to have male friends. Except Creighton was obviously a friend. Or was his wife her friend, and he just came with the bargain? Did *any* of that matter?

"I would like that." She gave him an arresting smile, and he began the disappointing process of telling himself not to react, either externally or internally. "Then I'll be able to visit Ash." She winked at him, and he nearly asked her not to do such things, that it wasn't fair. Except, he feared everything she did drew him to her.

"Perhaps you'd like to take a ride with me tomorrow?" he asked.

"I don't ride."

"Oh." Stupidly, he hesitated, as if he didn't know how to respond to her statement. Plenty of ladies didn't ride. "How about a drive, then? I'll bring Ash." That would actually be much better than a ride. He should have suggested it straightaway.

She stopped and turned toward him, her eyes narrowing slightly. "I'd planned to see you tonight and ask my favor regarding your brother and his wife. That was supposed to be the end of our association."

"You just said you wanted to be friends."

"I do, which is surprising and perhaps a little frustrating. After hearing Lady Witney the other day, I'd decided to avoid your family entirely."

"While I can appreciate your desire to stay clear of Susan —Lady Witney—I can assure you that I am nothing like her. Or my brother."

"I'm learning that." She studied him a moment. "Furthermore, you perplex me. You look as though you should be a confident rake swanning his way through London. Yet you are thoughtful, caring, and perhaps even a trifle, dare I say, awkward?" She shook her head. "Forgive me, that isn't the kindest word. I mean you seem slightly ill at ease."

Gregory couldn't help grinning. "I am most definitely awkward, particularly around fascinating, assertive women such as yourself. It was a problem when I was searching for a wife last Season."

"We can work on that." She pivoted back to facing forward in the direction they were taking along the path. "If you want to. I've been known to help people with certain things. Granted, they have all been women."

She was offering to help him? He *could* use guidance, particularly from a woman, if he wanted to find a wife. And it was an excellent reason to spend time with her. "You'll teach me the art of subtlety and flirtation? And not to be awkward?"

"I can try. Although, I'm not sure you shouldn't embrace your awkwardness. It's endearing."

A thrill shot through him. Gregory couldn't help feeling flattered. "I'll keep that in mind."

"Good. We'll start tomorrow when we take that drive."

They'd nearly finished their circuit of the garden. "I suppose we should go back inside," he said with great reluctance.

"I'm in no hurry. Let's go round again, and I'll do my best to convince you that your brother and sister-in-law must not come to dinner." She flashed him a coy smile.

"*That* looks like flirtation. Is that what I should do?"

"Certainly not. Men and women flirt differently. Believe it or not, many women find an aloof gentleman to be very attractive. Then, when you do cast your attentions toward a female, she'll be enthralled that you chose her over anyone else."

"That sounds rather manipulative."

"It is." She cocked her head as they started their second circuit. "I can see you aren't that sort of gentleman. You will woo a lady with your honesty and charm, your kindness and consideration. Conversation is your tool. You have the ability to put people at ease, I think. I predict you'll find an exceptional wife. That is your goal, isn't it?"

"Ultimately."

She slowed, her gaze settling on him for a moment. "Perhaps you aren't *entirely* forthcoming. I sense more to that single-word response. I won't press you tonight, but tomorrow, you can tell me what your real aspirations are." She'd seen through him.

"And if I don't know?"

Her lips spread into a breathtaking smile, and once more, he had to remind himself not to react on any level. "Don't you think it's time you find out?"

CHAPTER 3

*H*eloise held Henry on her hip. He had a terrifying grip on her coral necklace. "You're going for a drive with Lord Gregory?"

"Aren't you worried Henry is going to tear your necklace off?" Evie couldn't look away from the impending disaster.

"He hasn't yet. It's the coral. I need to find his gummy." Heloise carefully pried his fingers away. "Are you trying to avoid answering me?"

Evie nearly laughed. "You would never let me get away with that."

"Doesn't stop you from trying. Why are you going for a drive with Lord Gregory?"

"If you must know, I am teaching him how to flirt. He's also bringing the dog we rescued so I can visit with him."

Heloise gaped at her. Henry grabbed her necklace again. This time, he leaned forward and tried to put it in his mouth. Once more, Heloise expertly extricated him from causing damage, all while keeping her focus on Evie.

"Is he courting you? It sounds as though he's courting you."

"He is *not*."

"Does *he* know that?" Heloise asked wryly, transferring Henry to her other hip.

"He knows I am content to be a widow."

"Which you are not," Heloise muttered. "A widow, that is. I'd argue you are also not content."

Evie pinched the bridge of her nose. "Can we not debate that again? This is why I didn't tell you I'd met him the other day."

"Because you thought I'd immediately cast you in a relationship together?" Heloise scoffed.

Henry reached for her necklace again, and Heloise clutched his chubby hand. "Where is your gummy?" She glanced about the drawing room, then strode swiftly to the settee. Plucking up the coral stick, she presented it to him with a wide grin. "Here we are!" She transferred her attention back to Evie and walked toward her while Henry stuck the coral into his mouth.

Heloise narrowed one eye at her and cocked her head. "You didn't tell me about him because you *liked* him. You didn't worry I'd cast you in a relationship—you worried that *you* would." She gave Evie a sympathetic smile. "It wouldn't be the worst thing in the world, you know."

Thankfully, the butler came in to say that Lord Gregory had arrived.

"See you later." Evie turned and breezed from the room, ignoring what her sister had just said.

Snapping up her hat from a table in the entrance hall, Evie set it atop her head, then grabbed her gloves. A footman opened the door, and she stepped outside into the cool gray afternoon.

Lord Gregory stood next to a smart gig. He wore a dark blue coat over brown wool breeches. His waistcoat was also blue, nearly the exact same shade as the coat. His cravat was simple, but she liked that. It was a welcome contrast to the fussier styles she typically saw in London.

"I think someone is excited to see you." Lord Gregory stepped aside to reveal Ash sitting in the gig.

Evie instantly forgot about Lord Gregory and strode straight to the puppy. "There's our boy! Have you been such a good pup?"

Ash barked in response, his brown eyes fixing on her as she stroked his head, glad she hadn't yet put on her gloves. After repeating more happy puppy nonsense, she finally recalled that Lord Gregory was there. "I suppose we should go."

"Or we could just stand here and fawn over Ash. I don't mind."

Evie smiled at him. "You are a patient man."

"Yes, but mostly I am just as smitten with Mr. Ash as you are."

Evie wanted to disagree. She really didn't want to be smitten with the dog. Or with anyone.

In the end, she said nothing as Lord Gregory handed her into the gig. As soon as she was seated, Ash climbed onto her lap.

"That's how it is, then?" she murmured, petting the back of his neck and shoulders.

Lord Gregory chuckled as he climbed in beside her. "That's how we drove here. Him sitting on my lap."

Evie set her gloves on the seat between her and Lord Gregory. Though it was chilly, what was the point in wearing them when she was going to be snuggling a puppy?

Smitten, her mind whispered. She clenched her teeth.

The gig moved forward, and Ash sat up to look out at the passing scenery.

"He seems to appreciate the view," Evie said.

Lord Gregory nodded as he steered the gig along the

drive. "Yes. If you want a blanket, there's one tucked behind the seat." He glanced over at Evie. "Since you overheard Susan the other day, you must have heard what she said about Ash."

"I did. That's why I tried to subtly ask you about where he was sleeping."

"The subtlety you were telling me about in action." He smiled. "I wouldn't ever let her dictate what I do with our dog."

"*Our* dog?"

"We found him together, didn't we?"

"Yes, but we can't share him. He's your dog." She stroked Ash's back lest he think she didn't care about him. "I will simply visit as long as we are neighbors."

"Then I shall have to endeavor that we are neighbors when we are both in London. What is your address?"

She slid him a look of appreciation and let out a short laugh. "Now, that is some smooth flirting."

"I didn't even realize."

She suspected he really didn't. "I probably shouldn't tell you my address." She definitely wouldn't if he were any other man.

"Why not?"

"It isn't terribly seemly."

"I don't plan to advertise it. On the contrary, I will guard it like my very own special secret." He cast her a sidelong look, his eyes glittering with a distinct heat that she felt all the way to her bones.

"I live on Charles Street in St. James's." Stiffening, she kept her attention on the road in front of them so she wouldn't see his reaction.

Good heavens, she was fast coming to sixes and sevens. Perhaps if she'd lain with a man at some point in nearly three years, she might not be so affected by Lord Gregory. Yes, that was it. Not that he was singularly alluring. Or that she hadn't been affected by any man in nearly three years.

He was, apparently, different. The desire she'd felt for men who'd become her protector wasn't the same as what she was experiencing now. But then, she really couldn't compare. She'd only ever been with men who'd paid her for the privilege.

Evie pushed those thoughts away. Straightening her spine against the seat, she asked, "Are your brother and sister-in-law coming to dinner tomorrow?"

When he didn't immediately respond, she looked toward him. His jaw was tight.

"They're coming, aren't they?" She sighed.

"I'm sorry. Susan is rather fixated on the Phoenix Club and Clifford's exclusion from it."

"Does she think I'm somehow going to help her?" If so, she'd be sorely disappointed.

Lord Gregory glanced toward her, his eyes glinting with humor. "I think so. I tried to tell her you are not the sole decider when it comes to membership. But of course, I have no idea if that's true. Perhaps you do have the final say."

That made Evie laugh. "There is a membership commit-tee. It's secret, however, so I can't tell you who's on it." Nor could she tell him that the club's owner, Lord Lucien West-brook, actually had the final say, even if he tried to pretend that he didn't.

"You're a member." He didn't ask it as a question. "I mean, you're a patroness, so you must be."

Evie was the only patroness on the committee, and that was a secret not even the other patronesses knew. However, Evie typically took their opinions into account when she cast her vote on invitations. Well, two of the three of them. She almost entirely ignored Lady Hargrove's overzealous and often self-serving input.

"You're not going to respond to that, are you?" Lord Gregory asked.

"Did you ask a question?" She kept her hand on Ash's back as he settled into her lap for a nap. "I can't believe how well behaved this puppy is."

"I see we're changing the subject." He laughed. "He isn't really. Well, mostly he is, but he's still a puppy. He ran around the stables about fifty times before I drove to Threadbury Hall. He's just tired. After a snooze, he'll be clamoring for another runabout, I expect."

"To return—briefly—to the subject of your sister-in-law's interest in the Phoenix Club, it isn't the right place for someone like her or your brother. It's for people who aren't offered every invitation as they are."

"But they aren't. They don't have one to the Phoenix Club."

"You aren't advocating for them, are you?" Evie supposed it was a difficult situation. The marquess was his brother after all. Perhaps he wasn't as pompous as his wife. Except, Lord Gregory had indicated he wasn't without fault. Then again, who among them was?

"I'm not," he said firmly. "In truth, it's nice to have a club where I know I won't encounter them."

Then Evie would endeavor to ensure it stayed that way. "I'm sorry you and your brother aren't close."

He lifted a shoulder. "That's just the way it is. We are nearly complete opposites."

"You have nothing in common?"

There was a moment of quiet as Gregory's brow furrowed with contemplation. He finally said, "We both like horses."

"That can't be everything. Aren't you close in age? Surely you played together as children?"

"Yes, we are only eighteen months apart in age, but the

divide between us is much wider. I suppose it started when we were children, precisely because we didn't play together. We did at first, but we didn't enjoy the same things—just riding. I liked to read and draw and climb trees. He preferred to shoot and hunt and devise schemes to pilfer sweets from the kitchen, much to the cook's dismay and our mother's frustration. That is likely because he was so often sent to bed without dessert because he'd committed some offense, such as using my mother's figurines for target practice."

Grimacing, Evie wasn't sure how she would manage such a sibling. She and Heloise were so very close and had many wonderful memories from their childhood, despite losing their mother and living with so little security. She almost told Gregory about that—she didn't have to mention her sister's name—but it somehow didn't feel right. Why tell him about her beloved sister when his relationship with his brother was fraught? "I wish things were different for you."

His gaze warmed with gratitude. "I used to too, but as I said, this is just how things are. I've made peace with that for the most part."

"Does he have anything to do with the plans you alluded to last night?" She'd been looking forward to this discussion.

"Not really. He doesn't give a fig what I do."

Evie shifted herself toward him, careful not to jostle Ash too much. "So, you'd 'ultimately' like to wed. I had the sense you might wish to do other things first. Is that true?"

"Perhaps. I don't really know. I just know that I see myself married at some point. With children. And a dog." He tossed her a grin that made her breath catch.

Ignoring her body's reaction to him, she kept her mind focused. Or tried to anyway. "You mentioned a career in architecture, but that your father steered you toward the church. Are you ordained?"

"No. My father was hoping I would take that step this year."

"You sound hesitant."

He exhaled, his mouth pulling into a slight frown. "My father's fondest wish was that I become a bishop."

"It doesn't sound as if you shared that hope."

"I did consider it. I also studied the law. The truth is that I like to learn. I taught at Oxford for a year, and I enjoyed that."

"You haven't mentioned architecture."

"I studied it, but not officially. I was quite content in the law, actually. I was called to the bar, but I didn't end up practicing."

She heard the regret in his voice. "Was that because of your father?" she asked softly.

He narrowed one eye at her with a quick look. "You're very astute. Yes. He'd already had discussions with people about me becoming a bishop. Not immediately, of course, but the path was laid."

"Astonishing," Evie muttered, feeling suddenly sour. The privilege given to people who were already born with every advantage was extraordinary. And yet it could disappear in a moment if things went badly. She'd been born with the same privilege until it had become a liability. Then she and her family had been forced to live in poverty and anonymity. She was alive, however, unlike her parents, and for that she was grateful.

"But you aren't going to follow that path," Evie said. "Can you change your mind about the bar?"

"I don't know. I think I might actually like to work in a government post. I thought about trying for a seat in the House of Commons, but I like our representative and don't wish to challenge him."

"I'm sure you could find a rotten borough to purchase,"

she said sardonically.

He gasped. "You can't imagine I'd do such a thing?" His exaggerated expression when he turned his head toward her indicated he was jesting.

"I don't, which I think you realize. And that makes you remarkable—at least in your class."

"You sound cynical," he observed.

"Am I wrong?"

"Probably not. It's a shame that's the case, however." He shook his head.

"You like to believe the best of people, don't you?"

"Until they've proven there's no point in doing so. I do not waste my energy on those who don't deserve it."

Evie wondered if he was referring to his brother. "When you return to London, I'll arrange for you to speak with Lucien and a few other gentlemen—possibly his brother Lord Aldington, though he recently became a father for the first time, so he may be away from town, and his good friend Lord Overton. They are in the Lords and could recommend you for positions."

"I am not sure Overton would want to help me. I was almost courting his wife for a short time."

"He's not the sort to hold a grudge. Anyway, he is happily married to her, and you are not," she added with a playful smile.

A sharp laugh burst forth from Lord Gregory's lips. "You wound me." He reached over and brushed his fingertips against her pelisse. "Not really."

He'd grazed her, and there'd been layers of clothing, yet she'd felt the connection as if he'd touched her bare flesh. She ignored the ripple of awareness that passed through her. "If you're truly interested in a government position, those gentlemen can likely make it happen." Once again, privilege would ensure victory.

"I appreciate your assistance. Why are you so interested in helping me?"

"One of the reasons Lucien started the Phoenix Club and why I agreed to support the endeavor was that he wanted to help people. He would offer anything to someone in need."

"Why? He doesn't know me."

"Because he's the kindest person I know. I assure you, he has no ulterior motive."

"I look forward to getting to know him. Do I get to flirt with you now?"

Evie laughed, causing Ash to startle. He lifted his head and yawned. "Sorry to wake you, sweet lad." She stroked his head until he settled back down.

Contemplating how to begin, she wondered if he even needed her help when he had her hanging on his every word and wishing he would chance to touch her again. "You have me thinking about the art of flirtation and how everyone responds to it. What works for some won't work for others. But I suppose that's what makes it an art and is how people find their match—you're either drawn to that person and their manner or not. Perhaps this is a futile exercise. You should just be yourself, and doing so will attract the best partner for you."

"You've a thoughtful, intelligent mind, Mrs. Renshaw. Just the same, I think I'd like you to teach me the basics of general flirting. I understand it may be what *you* would respond to. I am more than content with that." His gaze met hers, and she realized she was responding to just him looking at her. Rather, it was the way in which he was doing so, as if he wanted to touch her as much as she desired him to.

She desperately needed to cool this heat surging between them, but if she were to teach him to flirt, she ought to flirt with him. "A demonstration is in order, I think," she said demurely, holding his gaze as her lips curved into a provocative smile. "This is one way to flirt."

He swallowed and didn't look away. "How is that?"

"Eye contact." She glanced toward the road. "Though in this particular setting, you may wish to look at where you are driving, at least periodically."

He muttered something indistinguishable under his breath and jerked his head forward. "My apologies," he said in a louder tone.

"It's quite all right. We are having a lesson. You can see how exchanging looks can be stirring. There are different ways of using your eyes to convey interest and to flirt."

Glancing her way, his eyes held a fervent sheen. "What ways are those?"

"If you look at a lady many times throughout an evening —or whatever the occasion is—that will signal you are interested. Lingering looks are another way."

"Is that what you just did?" he asked.

"Yes, along with applying intensity."

He nodded. "It seemed urgent that I continue to look into your eyes."

Evie laughed. "Then I was successful. However, I should not have distracted you from your task. We'll save further lessons on that front until you are no longer driving."

"An excellent idea. What else can you teach me now?"

"There is conversation, of course. Depending on what you hope to achieve, you can choose words and a manner of speaking to flirt."

"Achieve…I hadn't considered that. I suppose my aim would be to simply spend time with the lady, to get to know her better and determine if we would suit. What else would there be?"

"Some men flirt for more…scandalous reasons. They hope to steal a kiss. Or more." In truth, it was *most* men in her experience. "A great many men seek to have a bit of sport and nothing more."

His lips pressed together, and his eyes narrowed slightly. "I understand. I was looking at this with mostly myself in mind. I am well aware that some men—too many of them, in fact—seek to take more than they should from a woman."

She heard the anger in his voice, and damn if that didn't have the same effect as flirtation on her. "Have you witnessed this?"

"More often than I would like to admit. I am embarrassed to say that it took me a while to step in on a woman's behalf."

"When you did, was your interference welcome?"

He shot her a look of surprise. "Not always. And I can't claim to understand why."

Because just as some men were eager to satisfy their baser urges, women were not immune to those desires. Or, perhaps more accurately, they were not able to decline—for a variety of reasons.

"Women sometimes make choices because they feel they have to, that there is no other way. It was good of you to try," she said softly. "Now, where were we? Conversation, I believe. If you are just getting to know a lady, I recommend listening carefully and looking for things you have in common. Speaking with her about subjects that are of interest to you both will allow for natural flirtation. I daresay you already do this without realizing."

"Did I last night?"

She found him utterly engaging and alluring, so she didn't trust her judgment in the slightest. Furthermore, she hadn't been looking for that. "I wasn't assessing your behavior in that way. Should I do that going forward?"

"It might be helpful. You mentioned last night that aloofness is attractive to some women. Should I attempt that?"

"I think I also said I didn't see you as that sort of gentleman. Women like a man with a strong carriage—someone who can command a room. Sometimes aloofness conveys that strength even if it doesn't really exist."

"I see what you mean. I have known men who display a bravado that hides their true selves."

"Exactly so. I can't imagine you would need to do that."

"Are you saying I already possess a strong carriage and that I can be commanding?"

"You carry yourself with confidence, and I have no trouble believing you could command a room, should you choose to do so." She could see it clearly. "Didn't you have to do that when you were studying the law?"

"I did, in fact. It was one of my most compelling aspects when I was called to the bar, or so I was told."

She imagined him speaking in court, his intelligence and passion captivating everyone in attendance, and found the notion rather stirring. "Then conversational flirting will no doubt come quite easily to you—and I maintain that you already do it without realizing."

"Because it's subtle." He nodded. "I think I understand. You're saying I needn't try to practice more overt flirtation where I compliment a woman's appearance or wit?"

"Well, it is universally acknowledged that a lady *always* appreciates a compliment," she said with a laugh.

Ash stretched on her lap, then rose to a sitting position. He looked about, then left her to take a position on Lord Gregory's lap.

"I've been forsaken," she said, her lap feeling cold now that the puppy was gone.

Lord Gregory transferred the reins to one hand and briefly stroked Ash's head. "He's just looking to see if the view is any different over here."

Evie found the sight of Ash sitting on Lord Gregory's lap incredibly endearing. Even if she wanted the puppy for herself, she wasn't sure she could take him from Lord Gregory.

Looking forward at the road, she said, "We've discussed eye contact and conversation, so I suppose we should review touching."

"Touching?" He sounded surprised. "Is that allowed?"

"How do you dance if you don't touch?"

"That's dancing, not flirting."

She laughed softly. "Dancing *is* flirting if you want it to be. You can do all of it at once—use your eyes, words, and body to show you are interested. Whenever you touch in the dance, hold her for a moment longer than necessary or graze your fingertips along a part of her body as you pass one another. If you promenade, you can situate yourself closer to her side as you walk. Or you can take your free hand to touch the hand she has curled around your arm."

"My mind is positively swimming with potential ideas, but I fear I would be nervous to overstep. A moment longer than necessary seems like a breath away from potential scandal."

"I'm not advising that you sweep her into your arms and kiss her in plain sight of people."

"I suppose that's one way of assuring I'm successful in obtaining a wife." He made a face and twitched his shoulders. "I could never do that."

He assumed he would always be in complete control. She'd yet to meet a man who was. Even Lucien had succumbed to uncontrollable desire a time or two. "What if you were absolutely overcome with passion? And you didn't realize anyone could see you. What, then?"

Ash whimpered, then hurried over to Evie's lap, where he looked rather longingly to the side of the gig.

"I think we should stop so Ash can relieve himself." Lord Gregory steered the gig to the edge of the track. He quickly stepped down, then came around to pick Ash up. "This is a wonderful opportunity for us to practice what you've been teaching." His gaze met hers with a subtle but certain intensity—as she'd discussed. He lifted his hand to help her from the gig, and the combination of his touch and captivating stare provoked her belly to clench with anticipation as to what he might do next.

When she was on the ground, he didn't release her immediately. The moment stretched between them and a delightful heat snaked up her arm. "You've paid close attention to what I said," she murmured.

"My father always told me I was a good listener." Gregory winked at her as he released her hand. She was sorry to lose his touch, but recognized that Ash was squirming in his other arm.

They walked to the field, where he set Ash down. The puppy immediately dashed off until he found a stand of trees.

Evie turned to Gregory and braced herself. She was already incredibly attracted to him, and he hadn't been employing what she suspected would be devastating skills of seduction. No, not seduction, *flirtation*. This was an exercise, and nothing more. "All right, then, let's pretend to promenade, and you can demonstrate what you've learned."

He offered her his arm. Taking a deep breath, she tentatively grasped his sleeve. As they began to walk toward the trees where Ash was now running around, she felt him press gently against her side. Oh dear, that felt lovely.

"I must tell you how grateful I am for your expert tutelage," he said smoothly. "You are rather brilliant at this."

He didn't know of her past, how she was quite literally an expert. What would he think of her then? She didn't want to know. Nor did she ever need to find out—she preferred to leave that part of her life behind, even if it meant hiding her true self and lying about her relationship to her own sister.

His gaze caught hers, and she noticed a faint tawny ring around the pupils. As the darker brown graded to a lighter color, it was as if his eyes were…smoldering. She couldn't look away.

"Is this right?" he asked softly. "Or should there be more?" He arched one brow and leaned slightly toward her, his gaze becoming so intense as to be…comical.

Evie burst into laughter. "Too much." She put her hand over her mouth to stifle the guffaws.

He grinned and then laughed with her. Ash barked, seeming to join in their joyful noise, and ran toward them.

"What you did when you helped me from the gig was perfect," she said.

He inclined his head as they continued walking. "Noted."

As they progressed, Ash ran right into Evie. Trying to avoid stepping on him, she lost her balance and pitched toward Lord Gregory.

He caught her, but the momentum was too much for them to stay on their feet. He cushioned her fall, holding her against his chest as they lay in the grass. "Ash!" Lord Gregory admonished. He looked up at Evie with concern cooling the heat that had been in his eyes. "All right?"

"Yes. How about you? You've taken the brunt of this fall."

"I've had worse."

Evie was overwhelmingly aware of Lord Gregory's arms around her, of his hands clasping her back and…lower. Indeed, he was clutching her backside, and she wondered if he knew it. Consequently, her pelvis was pressed into his, igniting a sharp, encompassing desire. Everywhere they touched was a point of arousal—her hands on his shoulders, her breasts against his chest, her legs between his so she was nestled into his thighs. He was doing extremely well at the touching part of their lesson.

Without even trying, she would wager. He thought he

needed help attracting a wife when the reality was that any woman with a brain between her ears and even the slightest sense of sexual desire would be drawn to him. Perhaps he'd already disappointed an army of women without even knowing it.

"I think you've accomplished the bit about touching someone a moment longer than necessary," she murmured.

Alarm flashed over his features. "My apologies. I'm trying to determine how to help you up."

Ash decided this was a good time to lick Lord Gregory's chin. Which led the dog to lick Evie's cheek next. They started to laugh again.

Evie was grateful for the break in whatever had transpired between them. Unless it had been a single-sided connection. It was best she endeavor not to think about it in any case.

Sliding to the ground on her side, she worked to stand. Lord Gregory moved quickly, helping her up so they both stood, facing each other.

This time, he let her go rather quickly. She buried her disappointment.

"I suppose we should return." She turned toward the gig without waiting for his response.

He walked beside her, but didn't offer his arm. That was for the best, she decided. Her body was practically singing with desire—a sensation she generally had to coax into fruition. But even then, it had been different. She'd been employed by those men. With Lord Gregory, there was absolutely no reason for her to feign interest. Quite simply, she wanted him. Not because of a paid arrangement, but because she couldn't help herself.

How was she going to make it through the next few weeks as his neighbor without succumbing to her own passion? She'd no idea, but it had to be done.

"You have been an excellent student, Lord Gregory. I think you are probably better at flirting and have left an impression on more ladies than you realize."

"I appreciate you saying that. But then, I've had a good teacher. Perhaps tomorrow night at the dinner, we can practice more. A social occasion will lend itself to honing my skills."

Oh no. She wanted to say it was unnecessary, because truly it was. However, the thought of having his attention, even if it was manufactured, for just one night, was too enticing to refuse. Furthermore, it would be something to look forward to while enduring the presence of his abhorrent brother and sister-in-law.

"I daresay you don't require much more practice, but yes, you are welcome to finesse your flirtation." She stopped walking as they'd arrived back at the gig.

He helped her onto the seat, then bent to pick up Ash, who'd trotted along beside them, and deposited him in her lap. Glancing at the sky as he climbed in beside her, he noted, "It may rain. I shall quicken our pace on the return."

Evie looked at the roof of the gig that arched over the seat. "We'll stay fairly dry in here, won't we?"

"Fairly." He cocked a brow at her. "Just in case, I shall demonstrate my excellent driving skills."

"Well done, Lord Gregory. You are fast becoming a master flirt."

"The credit, my lovely Mrs. Renshaw, goes entirely to you."

As he turned the gig, Evie worked to keep from looking at him, focusing all her thoughts and energy on Ash. Things were far simpler that way.

And Evie preferred simple.

CHAPTER 4

*A*s when he'd gone to the assembly two nights earlier, Gregory left Ash in the care of his valet. At first, Harris had wrinkled his nose and asked if a footman or stableboy might be better suited for the responsibility, but Gregory had explained that they didn't work for him. At Witney Court, it was all too possible, if not likely, that Susan would object to a footman wasting his time with a puppy, and Gregory didn't want to consign Ash to the stables. The lads there worked hard enough as it was.

It had taken less than a quarter hour for Ash to win Harris over. Indeed, he reminded Harris of a dog from his youth, and now Gregory wondered if Harris secretly enjoyed having Ash to himself on occasion.

"It's rather unimpressive, isn't it?" Susan remarked as their coach came to a stop in front of Threadbury Hall.

Built in the late seventeenth century, the house was probably half the size of Witney Court. Even so, it boasted an attractive, symmetrical façade made of Portland stone featuring tall windows and a dormered top story.

"It's charming," Gregory said, refusing to let Susan

provoke him. Not tonight when he was going to spend the evening in the company of the divine Mrs. Renshaw.

Susan sniffed. "I suppose."

"You have to admire the man," Clifford said as the coachman opened the door. "Creighton, I mean. He didn't inherit this."

She pursed her lips at Clifford. "I do not have to admire vulgarity."

Gregory exhaled sharply. "What could possibly be vulgar about a family working to better its prospects?" He was instantly sorry he'd taken her bait.

"Well, we don't have to befriend them. At least not in London." She stepped out of the coach, and Gregory had an exceedingly uncharitable thought that perhaps she might trip and hurt her ankle so that she would return to Witney Court.

Alas, she made it to the ground without issue, and Gregory silently admonished himself to be kinder than she was. Clifford followed her out, and Gregory climbed down last. They made their way to the front door, where a smart, liveried footman greeted them.

The butler—Gregory assumed his identity since he possessed the confident carriage of any butler—stood in the center of the entry hall, with its shining marble floor and polished wood paneling. "Welcome to Threadbury Hall. Allow me to escort you to the formal drawing room."

The footman took Gregory's and Clifford's hats and gloves and Susan's cloak. Gregory trailed them as they fell in behind the butler, who led them through the staircase hall. They passed through two more rooms before entering the large formal drawing room.

The space was elegantly, if a bit spartanly, decorated and contained their hosts along with perhaps a dozen other people, including Mrs. Renshaw. Gregory spotted her immediately. She stood near the center of the room speaking with the vicar. A purple gown embroidered with gold flowers draped her frame, and an amethyst necklace sparkled against the flesh of her upper bosom. He could scarcely wait to begin his campaign of flirtation.

To what end? It was all practice with no hope for anything real between them. He'd realized last night as he'd tossed and turned, his body in a state of unrepentant arousal, that he wanted more. He thought of her almost constantly and looked forward to when they would next be together. After tonight, he didn't know when that would be, and that was unacceptable. Thankfully, he had Ash to tie them together—at least he hoped that connection would continue. What would happen when they both ultimately returned to London?

"Remember, I am going to secure an invitation to the Phoenix Club before the night is out," Susan whispered to both him and Clifford.

"I told you, I don't think Mrs. Renshaw can do that."

Susan stared at him as if he were daft. "She's a patroness. Of course she can."

Gregory gave her a slight smirk. "You think you understand the workings of the Phoenix Club better than she does?"

"Well, no," Susan admitted. "But I refuse to believe she doesn't carry enough weight to ensure our inclusion. She must."

"And yet you were so eager to denigrate her dear friends the Creightons," Gregory murmured.

"Let's hope Mrs. Renshaw isn't aware of that," Clifford said with a flash of a smile.

Gregory stared at his brother a moment, wondering if he possessed any self-awareness whatsoever. He couldn't possibly. Biting his tongue, Gregory quickly made his way to the Creightons.

Their hosts greeted Gregory, his brother, and Susan with warmth and smiles. "So glad you could come," Mr. Creighton said. "I do plan to bore you with my refurbishment plans after dinner over port."

"I won't be at all bored," Gregory assured him.

"Lord and Lady Witney, it's our honor to welcome you this evening," Mrs. Creighton said with a curtsey. Diamonds adorned her ears and neck and nestled in her artfully styled light-brown hair. She looked every bit the part of Society, not that it would matter to Susan.

"We appreciate the invitation," Clifford said. "I shall also enjoy hearing about your refurbishments. Lady Witney and I are considering improvements to Witney Court."

Gregory hated to think of them altering a thing about his childhood home, but it wasn't really his home anymore, even if he would always be welcome. Indeed, he wasn't at all certain Susan would extend that courtesy in the future, particularly after she and Clifford had children. Anyway, he had his small terrace house in London, and that would be enough.

Susan glanced about. "I'm keen to speak with your guest, Mrs. Renshaw."

"Please do," Mrs. Creighton said, gesturing toward where Mrs. Renshaw stood. "Do you know each other?"

"We met at the assembly," Susan explained. "I look forward to deepening our acquaintance."

But not yours.

Gregory couldn't tell if Mrs. Creighton had gleaned that from Susan's demeanor and sincerely hoped she hadn't.

"You'll understand if I just go and speak with her now." Susan gave her a condescending smile—hopefully, Mrs. Creighton wouldn't recognize it as such—and went toward Mrs. Renshaw. Clifford followed in her wake.

Torn between racing to protect Mrs. Renshaw from their

attack and being polite by staying longer with his hosts, Gregory's shoulders tensed. He watched as his brother and sister-in-law reached their quarry. At least they'd have to converse with the vicar too. That would hopefully moderate Susan's behavior.

But it probably wouldn't.

"What is your brother planning for Witney Court?" Creighton asked affably.

"I don't know." Gregory couldn't keep from glancing in Mrs. Renshaw's direction repeatedly. "He doesn't involve me in his plans. It may be that Lady Witney has ideas. She's eager to make her place as the marchioness."

"She also seems eager to befriend Mrs. Renshaw." Mrs. Creighton kept looking toward them as well, and Gregory noted the woman's brow puckered slightly. Was she concerned for some reason? Perhaps she'd seen straight through Susan. It wasn't hard since she was so incredibly shallow.

"Lady Witney hopes to persuade Mrs. Renshaw to secure invitations for herself and my brother to the Phoenix Club."

Mrs. Creighton's brows shot up. "Indeed? Well, Mrs. Renshaw can't do that on her own. Lady Witney would do better to take it up with Lord Lucien."

"I told Lady Witney that, but she seems to think she knows better." Gregory could tell that Mrs. Creighton was well informed on the matter, more so than Susan, which would irritate her greatly. "I take it you are members?"

"We are," Creighton said. "Lord Lucien is a splendid sort. The club is magnificent."

Gregory nodded. "It is indeed. I am also a member." He looked forward to annoying Susan later with the news that the Creightons had already received invitations.

No, he wouldn't sink to her level, as tempting as that was.

"Perhaps you should go join their conversation," Mrs. Creighton said.

"I should be delighted." He bowed to them both, then hastened to the middle of the room where the vicar was giving a preview of next Sunday's sermon. He planned to discuss humility.

How appropriate.

Gregory could see that Susan was feigning interest. Her body was turned toward Mrs. Renshaw, and it was clear she was eager to speak.

At last, the vicar took a breath. Susan pounced. "Mrs. Renshaw, I wonder if we might discuss the Phoenix Club. Witney and I would very much like to see it for ourselves when the Season starts."

"You cannot see inside without receiving an invitation of membership. You could attend one of the Friday assemblies during the Season if someone in your family who is a member invites you as their guest." Mrs. Renshaw looked to Gregory, and while there was nothing provocative about her gaze, he still felt entranced. "I suppose you'd have to rely on Lord Gregory, since he is a member."

"We could, but it would be ever so much more efficient if we had our own membership," Susan said sweetly. "Is there anything we should do to indicate our interest?"

"I think you've done that." Mrs. Renshaw's tone and expression were both wry. "If the membership committee wishes to invite you to join, they will."

Susan smiled widely—and insincerely by Gregory's estimation. "I have to believe a good word from you would ensure our success."

Mrs. Renshaw lifted a shoulder. "I don't suppose it would hurt."

The butler entered then and announced dinner. Gregory turned to Mrs. Renshaw. "May I escort you into dinner?"

She put her hand on his arm. "That would be lovely, thank you."

Because of their rank, Gregory's brother and his wife went first. That suited Gregory just fine. He leaned his head toward Mrs. Renshaw's. "My apologies for Lady Witney." Whispering as near to her ear as he dared, he employed what she'd taught him about flirting. He would normally never have moved so close.

Mrs. Renshaw turned her head, surprise or something similar flickering in her eyes. "Careful, or you're going to spend the rest of your life apologizing for her."

As they moved forward, he kept his body close to hers. She smelled of flowers and spice, and the scent was wholly intoxicating. "Unless I can find a way to avoid her presence." He continued to speak in a low tone. "I'd planned to remain at Witney Court through the holidays, but I now wonder if I ought to return to London." He tipped his head toward her. "When are you returning to town?"

Her eyes narrowed slightly. "In January. The Creightons were kind enough to invite me for the holidays."

Then he didn't want to leave either. "You present a compelling reason to stay," he said with a smile.

She hesitated, then spoke measuredly. "Please don't make your decisions based on me."

"I'm flirting," he murmured. "How am I doing?"

They entered the dining room, and she sent him an amused glance. "Well enough that I was completely ensnared."

He helped her into her chair, which was to Mrs. Creighton's left. Gregory was pleased to see that he would be seated to Mrs. Renshaw's left. He would thank his hostess, but then that would draw attention to the fact that he was quite desperately interested in spending time with Mrs. Renshaw. As he pushed her chair toward the table, he allowed his fingertips to brush the tops of her bare collarbones.

When he sat beside her, he noted a faint blush in her cheeks. Had he caused that?

Throughout dinner, he could tell Mrs. Renshaw and Mrs. Creighton were very close friends and had to have been for some time. He was again struck by a vague similarity between them, but he recalled a pair of lads from Oxford who looked as though they were brothers when, in truth, they had just been friends for years. Perhaps if you spent enough time with someone, you began to look a bit alike.

Gregory was particularly glad that his brother and sister-in-law were seated at the other end of the table on the opposite side. Clifford sat on their host's left, and Susan was on his other side. She did send occasional glances toward Mrs. Renshaw, her gaze shadowed with consternation, as if she were trying to strategize how to get closer to the woman.

At one point, he leaned toward Mrs. Renshaw and whispered, "Will you really put in a word for my sister-in-law?"

"I didn't say that I would."

No, she hadn't. She'd been very clever with her words. "You continue to astonish me," he murmured with a smile. "I daresay you'd best be wary of her trying to corner you after dinner."

"Never fear, I have a plan," she responded softly, her eyes glinting with mischief.

"Do tell."

"We'll play a game that will likely take as long as you gentlemen are lingering over your port. However, if I may be so selfish as to ask that you don't linger *too* long, I would be appreciative."

"I will ensure we drink with haste. What sort of game?"

"One involving embroidery. Each player has one minute

to stitch a representation of a word everyone else must guess. Something like 'tree' or 'rabbit.'"

"That could be very simple or incredibly difficult, depending on the word."

"And one's embroidery skill. Mine is atrocious. But I can typically get by with 'tree' or 'flower' or 'house.' Do you happen to know if Lady Witney possesses any skill with a needle?"

"I do not. I am sorry I'm going to miss this."

"Well, if you joined us, you'd have to play. Those are the rules."

Gregory wasn't sure Susan would go along with this scheme. "And if someone refuses?"

"They typically don't, but I imagine we'd try to coerce them. Failing that, we'd make them move to another part of the room so as not to interfere."

Susan wouldn't like that either. "I've no idea what Lady Witney will do, but it sounds as though you have things well in hand."

As the final course was served, Gregory wondered if he might be able to take Mrs. Renshaw onto the terrace later. It was bloody cold tonight as they neared mid-December, but he wanted just a few moments alone with her.

No, he wanted much more than that. To that end, an idea had formulated in his mind—a wild, shocking, sure-to-be-rejected scheme—that he couldn't dispel. He only hoped he didn't horrify Mrs. Renshaw with the suggestion.

Dinner drew to a close, and the ladies rose to adjourn to the drawing room. Gregory helped Mrs. Renshaw from her chair and wished her luck with the game—and, more importantly, with keeping his brother's wife at bay.

After the women left, Creighton invited Gregory to take the now-empty seat to his right. Over port, he described the refurbishments he had planned, including the addition of an orangery.

Clifford jumped into the conversation at every opportunity, to the point that Gregory stopped trying to say anything. Creighton seemed to notice this, his expression patient with a mild, almost imperceptible edge of frustration.

Mr. Wadleigh, the constable, sat to Gregory's right. In his forties, he sported thick graying hair with even thicker brows. Speaking so only Gregory would hear him, he said, "His lordship has a great deal to say. How do you ever get a word in?"

"It can be difficult. Occasionally, I just abandon hope."

"We all certainly miss your father around here." Wadleigh's tone was sympathetic. "Dare we hope you'll be staying at Witney Court for some time?"

"Only through the holidays." After nearly nine months since his father's death, it was time to get back to his life.

Wadleigh lifted his glass to Gregory before draining what little was left. "I hope you'll visit."

Gregory finished his port as well, which ended up being timely. Creighton stood, saying it was time to join the ladies. Presumably, he'd had more than enough of Clifford's verbosity.

The ladies were indeed playing the embroidery game. And it was Susan's turn. Her face was splotched with red, making her look angry or discouraged or both as she furiously poked the needle through the linen.

"Time's up!" Mrs. Creighton called, eyeing a small hourglass on the table beside her.

Susan's shoulders slumped and she let out a soft hiss, sounding like a snake that had missed its prey. "Is this better?" she asked, holding up the linen.

There were two...shapes. One looked somewhat like an oddly formed bean. The other, from which the needle was still protruding, looked as though it might be half of a... hand? Were they both supposed to represent the same object, or was she on her second turn? No, she'd asked if this was better, which seemed to indicate she'd made more than one attempt.

"Is it a hand?" someone asked.

"It's a *leaf*." Susan tossed the needlework onto a table. "This is a terrible game." Her gaze drifted toward Mrs. Renshaw. Was that because she'd suggested it? Or was she merely marking her target for when the game was dismissed, which would likely be now since the gentlemen had arrived.

"Well done, Lady Witney," Mrs. Creighton said. "This game can be quite daunting the first time you play." She looked to her husband, who came up beside her chair. "Shall we play cards instead?"

Gregory saw Susan's eyes narrow at Mrs. Renshaw in a decidedly predatory manner. He didn't hesitate. Moving swiftly to Mrs. Renshaw, he offered her his hand. "Shall we take that stroll on the terrace?" He spoke as if they'd planned it.

"Yes, thank you." She placed her hand in his, and he relished the surge of anticipation that shot through him.

When she stood, he whispered, "Where is the terrace?"

"Just through here." Taking his arm, she guided him to the next room and out the door to the terrace, where a brisk, cold breeze greeted them.

"It's too cold," he said, trying to hide his disappointment. "You don't even have a wrap."

"One moment." She stepped back inside and returned with a thick shawl draped about her shoulders. "Heloise keeps a few shawls by the door for just this purpose. One never knows when the urge to go outside will strike."

"Ingenious. We won't linger too long. I don't want you to catch cold."

"I may pretend that I do so that I may retreat to my chamber in order to avoid Lady Witney."

"That's why I swept you out here. I recognized the predatory glint in her eyes."

"I wondered." Mrs. Renshaw shot him a grateful smile. "I appreciate it."

They walked to the end of the terrace. He would have suggested they continue into the garden, but it had rained earlier, and the ground was likely quite soft. Instead, they turned and started back.

Gregory was right—he couldn't keep her out here too long. It was now or some other time, and he still didn't have a future engagement planned with her. "I hope you won't think me too forward, but I have a proposition for you."

She stiffened, and his nerve started to falter. "What sort of proposition?" Her voice sounded stilted.

"I like you—a great deal, in fact. If you hadn't made it clear that you aren't interested in marrying again, I would have asked to court you. But since that is not an option, I wondered if we might still spend time together as friends." He worked up his courage. "Very *good* friends."

Blast, that wasn't at all what he'd meant to say. He couldn't seem to form the words. Because it was too brazen. It was almost scandalous.

She stopped and took her hand from his arm. "I sense you are nervous."

He relaxed slightly. "I am. Thank you for noticing. Why do I feel as if you already know me better than almost anyone I've ever known?"

"I'm sure I couldn't say," she murmured.

"I've particularly enjoyed our mock flirtation, and in the interest of honesty, I should tell you that it hasn't been practice for me. I mean, it has, but it's also been genuine. I find myself attracted to you in ways I've never experienced. I've never wanted to be…intimate with a woman before."

Her eyes widened briefly. "Oh. Well." Pink bloomed in her cheeks. "Never? As in, you haven't…?"

Gregory shook his head. He sometimes felt embarrassed about his choice to remain celibate, but it depended on the company he was with. His father had encouraged him to do so, saying he would make a better bishop if he waited until he was wed. That sentiment had been encouraged by Clifford's excessively profligate behavior after he'd left Oxford. Both their father and mother had been horrified by his gambling, drinking, and philandering. They'd cautioned Gregory against following his brother's path, and Gregory hadn't wanted to emulate his brother in any way. It had helped that Gregory truly hadn't been moved to even try to bed a woman.

"I want to make sure I understand," Mrs. Renshaw said. "You're a virgin?"

"Yes."

"Are you hoping to change that state?" She paused, her entrancing blue eyes holding his. "With me?"

Now he grimaced. "This is really too beastly of me. Forget I mentioned anything." He started to turn, but she closed her hand around his forearm.

"No. I'm flattered. The truth is that I am also attracted to you. In ways I haven't been in a very, very long time. Perhaps ever," she added so quietly that he wasn't entirely sure she'd said it.

Now it was his turn to feel a rush of heat to his face, and he wondered if his cheeks were also turning pink. "That's rather lovely to hear. What should we do?"

"I think, perhaps, we ought to start with a kiss."

CHAPTER 5

*R**un. Away.***

The words repeated in her mind, growing louder but still not able to drown the persistent thrum of desire that had overtaken Evie. She was standing on a precipice facing something she'd never encountered: her own passionate response to someone.

"Have you ever kissed anyone?" she asked, feeling as though she hadn't, which was of course absurd. But the nervous tilt of her stomach, the heightened speed of her pulse, and the perspiration beneath her arms and between her breasts reminded her of when she was young, of when she'd been faced with the decision to sell herself.

This was wholly different, even if some of her body's responses were similar. She knew what would come next physically, but for the first time, she understood there might be more to it than that.

The word "smitten" came back to her from the day before.

"Yes, I've kissed someone—rather, someones—before," he

said, his eyes dark with his own desire. "But I want to know how *you* want to be kissed." Oh, this was dangerous.

Stepping close to him so that they almost touched, she gingerly placed her hand on his chest. Though she'd done this more times than she could count, she was apprehensive. Her mind kept screaming that this was different. That Lord Gregory was different.

Lord Gregory.

She looked up into his face. "Would you mind if I call you Gregory? You may call me Evie."

"I would like that very much." He put his hand on her waist. His touch was light, not nearly what she craved.

And what was that?

For him to grasp her in his arms and haul her against his body so that she could feel him through their clothing. Then to claim her mouth in a searing kiss. Except she was supposed to be the one teaching him.

She had to stand on her toes so she could reach her hand up to cup the back of his neck. "Lean down," she murmured, heat pooling between her legs, making her sex pulse with want.

He did as she said, lowering his head. His breath was fast, which made hers come even faster.

"Hold me closer," she said. "With both hands."

He put his other hand on her waist and pulled her to his chest. It still wasn't quite enough.

She pressed her fingers into his nape. "You won't break me. I want to feel you."

He swallowed, his Adam's apple bobbing. "Where?" His voice was a low, seductive rasp.

"Everywhere." Evie put her other hand on his cheek. "When you kissed before, did you use your tongue?"

"Yes." He stared at her mouth, and she licked her lips. The

faintest gasp slid from him, cloaking her in sensual longing. "Do you want me to use it now?"

"Please." Holding his gaze, she put her mouth on his, her lips slightly parted.

He gripped her harder, lifting her slightly as he pressed his lips to hers.

His scent of pine and mint washed over her, and she slid her hand down to his neck, her fingers tangling in his cravat. She wanted to tear it from him.

Wait.

Did she really want that? He expected nothing. He wanted what *she* wanted. She'd never allowed complete indulgence. The primary goal was always to give pleasure. If she was lucky, and she'd been fortunate to mostly have been, her lover was courteous enough to provide her pleasure in return.

Pulling back the barest inch, she searched his face. "You truly want to know what I desire?"

"More than anything."

She couldn't put it into words, but what he'd just said was exactly what she'd wanted to hear. Again, her mind registered the danger ahead. She ignored the warning. "Just kiss me."

Clutching at his head, she pulled him to her, and their mouths collided. She pushed her tongue into his mouth, where he met her eagerly. The kiss was deep and furious. But then he gentled, his hands moving over her back. His tongue glided along hers before he retreated. Angling his head, he kissed her again, his lips and tongue playing merrily with hers.

It was a joyful interaction. *Joyful.* She removed her hands from his neck and took a small step back. Hand shaking, she put her palm to her mouth and stared at him. This danger was very real. Having an affair with him would be completely uncharted territory.

"Did I do something wrong?"

She lowered her hand to her side. "Not in the slightest. I must ponder your proposal." She needed to find a way to refuse him. To do anything else would be to risk too much. Her life was finally her own. She didn't want to share it with him. She didn't even want to share it with an adorable puppy!

He nodded slowly. "I understand. Can I see you tomorrow?"

She wanted to say no, but the sooner she summoned the courage to deny him, the sooner she could reclaim her independence. "Let's take a drive to the village."

He smiled. "I'll bring Ash."

Good. She could bid him farewell too. Her heart twisted.

"Forgive me, I am rather cold. I think I'll go upstairs." She walked past him to the house.

"Thank you," he said, prompting her to turn to face him once more. "For trusting me to kiss you."

Trusting him.

How in the hell did he know exactly what to say to make her melt into a puddle? "Good night, Gregory."

"Good night, Evie."

She went into the house and hurried upstairs, not stopping until she reached her chamber. After closing the door firmly, she rushed to the fire and stood as close as she dared. The truth was that while she was cold on the outside, she was aflame with want on the inside.

There was no doubt in her mind that an affair with Gregory would be extraordinary. He would allow her to direct everything. Indeed, he'd likely insist upon it. She might never have such an opportunity again.

At some point in her meditation, she sat in a chair while

she continued to stare into the fire. This was how she was situated when she heard a rap on the door.

"Evie?"

Recognizing Heloise's voice, she said, "Come in."

"Are you all right? Lord Gregory said you'd gone upstairs because you'd caught cold outside. He felt rather badly about that."

"Has he gone home?"

"Yes, everyone has. It's late."

Evie blinked toward the clock on the mantel. It was indeed late. She'd been sitting here considering Gregory's proposal for a long time.

Heloise pulled another chair toward Evie and sat down. "Are you ill?"

"No."

"Then why do you look like that? As if you're unsettled?"

"Because I am." Evie thought about not telling her, but she needed her sister's counsel. Heloise had been the one to guide Evie throughout their lives, and she needed her now more than ever. "Gregory proposed we have an affair."

Heloise's eyes rounded, and she sat back against the chair. "*Oh.*" She took a deep breath, and her expression relaxed. "What did you say?"

"I haven't given him an answer. I asked him to kiss me."

"And did he?"

Evie nodded.

"Was it a test? And if so, did he pass?"

"I hadn't intended it to be, but I suppose it was. He was quite spectacular, particularly when you consider that he's a virgin."

"He *isn't.*" Heloise sat forward, her features once more widening in surprise.

"He is."

"But he doesn't want to be any longer?"

Evie lifted a shoulder. "Apparently not."

"Perhaps this is a silly question, but did he make that decision before or after he met you?"

It wasn't silly. "That's actually a very astute observation. I shall ask him."

"Does it matter? That is, will his answer determine what your answer will be? Or have you already made up your mind?"

Evie groaned and tipped her head back to stare at the ceiling for a long moment. "I haven't decided anything."

"Do you want him?"

It took several breaths for Evie to summon the nerve to answer. She lowered her gaze to Heloise's. "I do. And that is what frightens me."

Heloise reached over and took Evie's hand. "I understand. It was the same for me and Alfred. Not at first. But within a fortnight of our arrangement, I felt differently with him."

It hadn't even taken Evie two days, let alone two weeks. From the moment she'd encountered him at the hedgerow, she'd felt as if she'd fallen under a spell.

Brow pleating with concern, Heloise looked at the fire. "I confess I'm disappointed he proposed an affair instead of marriage." She snapped her gaze to Evie's. "He doesn't know about you, does he?"

"How could he?" Evie smoothed her hands over her lap. "He proposed an affair because I made it clear I'm not interested in marriage. He would have liked to court me, actually."

"Oh, Evie," Heloise whispered, her tone tinged with sadness. "He seems lovely. Why wouldn't you want him to court you?"

A burst of fury rushed through Evie. "I am not you, and you need to stop thinking I want the same things. I do not want a husband or children or what you think of as security. I have that now—a home, employment, and standing."

"You'd have a home and perhaps even greater standing as the wife of Lord Gregory," Heloise said evenly.

Evie stood and paced away from the fireplace. The spike of anger had dwindled—she was often quick to emotion and nearly as quick to let it go. When she turned, she fixed a cool stare on her sister. "I forgot the most important thing I possess: independence. My life is entirely my own, and that's precisely how I prefer it."

Heloise exhaled and also got to her feet. "I do understand. I suppose I worry. Don't bother telling me not to. As your older sister, that is my responsibility."

"I wouldn't." Evie knew Heloise would always be concerned for her. She'd fought so hard against Evie following her into the sex trade. Her plan was to provide for them both so that Evie could find a respectable occupation and hopefully a respectable husband.

"I appreciate that you've always looked out for me," Evie said quietly. "But we're different."

Heloise walked slowly toward her. "I know. I wish Nadine hadn't died."

"She was old. And sick." Evie had cared for her, the woman who'd been the only parent to them after their mother had died, ill and heartbroken more than a decade earlier, a few years after they'd escaped from France. Nadine had been their mother's maid. Skilled with a needle, she'd worked as a seamstress to provide for them, including paying for reading and writing lessons, continuing what their mother had started before she'd died.

"You still sound so dispassionate," Heloise said sadly. "I know how much losing her hurt you. It hurt me too."

"You were gone." Evie didn't blame her. When Nadine had died, Heloise had already been working a year in a fashionable brothel frequented by Society gentlemen. Soon after that, she was settled in her first arrangement with a protector. Draped in lush gowns and sparkling jewels, she'd enjoyed extravagant food and slept in a large, comfortable bed. She was elegant and happy, basking in a life of ease they'd never known. Perhaps not ease—Heloise had paid a rather high price. Evie had been willing, no eager, to do the same. She looked at her sister without remorse. "I wanted what you had, not what you wanted for me."

"I know." A faint smile teased Heloise's lips. "And here we are."

"Both of us happy," Evie said. "I am *truly* happy. I love my position at the Phoenix Club, and I have so many wonderful friends—plus you and Alfred. And Henry."

"Now you have Lord Gregory." Heloise arched a brow, which never failed to make her look enigmatically attractive. It was no wonder she'd found such success as a courtesan. "And a dog."

"I don't 'have' him," Evie said. But she could. At least temporarily.

"You want him. He's offered himself to you. The only thing in your way is you." Heloise stood before her, hands clasped at her waist. "I can find a vacant cottage for you on the estate in which to meet. We'll spruce it up so it's comfortable."

"You would do that?" Of course she would. Evie shook her head. "Forget I asked that. You are the very best sister."

"You're going to say yes? I hope you do. When have you ever taken a man to your bed simply because you wanted to?"

"Never." With that one word, Evie made her decision. "I will be clear that this will be a limited affair—just so long as we are here for the holidays."

Heloise cocked her head, her eyes warm with care. "What if you don't want it to end?"

"It must end." She shook out her shoulders, glad to have made the decision. A thrilling anticipation raced through her. "I'm taking a trip to the village with him tomorrow. When do you think you can find a cottage?"

"I'll speak with Alfred about it before bed. I won't tell him the purpose, and he won't ask."

Evie took her sister's hands. "Thank you. I love you."

"I love you too." Heloise embraced her tightly. When they broke apart, she said, "This will be a marvelous time for you. I like Lord Gregory very much. I can't believe he's a virgin. I confess I'd like to hear what happens." She giggled softly and pressed her fingertips to her mouth.

Evie laughed too. As sisters, they shared a great many things. "It will certainly be a first for me." She was equal parts excited and nervous. Not just because of him, but because this was new territory for her too. It would be a revelation for them both.

CHAPTER 6

The mid-December afternoon was surprisingly sunny. It was also very cold, so Gregory had picked Evie up in a coach instead of the gig. They sat together on the forward-facing seat. At the moment, Ash was standing on Evie's lap with his front paws braced against the window while he looked out at the passing scenery.

"I think he'd rather be in the gig," Evie observed with a smile.

Gregory's breath caught. Did she know how incredibly captivating she was? Even during a mundane conversation about a dog? He looked fondly at Ash. "Only until the breeze picks up and he begins to shiver."

"He needs something to wear. I'll knit him something."

She surprised him yet again. "You knit?" he asked.

"Occasionally." She stroked Ash's back and looked out the window with him.

"How did you learn?"

She flicked him a glance as she continued to pet the pup. "My mother's maid taught me. I wanted to make a dress for my doll, and I am rubbish with a needle."

"I imagine knitting is a very useful skill. Particularly since it will provide our dear Ash with a cozy covering when he goes outside. I wonder, however, if he'll take to wearing it."

"Once he realizes how much warmer he is, I daresay he'll allow it." She leaned her head down to Ash's. "Won't you, dear?" Ash licked her chin.

Evie hadn't said a word about Gregory's proposal, and he didn't want to badger her. Which all amounted to him feeling as though he was stumbling through the darkness, uncertain of where his path led.

"I suppose you're wondering if I have an answer for you today," she said slowly.

"It's as if you stepped inside my mind." He flashed a smile. "I admit I am most eager for your response." He'd barely slept last night in want of it. In want of *her*.

"Then I shan't keep you waiting any longer. My answer is yes." She paused, as if she knew his insides were careening with joy and he needed a moment to rein himself in. "However, it's important to me—imperative, really—that we set boundaries. This will be entirely between us, meaning there will be no public displays of our...association. All interactions between us will take place at a vacant cottage on the Threadbury Hall estate. Lastly, our affair will end after the holidays—when we return to town."

"That is more than acceptable. May I ask when it is that you plan to leave?" He wanted to know how long they had together.

"No later than Epiphany, but I may decide to return to London sooner. I'm sorry, but I can't be more specific than that."

"I shall expect at least Christmas, hope for the new year, and pray for Epiphany." He winked at her. "Truly, I am honored that you accepted. Any time we spend together will be a gift that I will treasure always."

"That's lovely of you to say," she murmured. Turning her upper body toward him, she asked, "I wonder if you'd answer something for me? I'll understand if you'd rather not."

He also pivoted in her direction. "What is it?"

"Why are you celibate?"

He'd expected she would ask. "The easy answer is that I've never been attracted to anyone enough to pursue an encounter. My parents also strongly urged me to live with virtue so that I could undertake my religious studies with a clear heart and mind. The more complicated answer includes the fact that my brother was the opposite of celibate, which disgusted our parents. I never wanted to disappoint them."

"I see. You were the good son, while your brother was...not."

"Mostly. But you must understand that I didn't see my celibacy as a sacrifice. I truly haven't wanted to bed anyone." His gaze held hers as an electric current passed through him. "Until now."

"So, your decision to end your celibacy was prompted by me?"

"Entirely."

Her lips parted, and he was struck with an overwhelming urge to kiss her. This wasn't a public space, so he could do that, couldn't he? He wasn't sure he dared. Not yet. They'd agreed to an affair, but did that mean it had already begun?

He chose to deepen their emotional connection instead. Sharing his reasons for celibacy with her made him feel as though they were growing closer. He hoped she felt the same way. "May I ask you a question now?"

"Yes."

Ash settled down into her lap and rested his head on his paws. She stroked his ears, and Ash's eyes nearly closed in apparent delight.

Gregory moved his attention from the dog to Evie. "Why

do you prefer to remain unwed? Was your marriage unhappy?"

Her hand stilled, flattening against Ash's back. "No. It was…fine. It wasn't a love match, but we got on well enough. He was quite a bit older than me."

"Why did you marry him?" He saw her nostrils flare slightly and rushed to add, "You don't have to answer that."

"I wanted security. He gave me that. He'd hoped I would give him a child, but that was not to be. He died just over a year after we wed."

He'd hoped for a child. Did that mean she hadn't? He wanted to ask more questions. He wanted to know everything about her. But he *didn't* want to make her uncomfortable. "I'm sorry you didn't have much time together."

"I don't have any regrets," she said staunchly, then flashed him a smile to underscore the sentiment.

While her marriage sounded…fine, he couldn't detect even a bit of passion. He silently vowed to give her that.

"I should tell you about the cottage," she said, signaling she was finished with the subject of her marriage. At least for now. Gregory would hope for future revelations. Indeed, he was thrilled by the idea that he'd learn things about her throughout their association. And hopefully beyond. He didn't want to think that their friendship would end in a few short weeks.

"How did you manage to secure a vacant cottage?"

"I asked Heloise if there was a place we might meet to play with Ash. It's too cold outside for extended encounters."

"She didn't suggest we just meet at Threadbury Hall?" Gregory asked.

"She did, actually, but I said it would be nice to have a smaller dwelling so that Ash could go in and out easily."

He contemplated her with admiration. "You thought of everything."

She laughed softly. "I tried to. The cottage isn't far from the hedgerow where we found Ash. It's compact, with only a few rooms and a small garden."

"I take it you'll walk there since you don't ride?" he asked.

"Yes, it's not quite a half mile from Threadbury Hall. We can meet there tomorrow if you like."

Tomorrow. His body thrummed with anticipation. More specifically, his cock had an annoying habit now of trying to harden whenever he was in her presence. It took concerted effort for him to keep his desire at bay. "Why not tonight?"

This drew her to send him a sharp look. Blast, he sounded desperate. "Tomorrow would be fine too," he added somewhat lamely. "I was only thinking, why wait?"

"You'd want to spend the night at the cottage?" Her features softened. "There is something about sleeping together that goes beyond the act of sex. It's even more intimate."

He could easily envisage that. Just as he could see her sleeping beside him, her lashes curled against her cheeks in slumber, her lush lips pursed as she dreamed. There went his cock again.

"Would that be acceptable to you?" he asked, wondering if his voice sounded a bit higher than normal. "Oh, but what would you say to the Creightons about being gone overnight?" Disappointment dimmed his enthusiasm.

"I'll come up with something," she said confidently, lifting him back into full anticipation. "What about Ash?"

Gregory glanced toward the pup, still snuggled down on her lap, his eyes closed. "I could bring him."

Evie gently scratched Ash's shoulders. "While I always love to see him, I think it might be better if you left him at Witney Court this first time. He could be…distracting." She looked down at Ash. "Sorry, sweetheart. Next time."

Next time. Gregory realized there would be many times,

probably, before they parted. He could hardly wait for the first time.

"We wouldn't want distraction," he murmured.

Her gaze locked with his, and it was one of those intense, lingering looks she'd taught him about. "I don't think so. Especially not this time."

The tone of her voice was low and rich, sweeping over him like velvet. He couldn't look away from her. He wanted to kiss her. Touch her. Claim her.

Tonight, he would do all those things.

"I eagerly accept your counsel. I will follow you in all things."

Her eyes glinted with sensual promise. "How marvelous. Tonight, then."

How was he going to endure the entire afternoon? He was glad to be with her, but she was just out of reach. Temporarily. Soon, she would be his. And he would be hers.

He'd never wanted anything more in his life.

~

*E*vie arrived at the cottage well before Gregory. Heloise had insisted on accompanying her so they could make everything comfortable and enchanting, or as Heloise had said, "perfect." Evie wasn't sure she agreed with that. Nothing was ever perfect.

The cottage boasted five rooms: a parlor, a kitchen with eating area, two bedrooms, and a small room that could be used for storage or any number of things. There was furniture, but not much of it. They'd focused their attention on the larger of the two bedrooms, dressing the bed in soft bedclothes and adorning it with more pillows than they probably needed.

They'd built a fire in the bedchamber and lit several

candles. Heloise reasoned they could extinguish them later, if they wanted. Evie had always preferred the room to be as dark as possible. Would that continue with Gregory?

An unexpected apprehension had gripped her as they'd driven a cart with the furnishings along with some food and drink to the cottage. Now, as Gregory was shortly expected, she found she was practically quivering with nervous energy.

Heloise stepped back from the small table near the fire where she'd set out the bottle of wine that they'd brought along with two glasses. The basket with a small, cold supper sat on a dresser in the corner. "Is there anything else we should do?" she asked.

Evie took a deep breath that really wasn't that deep. Her lungs couldn't seem to expand enough. "Nothing comes to mind. Thank you for everything."

"I should go before Lord Gregory arrives." Heloise wriggled her brows at Evie. "Sleep well! Or not." She smirked before leaving, taking the cart as they'd arranged.

Evie went to the parlor and looked out the window to watch her sister drive away in the cart. Or perhaps she just didn't want to stand in the bedchamber any longer.

Why was she nervous? It wasn't as if she hadn't done this thousands of times. Thinking that made her cringe. What would Gregory say if he knew that about her?

She wouldn't ever know because she wasn't going to tell him. Some might think that cold of her, but she didn't owe him any explanation about her past. Nor did she expect anything from him. Why, then, had she asked why he'd remained a virgin?

Because curiosity had got the best of her. A celibate man was a rare discovery and one she hadn't made before. It made sense, she supposed, since he'd at least considered entering the church. And his family had made a deep impression on him, both good and bad. Between his parents' encouragement and his brother's behavior, it seemed he was bound to remain a virgin until he wed.

Movement outside jolted her from her reverie. He was coming up the path to the door. A wave of heat and anxiety swept over her. She tried to take another deep breath and failed. She had to regain her wits. What would he think if she acted as if this were her first time too?

In some ways, it was. This would be the first time she gave herself to a man because she wanted to. For herself and nothing else.

And for him. She had to admit she was quite eager to take him to bed, to show him pleasure.

Evie hurried to the door and pulled it open. "Come in before you freeze."

He stepped inside, and she closed the door firmly. Rubbing his gloved hands, he blew out a breath. "I wasn't in danger of freezing, but it was cold. I kept up a brisk pace to get here." He gave her a brilliant smile that nearly made her sigh. She was really becoming quite silly about this. Glancing toward the dark hearth, he frowned slightly. "No fire? I saw smoke from the chimney."

"In the bedchamber. I didn't see a point in lighting one here. Come." She almost took his hand, but she still felt too apprehensive. So, she led him to the bedchamber, which was much cozier. "This should be better," she said with a smile.

He moved into the room and went to the fire. "Much better."

Evie closed the door to warm the space even more. "Can I take your cloak?"

Unfastening the clasp, he shrugged out of the dark wool. She caught the garment and moved to hang it on a hook near the door. When she turned back toward him, he'd removed his hat and was in the process of stripping away his gloves. The simple act of taking them off made her mouth go dry.

The rest of his clothing would soon follow. She imagined the hard planes of his body glowing in the firelight.

Shaking her head, she walked to the table. "Would you like claret?"

"Yes, thank you."

She poured two glasses. He reached for one, and their fingers brushed against each other. Another jolt of heat stole through her, and thankfully, less of the irritating nervousness. Still, she took a long drink of wine, hoping it would ease her anxiety.

He sipped his claret, standing on the opposite side of the table from her. His dark eyes glimmered with anticipation as his gaze moved over her. She'd dressed simply so it would be easier to disrobe, but now wished she'd taken more care.

Why? It wasn't as if she needed to lure him. He wasn't a future protector. He would be her lover, and he was already eager to bed her.

Another surge of disquiet sent her to the basket on the dresser. She had to walk by him and made sure to leave plenty of space so as not to brush him as she passed. "There's food too—ham, bread, cheese, apples, and biscuits. What can I get for you?" she asked, keeping her back to him.

Setting her glass on the dresser, she opened the basket. The touch of his hand on her shoulder made her jump. She let out a soft gasp and turned.

"Evie?" He looked at her with gentle concern. "Is everything all right?"

She pressed her back against the dresser. "It's fine."

"You don't seem quite…fine. You appear agitated. Have you changed your mind?" He searched her face as if he could discern the answer from her expression.

"I haven't." She put her hand on his chest, and it was almost as if she'd been burned, but with only the shock of heat and none of the pain.

Her hand on him was the only place they touched, but it was as if they were bare against each other. Perhaps it was the way he stood before her, effectively pinning her to the dresser. She knew she could move, and he would allow her to. Part of her wanted him to hold her there, to take her in his arms and kiss her, then toss up her skirts and make her come.

Her sex fluttered with want, a sensation she never felt this early in an encounter. It typically required work to arouse her to this level. With Gregory, it was effortless. He had only to look at her, to be close—and not even that close. She was fairly certain he could be on the opposite side of the room, and she would want him just as fiercely.

Perhaps, then, they should get to it.

"Do you want to eat?" she asked, her voice suddenly husky.

"Do you?"

She considered making a ribald jest, but didn't want to have to explain it. "No. Gregory, how much do you know about what's to happen?" She knew he could kiss, but what else could he do? What else had he done?

"If you're asking whether I am aware of the mechanics, I am. It's hard not to notice animal behavior if you spend any time outside on an estate."

She thought about that a moment. "Do you think…that is, are you expecting to enter me from behind?"

"No. I mean, I'm aware it's typical for the gentleman to be on top. However, I also know that I *could* take you from behind. If you wanted that."

God, she wanted that and everything else. Right this second.

She'd never craved specific acts. She knew better than to expect anything. Her job was to see to her employer's pleasure, not her own. Granted, some of them took that into great account, notably Lucien, but it was still trans-actional.

"I do have an idea for tonight, but it's neither of those things." She'd thought to ride him so that she could show him how to set the pace, as well as how to control things. However, she began to wonder if she would actually need to teach him that. He exuded sensual confidence. And here she was, a quivering mess of tension.

He held up his hands and smiled. "I am at your command. I am rather desperate to touch you, though, so I do hope your commands will come soon."

That made her laugh—short and light, a release of stress that calmed her somewhat. "Take off your boots. If you're warm enough now."

"I am." He left her, and she wished she'd kissed him before he'd gone.

She watched as he sat on the edge of the bed and removed his boots. His feet were rather large, but that made sense because he was tall. Usually, large feet indicated a large cock, but not always. In any case, size wasn't the indicator of plea-sure or skill that many thought it was.

"What's next?" he asked.

"Your coat." When he'd removed the garment, she moved to take it from him. There were more hooks on the wall on that side of the bed. She hung it there, then moved to stand before him.

He looked up at her. "Waistcoat?"

"In a moment." She squeezed between his knees, and he spread his legs. Holding his gaze with her own, she unknotted his cravat. "You wear this plainly."

"My valet is always trying to get me to try something fancier, but I don't like fussy."

"I don't either. I prefer simple." She gave him a slow, seductive smile—not because it was a part that she was playing, but because she was entirely in this moment with him. "It's also easier to remove."

"May I touch you?"

"Not yet." She wanted him to, but feared that when he did, she would begin to lose her control. That in itself was a terrifying thought. She almost never lost herself completely. In fact, she could count the precisely two occasions, and they'd scared her enough to work hard to avoid it. Still, she wondered if she could do that with him. This was different. *He* was different.

Pulling the cravat from his neck, she pivoted to hang it on another of the hooks.

"You needn't be so careful with my clothing," he said.

"I'm always careful with my things." Because for years, they'd had very little. Carelessness meant not having two stockings to wear.

"I appreciate your concern."

She began to unbutton his waistcoat. He leaned back to give her more access. When she opened the garment, she brushed her knuckles against his abdomen, partly to see if his muscles there were stretched taut as she expected them to be in this position. He was hard, with spectacular ridges. She could hardly wait to remove his shirt. To touch him. To kiss him.

What *was* she waiting for?

Lowering her head, she kissed him. The moment her lips met his, a fire ignited within her. She nearly whimpered with want.

She clasped his face and slid her tongue deep into his mouth, desperate to taste every part of him. He kissed her back with equal passion. But why wasn't he touching her?

Because she hadn't told him he could.

Breaking her mouth from his, she took deep breaths to slow her racing heart. "Touch me. I am giving you permission to do whatever you like. Ask whatever you like. Take… whatever you like."

His eyes narrowed, and his resulting sensual expression made her clench her thighs together. "I want your hair down."

Reaching up to her head, she began to pluck the pins out. Locks fell until she held all the pins in one hand. She hastened to put them on the dresser next to the food basket.

As soon as she was back between his legs, he slid his one hand along her neck to her nape. Then he thrust his fingers up into her hair, cupping her head. He pulled her down for another kiss, holding her in just the way she wanted.

But it wasn't enough. She needed to feel him against her, his sex pressing into hers. Pushing him back onto the bed, she climbed over him, straddling his hips. She hiked her skirts and sank her pelvis onto his. The ridge of his cock stroked her, and she renewed their kiss, her lips and tongue desperate to memorize every part of him.

He gripped her hips with both hands and arched up into her. She'd never come like this, but wondered if she might. No, it could never be that easy. Could it?

She reached down to pull his shirt from the waistband of his breeches. He helped her get the garment over his head, and this time, she paid no mind what happened to it. The gorgeous expanse of his chest was far too distracting. It commanded her full attention.

Running her hands over him from shoulders to nipples to lower belly, she skimmed her fingertips along his muscles. Unsurprisingly, he was splendidly formed. She almost thought it a shame that no woman had experienced this before. But then she felt a surge of joy that it was all for her.

"Has anyone ever touched you like this?" She looked into his slitted eyes.

"No," he rasped.

She reached lower, stroking her fingers over his cock through his breeches. "What about here?"

"The only person who's ever touched that is me."

"Do you pleasure yourself?"

"More in the past several days than ever before," he said wryly, grimacing slightly.

Another absurd burst of pride and pleasure surged through her. She moved her hand and ground down against him, reveling in the sensation of him rubbing her. "This is what we're going to do," she said, bracing her hands on his chest. "Without clothing."

"Can we get to the no-clothing part? I want to see you. How does your gown work?"

"I dressed for ease of removal." She continued to move against him, undulating her hips in slow, measured rotations. Lifting her hands to her bodice, she unfastened each side and dropped the front. Then she reached behind herself and loosened the tie at her waist.

He helped her pull the garment over her head. Again, she tossed it away without concern. Despite the cold, she'd gone without a petticoat, though she'd brought a thick one to wear on the walk back to Threadbury Hall tomorrow. Her corset was light, but before she could loosen the laces in the front, he was already at work. It soon joined her gown.

She started to pull up her chemise, but he shook his head. "Wait. I want to look at you. To touch you." He traced his fingertips along the upper curve of her breasts. He lifted his gaze to hers. "Is this all right?"

"More than." It also wasn't enough. "Cup them. Like this." She showed him, putting her hands beneath the globes and lifting them. Loosening the tie holding the chemise closed against her, she made the garment gap so she could pull her breasts free. "Now you can see them." She held them above the top of the chemise as he feasted his gaze on her.

"Absolutely beautiful."

She took his left hand and put it beneath her right breast, showing him how to cup her. His palm was warm against her flesh, his touch gentle. "You can squeeze," she said. He encircled her with his hand and compressed. "Touch the nipple."

He moved his thumb over the pebbled tip, and they both gasped softly. "It's getting longer," he murmured.

"With arousal, it behaves somewhat like your cock."

His gaze lifted to hers. "You're aroused?"

Surprisingly so. "Very." More than she'd ever been. "Take your fingers and pinch the nipple."

His brows rose slightly as his eyes shifted downward once more. He brought his fingers together and squeezed softly.

"More firmly. You won't hurt me."

His gaze shot to hers again. "I wouldn't ever want to do that."

She put her hand over his and used her fingers to show him just the right pressure. "Like this." She moaned as pleasure arced through her, flooding her core with a desperate need.

"Can I put my mouth on you?" He sounded genuinely curious.

"If you wish. I like to be suckled." She wrapped her hand around his nape and drew his head to her while holding her breast for him with her other hand.

He moved to cup her once more, his fingers over hers, then took her nipple into his mouth. He was tentative at first, and she let him explore her with his lips and tongue. After a moment, she pressed her fingertips into his neck and the base of his scalp, urging him to suck her. His mouth closed over her, and he drew on her flesh. She thrust both hands into his hair, messing his blond locks as she closed her eyes and surrendered to the delicious ecstasy rioting through her.

She didn't have to think to move her hips, because she

couldn't keep herself from seeking relief as a thundering lust pulsed in her sex. He put his other hand on her other breast, massaging and squeezing her. There was no gentleness, no hesitation, just his bare need to touch her. Evie cast her head back, moaning louder as he transferred his mouth to her other nipple and feasted anew.

She ground down hard, her body tumbling toward orgasm. How could that be? She had never come like this. And she didn't want to, at least not tonight. She began to think she might find her climax when he was inside her, which rarely happened. Everything about him had been different, so why not that too?

With a sharp groan, she pushed him back on the bed and whisked the chemise over her head. She ought to remove her boots and stockings, but she didn't really want to spare the time. Instead, she climbed off him and stood between his legs once more. Hands shaking with want, she unbuttoned his fall and pulled his breeches off, then his smallclothes, revealing his cock.

It did look longer than most, and it was certainly gloriously erect. When she'd tossed his clothing to the floor, she encircled the base of his shaft and slowly brought her hand to the tip.

His hips jerked up off the bed as he moaned loudly. His hands gripped the coverlet as if he would tear it to pieces. She considered taking him in her mouth, something that she usually viewed as a task to be performed, not a mutually delightful act she wanted to share with someone.

But not now. Now, she wanted him inside her.

"Move onto the bed." She didn't recognize the deep gravelly tone of her voice. She sounded commanding and confident. It made her feel powerful, and she reveled in the sensation.

He pulled his legs fully onto the mattress and rotated his

body so that his head was on the pillows. "Are you joining me?"

"I'm contemplating whether I want to bother removing my boots and stockings. I don't really want to take the time."

"Would you mind? Perhaps I'm being too pure of mind, but I envisaged having you completely nude. At least this first time."

She looked forward to other encounters when they might be fully clothed. Perhaps he'd thrust her skirts up to her waist and bend her over a table to take her wildly from behind. Moving quickly, she unlaced her boots and kicked them off. She fumbled a bit with her stockings and garters, and he took over on the second one, moving across the bed like a predatory cat. His fingers deftly untied the garter, and the act of him removing the stocking was more sensual than anything anyone had ever done to her before having sex.

His fingertips whispered across her flesh. He lowered his head, his breath caressing her. He kissed the inside of her knee, her calf, and the middle of her foot, where it arced inward. "You have very pretty toes."

"Some men like to suck them." Oh God, had she really said that? "Or so I've heard."

He looked up at her as he set her stocking aside. "Should I try that some time?"

She hadn't ever enjoyed it much, but she was fast realizing that everything she'd done before was moot with Gregory. She had to consider this experience with him would be entirely new. It made her speechless. She tugged gently at his hair.

He climbed back onto the bed and assumed the position she'd told him to take a few minutes earlier. She moved to his side, her gaze devouring the length of his body. Sweeping her eyes from his large feet over his muscled calves and thighs, she spent a moment appreciating his cock before traveling upward to enjoy the planes of his abdomen and chest. When she at last settled on his face, she saw that he was watching her too. His lips were parted as he drew rapid breaths. His eyes were glazed with desire, the lids drooping in sensual promise.

Evie straddled his thighs as she wrapped her hand around his shaft once more. Pushing back his foreskin, she ran her thumb over the tip, feeling the moisture there. She'd already placed a sponge inside herself so she wouldn't have to ask him to pull out of her body.

"Another time, I'll take you in my mouth and suck you until you come. Would you like that?"

He stared up at her, his eyes slitted. "I will like everything and anything you wish to do to me."

"What I want is to ride you."

"Can I touch you first? Your sex, I mean."

She took his hand and pressed it at the apex of her sheath. "This is the clitoris. It's where I feel the most pleasure. There's friction against it when we come together. You can also use your hand."

"What about when you masturbate? What do you do?" He smiled briefly. "Perhaps I shouldn't assume you pleasure yourself."

"Of course I do." It was how she found the most pleasure. Until now, perhaps. "I even have implements I can use to help."

"Will you show me sometime?"

"If you'd like." An image of him using one of them on her, of him bringing her to orgasm brought a fresh flood of desire. "Rub your fingers against me there." She showed him how.

The heel of his hand brushed against her pelvis as he worked his fingers on her. "What about me putting my mouth on you? I understand that is pleasurable?"

"Usually." If the gentleman knew what he was doing.

"You can show me how another time. The more I touch you, the more I think about tasting you." His finger slid lower. "You're wet."

She couldn't help smirking. "Quite. That comes with arousal and will make our coupling that much more enjoyable." She'd learned over the years to use things to help with lubrication when necessary, which in her line of work had been not infrequent.

He moved even lower on her sex, his finger sliding slightly into her sex. Her muscles clenched, and she nearly pressed down to take him inside her. She also moaned softly.

"You like that?"

"Yes. I'd like more. Put your finger inside me." She looked into his eyes, and their gazes held as he did what she said.

He stroked into her, slowly, and her eyes narrowed with an equal slowness as her hips rocked forward. He did it again, moving a bit faster.

"Yes," she hissed.

Somehow, he knew to rub his thumb against her clitoris as he thrust again. Evie cried out, bracing one hand on his chest.

"Faster?" he asked.

"And harder. Two fingers, please."

He complied, pushing two fingers deep into her sex as he continued to work her clitoris. Her orgasm was so close. She pulled his hand away. "It's time," she rasped.

Scooting up over his thighs, she clasped his cock and positioned herself over him. She carefully took him into her sheath, lowering her hips until her thighs met his hips.

When he was fully seated inside her, she paused, her body accommodating to him. "How does that feel?" she asked, that power she'd felt earlier surging through her once more.

His eyes were closed, the muscles of his neck and jaw

strained. "I don't know that I can describe it. You feel so good around me. I think I could die now and have no regrets."

Evie laughed. "I can only imagine how you'll feel when you come." She began to move, slowly rocking her hips against him.

He moaned low and deep, his eyes opening the slightest bit. "Evie," he breathed, whispering her name over and over as he clasped her hips.

"I'm going slowly at first," she said. "But I'll go faster. And faster." She picked up her pace, grinding down hard to feel the friction of him against her clitoris. Sensation streaked outward from that very point, and she was suddenly moving at a greater speed, her body desperate for release.

She'd wanted to control this, to bring him to a magnificent orgasm. But she found herself unable to keep herself in check. Her body was suddenly frenzied to reach that pinnacle that so often eluded her, especially at this moment of connection.

"Gregory, I can't—" She whimpered as she bent over him and surrendered to her desire.

Again, he somehow knew precisely what to do. He moved one hand to grasp her breast and the next thing she felt was his mouth on her nipple, his teeth and tongue pulling on her flesh.

She couldn't hold on any longer. Her entire reality splintered as lights danced behind her eyes and her body quivered with release. He kept moving, his hips thrust up as his cock continued to spear into her, drawing out her orgasm and making her cry out in frantic desperation.

"Evie? Is this the moment?"

She felt his thighs clench and found the ability to move again, riding him fast until she felt him stiffen. "Yes, Gregory. Come now. Give me all of you."

Falling forward, she kissed him, cupping the side of his

head as she stroked her tongue into his mouth. He clutched her backside as his movements began to slow. She tore her mouth from his, allowing him to cry out over and over.

Evie smiled against his cheek, the pleasure of seeing and feeling his joy as satisfying as her own release. Which she'd enjoyed while he was inside her. That almost never happened.

She pulled her hips up until he slid from her body, then moved to his side. Her heart was still trying to find its regular rhythm. He turned toward her and kissed her forehead, her cheek. "Thank you. That was an extraordinary gift."

"You have no regrets, then?" She snuggled against him, content to revel in this moment in a way she never had before.

"Absolutely none. I hope you don't either."

She shook her head, her throat tight. She slipped her arm over him and held him close. She didn't ever want to let him —or this serenity—go.

CHAPTER 7

G regory stirred and became instantly aware of the warm body beside him. What a new and wholly pleasing experience. He blinked his eyes open and turned his head. She was precisely how he envisioned she would be in sleep—perfection. He gently stroked this thumb from the corner of her mouth to her temple.

They might be warm in the bed, but the chamber had chilled. He glanced at the fire, which had diminished to smoldering embers. It was still dark, but then the nights were long. Whatever the time, he decided to slip from the bed and rebuild the fire.

Before doing so, he kissed Evie's brow, murmuring, "Be back directly."

She sighed softly, and he smiled to himself. This was the happiest he'd been since his father had died. Perhaps the happiest he'd been in his entire life.

His body twitched as a chill passed over him. Moving quickly, he built the fire up, his mind drifting to last night when he'd arrived. Evie had been nervous. He found that somewhat flattering. He'd expected to feel anxious, but he'd only felt a joyful anticipation. And everything had exceeded his imagination.

As he made his way back to the bed, he saw that Evie's eyes were open. "You're awake," he said.

"Barely. I was enjoying the view as you worked."

He chuckled as he slid back into the bed. "I'm glad."

She moved close to him and gasped. "You're so cold!" Immediately, she began to rub her hands over him. Then she pressed her chest to his, giving him her heat.

He wrapped his arms around her and kissed her temple. "Thank you. For everything. It—and you—were astonishing."

"Do you regret waiting so long?" she asked, nuzzling her head beneath his chin.

"Not at all. Last night was perfect. I couldn't have dreamed of anything more. I think I was meant to wait for you."

She stiffened briefly, and he wondered what he'd said to trouble her. "This is a temporary affair, Gregory." She spoke slowly, quietly.

"I know." Even though it made him sad. He would take what he could. She was worth any time they had together—and the heartache he would suffer when it was over. "I didn't mean to make you uncomfortable. I confess I would be quite happy to extend our time together past what you originally discussed. I am incredibly grateful for this connection we've made, for however long it lasts."

A look of mild amusement passed over her features. "Are you always so optimistic?"

"Usually, yes. My mother used to call me Sir Cheerful."

Evie giggled. "Sir Cheerful. My goodness, but that is sweet. You must miss her."

"I do. What of your parents? You've never mentioned them."

"I don't remember my father at all. He died when I was

very young. My memories of my mother are vague. I know she loved me." She tipped her head toward his chest. "But she was sad after losing my father."

Gregory held her closer. "I'm sorry to hear that. How did you manage after losing your parents so young?"

"Family cared for us."

He wanted to know more, but wouldn't press. He sensed she didn't like to discuss her family too deeply. "My father was devastated when my mother died. It gives me peace to know they are together now."

"Yes, I think you simply *must* find the best view of everything," she murmured. "What a charming attribute, Sir Cheerful." She kissed the hollow at the base of his throat, and he went instantly hard. Not that it had taken much, for he'd been in a state of half arousal since returning to the bed with her. She seemed to notice, because her brows arched. "Perhaps I should call you Sir Ready."

"It's still the middle of the night," he said. "We should go back to sleep."

Her hand moved down over his backside, then over his hip to caress his cock. "Why? We're here, and it would be a shame to let this go to waste." Her eyes narrowed seductively, and he was lost.

He kissed her, pressing her back into the mattress as she stroked him. She nipped at his lip, then kissed him again and again, short, sensual kisses that enflamed his desire. He followed her lead, using his teeth and tongue to explore her mouth. She gripped his nape with her other hand, holding him fast.

Wanting more of her, he moved his lips along her jaw, then down her neck. "Yes," she rasped, urging him to continue his survey of her body. As he moved his head down, she released his cock. Her other hand remained on his head, guiding him to her breast, where he took her nipple deep into his mouth and sucked. He fondled her other breast as she arched up, letting out soft mewls of pleasure.

After lavishing equal attention with his hands and mouth on both breasts and thrilled to feel her body quivering beneath him, Gregory moved lower, trailing his tongue from between her breasts to her navel. She writhed at his touch as he caressed her sides and hips. He brought his hand over her thigh and gently stroked her sex. She was as wet as earlier. He licked his lips as the urge to taste her nearly overwhelmed him.

"Can I put my mouth here?" He ran his finger from her clitoris down into her folds.

She parted her legs. "Yes."

"Tell me what to do." His body shook with need, not for himself, but with the breathtaking desperation to give her pleasure. He wanted to hear her cry his name, to come apart in his embrace.

"What do you want to do?"

"Lick you. Suck you."

"Do it. All of it. Use your lips, your tongue, your fingers."

Her words only fed his arousal. "You'll tell me if I do something wrong or that you don't like?"

"You won't."

He couldn't help smiling. "You sound confident."

"I have every faith in you." She tangled her hand in his hair and pressed him against her.

Needing no further urging, he tentatively licked her clitoris. She exhaled sharply. Emboldened, he used his thumb to part her sex and lick where she was most wet. Her fingers dug into his scalp.

She'd said to lick and suck. He sucked her clitoris next, provoking her to buck her hips from the mattress. Smiling, he did it again, but harder. She'd also said to use his fingers. He knew she liked it when he put them inside her, so he did that, using just one at first. Her muscles clenched around him, just as they'd done when his cock was inside her earlier. His body throbbed in response. He wanted to give her pleasure, but the wonderfully surprising truth was that this gave him just as much ecstasy.

Removing his finger, he thrust his tongue into her. She arched up, her hips remaining elevated. He moved his hand to her backside, cupping the globe of one soft cheek. She moaned his name over and over, and it was the sweetest sound he'd ever heard. He continued his feast, licking and sucking until she began to move wildly against him. Her thighs settled on his shoulders, pinning him to her sex, but there was nowhere else he would rather have been.

He felt her muscles clench—thighs, buttocks, sex—and knew her release was close. He drove deep with his tongue and stroked her clitoris with a feverish pace. She made a thoroughly animalistic sound and shuddered around him. He didn't leave her, not until her body began to settle from her orgasm.

"My God," she breathed, her hand still clasping his head as she sprawled beneath him, seemingly spent. "Are you sure you've never done that before?"

It was impossible not to feel a burst of pride at her question. Or perhaps it was just that he'd never felt so amazing in his entire life. He kissed the inside of her thigh. "Never."

He almost added that he feared she was ruining him for other women, but decided that would dampen the mood. She'd made it clear this was temporary, which meant for him, there would be other women. Would there be other men for her?

Rolling to his side next to her, he asked, "Have you had other affairs?"

She glanced toward him, her eyes half-closed. "I'd rather not answer that."

"Fair enough."

Turning toward him, she opened her eyes completely. "You truly never considered losing your virginity before you met me?"

"Until you, the idea hadn't entered my mind."

"You've *never* lusted after anyone else?"

"My body has felt desire, or at least the need to be satisfied." He gestured toward his still-hard cock. "I've had to deal with this for a very long time."

She frowned exaggeratedly before smiling. "Poor thing. Shall we help it along?"

"We should sleep. I just exhausted you."

"Hardly. If you're ready for another lesson, I'm more than game. This time, you'll be on top. If you want."

He wanted anything she was willing to give. "Show me what to do."

"Kneel between my legs."

When he was in position, she stroked his cock. He closed his eyes briefly and surrendered to her touch. It would be so easy to let himself come like this. But then he'd make a mess all over her. Something about that actually made him harder. Would she mind?

"We're going to guide you into me together. Put your hand on mine."

He wrapped his fingers around hers. She scooted down toward him, and they slid him into her tight sheath. Gripping his hips, she arched up, encouraging him to push deep.

"Yes, like that." She moaned softly. "You can stay like that, or you can come forward, so our chests are touching. If you do that, I'll wrap my legs around you."

"Which do you prefer?" He liked the sound of her legs around him.

"I'd like to feel as much of you as possible."

He felt precisely the same. "I won't crush you?"

She shook her head as she moved her hips. "Go as slow or fast as you like."

"I assume fast is preferable."

"Not always. Sometimes slow can be incredibly intoxicating."

His throat went dry as he listened to her talk about such things. He realized he wouldn't be able to walk away from her without trying everything she said. "Then I'll see what feels good."

Her lips spread in a gorgeous smile as her gaze met his. "Yes, that is always the best plan. Now move. Please," she added sweetly.

He leaned over her until her breasts grazed his chest. Gasping softly, he brushed her hair back from her cheek and kissed her there. She turned her head and claimed his mouth in a searing kiss. Then she wrapped her legs around him, and he nearly spent himself.

Grasping hold of what little control he possessed, he thrust into her, slowly at first. She moved with him, her hips rocking into his. He braced his hand beside her head and had to stop kissing her to catch his breath.

He began to stroke faster as their bodies became slick with perspiration. Her hands moved over his back and down to his backside, where she squeezed his flesh.

"Faster, Gregory," she whispered near his ear, her tongue sweeping over his lobe. "Harder. Make me yours."

"You are mine." He lifted his head and looked into her face, but her eyes were closed. "Look at me, Evie." She opened her eyes. "You are mine. For now, and for as long as we agreed. *Mine.*"

He'd never felt such a stark sense of possession, of absolute dominion.

Her eyes narrowed and she put one of her hands on his

cheek. "Yes. And you are mine. For now." She lifted her hips and urged him to set a wilder pace. "Take me."

He kissed her again, pouring all the apparently repressed lust he had into her. Into them and this moment. He let go of his control and plunged into her with relentless strokes. She cried out, her fingernails lightly scoring his back. "Yes, Gregory. Come now!" She shuddered beneath him, her muscles squeezing his cock.

Shouting her name, he surrendered to his orgasm. That first time with her had been a revelation and this was no different. He felt as though he were seeing the world and breathing its air for the very first time.

He collapsed over her, panting and hearing her do the same. "That was astonishing. But then, so was last time."

"I must agree," she said softly.

There was something in her tone that made him lift his head and look at her face. She looked rather blissful, her eyes closed and her mouth spread in a closed but beatific smile. He was so glad he could please her as much as she pleased him.

He kissed her cheek before pulling from her body and rolling to his side. "Now we should sleep."

"I concur," she murmured, rolling to her side so that her back was against him. She wriggled her backside, and he smiled again. Yes, this sleeping-together part was definitely wonderful. Could they just live together in this cottage until the new year?

"Won't your brother miss you?" she asked sleepily. Apparently, he'd asked that last part out loud.

"I suppose. I told them I wasn't feeling well and retired to my chamber early, then I stole from the house."

"Someone will have seen you." She yawned. "It's a large household. We can't do this every night. Indeed, it will be a few days before we can do it again, and even then, we should perhaps meet in the afternoon."

He tamped down his disappointment. He wanted to see her every day. "I'm at your command." He'd almost said, "My love."

He had to be careful. What he wanted was not the same as what she wanted. He needed to accept that he would be disappointed, that this would end.

Until then, he'd make the most of this. And he'd hope.

$\sim$

A few days later, Gregory made his way toward the cottage, whistling, as Ash trotted ahead of him. The pup stopped every now and then to sniff things and once or twice to dig at something. Gregory prodded him along as necessary, not because the dog was in the wrong, but because Gregory was anxious to reach his destination.

He'd met Evie at the cottage every day since that first night, and he only wanted more. More laughter. More conversation. More touching. More *time*.

"You spend an inordinate amount of time with that dog."

Gregory snapped his head up to see his brother striding toward him. Had Clifford followed him? No, he wasn't coming from the direction of the house. "Afternoon, Clifford. I enjoy the dog's company very much."

Clifford snorted. "If you're trying to elegantly say you prefer him to me, that was well done. But you're never that snide, not even charmingly."

"I leave that to you."

"Ha! You do have bite." Clifford chortled. "Perhaps you're loosening up now that Father is gone."

Gregory bristled. This wasn't the first time Clifford had

made such a comment. "I am the same person I was before Father's death, and I don't expect to change."

"I don't see you rushing to be ordained. You know, I could easily retire old Fairley and replace him with you."

The vicar in Witney was sixty and truly still in his prime, as far as Gregory was concerned. "You can't do that. We've known him our entire lives."

Clifford shrugged. "He'd probably welcome the opportunity."

"No." Gregory was all but certain Mr. Fairley would *not*. He was well liked and respected. "Everyone in and around Witney would revolt."

"Admit it, Gregory. You just don't want to be a vicar. You were only humoring Father. Rather callous of you, if you ask me."

"I am not asking you." Gregory wondered briefly if his brother was right, at least a little. No, humoring wasn't the right word. He'd truly explored a religious career along with others, and in the end, he didn't want to be a vicar or a bishop. While his father's death had helped him reach that decision, Gregory was confident he would have got there eventually. And he would have discussed it with his father, who would—Gregory believed—have supported him.

But there was no point in debating any of this with Clifford. He always chose to believe what he wanted, what fit his expectations and perspective.

Clifford glanced toward Ash, who was digging a hole near the hedgerow. "Where do you go with that dog?"

"Walking."

"Seems like you're gone a long time." Clifford waved his hand. "Or so Susan says. I don't pay a bloody bit of attention." He laughed heartily.

Gregory didn't like that Susan was noting his behavior. He'd make a point of doing something different tomorrow.

He'd take a ride and leave Ash at home. Hopefully, Evie wouldn't mind.

He had to think she wouldn't. Ash could be most distracting, especially at inopportune moments. He'd learned after the first day with him to bring a special treat. It was tucked into his coat pocket, tightly wrapped in paper so Ash couldn't smell it.

Clifford's brows drew together, and he grew serious. "Speaking of Susan, she wanted me to make sure you do your part to ensure Mrs. Renshaw attends the Yuletide party. It's the least you can do since you talked me into hosting the damn thing."

"It's your duty as the marquess. Don't you want to foster good will and cheer in the community?"

Making a face, Clifford grunted. "I don't give a damn about any of that. If Susan weren't keen to show off the house and play marchioness, I wouldn't bother."

Sometimes, Gregory couldn't believe his brother was so insensitive. "She isn't playing marchioness. She *is* the marchioness."

"You know what I mean." Clifford snorted again. "Always so bloody stiff. Back to Mrs. Renshaw. Seems like you and she are friendly, so if you see her, make sure she comes to the party." His brown eyes darkened with suspicion. "Just how friendly are you?"

Gregory understood what his brother was getting at, but refused to engage him on the matter. It wasn't just that he'd promised Evie to keep their affair secret. He had no wish to share his joy with Clifford. That thought made Gregory feel a bit badly. Was that what their relationship had become?

"If I see her, I'll do my best to convince her to attend." Gregory looked to his pup. "Come along, Ash."

Striding along the hedgerow, he walked past when he would normally have moved onto the Threadbury Hall estate. He carefully glanced back to make sure Clifford wasn't following him.

His brother's back was already disappearing from view.

Good.

Yes, he would need to be more careful when he met with Evie and would endeavor to do so.

A short time later—longer than he'd intended due to their detour—Gregory and Ash arrived at the cottage. As soon as it came into view, Ash bounded ahead, barking as he ran into the yard.

Evie opened the door and crouched down to pet the dog. Gregory could hear her talking, but couldn't quite make out what she said. Nevertheless, he smiled. Watching her with Ash gave him immeasurable joy.

That helped banish the icy sensation that had settled between his shoulder blades since he'd run into Clifford. Evie welcomed him into the warmth of the cottage and, as soon as the door closed, gave him a long, breathless kiss.

The heat and wonder he felt in her presence was at such odds with the environment in which he was currently living with his brother and sister-in-law. Was it any wonder he wanted to spend every moment here with Evie?

As Gregory stripped off his gloves, he noted that Ash had gone to the hearth where Evie had left some sort of treat. Seeing that he was quite occupied, Gregory dropped his gloves to clasp Evie against him and kissed her again. This time, he swept his tongue deep into her mouth and took what he needed with a near-reckless savagery.

She kissed him back with an equal ferocity, her hands clutching at his shoulders and neck. Then she pushed his hat from his head and thrust her fingers into his hair.

Desperate for her, for the pleasure only she could provide, he picked her up. She hiked her gown up so she could wrap her legs around him. His cock strained against his breeches and pressed along her sex.

He broke the kiss and put his mouth to her ear. "I want to take you like this. Against the wall. Now. Hard. May I, please?"

"You don't have to ask." She fixed her mouth against his neck, sucking and scoring her teeth along his flesh, stoking his already blazing desire. "Just take me, Gregory."

Turning with her, he pressed her to the wall next to the door, his left arm wrapped around her waist. She clung to him as he put his other hand between them and worked to open his fall. The buttons were especially stubborn, and he tore one off in his frustration.

At last, he had his cock in hand and guided it to her sheath.

She dug her fingers into his shoulders. "Come into me, Gregory."

He thrust into her, his shaft sliding easily into her wet heat. She clenched her legs around him, using her muscles to squeeze and ride him. He had to silently tell himself not to find his release too quickly.

Taking his hand from between them, he cupped her face and kissed her again. A wildness came over him, drove him to nip at her lips and tangle his hand into her hair. Pins fell against his wrist, a tangible sign of her coming undone. Good, because he was so close.

Tearing his mouth from hers, he groaned, his body rushing toward climax as his balls tightened. Her muscles constricted, and she cried out.

As her orgasm claimed her body, making her stiffen, he thrust hard and fast a handful more times before he came in a blinding flash of white-hot light. He slapped his palm against the wall as he moaned her name.

When the rapture began to calm, he put his arms around

her and eased her legs from around him. He slipped from her body, and her gown fell to the floor.

"Well, that was lovely," she murmured.

Gregory took in her flushed cheeks and her stilted breathing. He glanced down to tuck himself back into his breeches. "That was beastly. I tore a button off in my primitive haste."

"I rather enjoyed your 'primitive haste.'" She arched a brow at him and smoothed her skirts. "I would offer to sew your button on, but you know I can't."

He laughed. "It's all right. My valet will take care of it."

"I don't have a needle or thread in any case." She moved toward the two chairs near the hearth. "At least Ash remained distracted. Now, come tell me what came over you. I haven't seen this side of you, and I confess it's somewhat titillating."

Gregory removed his coat and hung it near the door, then he plucked up his hat and gloves and set them on a small table. "I'm glad to hear it. I was feeling upset on the way here. I suppose I let emotion—rather, passion—overcome me when I arrived." He dropped into the other chair and stretched out his legs.

"You were hoping I could ease your agitation? I'm flattered. Sex is an excellent way to soothe oneself. Or I should say, having an orgasm is."

He hadn't considered that, but she was right. He'd used self-pleasure in the past to relax. Doing so with Evie was even better and far more satisfying. "You more than eased me, you sent me into a state of complete bliss. That is no small feat since my brother typically annoys me to distraction."

"Did something happen with him?"

He realized he hadn't said. "I ran into him on my way here. He was just his usual sarcastic self. We're as opposite as anyone could be. Sometimes I wonder how we came from the same parents."

She turned toward him, her brow furrowed. "Did he ask where you were going?"

Gregory sensed a bit of apprehension on her part. "No. He could see I was just out with Ash." He decided not to mention what Clifford had said about Susan noticing Gregory's absences. He didn't think it was anything to worry about and didn't want to spark concern. Plus, he had already decided to take even greater care when he met with her. "Once he'd chastised me about talking him into hosting the annual Yuletide party at Witney Court, he asked me to make sure you would be there."

Her features smoothed as she looked down at Ash, who had finished his treat and was now gnawing on a piece of wood destined for the fire. "I saw the invitation that was delivered to Threadbury Hall yesterday."

"Do you and the Creightons plan on coming?"

"They do. I admit I'm torn. I'd love to spend time with you, of course."

He said out loud what she did not. "But my sister-in-law is a deterrent."

"Unfortunately, yes." She smiled at him. "Still, I think I can overcome the obstacle of her badgering me about the Phoenix Club, particularly if you persuade me."

He leaned toward her. "How may I do that?"

She gave him an alluring stare and ran her tongue over her lower lip, making his heart skip and blood rush straight to his cock. "I'd say you are already well on your way, my lord."

"Then allow me to finish the task."

CHAPTER 8

*T*he last week had passed too quickly. Though Evie hadn't planned to see Gregory every day, she had. She couldn't seem to keep herself from him, which she attributed to the finite aspect of their affair. Their time was limited, so she wanted to make the most of it. That made sense, didn't it?

She hadn't seen him today, however, knowing she would encounter him at the Yuletide party at Witney Court. In the end, he'd been most persuasive in his efforts to convince her to attend.

"It's quite spectacular, isn't it?" Alfred asked, interrupting her thoughts as the coach pulled to the front of the impressive house. Evie didn't know much about architecture, only that it looked quite old and sprawling. It was what came to mind when one heard the phrase "ancestral pile."

She wondered what it was like for Gregory to grow up here. Had her family's house in France been so large? Had her father welcomed people in during the holidays? Had he cared for people in the nearby village? Not only did she not know the answers to any of these questions, there was no one she could ask. Heloise always said their mother had never wanted to speak of their home in France or their father. Accordingly, Nadine hadn't told them anything either, not even after their mother had died.

They departed the coach, and as they walked toward the door, Heloise leaned toward Evie and whispered, "You seem pensive. Is everything all right?"

"Yes."

"Are you anxious to see Gregory?"

Evie managed not to roll her eyes. Heloise had been somewhat relentless in her efforts to match Evie with Gregory permanently. Oh, she'd tried to be subtle, but there was no mistaking what she hoped would come to pass. She wanted to see Evie wed.

"You mistakenly continue to believe that my happiness relies on him. It does not," Evie responded quietly but firmly.

"I do not believe it *relies* on him, only that it might be enhanced." Heloise gave her a warm smile, and Evie reminded herself that her sister only wanted the best for her. Even if she was biased due to her own wedded bliss about what that looked like.

The grand entry hall, cheerfully adorned with evergreen, welcomed them with warm polished wood and shining marble floors. The butler greeted them, then gestured to the receiving line. They waited several minutes in the queue before they met Lord Witney.

Gregory's older brother wasn't as tall as him, but he possessed the same brown eyes. However, his gaze seemed to lack the warmth that Evie always detected in Gregory's. Instead, Witney demonstrated a casual arrogance, his gaze assessing as if everything belonged to him or could, if he so wished. His hair was brown, which was perhaps the greatest difference—at least physically—between the two brothers. Gregory's was a golden blond, an often preferable shade, at least in Society. Had it signaled him as the chosen one? In that moment, Evie felt a rush of pity for the marquess. Whatever his behavior, did he deserve to be held in less esteem by their parents? Furthermore, was he aware and had that driven him to even greater depths of profligacy and haughtiness?

None of that was her concern. She barely knew the man and would have little to no association with him going forward. He was her sister's neighbor. And Heloise wasn't even really her sister, not as far as the public knew. That was the one lie that ate at Evie the most. She loved Heloise more than anything and hated that she couldn't shout to the world that Mrs. Alfred Creighton was her beloved sister. It meant hiding a part of herself, perhaps the truest part of herself. Because who was she really if not Heloise's sister? If everything else faded away, they would always have each other. This deception could one day take a toll. But Evie chose not to dwell on that. Ever.

"Welcome to Witney Court," the marquess said, his gaze traveling over Evie in a familiar, repulsive way that made her teeth grind together. Never mind that he should have addressed Alfred instead of turning his head toward her.

"Good afternoon," Alfred said, magnanimously ignoring his host's obnoxious behavior. Alfred was all that a noble and kind gentleman should be.

"Yes, welcome," Lady Witney intoned. She also looked first to Evie, despite Heloise and Alfred standing before her. "I'm so pleased you could come, Mrs. Renshaw."

"I'm delighted my wonderful hosts, Mr. and Mrs. Creighton, saw fit to include me."

A brief flash of horror passed over Lady Witney's face, giving Evie a swell of satisfaction. "But I sent an invitation directly to you."

"If not for the Creightons having me at their home during

the holidays, I would not be here to be invited, my lady, so I will appreciate them profusely." Evie gave the marchioness a sickly sweet smile.

She realized Gregory, who stood on Lady Witney's other side, had finished speaking to whoever had been before them. He stifled a smile, clearly hearing what Evie had said.

Finally, Lady Witney looked to Heloise and Alfred. "Why yes, of course, we must thank them. They are the loveliest of neighbors. I do hope we'll get together in the new year." She reached out and took Heloise's hand, giving it a quick squeeze before releasing her. That, coupled with the appallingly fake smile the marchioness displayed, made it clear she was putting on a display for Evie. If she was nice to Evie's friends, perhaps Evie would put in a good word for her at the Phoenix Club.

"I'm sure we will," Heloise said vaguely, moving on to Gregory, who took her hand with a warm smile. It really was too bad he wasn't the marquess.

For his part, Witney was less obviously fake when he spoke to Alfred about his plans to refurbish Witney Court. In fact, he seemed genuinely interested in Alfred's opinion. "I hope you'll have time today to humor me for a short while. I'm keen to know which architectural firm you hired and how you selected them."

"I'm happy to help if I can," Alfred said evenly. He might not be happy to do it, but he would because he possessed a thoroughly compassionate nature.

Alfred moved on to Gregory, which left Evie face-to-face with Lady Witney. The marchioness gave her a less fake smile—she was getting better at pretending. "When will you be returning to London?"

"Soon." Evie wasn't going to give her a date. She resisted glancing toward Gregory. It was bad enough that she was going to have to give him one.

"We should be there by the end of January, perhaps sooner. I may return without Witney if he gets too involved with his plans for Witney Court." She cast him a slightly suffering look and let out a shallow laugh.

"I should want to stay and be part of that, I think," Evie said.

"I'm afraid I adore London too much," the marchioness responded conspiratorially, as if they were friends.

"The good news is that London will always be there," Evie replied airily before directing her attention to Gregory. Thankfully, Lady Witney greeted the person behind her.

"You did well," Gregory murmured, taking Evie's hand and stroking the back before releasing her.

"I feel as though I'm running the gauntlet."

His brows arched. "Hopefully not with me."

She barely smiled, not wishing to draw attention to their exchange. "Of course not. I'll let you get back to your responsibilities."

He gave her an almost imperceptible nod, his eyes gleaming with promise. "I'll come find you."

There was a slight jauntiness to Evie's step as she departed the entry hall, trailing Alfred and Heloise, along with other guests, into a long, stately hall that seemed to be from the original iteration of the house. From her limited knowledge, she judged the beams to be Tudor, perhaps because several of the portraits dated from that time period. One thing she knew was clothing, and the female subjects of the paintings wore decidedly triangular gowns.

"You seemed almost incandescent when you spoke with Lord Gregory," Heloise whispered so that Alfred couldn't hear.

Evie nearly groaned. "Do stop. You are not going to change my mind about the duration of my association with him."

"I just enjoy seeing you happy."

"Have you considered that my happiness is due, in part, to the fact that this entire relationship with Lord Gregory is, for the first time, completely on *my* terms?"

"Yes, well…" Heloise trailed off. "I surrender."

"Truly?" Evie nearly clapped with glee but wouldn't until she was certain.

"Truly. I shan't mention him again."

Smiling broadly, Evie accepted a glass of punch from a footman passing by with a tray. "Excellent."

They spent time conversing with other neighbors, and Evie was glad she'd decided to come. There was a communal warmth in and around Witney, and it seemed, with the exception of Lord and Lady Witney, everyone cared for each other. She knew her sister and Alfred would be very happy here. And they were still far enough removed from London so as not to suffer the stain of the origin of their marriage. Unless Lady Witney chose to make things difficult. She'd already been a judgmental shrew. Evie's hackles began to rise. If she did anything to harm Heloise or her family, Evie would take whatever measures were necessary. She would speak with Lucien about Lady Witney when she returned to London. It wasn't a typical manner in which they helped people, but Evie wouldn't allow her sister to go unsupported.

A footman approached her and delivered a folded piece of parchment. "For you, Mrs. Renshaw," he murmured before inclining his head and taking himself off.

Evie unfolded the note. It read: *There is a retiring room on the first floor to the left of the stairs. Go there in a quarter hour if you'd like to see Ash.*

Of course she wanted to see Ash. But she couldn't help wondering if the author of the note had something else in mind as well.

In fourteen minutes, she would find out.

~

*G*regory stood in the doorway to the chamber next to what had been designated as the retiring room for the party. He watched, waiting to see Evie's dark green skirts. He didn't doubt for a moment that she would come. Ash was too compelling a lure to ignore, and Gregory hadn't been above using him to get her to come to the party in the first place. Not that he blamed her reluctance. Susan was absolutely dogged in her pursuit of Evie's favor.

Was he any different? Of course he was—his desire for Evie had nothing to do with what she could do for him and everything to do with what he wanted to do for and with her.

There she was at last, coming toward the retiring room. Gregory stepped out and gestured for her to come to him instead. A faint smile teased her familiar lips, and he was suddenly desperate to taste them. But wasn't he always?

"This way," he said, gently touching her lower back as they moved through a sitting room.

"Where are we going exactly?"

"To see Ash."

And where is he?"

"My chamber."

She stopped suddenly. "Lord Gregory, are you attempting to seduce me?"

He grinned at her. "Is it working?"

Laughing, she gently shook her head. "Take me to our dog."

Our dog. She'd been doing that more and more, and it only increased his hope that things might change, that their affair might go on longer than she'd originally intended.

He led her into a long gallery that stretched the length of this wing of the house that extended back toward the garden. His chamber was in the corner on the left. There were windows along two walls, which made the room bright and cheerful, even in winter, which he liked. Especially since it was decorated in dark blue with accents of gold.

The moment they stepped inside, Ash came bounding toward them. Unsurprisingly, he veered toward Evie. "He always does that," Gregory mused, smiling.

Evie had crouched down to greet the pup. "Does what?"

"Greets you first."

Looking up at Gregory as she stroked Ash with both hands, she quirked a brow. "Does he?"

"As if you didn't know that," he said with a laugh. "I'm not the least bit offended. I would choose you first too."

"Not over him," she said, sounding horrified before she nuzzled her nose against Ash's. "Do you like it here, Ash?" she asked. "Where do you sleep?"

Gregory gestured to a large pillow near his wide four-poster bed. "He has a designated place to sleep, but he usually prefers to slumber on my feet."

She continued to pet Ash as she glanced toward the bed. "It's certainly large enough to accommodate him. And probably several other animals. Or a harem."

"There is only one woman I want in my bed," he said, imagining her tangled in the bedclothes.

"And is that why you brought me here?" she asked coyly.

"While I would like nothing more than to…indulge ourselves, I can't see how that's possible. We don't have much time. Besides, you look far too ravishing to be, er, ravished."

She narrowed her eyes provocatively. "There are ways to indulge ourselves quickly and without damaging our appearances. Would you like to learn how?"

"With an offer like that, how can I refuse?" While his cock hardened at the prospect, his brain saw another obstacle. He looked toward their sweet pup. "What about Ash?" He'd proven to be rather problematic when they were intimate.

They typically had to shut him out of the room to keep him from interrupting.

"You can either put him in your dressing chamber or find him something to chew on, which may occupy him long enough. As you said, we don't have much time, so we'll need to be quick." Her gaze dipped to his pelvis. "I do hope you're sufficiently aroused."

"Every time I'm with you," he said, his desire surging.

She stood. "What do you want to do with Ash, then?"

Gregory had to rein in his thoughts. In his mind, he was already caressing her and considering how they were going to avoid ruining her appearance. He was fairly certain he knew, and the notion that he was moments from experiencing it with her was enough to make him far more than "sufficiently" aroused.

Moving quickly, he found one of the toys made of rope that Ash liked to chew. "Here you go, boy," he coaxed, drawing the pup near the hearth. There was another plump pillow there, and it was probably his favorite place to sit, particularly while Gregory read the newspaper in the chair beside it.

When he finished settling Ash, he had to look to see where Evie had gone. His jaw dropped as he saw her standing at the side of his bed. She'd lifted her gown to her waist, exposing the glorious pale globes of her delectable backside. Her eyes met his with glittering intent, and she wriggled her rear. He strode to her as if he were dying of hunger and she was a buffet of culinary delights.

"Stand behind me," she said huskily, her arousal evident in the deep, seductive pitch of her voice. "I think you can probably discern the rest."

He could indeed. He'd seen animals do this dozens of times. He was eager to see how it felt.

"Hurry," she urged, parting her legs so that he could see the lips of her sex. "Touch me."

He was already halfway there, his fingers reaching for her as he unbuttoned his fall with his other hand. Stroking her, he found her wet, her arousal as desperate as his. They wouldn't need much time at all.

"Touch me, Gregory. I can push against the bed and stimulate my clitoris. Put your fingers in me. Now."

He did what she asked, spearing into her and making her gasp.

"Grab my backside," she rasped, breathless, her hips moving with his hand.

He'd already freed his cock, but he clasped one of her cheeks as he continued to stroke his fingers in and out of her sex. Her muscles clenched, and he could tell she was moving quickly toward her orgasm.

Normally, he would take her there, but they were short on time. Grasping his cock, he guided himself into her heat. She instantly pushed back against him until the flesh of her backside met his pelvis.

"Yes, Gregory. That feels so good. You press so deep like this. It's glorious." She wiggled against him, and he had to close his eyes and count to five to keep from exploding within her.

He gripped her hips and drove into her, careless of his speed. She felt too good around him, and he knew she was nearing her climax. Her hand landed on his thigh, her fingernails digging into his breeches. She turned her head, her eye not quite meeting his. "Faster, Gregory. I'm so close."

He leaned over her and dragged his tongue along her neck. "Come for me, Evie. Hard." He pulsed in and out of her with relentless thrusts.

She buried her face in the coverlet and cried out as she clenched around him. Gregory followed her into ecstasy, his orgasm racing over him. He closed his eyes and cast his head back, surrendering completely to bliss.

"Ash!"

Gregory's eyes snapped open. Ash was on the bed in front of Evie's head, licking her face. She laughed. "Curious, naughty boy," she said between giggles.

Withdrawing from her body, Gregory couldn't help laughing too. He needed to tidy himself—and her—which only added to the humor of the moment. "Don't move," he said, rushing to fetch a cloth from the washstand on the other side of the room. Grabbing two, he hurried back and gave one to her.

"Thank you," she said, still laughing. Ash now sat on the bed and looked from her to Gregory and back again, his expression one of absolute inquisitiveness. "He would like to know what we are doing."

"Clearly." Gregory finished cleaning up and refastened his breeches. Taking her cloth when she was finished, he returned them to the washstand.

She turned a circle as he walked back toward her. "No damage done, I believe?"

"None. You're a bit flushed, however."

"That will fade shortly, but the memory will not." She gave him a wicked smile.

How was he going to survive without her? He'd never felt so wonderful. So *alive*. His gaze settled on her mouth. "We didn't even kiss."

"No, we didn't." She rose on her toes and pressed her mouth to his. He'd no idea if she'd intended it to be chaste, but he was incapable of that. Though they'd just coupled rather satisfyingly, he clasped her to him and kiss her ravenously. He kept it short, but by the time they parted, she was breathless.

"Careful, or we're going to be gone much longer than we should," she murmured.

He was so very tempted. Alas, they needed to get back to the party. Or, at least he did. "I realize I can't see you tomorrow with the holiday, but can we meet at the cottage the following morning?"

"Christmas morning?" she asked, sounding hesitant.

"I have a gift for you. Since I can't give it to you tomorrow, Christmas morning is the next best thing."

Her eyes rounded briefly. "Oh, Gregory. You shouldn't have done that. I don't have anything for you."

"That doesn't matter to me. I would have given this to you even if it wasn't Christmas."

"Well, now I'm intrigued," she said softly. "All right. I'll meet you."

Happiness bloomed in his chest as he gave Ash a farewell pat. "Be a good boy," he said.

Evie bent down to give him a kiss and thoroughly rub his head and back, then he rolled over so she could pet his belly. "How can I leave him like this?" she asked, pouting.

"You can always take him with you."

She rose with a sigh. "You'd miss him."

"Better me than you."

Her gaze met his. "You're too selfless."

Smiling, he strode toward the door. "Can anyone really be too selfless?"

"In your case, no. Because you are genuine, and most people are not."

"You're too cynical."

She blinked and her forehead creased. "Am I?"

"No, not *too*, but perhaps some of my optimism will rub off on you." He held the door for her. "You go down first. Just find your way back to the retiring room. You can say you were in the sitting room next door if necessary. I'll say I was looking after Ash."

"Of course you would have a plan." Her tone held a distinct approval. She blew a kiss to Ash before leaving the room.

Gregory closed the door, then resettled Ash near the fire with a treat of dried venison and his rope toy. "I'll be back before you know it," he said fondly. "And with any luck, you won't have to keep saying goodbye to Evie."

What did he mean by that? Did he hope she would change her mind about marriage? No, he never allowed himself to consider that. It was too painful, for he'd marry her in a trice if she were inclined. He supposed he thought she might yet change her mind about taking Ash, even if it was only temporarily—as if they truly could share him.

"She's right, though." Gregory stroked Ash's soft head. "I would miss you terribly." Nearly as much as he was going to miss Evie.

He stood and left the chamber, closing the door firmly behind him. As he made his way to the stairs, he encountered a maid tidying the sitting room next to the retiring room. Had she seen Evie? A ripple of unease rolled over his shoulders.

"Have you been here long?" he asked, unable to help himself in the face of his concern.

"No, my lord." She dipped a curtsey. "I was in the retiring room."

Relief relaxed his frame, and he gave her a faint smile. "You do excellent work, Teresa."

Her eyes widened briefly. "Thank you. I didn't realize you knew my name." Probably because his brother didn't. He only knew the names of his valet, his wife's maid, and the butler.

"Of course I do. You are much appreciated and valued at

Witney Court." Gregory felt a pang of remorse that he would soon spend little time here.

He nodded toward her, then continued on his way.

~

*E*vie stopped in the retiring room to make sure she wasn't *too* flushed. After splashing water on her face and ensuring her hair was still secure, she made her way downstairs. Within approximately one minute of returning to the drawing room, Heloise came gliding toward her.

"Where did you go?" she asked.

"The retiring room."

"Avoiding Lady Witney?" This was a welcome response since Evie had expected her to note that Gregory had also been absent.

"Whenever possible," Evie responded sardonically.

"She did ask where you were, so you will likely have to suffer her attention at some point."

"Then I shall require more punch. Or perhaps something stronger."

Heloise linked her arm through Evie's and led her to a cabinet, where a footman was pouring a variety of wine. Evie asked for madeira, and Heloise requested sack, then they moved away.

Upon taking a sip, Evie briefly squinted one eye. "Not as good as the Phoenix Club." As soon as she mentioned the club, she noticed Lady Witney watching her from across the room. They made eye contact, and Evie muttered an oath, jerking her gaze back to Heloise. "She Who Will Not Relent is coming this way."

"I will endeavor to help you keep the conversation away from the Phoenix Club."

Evie snorted softly. "I shall admire your efforts, even when they fail."

Lady Witney swooped in like a bird of prey. "There you are, Mrs. Renshaw. I thought perhaps you'd left."

"No, I'm quite enjoying your festive gathering." How could she not after her sojourn with Gregory upstairs? She noted him entering the drawing room at that moment, but did not turn her head.

Even so, her eyes must have given her away, because Lady Witney turned *her* head. "Ah, Gregory. I wondered where he'd got off to. He promised to help manage the guests today."

Evie didn't like that she'd noticed they were both absent. Hopefully, she wouldn't make any connection, though she'd wondered if anyone at Witney Court had noted Gregory's frequent absences. After so many months of mourning, was his behavior odd? She had to trust that he was managing the situation. He said he most often used the excuse of going for a ride.

Lady Witney drew Evie back to the present as she addressed Heloise. Evie stared at the marchioness in slight shock. "Mrs. Creighton, I hope you and Mr. Creighton are enjoying yourselves. I fear Lord Witney has been occupying your husband's time this past quarter hour or so. They're in his study."

"I'm aware," Heloise said. "Alfred is more than delighted to discuss matters of architecture and improvement. One of the reasons he purchased Threadbury Hall was for its potential, as much as for its rich history." She sipped her sack, looking every bit the respectable society matron she deserved to be. That she *was*.

Evie had to stop thinking, however privately, that she and her sister were pretenders, that they didn't belong because of the choices they'd been forced to make. They were of noble blood, and it wasn't their fault that they'd grown up in poverty. If they hadn't been forced from their homeland, they would have enjoyed lives precisely like the ones they were leading now. Except they would have been able to do so openly and honestly, and without fear of judgment or disdain. Instead, Heloise was the former courtesan who was unwelcome in many social circles, while Evie chose to hide her past and take on a new identity that didn't allow her to be her full self.

Alas, that was the price she had to pay to live in comfort and acceptance. She gave it without hesitation because it meant she belonged, even though it required deceiving many of those closest to her.

Lady Witney turned her gaze to Evie. She'd made her point of giving attention to Heloise and could now get back to her quarry. Evie took a long sip of madeira.

"How do you find the shopping in our quaint hamlet?" the marchioness asked. "It's not London, of course, but the milliner does make rather cunning hats."

"I've found that to be so," Heloise said. "In fact, I've commissioned several. I fear Mr. Creighton may ask me to limit my spending there." She laughed, and Evie joined her.

It took Lady Witney a moment to laugh too, and when she did, the sound was high and stilted. If Evie liked her, she would have offered to help her work on her polite conversation and reactions.

Evie suddenly felt rather uncharitable. Perhaps there was a reason for the marchioness's disagreeability and her desire to feel important. One never knew what another was coping with. It was possible that becoming marchioness had completely overwhelmed her. It was also possible that she really was a shrew.

"Do you have a favorite milliner in London?" Lady Witney asked, directing the question to Evie instead of

Heloise, even though it had been Heloise who had commented on the merchant in Witney.

"The one Heloise uses," Evie said with a bland smile.

"Oh, lovely." Lady Witney turned her expectant gaze to Heloise, who—Evie could tell—was gritting her teeth.

"Weaver's on New Bond Street."

A gentleman in his middle forties sporting bushy eyebrows and long sideburns, approached them. Evie resisted the urge to thank him for the interruption. "Afternoon, ladies. Pardon my intrusion, but I wonder if we've already been introduced?" He asked the question of Evie, his small, dark eyes focused on her, his gaze swiftly dipping to her bodice and back to her face again.

Perhaps this interruption was not all that welcome.

He did seem vaguely familiar, but Evie didn't particularly want to play the "how do I know you?" game with him.

"This is Mrs. Renshaw," Lady Witney said. "Mrs. Renshaw, perhaps you and Mr. Arbuthnot met in London?" The marchioness gave him a dazzling smile. "Are you a member of the Phoenix Club perhaps? Mrs. Renshaw is one of the patronesses."

Evie worked not to shake her head. The marchioness had been *so* close to not mentioning the club in this entire conversation.

Arbuthnot, whose name did not summon any recognition, shrugged. "I don't know anything about that. Spend my club time at Boodle's." He took a swig of ale.

That Evie couldn't place him was bothering her. "What brings you to the area, Mr. Arbuthnot?"

"My sister and her husband live on the other side of Witney. I'm visiting for the holidays."

That didn't help.

"Ah, here comes Mr. Creighton," Heloise said, her gaze on

the doorway where he was entering with Lord Witney. "Please excuse me."

"And me," Evie said. Arbuthnot's frequent glances toward her bosom were irritating. She accompanied Heloise toward her husband.

"I was hoping you'd come along," Heloise whispered. "I found Arbuthnot rather objectionable."

"As did I. He did seem familiar, however." Suddenly, she knew. A soft gasp bolted from her lips before she could stop it.

Heloise sent her a sharp glance. "What?"

"We met at one of Mrs. Farrow's balls. Thank goodness he didn't remember that." But what if he did recall meeting her at a ball hosted by one of London's most successful courtesans? Evie had encountered only a few gentlemen over the past two and a half years who'd known her as Mirabelle Renault, the courtesan. She'd been careful to keep the interactions brief and endeavored not to return to wherever she'd encountered them. Thankfully, none of those men had recollected her. She didn't like that this man was connected to Witney. It meant she might visit her sister even less and that when she did, she wouldn't stray far from Threadbury Hall.

Not for the first time, she wished Heloise and Alfred had remained in Nottinghamshire.

They reached Alfred, who apologized to Heloise for disappearing for so long. "I must say, Witney is keen to learn about building, even if he is a trifle insufferable." He grimaced slightly. "I don't mean to be uncharitable."

"Don't think poorly of yourself," Heloise said. "The Witneys are simply...complicated."

The three of them stared at each other a moment, then began to laugh. Evie caught sight of Gregory again, but he wasn't looking in her direction. Her pulse picked up speed as desire sparked. She'd really hoped that sensation would have faded by now.

He laughed at something the person he was speaking with said. Evie looked past him and realized who that was—Arbuthnot. They were friendly? Evie didn't need to understand the specifics. It was enough to know they were acquainted.

It seemed her decision to return to London early was a good one. She'd leave the day after Christmas.

She had a gift for Gregory after all: the date of her departure. Only it wasn't one he wanted.

CHAPTER 9

*S*ince they hadn't seen each other on Christmas Eve, Gregory was overcome with anticipation for his appointment with Evie on Christmas morning. He'd arrived at the cottage early and lit fires in the parlor and bedroom. He'd brought one of Ash's cushions from his bedchamber at Witney Court and situated it in the parlor. Gregory had made sure to bring Ash's favorite treat and a new rope toy that he'd got yesterday. They ought to keep him busy while Gregory and Evie were occupied.

As soon as she'd arrived, they'd fallen on each other and diverted straight to the bedchamber. Despite his plans for a slow, methodical coupling, they'd both reached their climaxes swiftly. He had no regrets, however, as it had been delightfully sensual.

Now they sat on a blanket in the parlor with Ash between them as he gnawed on his rope. Evie had donned her chemise and thrown a shawl over her shoulders. Her brown hair glimmered with gold in the firelight, a smile teasing her lips while she watched their dog.

"Are you ready for your gift?" Gregory asked.

"I suppose, but I still wish you hadn't done it."

"Nonsense. You're going to thank me." He'd put his breeches and shirt back on and now jumped up to retrieve her present.

He dashed into the kitchen where he'd set it on the table, then quickly returned to her. Sitting on the blanket, he handed her the gift wrapped in a red ribbon.

She gasped upon seeing it, lifting her hand to her open mouth. Her gaze lifted briefly to his before dropping once more to the portrait of Ash he'd drawn.

"It's Ash." She touched the frame. "I love it ever so much." She looked at Ash and scratched his head. He did not stop his chewing for even a moment. "Did you draw this?" she asked, her eyes meeting Gregory's again.

He nodded. "I'm better at buildings, but it's passable. I'd wanted to commission a painting, but there wasn't time."

"It is far more than passable." She set the portrait on the edge of the blanket. "You've a talent. Perhaps you *should* consider architecture."

"I may, but I think a government appointment is my preference. I'd like to be of service. Sometimes I think I should have bought a commission, but my mother rather vehemently insisted I follow the church instead, and I admit I preferred that."

"There's service in the church," Evie said.

"Yes, that's why I went along with my parents' wishes." He picked up his tankard and sipped the ale she'd poured earlier.

"Your parents were very influential."

"They were. I found myself missing them yesterday."

"That's understandable," she said softly. "It was your first Yuletide without your father. What did your family usually do on Christmas Eve?"

"When I was young, we went on a Yule log hunt. I tried to

get Cliff to do it again this year, but he declined. Apparently, Lady Witney doesn't like to be cold."

Evie found that ironic since the woman was incredibly frigid with regard to her personality. "You should have gone without her."

"That was my suggestion," he said wryly.

She patted his hand. "I would have gone with you."

He was suddenly annoyed with himself for not thinking of that. "Forgive me for not asking."

"I'm not sure it would have been wise. We already risk a great deal coming here, even though the cottage is rather removed. And we've taken several outings together."

Yes, they'd taken drives and gone to the village a few times. Were people talking about them? "Has someone said something to you?" He recalled the day he'd encountered Clifford on his way to meet Evie at the cottage. Had Clifford or Susan noticed anything more? He hoped not.

"Heloise noted our time together, which makes sense because I am staying with her. She asked if I'd changed my mind about courtship and marriage."

"And have you?"

She shook her head and glanced away. "I told her that I have not."

He wasn't surprised. "My perennial optimism demanded I ask. In keeping with that, allow me to ponder a Yule log hunt for next year. For us—not here." He half expected her to remind him that they wouldn't be together next year.

Instead, she leaned toward him, her eyes dancing. "Where would we go?"

The hope he tried to curb unfurled inside him and spread. If he wasn't careful, he might think this could actually happen. "North, where there is a greater chance of snow. Perhaps Yorkshire. I'd lease a cozy cottage like this, and we'd spend a fortnight, no, a month, there—just you, me, and Ash."

"Who would cook?"

"I'm sure we could find a local woman to take care of the kitchen duties as well as tidying the cottage."

"*I* can tidy the cottage," she said in mock defense. "And I can take care of rudimentary cooking. Just don't expect a syllabub."

He grinned. "What about pudding?"

"I've attempted them in the past, but they are not my forte." The last word rolled off her tongue as if she were a native French speaker.

"Your French accent, even on just that one word, is flawless."

"Is it?" She shrugged. "My mother's maid was French, so I learned to speak the language. I don't use it very often, however."

He loved learning new things about her. In French, he asked if she spoke any other languages.

She responded, also in French, that she did not. "What about you?" she asked in English.

"Latin, Italian, and, strangely, some Welsh. I enjoyed languages, and I've always liked a challenge. Welsh seemed especially challenging."

"Perhaps that will be useful in your new government position," she said with a wink. Her gaze strayed to the drawing of Ash. "Thank you again for the portrait. It's the best gift. This is going in my bedchamber so I may see it every morning when I wake."

"I'm still willing for you to take Ash when you return to London," he offered, though it would be difficult. He and the pup had established a happy routine of walks and play. Ash had been Gregory's best companion since his father had died —not including Evie.

She looked toward the fire. "I've been thinking about that actually. I do love Ash, and it will be hard to be apart from him. However, I imagine the two of you have developed a close bond, and I shouldn't want to disturb that." She flicked a glance at him. "I know you want to visit when we are back in town, but I think it may be best if we don't see each other."

Gregory felt as though he'd been punched in the gut. He struggled to find words. "At all?"

"Yes. I know I said I wanted to be friends, and I do, but this… Our time together has been more intense than I'd anticipated."

Hope resurged in his chest despite what she was saying. "I feel the same. I despair at parting from you."

She settled her gaze on him, and it was surprisingly cool. His hope dissipated. "I was clear from the start, and, as I just told you, I haven't changed my mind. This was a temporary affair."

Was?

"Are you leaving soon?" His voice sounded tight, reflecting the tension that now gripped his body.

"Tomorrow. I need to get back to my responsibilities."

So soon? She was a patroness at the Phoenix Club. What could she possibly need to do? "It's not as if it's the Season." He smiled, though it wasn't entirely genuine—he was just trying to lighten the mood.

"My duties are not only during the Season. I help Lucien with the management of the club. I realize that's difficult for most people to grasp—or approve of—which is why I don't typically share that information." Her tone grew even colder.

He hadn't meant to disparage her. "I find it quite admirable." She had an occupation, while he was completely idle.

She visibly relaxed, her features smoothing. "My apologies. Sometimes I feel a bit defensive about my position. It's unusual for a woman to be involved in a membership club as I am."

"From everything I've seen—and learned from you—the Phoenix Club is not a typical membership club."

"No, it is not. Lucien has worked to make it something different, a place where the members can truly be at ease and where character matters more than circumstance."

"What a lovely turn of phrase," Gregory murmured, his esteem for her growing with every moment they spent together. She inspired him, he realized. Now he was anxious to return to town as well, and not just because she was going. "I am keen to find my own way when I get to London. If you're still inclined, I would be grateful to you for speaking with Lord Lucien on my behalf."

Her gaze snapped to his. "Of course I will. I do want to be friends, Gregory. We *are* friends. I just… I need some time to myself. I hope you can understand that." She grimaced slightly, and he sensed this was difficult for her. Perhaps her earlier coldness was an attempt to disguise how she really felt.

All he wanted was to be closer to her. The idea of space between them was wholly unappealing. Yet, he'd known this was coming even if he hadn't expected it this soon. "I'd hoped we would have more time," he said quietly, reaching for his tankard of ale for a long needed pull to quench the desert in his throat.

"I'm sorry. To me, our time together has been wonderful."

"To me as well."

She smiled suddenly. "Let us not mourn, for we are here today, and we are together." She reached over to pet Ash, who rolled onto his back so she could rub his belly.

Gregory struggled to move on and to pretend that his heart wasn't breaking. His heart? Yes, for he was fairly certain he'd fallen in love with her. He was glad he hadn't told her that. Until that moment, he hadn't allowed even himself to know.

Still, he didn't want to squander a moment of their time together, and especially not with self-pity. "When do you need to return to Threadbury Hall?" he asked.

She glanced toward him. "Not for a while yet."

"Good." He reached for her, eager to show her just how good they were together. He'd give her the space she needed, but he wouldn't abandon her completely. He couldn't.

Pulling her onto his lap, he caressed her face. "Ash and I won't disappear forever. We *are* friends, and we will remain such."

Their gazes held for a long moment before she nodded slowly in response.

"I'll remind you, Evie, that I am an optimist." Cupping her neck, he kissed her, losing himself in the bliss of holding her. He couldn't believe this would be the last time.

He wouldn't.

~

our days later, a footwoman opened the door to the Phoenix Club for Evie. As soon as she stepped inside, the familiar scent of pine, sandalwood, and citrus—a distinctive fragrance Lucien had commissioned in order to give the club a unique and identifiable smell—welcomed her. A month was too long to be away, and yet she couldn't deny feeling refreshed and invigorated.

Though, she doubted that was due to being away. She owed it to Lord Gregory Blakemore and his divine attention.

"Good morning, Amanda," Evie said with a smile.

The young woman had worked at the Phoenix Club over a year now and was exceptional at getting to know and remembering all the female members. On the ladies' side of the club, they employed women as footmen, just as there were cleaning men on the men's side.

"Welcome back, Mrs. Renshaw. I trust you had a nice holiday."

"I did, thank you. And you?" She'd felt badly for not being here for their celebration the day after Christmas in particular, but Lucien had overseen the event and assured her all would be well. There was still the Epiphany party they would host next week, and Evie looked forward to that.

"We had a lovely time here at the club," Amanda replied. "Lord Lucien takes such fine care of us."

He did indeed. Everyone who worked here had needed a second chance, an opportunity to find a place to not only work but to belong—a home.

"I'm so glad to hear it," Evie said before continuing into the club. She passed the ladies' dining room and the library on her way to the staircase that took her up to her office on the first floor. Situated in the corner with a lovely view of the back garden, it was her home away from home, a place where she absolutely belonged. Also thanks to Lucien.

When he'd offered her this opportunity almost three years ago, she'd been more than surprised. She'd ended their contract—he'd been her last protector—and she'd been contemplating what to do next. He'd believed in her, and that had made all the difference.

She was halfway through her stack of correspondence, having just picked up a missive from another patroness, Lady Hargrove, when Lucien poked his head into her office. "Morning, Evie."

It was remarkable to her that he never, ever slipped up and called her Belle. He wouldn't now, not after this much time, but even in the beginning, he was perfect in his address.

She smiled at him. "Good morning, Lucien. Thank you for managing everything while I was away."

"It was my pleasure. Ada was here twice, so that is why everything is perfectly orderly."

Ada Hunt, the Viscountess Warfield, was the club's book-keeper. They'd met while Evie had left London to reinvent herself as a widow. Ada had been in need of a new beginning, and she was exceptionally clever. So clever that Lucien had sent her to help organize his friend's estate. Injured in the war in Spain, Warfield had been in a bad place and in need of assistance. He hadn't wanted it, but then he'd fallen in love with Ada. They'd wed this past summer, but Ada had retained her position. They lived about a day's ride from London, so she came to town often. They would come for the Season since Max, her husband, sat in the House of Lords.

"She wrote to me with updates," Evie said.

Lucien deposited himself in a chair next to Evie's desk, stretching his legs out. "Of course she did. How is Heloise and her family?"

Lucien was one of very few people who knew of their true relationship. "Very pleasant, thank you. Henry is getting so big. How was your holiday?"

"Happily focused on the new heir. My father absolutely doted on baby Robbie." Lucien spoke of his nephew who'd been born in late November. The only letter he'd sent to Evie had been about that. Lucien was a terrible correspondent. "I am quite relieved to no longer be the spare."

"I can well imagine." Nothing would have horrified Lucien more than to inherit his father's dukedom. Because nothing would have horrified his father more. Lucien's older brother, Constantine, was the favorite son and now that he and his wife finally had an heir, he was likely even more beloved. "Did His Grace actually *dote*?"

"I know it's difficult to conceive." A pained expression flashed over Lucien's face. "It was almost revolting."

"I'm glad for Con and for his son." She knew that Lucien was only revolted because that kind of behavior from his father was foreign to him. And it hurt. Not that Lucien would characterize it like that. He buried his pain so deeply that Evie sometimes wondered if he even remembered it was there.

"I'm surprised you're back this soon."

"You knew I'd be here for the Epiphany party."

"Which isn't until next week," he said, fixing her with a probing stare. "What happened?"

"Nothing happened. I just missed being in town." She wasn't going to tell him about her affair with Gregory. Never mind that he occupied many of her thoughts, mostly when he would arrive in London. She also couldn't stop thinking of Ash. The drawing of him was a poor substitute. "There was one thing."

One of his dark brows arched, and he drew his legs up, sitting straight and angling his body toward her. "Oh?"

"Threadbury Hall borders Witney Court. Alfred and Heloise hosted a dinner and invited the new marquess and his wife. Once she learned I was a patroness of the club, she became fixated on securing an invitation for herself and her husband."

"Fixated?"

"Every time I encountered her, she attempted to win my favor and spoke of their wanting to be members."

Lucien stroked his jaw. "I hadn't considered Witney. His brother, Lord Gregory, is a member and much more in keeping with whom we include. Honestly, in all my interactions with Witney, I found him somewhat insincere."

"I agree with everything you just said. The marquess, and his wife in particular, don't seem the sort to be Phoenix Club members." She frowned. "I overheard her disparaging Heloise and Alfred. She knows of their backgrounds and finds them horribly lacking, of course. She was dismissive of them until she realized I was their guest and a dear friend.

Then it became apparent that courting their favor might help her campaign."

Lucien smirked. "And did it?"

Evie rolled her eyes. "You know it did not. I found it repulsive."

"Indeed," Lucien murmured, sitting back in the chair and studying his fingernails a moment. "Rest assured. They will never be members."

"You say that with such finality, as if you possess the sole discretion when it comes to membership."

Lucien swung his gaze back to her. "You know I do not."

"Ah yes, will the two anonymous members of the committee agree with you? You seem rather confident." She watched his brow tighten briefly. "Despite what you say— what you've always said—I wonder if you really do have the power to make the final decision. I suppose if I knew who those two members are, I might have a better idea."

Exhaling, Lucien folded his arms over his chest. "I do wish I could tell you. But I can't."

"I know, and I understand." Even if she didn't like it. She and the other members of the secret membership committee, which included Ada as well as Lords Overton, Wexford, and Fallin, sometimes grumbled to each other that they weren't allowed to know the identities of two of their number. But they all trusted Lucien. Furthermore, they knew he was bound to secrecy. What perplexed them most was *why*.

Lucien unfolded his arms and nodded toward the stack of letters before her. "Anything interesting in that pile?"

"I was just about to read one from Lady Hargrove."

"Do read it aloud, if you don't mind."

Lady Hargrove was the least likeable of the four patronesses. Her husband was friendly and personable, but she was perhaps too haughty for the Phoenix Club. The membership committee hadn't realized that two years ago when they had established the patronesses before the club opened. Lucien had wanted three respectable ladies in addition to Evie. Lord Hargrove often supported the working class, and Lucien enjoyed his company. That his wife came from a very old family and was accepted in the highest circles gave the club credibility and a note of prestige. At least, that was the reason Lucien gave for inviting them. Evie had a sudden, curious thought—what if the anonymous members had been the ones to invite them?

At first, Lady Hargrove had been fine, but over time, she'd begun to gripe about certain members—never directly to Lucien, but to her fellow patronesses, which of course included Evie. One thing Lady Hargrove did not particularly approve of was allowing unmarried women membership, even though they were of a certain age and generally regarded as spinsters. It wasn't as if they offered membership to young ladies in their first Season. Even Lucien's sister hadn't received an invitation until she was wed.

The name Witney jumped out at Evie from Lady Hargrove's letter. She groaned inwardly before she began to read aloud.

I wish to recommend Lord and Lady Witney for membership. It is astonishing to me that Witney is not yet a member, since his younger brother already enjoys the privilege. As the new marquess, Witney will be an excellent addition to the club. Furthermore, Lady Witney is a lovely, engaging young lady. I could even see her as a future patroness. I look forward to discussing this at our next meeting.

Evie's lip curled as she set the letter aside. "If Lady Witney is ever made a patroness, I have to assume I will no longer be here."

"I just told you that she and her husband would never be

members," Lucien said evenly. "I confess I'm amused that Lady Hargrove thinks a sibling relationship offers any assurances for membership."

"She must not have been paying attention to the fact that your own brother wasn't invited until last spring."

"Precisely. Anyway, Lady Hargrove takes it upon herself to recommend a great many people, the vast majority of whom are never even discussed by the committee."

He made a good point. This wasn't the first time Lady Hargrove had written a note like this to Evie. "Because we don't present them. We'll just ignore this one as we have the others." Lady Hargrove would complain, but when she failed to receive any attention, she'd grudgingly move on.

Lucien nodded, his mouth twisting into a frown. "I sometimes wish she would resign in frustration."

"You could ask her to."

His gaze snapped to hers. "How would that look?"

Evie sighed. "We're apparently stuck with her, then."

"Unless we can manipulate her to quit." He narrowed his eyes toward the windows as he seemed to contemplate that idea. "That is not how I typically care to apply my efforts, but I think I must consider it. How do the other patronesses feel?"

Evie lifted a shoulder. "There is a general consensus among me, Lady Dungannon, and Mrs. Holland-Ward that Lady Hargrove likes to complain and honestly just enjoys the sound of her own voice. We also know that she is highly esteemed among the *ton*, so we don't wish to cause trouble."

Lady Dungannon's husband was striving to repair a bankrupt viscountcy. His father's mismanagement and suicide had plunged the family into scandal. Mrs. Holland-Ward's family's fortune came from trade. That she'd wed a landed gentleman had negatively affected her husband instead of elevating her. Both women were mostly accepted in Society now, but not entirely. Lady Hargrove gave them all a stamp of legitimacy.

Lucien eyed her intently. "If you can find an opportunity to discuss her…departure that might be helpful. Would they be in favor of that?"

Evie couldn't imagine how she could broach that topic without causing surprise and even concern. "Perhaps we ought to consider adding a fifth patroness? Someone Lady Hargrove wouldn't want to work with?" And who would provide the same credibility.

"She'd have to be someone with her credentials." Lucien fell silent for a moment. "Let me think on this."

"You could ask the anonymous members," Evie suggested.

"I may do just that." He gave her a bright smile. "Hiring you was the best decision I ever made."

Evie shook her head. "Founding this club was."

"You are a very, very close second, then." He started to get up, but Evie waved him back down.

"I've one more thing to discuss with you. I spoke with Lord Gregory over the holidays, and he is in want of a government position."

"I thought he was going to become a vicar."

"That *was* his plan, rather his father's plan, but he prefers to work with the government. He studied at the Inns of Court and was called to the bar, but didn't practice law."

"I didn't realize that. What draws him to government?"

"He wants to be of service, but not with the church. I thought you might be able to help him. You certainly know the right people."

"I do," he said slowly. "I'll consider how I may be of assistance. Is he back in town?"

"I wouldn't know," she said rather quickly, drawing Lucien to look at her perhaps more closely than he had been.

"I know he plans to return to London for the Season, but I don't know when."

Lucien nodded as he got to his feet. "Anything else?"

"Not at the moment, thank you. I'll let you know if I need anything for the Epiphany party."

"I'm sure you and Ada have it well in hand." He turned and started toward the door, but stopped abruptly. He faced her once more. "Are you still happy here, Evie?"

"Of course. Why would you ask?"

"I was thinking about Ada and how happy she was as our bookkeeper and how she's happier still now that she's wed to Max."

Evie scowled at him. "You aren't suggesting I should marry, are you?"

"Not at all. I just wondered if you might be…missing something from your life. I don't think you've taken a lover since we parted."

"How would you know?" Her voice rose more than she liked. She took a breath to calm herself in the face of his intrusion. "You must realize that for those of us who know you well, we have begun to call you the Meddlesome Match-maker. Some even add 'of Extreme Officiousness' at the end."

Lucien snorted. "Right up until they fall in love and are ultimately grateful for my help."

"I am not one of those people, Lucien," she said firmly. "I do not want, nor do I require your 'help.' I believe I was very clear with you nearly three years ago when I ended our arrangement that I prefer my independence."

"You did. That doesn't mean you can't allow yourself some indulgence. No one deserves it more." He hesitated before adding, "And frankly, I have a hard time imagining how a woman as sensual as you could—"

She slapped her hand on her desk. "Stop. You aren't allowed to discuss that with me. That is the past. I believe our business is concluded for the moment." She summoned a thoroughly false and rather agitated smile.

"My apologies. It's just that I care for you so much. Of all the people I've helped, you're the one whose happiness matters the most to me."

That softened her. He'd never said that to her before. "Thank you. But while I appreciate that sentiment, you do not have permission to bother me about such things."

"I understand. Just know that I will always care for you—as a dear friend."

"I know." She waved him off. "Now leave me to work."

He dipped his chin and spun about, striding from her office.

Evie frowned after him. They'd meddled together in bringing his brother Con and his estranged wife, Sabrina, together, but that wasn't typical for Evie. It was for Lucien, though, and while he'd promised to try to refrain after the situation with Con—despite the fact that their meddling had resulted in a delightfully blissful marriage—he hadn't been entirely successful. He just couldn't seem to keep himself from…*helping* others. If he had any notion that she'd conducted an affair with Gregory, he'd be relentless in his pursuit of a match—if he thought Evie loved him. Which she did not. She did, however, care for him a great deal and had meant what she'd told him on Christmas Day. Their liaison *had* been more intense than she'd anticipated. She enjoyed his company far too much.

She needed to keep her distance. Yet here she was helping him. She could do that without becoming involved.

Why, then, did she have a troubling suspicion she was fooling herself?

CHAPTER 10

*G*regory had spent a great deal of time working with Ash on walking together so that when he took the pup out in London, he would not run off. He'd tried to get Ash used to walking near a moving vehicle, having his groom drive his gig next to them. Over the past three weeks that they'd been in town, Gregory had watched Ash's behavior improve until he could accompany Gregory on a walk without dashing off.

And so it was today that Gregory felt confident enough to walk with him in St. James's. Or perhaps it was that Gregory was overcome with waiting to try to catch a glimpse of Evie.

He wasn't sure which house was hers on Charles Street, so his intent was to walk up and down it a few times. It was unlikely they would see her, but he was, of course, ever the optimist.

Walking closer to the street than Ash, Gregory kept his eye on the dog. He'd grown quite a bit in the last month since Evie had seen him. As much as Gregory longed to see her for himself, he was also anxious for Ash to see her. Though dogs couldn't really communicate, Gregory knew he'd missed her.

On his way back toward St. James's Square, he recognized a gentleman coming toward him: it was Lord Lucien. As they neared one another, Lord Lucien smiled. "What a marvel to run into you here, Lord Gregory. I trust you have been well, though perhaps it's been a difficult time these past months."

"Thank you. I am quite well and glad to be back in town. And you?" Gregory was anxious to hear why their meeting was a "marvel."

"Very well, thank you for asking. I am just on my way to see Mrs. Renshaw, whom I understand you became acquainted with while she was in Oxfordshire."

Gregory kept his features impassive. What did Lord Lucien know?

"I live just down the street, you see," Lord Lucien continued as he gestured behind himself. "I often call on Mrs. Renshaw as it pertains to the Phoenix Club."

Gregory felt a surge of jealousy that Lord Lucien lived so close to her and was welcome to visit regularly. "How convenient."

"Yes. You should join me. I'm sure Mrs. Renshaw would be delighted to see you." His gaze moved to Ash, who had moved forward to sniff the man's boot. "Who's this?"

"Ash. Perhaps Mrs. Renshaw mentioned him?"

Lord Lucien's gaze shot up to his. "She did not."

"Ah, well, we found him stuck in a hedgerow."

"And saved him, apparently. You did this together?" At Gregory's nod, he smiled. "How charming. I'm surprised she didn't mention that."

If she hadn't told Lord Lucien about that, what had she told him about their "acquaintance"?

"Her house is just here." Lord Lucien indicated the smart terrace in front of them.

"Come, Ash," Gregory beckoned. He almost asked if he was ready to see Evie, but her name would send him into a fit of excitement, and that would no doubt provoke Lord Lucien's curiosity. Furthermore, what if she wasn't home and Ash was disappointed? Except it seemed Lord Lucien might be expected.

Gregory accompanied him up the short set of stairs to the door. Lord Lucien rapped on the wood, and a moment later, an attractive young man opened the door. This was her butler? Gregory felt another surge of jealousy, but it was entirely different from what he'd felt when Lord Lucien had revealed the proximity of his residence.

"Afternoon, Foster," Lord Lucien said pleasantly. "Would you tell Evie I am here along with Lord Gregory Blakemore?"

Everything after Evie was drowned out by Ash, who'd begun barking. He dashed inside and stopped to sniff everything madly.

The butler's pale brows climbed his forehead, but he said nothing.

"Pardon me," Gregory said, moving inside and rushing to pick Ash up.

"Did I hear a dog?" The familiar feminine voice came from the top of the stairs, prompting Ash to start barking anew. He struggled to get free from Gregory's arms.

Suddenly, she was there at the top of the stairs. A vision in lavender, her gaze meeting Gregory's and widening in surprise. But then she looked to Ash, who managed to wrest himself from Gregory's grip, probably because Gregory was wholly focused on Evie.

Ash bounded up the stairs, and Evie bent down to hug him, bringing him to her chest. "I have missed you so!" She nuzzled his head, and Gregory realized the last month of separation hadn't diminished anything he—or apparently Ash—felt for her.

After a long moment, she looked down toward the butler. "Foster, will you have tea sent up to the drawing room?" She rose, scooping Ash into her arms as she went. "My goodness, you have grown very big. Soon, I may not be able to lift you this easily." She turned and disappeared.

Lord Lucien started toward the stairs. "I think that's our cue to go up."

Of course. Gregory was too busy trying to overcome his elation at seeing her. Swallowing, he willed his heart to calm its frantic pace as he followed Lord Lucien up the staircase.

Evie's drawing room was as feminine and beautiful as one might expect. There were floral patterns and a gorgeous arrangement of actual flowers—in late January—on a cabinet. And another smaller one on a round table near the windows that overlooked Charles Street.

She'd situated herself on a rose-colored settee with Ash on her lap. The dog was quite content to be with her, and that made Gregory inordinately happy. He considered taking a chair, but ultimately decided it would be best if he sat on the other end of the settee. That way, Ash could move to him if he wanted. Or, perhaps more accurately, Gregory just wanted to be near Evie.

"Apparently there's a story here as to how you found this dog?" Lord Lucien prompted, addressing Evie.

"I suppose there is. We discovered him caught in a hedgerow. Lord Gregory determined where he came from, but they were happy to allow him to keep Ash."

"Who named him?"

"Mrs. Renshaw did," Gregory answered. "There was an ash tree along the hedgerow."

"How charming," Lord Lucien murmured, his eyes twinkling as he looked at Evie. "I'm surprised you didn't tell me about it."

Evie's brows arched briefly. "Didn't I?" She stroked Ash's head. The dog stared up at her adoringly, and Gregory wondered how he was going to get him to leave.

"Looks as if you've quite a bond," Lord Lucien observed. "I never would have taken you for someone who would have a pet."

"And I do not," Evie said, though she grimaced faintly as she glanced at Ash and now used both hands to pet him.

Foster entered with the tea tray and set it upon the round table near the windows. "Shall I pour, Mrs. Renshaw?"

"Yes, please. Lord Gregory takes milk but no sugar." She turned her head toward Gregory. "Did I remember that correctly?"

"Indeed, you did," Gregory said, having no doubt she was saying that for Lord Lucien's benefit. There was no way she didn't recall how Gregory liked his tea.

Lord Lucien rested his elbow on the arm of his chair as he looked to Gregory. "Lord Gregory, I understand you are interested in a government appointment."

Gregory was thrilled to know that Evie had already mentioned this to him. "I am."

"Do you have a particular area of interest?"

Foster delivered Evie's cup of tea and, then Gregory's.

"I have experience with the law and somewhat with architecture," Gregory replied.

Lord Lucien took his cup from the butler with a nod before transferring his attention back to Gregory. "Also with religion, if I recall?"

"Yes, but I am more interested in the law and building."

"That is good to know," Lord Lucien said. "I may be able to arrange some meetings for you, if you'd be interested."

"I'd be delighted, thank you." He glanced toward Evie. "And thank you," he said softly.

"I was happy to speak to Lucien on your behalf." Evie sipped her tea. Ash had moved off her lap and was now snuggled beside her, his head on her thigh. Gregory thought that an excellent place to be.

Lord Lucien drank from his teacup before balancing it back on the saucer. "It's also come to my attention that your brother and sister-in-law hope to gain membership to the Phoenix Club. That does not look as though it will happen. I hope that won't cause strife within your family."

"It's none of my business," Gregory said, secretly glad they would not be members. "I don't spend a great deal of time with them."

"You don't reside at Witney House?" Lord Lucien asked.

"I've a terrace on Avery Row." He wondered if Evie would appreciate knowing that. She hadn't ever asked where he resided in London.

"Charming address." Lord Lucien took another drink, then stood abruptly. "Evie, our club business can wait until later. I'll let you catch up with Lord Gregory and…Ash. Who is not your dog," he added with a smirk.

Evie sent him a long-suffering stare. "I'll see you later at the club."

After depositing his cup on the tray, Lord Lucien turned back to Gregory. "I'll let you know about a meeting. Perhaps I'll see you at the Phoenix Club soon?"

"Definitely. I am grateful for your assistance."

"It's my pleasure." He departed, leaving Gregory alone with Evie. And their dog.

Gregory finally took a drink of his tea. "I encountered Lord Lucien on the street." She hadn't asked for an explanation as to why he was there, but he assumed she would.

"You just happened to be out with Ash in St. James's when you live on Avery Row?"

"Er, yes." Exhaling, he set his teacup down on a table next to the settee. "I had hoped I might see you. For Ash's sake. He's missed you, or can't you tell?" It wasn't a falsehood, but he was lying by not telling her he had also hoped to see her for *his* sake.

"I missed him too," she said softly, smiling down at the pup as she stroked his fur. "I have his tunic." She lowered her voice and spoke directly to Ash. "I'll be right back. Don't go anywhere."

She got up from the couch, and Ash barked after her. "I promise I'm coming right back!" She hastened from the room.

"She did promise," Gregory said, trying to reassure the dog.

A moment later, Evie returned with a small light-blue knit tunic. Sitting down beside Ash once more, she set the garment on her lap. "Here we are. This will keep you warm when you are out on a day like today."

He sniffed the tunic, then began to gnaw on the edge. She whisked it away with a soft laugh. "It's not for chewing, sweetling. It's for wearing." In one quick motion, she pulled the garment over Ash's head. He whimpered and shook his shoulders as if he could wriggle out of it. However, Evie handled him expertly, pushing his legs through the holes in the garment.

"You're truly certain you've never had a pet and don't wish to have one?" Gregory asked.

"Yes." She adjusted the tunic around Ash and frowned slightly. "I should have made it a bit larger. Ah well, I am already working on another, and I'll ensure it will fit as he grows."

"You look very smart, Ash," Gregory noted with a smile. Ash seemed to understand, because he tossed his head and marched onto Evie's lap where he stood straight and tall.

Evie laughed, and Gregory's chest constricted at the sound—he'd missed her so very much. He nearly said it aloud.

Evie hugged Ash, and he settled onto her lap. She looked

over at Gregory. "Do you think he might want to come and spend the night with me?"

For the barest moment, Gregory thought she was asking *him* to spend the night, but of course she wasn't. "I think he would love that. Though, I'll have to fetch his things."

"Not tonight," Evie said, frowning slightly. "I'll need to prepare the household. And not tomorrow night as I will be at the Phoenix Club rather late since it's Tuesday. Would the following night be amenable?"

"Yes. What time would you like me to bring him over?"

"After dinner? Perhaps you might send him with a groom to be more discreet?"

She didn't want him to be seen visiting her at a late hour. He supposed that made sense, even if he suffered a flash of disappointment. "I don't know that he'll want to go with a groom. Ash is particular about whom he trusts. What if I dress inconspicuously and bring him down to the servants' entrance?"

"I suppose that will have to do." She leaned her head down toward Ash. "Are you a particular boy? I can understand that. We can't trust everyone even if we want to." She looked back over to Gregory. "He's been well?"

"He has. The journey to London was quite eventful. There were children at the inn where we stopped overnight, and they absolutely wore him out playing in the yard." A light smile teased his lips as he recalled how much fun it had been for Ash.

"That sounds lovely," Evie murmured.

As she continued to dote on Ash, Gregory couldn't help feeling a trifle awkward. "I hope you don't mind that we are here."

She shot him a grateful look. "I am glad to see you both. Truly. Have you been well?"

"I have. And you?"

"Very, thank you. Have you been in town long?"

"A few weeks. I couldn't stand to remain at Witney Court any longer. And now my brother and Lady Witney are in town. They arrived yesterday. I hope Lady Witney doesn't make too much trouble with her Phoenix Club obsession."

"Another of the patronesses advocated for her membership, but there isn't any support for her." Her features creased in a faint grimace. "Or your brother."

"You can't think that would bother me," he said lightly.

"No, I didn't think it would. Now tell me about how these children fawned all over Ash, then we shall take him for a turn about my small garden."

"It would be my pleasure." Gregory had thought she might try to keep their time together short. That she didn't gave him hope.

And he'd never let that go.

~

Evie stifled a yawn as she made her way to the gentlemen's side of the club. It was early yet, before the club was very busy, so she shouldn't be tired. But she'd tossed and turned for quite a while last night. She blamed Gregory's visit.

Just when she'd exorcised him from her mind, he reappeared. And damn if she hadn't been thrilled to see him. And Ash! She'd nearly wept upon seeing the dog and had worked hard to hide the depth of her emotion. The fact that she'd asked to have him stay the night with her was revelatory enough. Thankfully, Gregory hadn't probed her about it.

She expected, however, that Lucien would interrogate her about Gregory and Ash—and more importantly, why she hadn't told him about any of it. So far, she'd successfully avoided him today. But she knew that wouldn't last.

So, she strode into his office and closed the door behind her. He looked up from his desk. "Is something amiss?"

"I know you want to ask me about Lord Gregory and the dog, but let me assure you that there is nothing notable to share. I confess I missed Ash more than I expected. If I didn't think it would pain Lord Gregory—and Ash—I might even ask to keep him for myself."

Lucien stared at her. "Extraordinary." The word was barely audible. He was behaving as if he'd just discovered some sort of new species.

Evie crossed her arms. "That's all you have to say?"

"No, but I don't think you'll answer my questions." He clasped his hands atop his desk and cocked his head. "Am I to believe there is nothing between you and Lord Gregory besides a dog?"

"That's right."

"And the fact that you asked me to help him with a government appointment. Then there is the pesky issue with Lady Witney. You seem rather...tangled up with Lord Gregory." Lucien actually looked smug.

Evie groaned low in her throat. "Stop it. There is no entanglement. We became friends caring for Ash in Oxford-shire, nothing more."

"I wonder if Lord Gregory knows that," Lucien quipped. He leapt to his feet.

"Why would you say such a thing? Please cease being meddlesome."

Lucien held up his hands. "I am hardly being meddle-some. I was merely walking down the street, minding my own business, when I encountered Lord Gregory. You should have seen the look on his face when I told him I was going to your house."

An absurd thrill shot through Evie's chest. "Don't even think of making a match." Between him and Heloise, Evie was beginning to wonder if she ought to escape their interference and return to Cornwall where she'd gone to reinvent herself. She'd enjoyed several lovely months there as the newly widowed Mrs. Renshaw.

Except she loved London far too much to leave. And her friends, who were—mostly—here. She also loved the Phoenix Club, especially on nights like tonight when it would be teeming with people she knew and who accepted her completely. Would they do so if they knew the truth?

Where the hell had that come from? She rarely thought of her past life and whether it might become known. Enough time had passed that she felt comfortable in her new situation. Perhaps it was her encounter with Arbuthnot.

Or, mayhap it was her affair with Gregory. She'd let down her guard with someone in a way she never really had before. For the first time, she wondered if she could truly reveal herself and all her secrets. The thought of doing so was terrifying.

Lucien held up his hand, palm out. "Evie, I solemnly swear I will not try to match you with anyone, least of all Lord Gregory."

"Thank you."

"But if you wanted to shag him, I'd encourage it wholeheartedly," he said, eyes twinkling.

She put her hand on her hip. "Do I give you suggestions for whom you ought to take as a lover?"

"In fact, you did two years ago. When I didn't take a new mistress after you, I distinctly recall you saying I needed to find a new one. If I remember correctly, you gave me several names."

Evie pursed her lips. "Well, I haven't done it since. And now you've had your fun—no more. My romantic life is none of your business."

He put his hand to his chest. "You wound me, my dear.

We are the best of friends. I only want your utmost happiness."

She was perhaps overreacting slightly. Because he'd seen right through her attempts at hiding what had happened. And he was indeed her best friend. Along with Ada. "I care for Lord Gregory, but there is nothing between us. Anymore," she added very quietly.

His eyes widened almost imperceptibly. "You have my complete support however you may need it. You are a kind friend to help him find an appointment."

"He's a good sort." That seemed a wholly inadequate description of the man, but Evie wouldn't expound on her sentiments. Nor would Lucien ask her to—she was certain they'd just come to a silent agreement. There would be no more discussion of her and Gregory.

"Shall we venture into the club? Ada is returning today, isn't she?"

Allowing her shoulders to relax with relief, Evie went to the door. "Yes, they got to town yesterday. She sent me a note."

"Splendid. I'm sure Max is terribly excited to attend the Lords when it opens in a few days."

"Terribly." Evie flashed a smile as Lucien opened the door for her. They went to the members' den, which was on the same floor as Lucien's office, and chatted with several members. Lucien ended up speaking with someone at length, and Evie made her way to the library, where their closer friends tended to congregate, particularly on Tuesdays.

Ada and Max were there, and Evie rushed to embrace her friend. Then she did the same to Max, who'd learned to accept the demonstrative affection of Ada's friends, who were really more like her family since she didn't really have one.

"How were your holidays in Oxfordshire?" Ada asked.

"Pleasant, but I missed London."

"You always do." Ada leaned close and whispered. "I do too."

"I heard that," Max said. "You come once a month. At least. And now we're here for the bloody Season."

"Your lack of enthusiasm is palpable," Evie said cheerily. "At least you have a wonderful wife to care for you."

"That I do." His gaze moved lovingly over Ada, who stood at his side.

"How are things at Stonehill?" Evie asked.

"Absolutely brilliant." Max beamed at his wife. "Thanks to Ada and Mrs. Tallent."

Mrs. Tallent had been a widowed tenant and was now the steward. Ada was always singing her praises.

Lucien came in then, and they all spoke for a few minutes before the men broke off to have drinks. Evie and Ada left the library to go down to the ground floor. They liked to walk about the club on Tuesday evenings to ensure everything was running smoothly.

After speaking with the head footman positioned in the dining room, they moved on to the gaming room, which was quite busy. Evie noticed Lady Dungannon, another of the patronesses on the opposite side of the room. She wasn't playing but was watching her husband.

"Let us speak with Emma," Evie said, referring to Lady Dungannon by her first name, which the patronesses typically used among themselves. "I have a proposition."

Ada blinked at her. "You do?"

"Lucien and I were discussing how Millie is becoming a bit of a nuisance." Millie was Lady Hargrove. Evie kept her voice low so they would not be overheard. "I suggested adding a fifth patroness."

Ada's eyes lit with understanding. "That may provoke her to resign." She was quiet a moment, her eyes moving over the gaming room. Then she smiled and refocused on Evie. "What about Lady Edgemont?"

Evie drew in a breath. "Brilliant. Lord Edgemont's title is old and revered, and he's quite wealthy. Lady Edgemont also comes from a pedigreed family. They are highly respected, and their invitations are sought after. Millie sees her as a rival. But will she leave, or will she be driven to prove she is a better patroness?"

Ada snorted. "I've sensed her growing frustration. If she's uncomfortable enough, she'd surely leave, wouldn't she?"

"Doubtful," Evie said with resignation.

"Pity. Shall we?" Ada started toward Emma, and Evie followed.

In her late forties with auburn hair and bright blue eyes, the petite Emma possessed a level head and a considerate nature. Her husband, an Irishman, was known for having a bit of a temper, but his wife kept him in hand for the most part.

"Good evening, ladies," Emma greeted them. "This is the busiest Tuesday we've had in some time. Because everyone's back for Parliament, I suppose."

"Yes," Ada agreed. "That is why my husband is here. I also needed to check in on the club, and he's usually kind enough to accompany me."

"He can't do without you, more like it," Emma said with a soft laugh. "We can all see the way he looks at you."

A faint blush tinged Ada's cheeks. "I am very fortunate."

"If you're going to converse, move away," Lord Dungannon grumped.

Emma put her hand on his shoulder. "Yes, dear." She bussed his cheek, then wished him good luck before leading Evie and Ada from the gaming room.

They moved into a vestibule behind the staircase hall.

"My apologies for Lord Dungannon," the viscountess said. "He becomes awfully fixated on his gaming."

Evie waved her hand. "No need to apologize. We are well acquainted with his brusqueness and don't take it personally."

Emma's brow puckered. "Evie, I've been wanting to speak with you outside our next patroness meeting." That was scheduled for later in the week. "Millie has been carping about her membership recommendations being ignored. She is particularly annoyed about her most recent suggestion—Lord and Lady Witney."

"I can imagine," Evie said. "Millie's recommendations do not often lead to invitations. I do wonder sometimes if she's happy being a patroness here."

Emma nodded slowly. "I've wondered the same. But she'll never resign—even if we install a fifth patroness whom she doesn't like. She has no hope of becoming a patroness at Almack's, and this is the next best thing."

"Is it?" Evie hadn't realized. The Phoenix Club was *nothing* like Almack's.

"It's the exclusivity," Emma said.

"But we aren't that exclusive," Ada argued. "Indeed, we include those who aren't invited to Almack's and other places."

"We also exclude those who are invited everywhere," Emma pointed out kindly.

Ada frowned slightly. "I hadn't thought of it as being exclusive. I didn't think those people wanted to be members."

"Lady Witney does," Evie said flatly. "I encountered her over the holidays, and to say she was persistent with her expressions of desire for an invitation would be an understatement."

Perhaps, in the interest of the club's mission, the membership committee *should* invite the Witneys. Lucien could be clear about the club's purpose as well as the sort of condescending conduct that wouldn't be tolerated. Then, if they exhibited such behavior, they would be expelled. No, if they did that, they'd have to invite practically everyone, regardless of their attitude and treatment of others, and that wasn't the community Lucien had built.

Emma wrinkled her nose. "So, she turned to Millie. I do dislike when someone launches a campaign to be invited."

Evie looked earnestly to Emma. "I have a proposition that may help matters. What if we add a patroness? Specifically, I was thinking of Lady Edgemont."

"Oh!" Emma's eyes widened briefly before she smiled. "Aren't you clever. Do you think she would accept?"

"She was Ada's suggestion, actually." Evie glanced toward Ada. "I think it's highly likely she'd accept the offer."

Emma's expression darkened. "This will upset Millie."

"Yes," Ada acknowledged slowly. "But it may also dilute her voice, which would benefit us all."

"I can't argue with that," Emma said. "You have my support. I daresay Harriet will also agree." She referred to the fourth and final patroness, Mrs. Holland-Ward.

"She and Lady Edgemont are friendly, I believe," Ada noted.

"Yes. That should help matters." Emma fixed them both with a serious stare. "Is your goal to drive Millie out? As I said, I don't think she'll resign."

Evie didn't want to be completely transparent, not with anyone other than Ada and Lucien. "Our goal is to establish a more pleasant atmosphere."

Emma smiled. "I can't find any fault with that. Do we need to speak with Lord Lucien or have the membership committee approve this appointment?"

"Lady Edgemont is already a member, so we won't need any input from the committee," Evie said. "We've never added a patroness, so I'm not entirely certain what's required. I suspect we'll be making it up as we go." She smiled. "I'll go and speak with Lucien now, then find you later to confirm that we patronesses are able to add someone."

Emma cocked her head and looked at Ada. "Why aren't we also adding Ada? She would be an excellent patroness. She already comes to most of our meetings during the Season, and we truly couldn't do without her input and expertise when it comes to planning events. Furthermore, a sixth patroness will only lighten the atmosphere even more."

Evie suddenly wanted to bang her head against the wall. *Of course* they should add Ada. She was Lady Warfield, for heaven's sake! Not that a title was necessary to be a patroness. Adding her would only needle Millie further. "That is an *excellent* idea, isn't it, Ada?"

Ada gaped at them for a moment. "I'm speechless, which doesn't happen often."

Evie and Emma laughed, and Ada joined in.

"You must," Emma insisted.

"I would be honored," Ada said softly. "But I know you need Mrs. Holland-Ward, at least, to agree."

Evie didn't think any of them expected Millie to support either addition, but all they needed was a majority.

"She will," Emma said with confidence. She turned to Evie. "You'll speak with Lucien."

"I will." He would be as annoyed with himself as Evie had been for not thinking of Ada at the start. "He may also have suggestions," Evie added, thinking of their conversation and his intent to speak with the secret committee members.

"Then we are in motion." Evie regarded them with a slightly narrowed eye. With any luck, Millie would find her way out.

CHAPTER 11

$\mathcal{T}$hough Gregory had visited the Phoenix Club only a handful of times before leaving London the prior Season, he felt instantly at home as he climbed the stairs to the first floor. The pleasing scent of sandalwood and citrus and the comforting murmur of conversation enveloped him, provoking a smile.

"You look enchanted," Lord Lucien noted at the top of the stairs, as if he waited there to greet those arriving.

"It's your club," Gregory said. "It's hard not to be. Do you stand here as a sentry?"

Lord Lucien laughed. "Hardly. I was going downstairs, but now that you're here, perhaps we might have a drink in the library so I can tell you about the meeting I've set for you."

Gregory grinned. "Brilliant." As he followed Lord Lucien into the library, he glanced about, hoping to catch sight of Evie. Unfortunately, he didn't see her, nor was she in the library.

Situated at the front of the building and overlooking Ryder Street below, the room was warm and inviting. It was also far less busy than the larger members' den, which occupied most of the space on this floor.

"Whiskey?" Lord Lucien asked. "We have Irish and Scottish. We also have gin, rum, and wine, if you prefer. And ale, lest I forget. The brewer would smack me."

"Scottish whisky, please." Gregory had had it only a few times and liked the flavor.

"Two Scottish whiskies, please," Lord Lucien said to the footman standing at the liquor cabinet. He poured two glasses and handed them off.

Gregory accepted his with thanks, then turned with Lord Lucien to follow him to a corner where a pair of chairs were situated. When they were seated, Lord Lucien spoke.

"Given your interest in the law, I've secured a meeting for you with the Lord High Chancellor's office."

Gregory could hardly believe it. "Indeed? That is astonishing. Thank you."

"It's just a meeting, but I daresay with your family connections, an appointment will be forthcoming. You'll be meeting with Lord Hargrove. Do you know him?"

"I don't believe we've been introduced."

"He may be here tonight, but I haven't seen him yet. He's a jovial fellow. You'll like him. I'll introduce you if he shows up."

"I greatly appreciate that." Gregory lifted his glass in a toast.

Lord Lucien did the same, and they both drank. "I'm curious why you veered from the church. When I mentioned your name to several people, they all believed you were headed for ordination."

"That was the plan. Rather, it was my father's plan." Gregory grimaced. "It pains me to think I might be disappointing him, but I hope he'd be proud of me in the end."

"Were you close?" Lord Lucien asked.

"Yes. He very much wanted me to sit in the Lords and reasoned that my becoming a bishop was the only way for me to do that."

"You're the spare. Your brother's death is another way." He winked at Gregory, who wasn't entirely sure how to take that. "I'm jesting," Lord Lucien clarified. "My apologies. I can have a rather dark sense of humor at times. Of course I'm not advocating your brother's untimely demise."

"Of course not," Gregory murmured. "The terrible truth is that my father might have laughed at that. He told me he wished I'd been his heir. He and my brother were...not close."

"That sounds like me and my father," Lord Lucien said, his tone frank and without emotion. "My older brother is, thankfully, the heir as well as being the favorite."

"I can't say I enjoy being the favorite. I wonder if my brother realized that. He never said."

"It's an open secret in our family. I have no illusions as to what my father thinks of me. I'm a disappointment and a general pain in his arse." Lord Lucien lifted his glass a second time, then took a drink, the length of which seemed to indicate he was at least a little bothered by his father's sentiments.

"How can that be true?" Gregory asked. "You're successful —with a decorated military background, I believe—and well liked. Any father would be proud to call you his son."

"Not mine. Don't feel badly for me. I accepted his dissatisfaction long ago. Besides, not everyone finds me so agreeable. Have you not heard that in some circles, I am called a devil?"

"Why?"

Lord Lucien shrugged. "My 'reckless' ways and my association with people who are beneath me." He leaned toward Gregory and lowered his voice to a stage whisper. "Because the Phoenix Club welcomes men who are in...trade." He widened his eyes as if he'd just imparted a horrible piece of gossip.

Gregory rolled his eyes. "I realize that bothers some people, but that makes them more in line with the devil than you, I think."

"Coming from a man who has engaged in extensive religious study, I shall take that as a compliment."

It occurred to Gregory that his brother could very well be in that circle who regarded Lord Lucien in that manner. Sipping his whisky, Gregory thought of Clifford and the fact that he'd have to pay a call on him and his wife at some point. Probably. He really should.

Thankfully, Evie walked in and interrupted those annoying thoughts. Her dark purple gown sparkled with what had to be crystals sewn into the embroidery on the bodice and around the hem. She always looked stunning, and he wondered if her appearance would ever cease to steal his breath.

"Ah, Evie has arrived," Lord Lucien said softly. "I'm sure you wish to speak with her."

Gregory darted his gaze toward the other man briefly, wondering at his odd tone. His eyes held a knowing glimmer that Gregory didn't want to contemplate.

"About the dog, I mean," Lord Lucien added. Gregory was all but certain that was *not* what he meant. What did the man know? Or think that he knew?

"Thank you again for arranging the meeting," Gregory said, rising.

"My pleasure."

Gregory finished his whisky and set the empty glass on a table before making his way to Evie. She'd entered with another woman. Petite, with dark hair and blue-gray eyes, she was very pretty. Gregory thought they might have met before but couldn't recall for certain.

Evie spotted him and smiled. "Lord Gregory, allow me to introduce my dear friend and the club's bookkeeper, Lady Warfield. Ada, this is Lord Gregory Blakemore."

Lady Warfield gave him her hand, and he bowed his head. "I think we met last Season," she said. "I am sorry for the loss of your father."

"Thank you." Gregory had already heard enough of that since his return to town to last him a lifetime. He was ready to move on. But he would never be rude about it. He looked to Evie. "I was hoping you might give me a tour."

"You've been here before," she mused, a smile teasing her lips and making him want to kiss her. Except, he nearly *always* wanted to kiss her.

"I didn't know you then," he said. "Perhaps Lady Warfield would oblige me."

Evie clasped her hands. "That might be best since I need to speak with Lucien about an important matter."

Disappointment swirled through him. Lady Warfield opened her mouth to speak, but Evie gave her a gentle nudge with her elbow. "Be sure to show Lord Gregory the mezzanine to the ballroom."

Gregory offered his arm to Lady Warfield. "Shall we, then?"

"Yes. And you can tell me all about how you and Evie became acquainted."

The barest flash of alarm passed over Evie's features. Surely, she knew he wouldn't be indiscreet. It also seemed her "dear friend" didn't know about his and Evie's "friendship."

Lady Warfield took his arm, and he turned his head, whispering to Evie, "I'll see you tomorrow night."

She didn't respond, but there was an unmistakable smolder in her gaze. That was enough for him.

For now.

$\sim$

*a*fter foisting Gregory off on Ada last night at the Phoenix Club, Evie had seen him a few more times over the course of the evening. She hadn't approached him, however. Their eyes had met once, and she'd nearly sent a note to him via footman asking him to meet her in the garden. There, she would have stolen him through the doorway that led to the ladies' side, where they would have privacy.

She'd done none of those things, though, and it had affected her sleep again. Her unsatisfied desire for him was not conducive to slumber.

It was, however, the reason she was glued to the window in her drawing room, watching the street below for his and Ash's approach. At last, she spotted them, a tall, athletic figure in a dark, indistinct costume and a small, white dog wearing a tunic.

Evie stood and hurried down to the kitchen level. She reached the door that led up to the street just as Foster let him in.

"Thank you, Foster," she said brightly. "I'll take over now."

The butler inclined his head and took himself off.

Ash barked happily, and Evie scooped him into her arms, cooing endearments as she nuzzled him.

"Your butler is rather young. And, ah, pleasing to regard," Gregory said, removing his hat.

"He's excellent." Evie had known him in their youth and had been thrilled to give him the position. About the same age as she, he'd been working as a footman in Golden

Square. She'd hired him and his sister, a scullery maid from the same household. Maggie was now Evie's very young, extremely talented cook.

Evie cocked her head at Gregory. "Are you jealous?"

"Of every moment everyone else spends with you." He flashed her a smile that made her knees weak.

"You've become an accomplished flirt. Have you been practicing what I taught you?"

"Not at all. It's easy to flirt with someone when you find them to be the most enchanting person in the world."

Evie rolled her eyes. "Really, you need to stop. That's excessive. Now, what did you bring for our boy?" She nodded toward the case he carried.

"His favorite pillow to sleep on, his favorite rope toy, and some food my housekeeper insisted on sending."

"My cook has already prepared his dinner. She was quite enthusiastic about it."

"Well, then he can choose which one he prefers. Or eat both, which is the most likely outcome if you allow it," Gregory said with a laugh. "Can I carry this upstairs for you?"

Evie realized she'd created a problem. She ought to have had Foster take the case, for she couldn't carry both it and Ash. She *could* set Ash down and take the case.

Or she could invite Gregory upstairs.

That seemed risky given her unceasing and rather provocative thoughts about him. She'd just have to send him on his way directly.

"Yes, thank you." Evie led him up to the ground level, then up again to the first floor. Eventually, the case should go in her bedchamber, but she stopped short of taking him there. Instead, she guided him into her private sitting room. Which was just outside her chamber, so was there really any difference?

After removing his gloves, hat, and greatcoat, Gregory set the case down and opened it. He removed Ash's things, and the dog wriggled in Evie's arms.

"You want to investigate?" she asked with a laugh, setting him down. "You know those are your things. But why are they here? Because you're going to stay with me."

Ash darted to where Gregory crouched down and immediately grabbed the rope with his teeth. Carrying it to the hearth, he sat down and gnawed, growling softly with his efforts.

Evie settled herself on the settee. "I finished the larger tunic. It's green."

"He'll look quite smart in that, I imagine. He dons it without fuss before we go outside."

"He knows he's warmer." Evie smiled at the pup. "Are you certain he should stay?" She turned her head toward Gregory. "What if he misses you?"

"Well, I could stay too." His heated gaze held hers, and she fell completely under his spell. But only for a moment. As tempting as it was to invite him into her bedchamber just a few steps away, she would not. She shouldn't even have invited him up here.

"You can't."

He stared at her mouth, and Evie's body felt as if it might ignite into flame. "What is it you're afraid of?"

"I'm not afraid of anything. I established the boundaries of our affair, and we are now outside them."

"Because we're in London? Or because it's past the holidays?" he asked softly, lowering his frame to sit beside her on the settee.

"Both."

He arched a brow at her as he put his arm on the back of the settee. His fingers were perilously close to her shoulder. "Those boundaries aren't moveable?"

"They are not."

"Pity, for I've not been able to stop thinking of you." He moved his hand, and the air he disturbed rustled over her flesh as if he'd touched her.

Evie shot up from the settee and moved to stand near a cabinet that held liquor. Perhaps she ought to have a glass of wine to steady herself, for she was feeling rather unbalanced. "A month is perhaps not enough time to…overcome what we shared."

"Is it for you?" He kept his arm along the back of the settee, and the pose made him look as if he'd claimed the piece of furniture. His features were also set in an enigmatic yet seductive expression. She'd never wanted to throw herself at someone before, but it was taking everything she had to keep away from him.

"I am quite busy with the club and my friends."

"That's hardly an answer." He glanced toward his hand as he flexed his fingers. "You avoided being alone with me at the club, which wouldn't really have been being alone with me at all given the number of people in attendance. Yet, you invite me here where we truly are alone. I find myself wondering at your expectations."

He met her gaze once more and stood, slowly, his body stretching like a cat after a nap. Then he prowled toward her, and she'd never felt more like prey.

Prey that wanted to be caught.

Hell, *Evie* didn't know her expectations.

"I invited you up here against my better judgment," she said, feeling almost faint with desire as he stopped just before her.

"Then I can deduce you have not, probably, *overcome* our liaison. I can tell you without hesitation that I have not. I think of you when I am awake, I dream of you when I'm asleep, and I long for you in every hour of every day." He caressed her cheek with two fingertips. It was the gentlest of touches, a tease of what could come next. She only had to ask him to stay…

Evie took a step back. "You should go. Before I change my mind and lose my nerve about keeping Ash overnight."

"Is that what you're going to lose your nerve about?" His hand brushed hers.

She shivered, desperate for more of his touch. But she would not surrender. This was the life she wanted—not one with a man, no matter how thoroughly he shattered her carefully laid defenses. "Yes. *Just* that."

Moving quickly, she went to pet Ash. She was not above using their dog as a barricade.

"What if I call your bluff?"

She narrowed her eyes at him. "Don't do that, please. You are going to anger me very shortly. I was clear about what I wanted from the start. You can't try to change the rules now."

He exhaled. "I don't wish to anger you. It's only that I sense whatever we shared is not yet over. You ended things rather suddenly—and please don't tell me you set expectations. You did, but I was still hoping for New Year's or Epiphany." He waved his hand, and she could see from his eyes that he was frustrated.

She couldn't think of anything to say to ease his agitation, nor did she think she should. She didn't owe him anything, and she wasn't responsible for his feelings.

"If you shared my opinion—that there is still more between us—I would hope you would allow us to see it through. I'm not asking for forever. I'm only hoping for… whatever feels right to us."

Dammit, but he made a compelling argument. Her only requirement was that no one could know. Her servants were completely trustworthy and would be discreet. There were only five of them anyway, and just three lived upstairs. The other two—a mother and daughter who cleaned—resided elsewhere and also worked for another household.

Wait, was she actually considering this? No. She would not. "Gregory, you need to let the past go. We had a lovely time together, but it's over. I do hope we can be friends, for Ash's sake if nothing else." The thought of having to say goodbye to Ash forever was surprisingly horrible. She didn't think she could do it. "What time should I bring Ash back to you tomorrow?"

Shadows flitted over his gaze, masking whatever he was feeling. "I can fetch him." Gregory went to retrieve his belongings, setting his hat on his head before donning his greatcoat. Lastly, he drew on his gloves.

Regret knotted in Evie's belly, but she wouldn't change her mind.

"Don't forget to take him outside so he can relieve himself," Gregory said, his voice stilted. "He'll let you know when, but it will be well before dawn. I'll be here around noon to pick him up if that suits you."

She would make sure to be elsewhere. "Perfectly. Thank you. Shall I show you out?"

"That won't be necessary. I can find my way." He smiled at the pup. "Good night, Ash. See you tomorrow."

Ash trotted over to him and nuzzled his leg, as if he understood. Gregory stroked his head, then took his leave without another word.

Walking to the closed door, Ash sat down and let out a soft whimper. Oh dear, it seemed he *did* miss Gregory.

Evie went to scoop him up, carrying him back to a chair near the hearth and setting him on her lap. "I know, my dear boy. I miss him too." At least she could tell the dog the truth, if not herself. And certainly not Gregory.

She missed him. She wanted him. She would eagerly rekindle their affair.

But she could not. He wanted her for more than that—she could see it in his eyes. It reminded her of the way Alfred looked at Heloise. The first time Evie had met him, when he was still Heloise's protector, she'd seen how he felt. She'd told Heloise that this man was different, that he'd formed an emotional connection. Heloise had rolled her eyes in response, but Evie had been right. Three months later, he'd proposed marriage.

Evie was not Heloise, however. A proposal of marriage wouldn't make her happy. This life—her job, her own home, independence—made her happy.

Gregory could bring her temporary joy, and he had. And now it was over.

CHAPTER 12

*L*ondon was dark and cold as Gregory hurried to Evie's. He hadn't wanted to wait for his horse to be saddled or his gig to be hitched. Her note had been short but terrifying: Ash was gone.

Gregory hadn't even bothered with a cravat or a waistcoat, and he'd run a good measure of the distance, heating his body so that he wasn't chilled in the slightest. Except internally, where fear for Ash kept his veins the temperature of ice.

The door to her house was answered almost as quickly as he'd knocked. A young woman with a blonde braid from which many strands of hair had escaped greeted him. "They're in the garden."

Gregory followed her to the back of the terrace, where the door to the garden stood open. Lanterns illuminated the darkness, making it easy for Gregory to spot Evie. She rushed toward him, a dark cloak billowing about her legs.

"Someone left the gate open. Just the barest amount. I didn't notice it." She looked pale and frightened. "I brought Ash out so he could relieve himself."

"He got out through the gate?"

She nodded as a shiver rolled through her. "I confess I closed my eyes briefly. He seemed to be taking a long time. When I went to see what he was doing, I couldn't find him. We've searched the garden thoroughly. Thrice. Foster has gone out through the gate to look."

Gregory gently clasped her upper arms and looked into her worried eyes. "We'll find him."

Clapping a hand over her mouth as tears pooled in her eyes, Evie nodded. Gregory resisted the urge to pull her into his arms—both because he doubted she wanted that, and because he needed to find Ash.

He looked to the young woman, certainly one of Evie's household, who'd let him in and inclined his head toward Evie. The servant moved to stand with Evie, and Gregory asked if there was a spare lantern.

"Here, my lord," another young woman said, coming toward him with her lantern.

Gregory thanked her and strode toward the gate, which opened into a narrow alley that ran behind the row of terrace houses. Glancing up and down the alley, he saw a light toward St. James's. That must be Foster. With long strides, he walked quickly to catch up to the butler.

"Foster, what say you?"

The man turned, his hat pulled low on his brow. "I've been looking for open gates in case the dog ran into another garden, but so far, they've all been shut tight. I mean to keep going to the end."

"What about the other direction?"

"Haven't been that way yet."

"Then that's what I'll do." Gregory spun about and hurried back the way he'd come, passing Evie's garden and her open gate. He paused and poked his head inside. "Will someone come stand here to keep an eye out in case Ash comes back this way?"

Evie rushed forward. "Of course."

Glancing toward the house, he asked, "Is there nowhere else he can get into the house besides that door from the library?"

"There's another door in the corner there, but it was closed and locked. Still, we checked the house thoroughly."

Gregory didn't doubt it. Ash had to have been missing close to an hour already. "Our search continues." He moved along the alley, checking the gates as he went and calling Ash's name as loudly as he dared. It wouldn't do to wake the neighbors. But perhaps they should. If Ash had gone into someone's garden through an open gate that had closed, he'd be trapped in a strange place. He'd be afraid.

He was likely afraid regardless. Poor boy.

Gregory shook such thoughts from his mind. They were not helpful in this moment. He moved slowly, careful to wait after calling Ash's name to see if he could hear any response. Finally, there was a soft whimper.

Excitement spreading in his chest, Gregory called the dog's name again and listened intently. Another whimper. The sound came from the left, but not from the garden he was standing outside. It was too distant. Unless Ash was being very quiet.

Moving to the next garden, Gregory tried the gate, but it was locked. The wall was also a good six feet. He set the lantern atop the wall and grabbed the top of the stone to haul himself up.

Pulling his legs over so he could sit on the stone, he held up the lantern. "Ash! Where are you, boy?"

The barking started just before Gregory saw the streak of white dart toward him. This was followed by a larger figure —also on four legs—with a darker coat. Ash stood on his hind legs and pawed at the wall beneath Gregory's feet, barking wildly.

"Shhh." Gregory dropped down into the garden and swept Ash into his arms. "There you are, boy. You're safe."

With his tongue lolling out the side of his mouth and his dark eyes wide with excitement, Ash didn't appear distressed. Indeed, Gregory would have said he looked quite pleased with himself.

Something moved against Gregory's legs, prompting him to look down. The dark brown dog was nuzzling his calf.

"I see you've made a friend, Ash. Who's this, then?" Gregory bent down to pet the dog's head.

"Gregory, did you find him?" Evie called over the wall.

"Yes. He's made a friend in here. Though I can't imagine how he got in." Gregory picked up the lantern and held it high, looking along the wall. He moved forward until he saw the small hole in the corner. "I see it now."

Doubling back, Gregory went to unlock the gate. Before opening it, he turned to the other dog. "We have to go now, but we'll be sure to speak with your people tomorrow. Sleep well."

He faced the gate. "Evie, I'm coming out, but we have to move quickly so I can shut the gate before the other dog gets out."

"Other dog? Oh, Ash's new friend."

Gregory opened the gate just enough to squeeze through the opening, then closed it again. Unfortunately, he couldn't lock it, but he'd explain its state when he called on the residents tomorrow. They really needed to fix the hole in their wall, unless they wanted visitors such as Ash.

"Ash!" Evie reached for the pup but stopped short, her gaze rising to meet Gregory's. "I'm a horrid pet mother." Her distress was evident and nearly caused Gregory to drop Ash and take her in his arms. But he did not. He would soothe her when Ash was safely in her garden.

Grabbing the lantern from the wall, Gregory handed it to Evie to carry. "You are not horrid. At anything." He clutched Ash with one arm so he could put his other around Evie's waist. "Come, let's get back to your house. I think Ash has had enough adventure for one night."

As soon as they entered the garden, Gregory closed the gate firmly. The two young women who'd been helping with the search voiced their relief.

"Take Mrs. Renshaw and Ash inside," Gregory said, giving the dog to Evie and taking the lantern.

"Can I be trusted with him?" Evie whispered. She took Ash into her arms and snuggled him close, dropping kisses on his head and murmuring apologies.

"Of course you can," Gregory said. "I'm going to find Foster and let him know the search is over."

Evie looked at him, her eyes fervent with gratitude. "Thank you."

Gregory waited until they were inside with the door closed before he left the garden once more. Striding quickly, he found Foster and informed him that all was well.

"It was my fault, my lord," he said brusquely. "I left the gate ajar when I came back from my afternoon off."

"I daresay you won't do that again." Gregory clapped the younger man on the shoulder and kept his tone light. "Don't abuse yourself. These things happen, and there was no real harm done. The worst of it may be a litter of puppies at the neighbor's."

The butler blinked at him. "Where did you find him?"

"A few gardens over from Mrs. Renshaw's. There was another dog, female, I believe, but it was difficult to tell. I'll call on them tomorrow to explain the situation—they've a hole in their garden wall they need to repair to avoid future visitors. Next time, it may not be a friendly creature like Ash."

"*You'll* call on them?" Foster asked as they made their way back to Evie's.

Belatedly, Gregory realized how that would look. Why would *he* be concerned with a dog when he lived nowhere nearby? "Mrs. Renshaw will do it."

They walked in silence until they were nearly to the garden gate. Foster stopped, prompting Gregory to do so as well.

"Lord Gregory, I feel I should tell you that we all care for Mrs. Renshaw very much. She is more like family to us than an employer."

Gregory wanted to ask several questions about his statement. Why were they like family? How had they come to work for Evie? What was the reason for their depth of feeling? Instead, he said, "How wonderful."

Foster went on, "I won't presume to guess at your relationship with Mrs. Renshaw, but you should know that we will all look out for her."

He sounded like a protective father. Gregory stifled a smile. Here, he'd been absurdly jealous that Evie's butler was a handsome young man. "She is lucky to have all of you looking after her. I care for her too." A great deal more than she wanted him to.

Foster smiled, and damn if he wasn't even handsomer than he'd been a second earlier. "That is good to hear, my lord."

"Shall we go inside, then?" Gregory asked pleasantly.

"Of course." Foster opened the gate and gestured for Gregory to precede him. "I'll make sure it's locked securely."

"Excellent." Yes, Evie was quite lucky to have such loyal and caring people in her household.

Gregory went into the library and was followed by

Foster, who asked if Evie required anything further, as if searching for a dog in the wee hours of the predawn were as regular as serving tea.

"No. Thank you, Foster. For everything. What would I do without you, Maggie, and Delilah?"

"Fortunately, you've no need to find out," Foster said with a reassuring smile. "Good night, then." He took himself off, leaving Evie and Gregory alone.

Well, not *alone*. Ash was asleep on a chair next to where Evie stood.

"He wore himself out with all that," Gregory said.

Evie looked down at Ash with a pained expression. "You should take him home."

"Not right now, I shouldn't. I practically ran here, which means I'd have to carry him all the way home. He needs to sleep."

"Can you carry him upstairs?"

"Certainly." Gregory gingerly picked Ash up, careful not to wake him, which likely wasn't even possible given the depth of the dog's gentle snores.

Evie led him upstairs to her private sitting room, but they didn't stop there. She continued through to her bedchamber, a gloriously feminine space decorated in various shades of rose and vibrant gold. It suited her perfectly, right down to the delicately turned posts on her bed.

"His cushion is there." Evie gestured to a spot right in front of the fireplace where it was warm and cozy.

Gregory set him down. Ash didn't flinch.

"Is that where he slept all night?" Gregory asked.

"He started there, but then he moved to the foot of my bed," Evie said, removing her cloak and draping it over a chair. "I am so sorry, Gregory. How on earth have you cared for him this long without losing him?"

"Well, he did like to run around when I took him out at

Witney Court. After two nights having to chase him down, I learned to bring a treat with me to lure him back inside."

She stared at him. "You could have told me that."

"I didn't think it would be an issue since your garden is enclosed."

Grimacing, she leaned against the side of her bed. "I am a total failure. I told you I wasn't meant to have a pet."

Gregory moved to stand in front of her. He was going to touch her but stopped himself. "May I take your hands?"

She nodded and reached for him before he could do so.

Holding her firmly, he looked into her eyes. "Listen to me. You are not a failure in any way. You've never had a pet, and you're right that I should have given you more guidance. Puppies in particular can be vexing. You mustn't blame yourself. All is well."

She squeezed his hands. "My sister always took care of me. I've never had to care for something—or someone —else."

"You care for your servants, and I can see you do an exemplary job. They are quite loyal to you. Indeed, Foster sounds like a sibling or even your father."

This caught her off guard. Her grip went limp for a moment, and she cocked her head. "Does he?"

"Yes. Surely, you must know this."

She was slow to respond. "I suppose I do, but why do you?"

"Foster wanted to make sure I knew that they cared for you. He mentioned something about not knowing about our relationship—"

Her nostrils flared. "What did he say?"

"Nothing specific, just that they care for and watch after you. They said you are more like a family."

"That's true," she whispered, her gaze dipping to his chest.

Cloaked in his greatcoat and with all his running about,

he realized he was quite warm. He either needed to remove the coat or be on his way.

"You aren't wearing a cravat," she said.

"There wasn't time to properly dress. I wanted to get here as quickly as I could."

She lifted her gaze to his once more. He saw naked desire in their depths, and it stole his breath.

They stood like that for a long moment during which Gregory's cock went completely hard. He licked his lips, for his mouth was suddenly dry.

"I'm actually quite warm," he murmured. "I should probably go."

She let go of his hands and slid hers inside his coat, running her palms up his shirtfront. "Or you could stay." She pushed the greatcoat off his shoulders. All he had to do was twitch his arms to make it fall to the floor.

"You want me to stay?" As soon as he said it, he regretted the words. Why question what he wanted more than anything?

"Yes." She brought her hands up to the sides of his neck and brushed her lips against his. "I want you to stay. Here. With me. In my bed. And not to sleep."

$\sim$

Surprise flickered across Gregory's face before he clasped her waist and kissed her, long and slow. Evie tugged his shirt from his breeches, desperate to feel him. Why had she denied herself—and him—this pleasure?

He backed away, and she thought he meant to leave. But he only moved to sit on the bed so he could remove his boots.

Evie stepped between his legs and stripped his stockings away, baring his feet. She ran her hands up the insides of his calves, her gaze on the rigid shaft visible just beneath his breeches. He pulled at the fasteners on her dressing gown, opening the front. She shrugged it off, letting it pool to the floor as she kicked her slippers off.

Pushing him back, she worked the buttons of his fall until they were all free. She slid her hands beneath him and pulled the breeches down his hips. He wriggled, helping her tug them free. The hem of his shirt drifted down to shield his cock. Evie gripped the hem in one hand and encircled him with the other just before she lowered her mouth to the tip.

Gregory gripped her head, his fingers tangling in her hair, loosening the ribbon that held it to the side. He lifted the mass and held it at the back of her nape, as she moved her mouth over him.

"Evie." He moaned her name over and over as she swallowed him to the back of her throat, her tongue gliding along the underside of his shaft. She held his balls, fondling the sac, then stroking her finger along the flesh beneath them.

He arched up, spearing into her mouth with eager thrusts. She wanted to finish him like this, to feel him spend himself into her. They'd done that once before, and it had been glorious, like nothing she'd ever experienced. He'd said the same thing.

But not now. She wanted him to take her, to dominate her, to make her forget why she'd kept him away.

She slid her mouth from his cock and straightened. He looked at her with slitted eyes from the bed, watching as she pulled her night rail over her head and cast it aside.

His lips parted, and she heard the sharp intake of his breath. His sculpted chest rose rapidly as he looked at her, making her feel more beautiful—and powerful—than anyone ever had.

"Touch yourself," he rasped.

Lust arced through her, making her breasts heavy and her sex wet. "Where?"

"Your nipples. Pretend I'm touching them, pulling them. Show me how you like it."

She loved when he talked to her like this. He'd grown bolder with every encounter, arousing her with his words as well as his touch. Evie squeezed her flesh and moaned.

"Are you wet with desire?" he asked, his gaze dipping to her sex.

"Yes.

"Show me."

She skimmed her hand down her abdomen until she met the curls on her mons, then she slipped a finger into herself, thrusting deep. She whimpered softly before withdrawing her finger.

He sat up and wrapped his hand around her wrist. Holding her stare, he brought her finger to his mouth and sucked it between his lips, his tongue licking it to the base before releasing her.

That was perhaps the most erotic thing anyone had ever done with her. He could have asked her anything in that moment, and she would have said yes. She was completely in his thrall, and there was nowhere else she wanted to be.

She gripped his shoulders and kissed him almost savagely as she surrendered utterly to her most basic need. In one swift move, he pulled her onto the bed and covered her with his body. Tearing his mouth from hers, he ravaged a path of kisses to her breasts as his hand moved between her thighs.

Stroking her sex, he sucked her nipples until she writhed beneath him, mindless, as she clutched at his head, her legs spread for his touch. He brought her nearly to release, then thrust his cock into her. Evie locked her legs around him and raked her nails along his back as he speared into her. She came almost instantly, her body singing with rapture.

He didn't slow or hesitate. Rocking his hips, he thrust hard and deep. Their bodies moved together as if they'd designed the choreography. He kissed her fast as he quickened their pace. The world spun out of control, making Evie wonder if she was still on the physical plane at all.

Another orgasm snatched her in its grip, and she cried out. He came with her, his muscles tensing as his backside went rock hard. She dug her heels into him as wave after wave of pleasure brought her back to earth.

When he was spent, he rolled to his side, panting as he worked to catch his breath. Evie smiled into the darkness, unsure if she'd ever felt more replete.

At length, he murmured, "That was unexpected."

Evie moved to her side to face him. "I hope that's all right."

He turned his head toward her. "It's bloody wonderful."

She'd never heard him curse before. "You don't usually talk like that."

His brow creased slightly. "Was it too much? When I asked you to touch yourself?"

Laughing softly, she was surprised to feel another surge of desire. "Not that—the swearing. The other talk was incredibly arousing. You may do that any time. The same with licking my finger." That provoked another swell of lust.

"Any time?" He asked the question quietly, with an edge of tension. "Does that mean we might do this again?"

How could she refuse? This made her happy. *He* made her happy.

"I would like that," she said slowly. "But nothing more. I'm not opposed to...coupling with you like this on occasion."

"I can accept that." He grinned. "It's more than I expected, but it's what I hoped for."

She knew that—he'd been clear. "We've established that you're an incurable optimist."

"Mmm." He took her hand and kissed her palm. "Will you tell your servants, or are we to try to hide this?"

"I suspect they may have heard the racket I made." She grimaced. "I feel badly about that. I already woke them to help me find Ash."

"Speaking of Ash, you're going to have to speak with your neighbors three houses toward the Haymarket."

"That's where you found him."

"That's where his friend lives. I suspect she could be more than a friend. If so, there may be puppies in the near future."

Evie gasped. "But Ash is still a puppy."

"Old enough to be a father, I think. But, I could be wrong. I just thought it was worth mentioning in case their dear pet is increasing."

"Oh dear." Evie giggled as she glanced toward the fire where Ash was snoozing. "What a rake."

Gregory laughed, and she realized she'd missed that as much as lying with him. He sobered rather quickly. "It has made me think…I know you typically use a sponge when we are together, but not every time, such as the party at Witney Court and tonight. You aren't concerned with conception?"

"Not particularly. I know how to take care of that should it happen."

He blinked at her. "What do you mean?"

"There are herbs a woman can take if she's not equipped to be a mother."

"Have you done that?" He shook his head. "Never mind. You've only been with your husband and now me."

"That's not true. I have had other lovers. And yes, I've had to use that before. It wouldn't do to have a child when unwed."

He was quiet, his brow creasing and relaxing, then creasing again. "While I can't argue with your logic, I wonder how you might have felt about it."

"I felt it was the right thing to do. I am aware of my courses, and they are typically reliable. It's possible a child may not even have come, but I wanted to make sure. Can you imagine how that would have been for the child, a bastard?"

"You're very careful."

"I try to be. It is challenging to be a woman."

"Yes. But you make it look magnificent." He scooted closer to her and kissed her. "Thank you for telling me that."

"Including about the lovers?"

He closed one eye and smiled. "I can't say I'm not envious of the time any man has spent with you, but you're with me now, and that's all that matters."

"Thank you."

"For what?"

"For being understanding." He was unlike any man she'd ever known. Most wouldn't have even asked about conception. Of her protectors, only Lucien had sought to have the conversation. Evie had just always taken it upon herself to ensure she was guarded. To be with a man who shared her burden meant more than he could know. "For supporting me." She kissed him back, wriggling against him. "And for not being angry with me about Ash."

"I could never. We are all human. We do our very best every day. Don't we?"

That was all Evie had done. She'd done her best to survive. Until she'd been allowed to do more than that. Now, she did her best to make the most of every day, to feel joy and contentment.

"Now we can sleep," she said, closing her eyes, suddenly exhausted.

Gregory made her feel both joy *and* contentment. And that scared her more than anything.

CHAPTER 13

G regory couldn't help feeling a tinge of awe as he stepped into the Palace of Westminster. He was shown to a chamber that resembled a sitting room with two seating areas. One was around a table, while the other was a pair of settees and four chairs assembled in a conversational style.

Not knowing where to sit as he waited for Lord Hargrove, Gregory lingered between the two areas. Instead of contemplating the interview ahead, he couldn't help thinking of last night, the second he'd spent in Evie's bed. Having stolen into her garden through the back alley, he'd departed the same way just before dawn this morning. This time, however, he'd left Ash at home.

A smile threatened, but he worked to keep his face sober. He felt giddy, and it wouldn't do to display that when Hargrove entered. That didn't stop him from continuing to recall the bliss of Evie's embrace until Hargrove at last entered the chamber.

"Afternoon, Lord Gregory," Hargrove greeted, offering his hand.

Gregory pumped the man's arm before releasing him. "Afternoon, Hargrove. Thank you for meeting with me."

"Happy to." Hargrove moved to the seating area and deposited his average-sized frame into a chair. His head was bare, revealing a thinning patch of light brown hair. His gray-blue eyes were sharp, while the blunt edge of his slightly upturned nose gave him a boyish look despite the fact that he was in his early fifties. "I had great respect for your father, and I'm delighted to help his offspring, if I may. So terribly sad that he's gone from us. Far too soon." He lowered his gaze for a moment.

Taking a seat on the settee nearest Hargrove's chair, Gregory angled himself toward the older man. "I appreciate your kind words," Gregory murmured. "He would be pleased to hear them."

Hargrove's head snapped up as he refocused on Gregory. "Would he be pleased that you are seeking this appointment? I'd thought he was eager for you to be ordained and follow the path to becoming a bishop. Indeed, he made no secret of that."

"I'd like to think he'd support me in whatever I choose." Which wasn't to say that Gregory believed he actually would. No, he feared his father would be disappointed. Gregory would have tried to explain to his father that he was doing what felt right and true to him. In the end, he hoped his father would support his choices because they were his—and he'd trusted Gregory, hadn't he? "I find I am more drawn to the law than ecclesiastical matters. If I do not work in the government, I plan to become a barrister."

"Ah yes, I seem to remember you were called to the bar."

"I was. I also taught at Oxford for a year, which I enjoyed very much."

"What did you teach?"

"History and religion."

Hargrove inclined his head. "Well done. You didn't care for that, or was there no opportunity for you to stay?"

"I was only filling in for the year. I might have stayed on if they'd asked me to."

"And now you find yourself seeking a position with the government. I might wonder why you haven't chosen to seek a seat in the Commons."

"In truth, I considered it, but I like the member from our constituency."

Hargrove chuckled. "That doesn't mean you can't run in another borough, particularly if you've the funds to just purchase one."

Gregory didn't laugh with him. He found rotten boroughs a despicable practice and supported reform to eliminate them. Voicing that opinion, however, would likely not gain him an appointment in the Tory government.

"What does your brother think of your change in pursuit?" Hargrove asked.

"We haven't discussed it at length."

"Lady Hargrove and I were fortunate to dine with Witney and his lovely new marchioness the other night. He didn't mention any of this."

Gregory stiffened, wondering what Clifford might have said. Or had he said nothing? "Did you tell him we would be meeting today?"

Hargrove nodded vigorously. "I did. Witney was surprised to learn you were interested in this type of work." His gaze met Gregory's. "*I* was surprised he didn't know."

"He's recently wed and new to the marquessate," Gregory responded, trying to keep his voice even. Would Clifford speak against him? Just because he'd enjoyed being contrary in their youth didn't mean he would sabotage Gregory now. Honestly, Gregory didn't know. After failing to understand what motivated Clifford, Gregory had instead worked to distance himself from his capricious brother. "I haven't bothered to trouble him with my plans." Gregory offered the viscount a bland smile.

"Very sensible of you," Hargrove said, giving Gregory some relief. "I do think there is a place for you here. Give me a week or a fortnight to secure things."

The anxiety that Clifford had somehow ruined this for Gregory dissipated. "Thank you. I appreciate your time and consideration."

Hargrove rose. "I'll send word soon." He flashed a brief, toothless smile, then departed.

Gregory exhaled as he wiped a hand over his brow. Did that mean he would soon be installed in the Office of the Lord High Chancellor? It certainly seemed so. Now, he allowed himself to smile.

Everything seemed to be going well at the moment. He had Evie, this appointment, not to mention a splendid pup awaiting him at home. The only thing better would be if Ash were waiting for him at Evie's and that it was Gregory's home too.

It was a distant dream, but he felt renewed hope after Evie had rekindled their affair. Perhaps she'd fall in love with him as he'd done with her. He certainly hadn't fallen out of love in the past month.

Feeling giddy once more, Gregory left the chamber and a moment later, encountered the equivalent of a sudden rainstorm.

"Afternoon, Greg," Clifford said with a grin. "Finished with Hargrove?"

Gregory steeled himself. "I am."

"Splendid. I hope it went well." Clifford's brow furrowed, but to Gregory, the expression looked forced. "I confess I was rather shocked to hear about this interest of yours when I dined with Hargrove earlier this week."

"As I told Hargrove, I didn't wish to burden you."

"But I can help."

"Can you?" Gregory asked, skeptical. If Clifford truly wanted to be of assistance, he would have done so when he was dining with Hargrove.

Clifford smirked at him. "You have the appointment, do you not?" So, he *had* advocated for Gregory, or at least wanted him to think so. Gregory suddenly felt beleaguered. He was tired of trying to guess at his brother's actions and motives. For all that they'd grown up together, they'd never shared confidences. They were simply cut from different cloth. Indeed, they didn't even have the same friends and hadn't attended the same college at Oxford.

"I believe so, but it isn't finalized. That will take a fortnight, perhaps less." Gregory decided to assume Clifford had supported him. "I appreciate you speaking on my behalf."

"I'm happy to do it. I would hope you would return the favor if possible."

Gregory's neck prickled. "Of course I would."

"I know Susan spoke to your friend Mrs. Renshaw about an invitation for us to join the Phoenix Club. However, one has not been forthcoming." Clifford frowned so that it almost looked like a pout. Yes, it was decidedly a pout.

Gregory gritted his teeth. "I'm sorry. I don't know how you think I can help."

"Well, *you* are a member of the Phoenix Club. That should recommend me, one would think." Clifford laughed, but it was fake, and he sobered quickly. "It's just that Hargrove, like you, is a member, and it seems important business may be conducted there—as it is at White's and Brooks's. It seems important that I, as a marquess with a seat in the Lords, become a member."

"I am confident not everyone in the Lords belongs to the Phoenix Club." That included Lord Lucien's own father.

Furthermore, Gregory and Clifford's father hadn't been a member either.

"Still, it would be a helpful advantage. I'm sure you agree." Clifford eyed him expectantly, and now Gregory knew he expected Gregory to do something on his behalf. Just as he had—allegedly—done something for Gregory with Hargrove.

"I don't think I can help you," Gregory said. "I'm only a member. I've nothing to do with who is invited—or not—to join the Phoenix Club."

"While that may be true, I know you are friendly with Lord Lucien, that he arranged this meeting for you today." He knew that much at least.

Gregory didn't like that his brother was involved in his affairs.

"All I'm asking for is a word of support," Clifford continued. "I think it would go a long way toward securing our membership." He smiled again, and it made Gregory's skin crawl. He wanted to tell his brother to leave off, but feared Clifford might say something to Hargrove to jeopardize Gregory's appointment before it could be finalized.

"I will say something, but don't be surprised if nothing happens."

Clifford clapped Gregory's upper arm. "Susan will be delighted."

Always Susan. Gregory clenched his jaw. "You'll have to excuse me now, as I've another appointment."

"Of course." Clifford stepped aside. "I do hope you'll call at Witney House soon. We'd love to see you."

Gregory waved before continuing on his way. The giddiness he'd felt earlier had been replaced by a sickening weight. Ultimately, there was nothing he could do to ensure Clifford and Susan received an invitation to join the Phoenix Club.

What would happen when they were still ignored? Would Clifford work to thwart Gregory at every turn?

While Gregory knew that working for the government would involve a certain amount of politics, he hadn't expected it from his brother. But, really, he should have done. As he left Westminster and stepped into the gray winter day, he heard his father's voice: *"Your brother's priority will always be himself—never forget that."*

Gregory would not.

~

The patroness room was on the second floor of the ladies' side of the Phoenix Club and was for the express use of the patronesses. The only nonpatroness who'd ever been inside, aside from the maids, was Ada.

But she wouldn't be here today since the primary topic of business would be the addition of new patronesses, one of whom would hopefully be Ada. Evie could hardly wait for her to join her in this lofty rank. They would laugh about how a former courtesan and governess had risen so high. Then they would count their blessings for the comfort they now enjoyed—which wasn't reliant on their position. They'd both worked hard and come a long way, and they were grateful.

As Evie looked over the refreshment tray, she wondered how Gregory's meeting with Lord Hargrove had gone. She looked forward to hearing about it later when Gregory came to spend the night with her. Well, a portion of the night, since he arrived after midnight and left before dawn.

He was careful to come in through the garden under the cover of darkness. Still, Evie had told her loyal servants that he would be visiting. None had batted an eye. In fact, her maid, Delilah, had told her she was thrilled to see Evie engaging in something that gave her joy.

The arrival of Emma, Lady Dungannon, drew Evie from her thoughts. "Am I the first one here?" she asked.

Evie stepped away from the table, where there was an assortment of cakes and biscuits, as well as the club's finest sherry, which was their typical drink of choice for these meetings. They'd long abandoned the pretense of putting out tea or lemonade when they all went directly for the sherry.

"I need a quick drink before we begin." Emma winked at Evie before pouring herself a glass. She also grabbed a biscuit before going to her usual chair near the windows that looked down on the garden. Evie's office was directly beneath this room, so she had the same view.

"Good idea," Evie said, pouring sherry for herself before moving to her regular chair, which was next to Emma's.

Harriet, Mrs. Holland-Ward, came in next. The oldest of the patronesses, she was a commanding presence as she was taller than average, and her deep blue eyes were rather piercing. "Afternoon, ladies," she said warmly. "I see you have sherry, so I must have some too. Oh, and my favorite almond cakes." She piled two on a small plate after pouring her sherry and joined them, taking her seat on Evie's other side.

"The weather has been unusually pleasant for this time of year," Harriet observed as she nibbled her cake, the plate balanced on her lap.

"Quite. I enjoyed a lovely walk in the park yesterday," Emma said.

"I'm here!" Millie, Lady Hargrove, announced as she sailed into the room. She was always the last to arrive. At least today, she wasn't late. Closing the door behind her, she went to the refreshment table and filled the last wineglass with sherry. "Must we always have such delectable-looking cakes?" she complained. "I am trying to guard my waistline from expansion." Exhaling, she took one and popped it into her mouth prior to taking her seat.

"Welcome, ladies," Evie said with a smile. "We've much to discuss as the Season begins to pick up speed." She set her wineglass on the table beside her and picked up the parchment with today's agenda. "Today, we'll propose ideas for our four themed balls." Every Friday during the Season, starting in March, they held an assembly. On the first Friday of each month, from March until June, it had a theme. "We will also discuss the addition of new patronesses."

"What?" Millie blurted the word, drawing the other three to pin their attention on her. "Who decided we needed new patronesses?"

Evie responded evenly, "Club membership has grown so much—"

Millie cut her off. "It would grow even more if my recommendations weren't ignored."

Continuing as if she hadn't been interrupted, Evie said, "Lord Lucien believes we require more patronesses to meet the needs of the club."

"Now you're going to ignore me just as my recommendations are overlooked?" Millie clucked her tongue.

Evie spoke slowly and calmly. "Millie, you know that Phoenix Club membership isn't for everyone. It is the same at every membership club."

"But why are *my* recommendations always ignored?"

"They aren't always," Emma said. "I recall Mr. and Mrs. Hathaway were invited last Season."

Millie pursed her lips. "A paltry few. I want to know why more of them don't receive invitations. Evie could tell me, but she won't."

"That isn't true," Evie said, keeping hold of her temper in the face of the woman's belligerence. "How the membership committee decides upon invitations is known only to them."

"But you are *on* the committee," Millie sniped. "You could tell us the process."

"You know the committee is secret." Evie resisted the urge to down the rest of her sherry in one long gulp. "In any case, may we please discuss the matters at hand? If you have complaints, I urge you to take them up with Lord Lucien." He would hate that, and yet it was his duty to deal with such things.

"I'll do that." Millie sniffed. "Who are these new patronesses to be?"

"That is what we shall discuss," Evie said, glad they were moving on, but bracing herself for what was likely to be another storm. "Due to the increase in membership last Season and the success of our Friday assemblies, Lord Lucien has advised we select ladies to join us. They must already be members. Does anyone have a name they'd like to propose?" This was all for show—for Millie's sake—since she'd already discussed this with Emma, and Emma had shared it with Harriet.

"I'd like to suggest Lady Edgemont," Emma said.

Millie's nostrils flared, but she said nothing.

"She'd be excellent," Harriet added with a nod. "What about Lady Warfield, since she is already employed at the club and is so intrinsic to the assemblies?"

"Disgraceful that a viscountess has employment," Millie muttered.

"What's that?" Evie asked, as Millie pushed her precariously close to her last nerve.

Never one to back away from her convictions, Millie spoke louder this time. "I find it distasteful that Lady Warfield hasn't resigned her position as bookkeeper now that she is a viscountess. It's unseemly for her to be *working*."

"It's absolutely in line with everything the Phoenix Club

stands for. *In individuality, we are one*," Evie said, quoting the phrase Lucien had written as the club's primary mission.

"I fail to see how that has anything to do with Lady Warfield," Millie said sharply.

Of course she didn't. Evie ignored her. "Shall we vote on the names presented?"

Millie sat forward in her chair. "I haven't made my suggestion."

Evie forced a faint smile. "I haven't made one either, so don't feel as if you must."

"But I want to."

"Who?" Emma asked, fixing her gaze on Millie.

Harriet also looked to Millie. "Yes, who?"

Millie sputtered. "I don't know yet. I haven't had time to properly consider this. How did you know to suggest Ladies Edgemont and Warfield?"

Emma shrugged. "Lady Edgemont came immediately to mind."

"And Lady Warfield seems an obvious choice," Harriet said, appearing faintly bemused.

"Well, I need time to think of just the right person." Millie settled back in her chair looking thoroughly disgruntled.

"All right, then," Evie said. "We'll vote on Lady Edgemont and Lady Warfield today, and we can—"

Millie interrupted her again. "That isn't at all fair. We shouldn't vote until I've made my proposal. If I didn't know better, I might think you're all trying to keep me from participating in this endeavor."

Harriet narrowed her eyes, her brows pitching downward. "If we meant to do that, would we have invited you at all?"

Millie sniffed again. "We can vote next week."

Evie didn't want to press the issue. Next week would be

soon enough. "Very well. Are we all agreed that we'll vote on our new patronesses next week?"

Everyone nodded in agreement, but Evie could tell that Harriet and Emma were as annoyed by Millie's behavior as Evie was. The truth, however, *was* that they were trying to keep Millie from continuing as a patroness. Or at least encouraging her to be on her way. Evie felt marginally bad about doing so, but Millie was becoming increasingly difficult to tolerate.

Nodding, Evie smiled warmly at the others. "Excellent. Please don't discuss the addition of patronesses. We don't want everyone buzzing with this information until after we've made the announcement of who they will be." She directed that last part at Millie, who was inclined to gossip. The others were not, and Millie knew this. If word got out, they would all know it was her. *That* would be grounds for immediate dismissal, at least in Evie's mind. They'd always discussed the importance of keeping their discussions and plans private until such time as they needed to become public. What fun was it to announce the themes of the monthly balls if they'd already been leaked through rumor?

"Shall we move on to discussing the themes?" Evie asked.

"In a moment," Millie said, straightening. "I am truly disturbed that my recommendations continue to be disregarded. My friends, who are members here, have begun to wonder if the Phoenix Club is worth belonging to if it ignores longstanding members of White's or Brooks's."

Any charity Evie had for the women was rapidly diminishing. "That is somewhat the point of the Phoenix Club. Its charter states that it is a haven to the unwelcome, the marginalized, the forgotten, and the downtrodden, that it will strive to lift people up, to engender kindness, tolerance, and understanding. If you can't see that this is precisely what the club does, then perhaps you are the one who is wondering if the Phoenix Club is the right place for *you*."

Evie stole glances at Emma and Harriet, both of whom seemed to be trying to stifle their expressions of approval for what she'd said. They both sat straight, with hints of smiles teasing their lips.

Millie opened her mouth, but snapped it closed again. It seemed Evie had finally made her shut up. At least for now. She wasn't foolish enough to think Millie wouldn't speak up again.

Evie feared she'd awakened the beast. She and the others would have to take great care to avoid her bite.

CHAPTER 14

"Now, tell me about your meeting," Evie demanded as she snuggled into Gregory's side.

Gregory kissed her temple, reveling in her scent. His heart rate had finally returned to normal after their sport. He'd arrived only a short while ago, but they'd fallen on each other in a desperation of lust. Now sated, they could discuss their days, which he was keen to do.

"I think it went well. Right up until I encountered my brother as I left. He knew about the meeting."

"That troubles you?"

"I don't like having my brother involved in my affairs. In this case, I've a right to feel that way because he's asking me —again—to speak with Lucien on behalf of him and Susan and their potential Phoenix Club membership. I assured him I have no sway, but he also knew that Lucien arranged today's meeting."

"He doesn't believe that you have no influence." Evie scoffed. "I'm sorry you're having to tolerate such nonsense."

"I only hope it doesn't adversely affect my chances for

this appointment. The reason he knew about the interview was because he dined with Hargrove earlier in the week. However, Hargrove seemed to indicate all was well and that I should expect confirmation within the fortnight."

"Then it likely will be," Evie said. "I know him, and despite his snappish wife, he is generally amenable and charming. I've never known him to be manipulative or cruel."

That gave Gregory a rush of welcome relief. "Well, that is comforting to know."

She tipped her head back and smiled widely. "Besides, I am confident he was thoroughly impressed with you and will see you appointed regardless of anything your brother might want."

"How was your patroness meeting?"

"Frustrating." She frowned. "But I was expecting it to be fraught. We were discussing a sensitive issue."

"What's that?"

She scooted back from him slightly so she could better see his face. "I'm not supposed to tell you. We keep our discussions private."

"Then I shan't pester you." He leaned forward to kiss her forehead.

"Did the dinner with Hargrove and your brother include their wives?" she asked.

"It did. Why?"

Evie scowled. "I don't like that the Hargroves seem to be close with your brother and Lady Witney. Lady Hargrove is becoming more vocal about the fact that the majority of her recommendations to the club, including Lord and Lady Witney, aren't given invitations. It seems she may be involving her husband in her crusade."

"What crusade is that?"

"To have more of her recommendations invited to join the club. Today, she indicated that her friends—those who are members—are beginning to think the Phoenix Club isn't for them." She grimaced. "Forget I said that."

Gregory put his hand to his bare chest. "I'll keep whatever you tell me completely inviolate. I can see why you're troubled. It does look as if they might be conspiring."

"Indeed." She shook her head. "I will hope that Lord Hargrove is the voice of reason. Still, I will share this with Lucien, if you don't mind?"

"I don't mind at all. It sounds as if Lady Hargrove is seeking to make herself heard."

"Oh, we hear her," Evie said sardonically. "We just don't *listen*."

Gregory chuckled. "An important distinction."

"Honestly, we'd like it if she'd resign from being a patroness. And at this point, I can't say I'd mind if she resigned her membership." Again, she grimaced. "I sound horribly uncharitable. But I hate that she may be speaking poorly of the club. Lucien has worked so hard to establish a wonderful, welcoming place."

Gregory stroked her shoulder and looked into her eyes. "She's one person. The Phoenix Club will stand against her complaints."

Evie relaxed, her features smoothing. "You're right, of course." She narrowed one eye at him. "What spell have you cast on me? I'm usually quite good at keeping secrets. Yet here I am in bed with you spilling all sorts of things I ought to keep private."

He laughed softly and drew her close once more, inhaling the fragrance of her hair. "I only know that I am completely under *your* spell, and I wouldn't have it any other way. I'm glad we can share our trials and concerns with one another."

"That is rather nice." She kissed the hollow of his throat, and his body roared to arousal, as if he hadn't just been utterly sated not long ago. "But at the moment, I'd rather we share something far more...primal." She moved over him, straddling his hips and rotating her pelvis against his rigid cock.

He thrust his hand into her hair and cupped her head. "There is nothing, at any given moment, that I would rather do." He pulled her down and kissed her.

There was no more talk of his brother or the Phoenix Club.

～

*E*vie stifled a yawn as she pulled on her gloves. She hadn't really slept until Gregory had left just before dawn. Not that she minded. She felt tired in that glorious, fulfilling way one did when one realized some things were simply better than sleep.

Foster opened the door for her as she stepped outside.

"I won't be too long," she said before turning to the right and walking to her neighbors' house to discuss the dog situation.

Mr. and Mrs. Kirby were in their later fifties, probably, their children grown with children of their own. More than once, Evie had seen them all walking together—a big, happy family. It had seemed so foreign to her.

She rapped on their door and was soon greeted by a housekeeper. The woman, in her thirties, with a long, slender face and businesslike mien, greeted Evie.

"Good afternoon," Evie said, presenting her card. "I'm here to see Mrs. Kirby. Or Mr. Kirby. Or both. It's a...sensitive matter concerning their dog."

The housekeeper's brows shot up briefly. She nodded. "Come in. They will see you in the drawing room."

The house was laid out almost identically to Evie's, but she followed the housekeeper upstairs to the drawing room. It was decorated much differently, of course, with muted colors of yellow and gray. A cheerful painting of daffodils graced one wall, and Evie went to inspect it.

A few moments later, the Kirbys arrived. Mr. Kirby was short and angular, his dark eyes assessing Evie. Mrs. Kirby was nearly as tall as her husband, but much softer. She smiled upon seeing Evie and welcomed her warmly. "Would you like tea?" she asked.

"No, thank you. I came to speak with you about your dog."

Mr. Kirby's brow had formed deep furrows as they all sat down. "Is there a problem?"

"I will hope not, but I wanted to inform you that my dog —well, not *my* dog, but my friend's dog whom I was watching overnight—stole into your garden. I'm afraid there's a hole in the wall. Perhaps you're not aware."

"We're aware," Mrs. Kirby said, her voice a bit tight. She sent a glance toward her husband, and Evie could almost hear the sentiment behind it. The hole was not only known to them, but Mrs. Kirby had been asking to have it repaired. Evie would bet on it.

"Well, my friend's dog got in—"

"How was your dog even able to do that?" Mr. Kirby asked. "Was he not contained in your own garden?"

"Don't be accusatory, dear," Mrs. Kirby said. She gave Evie a warm, expectant smile. While she was more polite than her husband, she clearly also wanted to know how Ash had found his way into their garden.

"I'm afraid one of my household left the garden gate

slightly ajar. When I took Ash—he's a puppy—out before dawn, he got away from me."

"Puppies can be such a handful," Mrs. Kirby said with a commiserative nod.

"Yes. I was quite worried when we couldn't find him. But we eventually tracked him to your garden, where he apparently made friends with your dog."

"Bess is very friendly." Mrs. Kirby called for the housekeeper, who was apparently just outside the drawing room. "Will you fetch Bess, please?"

The housekeeper took herself off quickly.

"Bess is a female, I take it?" Evie asked. "Ash is a male, and my concern is that they may have become *very* friendly."

Mr. Kirby exhaled sharply. "I shall hope not or that nothing comes of it. We had planned to breed Bess with another miniature greyhound belonging to a friend of ours."

"I see." Evie would also hope nothing came of it. She could see that Mr. Kirby was annoyed by the entire affair. "I am terribly sorry about it."

"I trust you will ensure your dog doesn't get out again?"

"He isn't my dog, and I don't expect he'll be staying at my house again." How that pained Evie. She missed him so. Later today, she would "happen" to encounter Gregory and Ash walking in the park.

The housekeeper brought in Bess, a brown miniature greyhound who was still bigger than Ash, but probably not for too much longer. "Here is our Bessie girl," Mrs. Kirby said with a smile.

Bess trotted over to her and nuzzled the woman's outstretched hand, then she sat down, her gaze moving inquisitively to Evie. She was impeccably behaved.

"Aren't you a pretty girl?" Evie asked. She longed to pet Bess. Apparently, she really liked dogs and had never realized. Or she had but had buried the memories of the street dogs she'd cared for in her youth.

"Go on." Mrs. Kirby pet Bess and give her a nudge.

Bess walked over to Evie, who removed her glove. Extending her hand to the dog, she let the animal sniff her before trying to stroke her soft, velvety head. "She's so well trained."

"Very important in a dog," Mr. Kirby said. "That's why she doesn't get out of our garden, even with the hole in the wall."

Mrs. Kirby pursed her lips. "It's because she can't fit through it." She looked to Evie. "Your dog must be very small."

"*My friend's* dog, Ash, is still a puppy." Evie wanted them to know he wasn't her dog. "He's a white terrier. I imagine he will soon be too big to fit through that hole. However, he won't have the chance to try."

"I think I saw your dog the other day—sometime last week," Mr. Kirby mused. "He was with a tall gentleman. That must be your friend?"

Evie tensed. She didn't want them to know her friend was a gentleman, and she certainly didn't want them to learn his identity. "I can't say for certain."

If they learned that Ash belonged to Lord Gregory Blakemore and that he entrusted the animal with Evie for a night, they might be curious as to the relationship between them. If they mentioned it to anyone, rumors could spread. She was so careful *not* to be the subject of gossip. The care she'd taken to reestablish herself as Mrs. Renshaw was monumental, and here she was, risking everything because she couldn't seem to stop seeing Gregory.

This would not do. People might not blink at a widow having an affair, even if it was with the brother of a marquess. However, if scrutiny directed toward her somehow unearthed her past—

No, she wouldn't even continue that thought.

Taking a deep breath, she rubbed Bess's head and told her what a good and sweet dog she was, then she looked to the Kirbys. "Well, I just wanted to come and speak with you about what had happened. I thought it important you knew." She rose from her chair.

The Kirbys also stood.

"We're so glad you did," Mrs. Kirby said. "Such a responsible and admirable thing to do. I'll make sure the hole in our wall is fixed posthaste."

"That's very kind of you." Evie drew on her glove and said goodbye to Bess.

Mrs. Kirby gestured toward the doorway. "I'll see you out."

They walked downstairs, and in the entry hall, she whispered, "Mr. Kirby has been promising to fix that hole for months. You must have been so distressed when your dog went missing."

"My friend's dog, but yes." Actually, perhaps Evie ought to stop mentioning her friend at all.

"Yes, your friend. I presume you made him aware of what happened?"

"They are aware, yes." Evie specifically chose a different pronoun. She wasn't going to confirm that Ash belonged to a man. In fact, she should have just said "she."

"I'll be sure to let you know if Bess is increasing following her...interlude with Ash. But I must tell you that Mr. Kirby planned to breed Bess with another greyhound belonging to a friend of his. They've an appointment to meet tomorrow."

"I see. I do hope Mr. Kirby's plans aren't ruined by Bess and Ash's chance encounter."

Mrs. Kirby waved her hand. "Bah. He's only himself to blame since he let that hole go unrepaired. In any case, there's no point fretting about things that are not yet certain.

We won't know if Bess is increasing for some time, and even then, we won't know if the puppies she carries belong to your—rather your friend's—dog or our friend's until they are born."

It seemed Bess was likely going to have puppies. It was just a question of who the father would be. Evie hoped it would be Ash, though that would probably anger Mr. Kirby. She preferred to think of Bess having puppies with the dog she'd chosen, not the one arranged by Mr. Kirby.

"I do hope you'll keep me informed. Your Bess is a lovely dog."

"Thank you. I adore her." Mrs. Kirby opened the door for Evie.

With a wave, Evie went on her way. Her stomach churned with anxiety as her mind returned to the possibility that someone would discover who she was. This was madness. Even if someone learned she was having an affair with Gregory, that didn't mean they'd determine her true identity.

Why was she so nervous? She realized she'd been that way the past month, perhaps because of her encounter with Arbuthnot at Witney Court. Since returning to town, she'd mostly kept to her house and the Phoenix Club. She'd even curtailed her shopping a bit, which was her favorite thing to do. And she hadn't accepted any invitations. She'd attributed it to being busy, but now she acknowledged that she'd been avoiding spaces and events where she might run into him again.

It would be best if she saw Gregory less. They didn't need to spend every night together. And as much as she wanted to see him—and Ash—in the park today, she'd send a note saying she couldn't make it. She'd also let him know not to come that night, that she was nervous the neighbors might notice.

He might ask why she would care. It wasn't unusual for a

widow to have a liaison. That didn't mean she wanted to flaunt it. He would understand.

And if he didn't... Well, this wasn't ever going to last forever. Nor was it even supposed to have continued when they returned to London—for precisely this reason. She'd curated a specific life here as patroness of the Phoenix Club.

She wasn't going to do anything to jeopardize that.

～

*E*vie's note informing him that she would not be meeting him in the park and that he should not visit her for a few nights had formed a ball of tension between Gregory's shoulder blades. She'd explained why—her concern that they'd be discovered—and he understood. He didn't particularly want their affair to become public either.

And why was that?

Because it was new to him? Because he cared about her? Because his father would have been horrified that Gregory was having an affair with a widow?

What harm was there in that, really?

None that Gregory could see, except for the fact that others might judge him, and that public scrutiny was something his father had preferred to avoid. Gregory shared that sentiment, likely because he was his father's son. He didn't particularly want to be fodder for gossip and innuendo. More importantly, he didn't want Evie to be.

Gregory walked up the stairs toward the members' den. Not long after a footman delivered him a glass of port, he contemplated a cozy chair by the fire. However, before he could sit down, Lord Lucien approached him, his gaze amiable but intent.

"Evening, Lord Gregory. I wonder if you might join me in my office."

"Certainly." Gregory followed him from the members' den.

Lord Lucien left his door only slight ajar. "Sit. I'll just pour myself a glass of something."

After fetching his drink, Lord Lucien joined him near the fire. "Evie told me about your brother and Lady Witney dining with the Hargroves. I am aware that your sister-in-law is on a crusade to garner an invitation to the club. It seems she is employing every means at her disposal to accomplish her goal."

"She is…tenacious." Gregory downed half his port.

"It sounds as if you and she are not close."

"Not at all, but I should just be satisfied that Clifford wed, I suppose."

"He wasn't expected to?"

"He never showed any inclination, much to my father's dismay. Always said he'd get around to it eventually. My father gave him an ultimatum, and Clifford finally committed to wed—while my father was on his deathbed. I remain astonished that he did indeed marry as he promised."

Lord Lucien grimaced as he sipped his drink. "My father is fond of those. He arranged my brother's marriage. Thankfully, it turned out exceptionally well, as they are deeply in love."

Envy stabbed through Gregory, but he managed to say, "How wonderful for them." Then he drank most of the rest of his port. "Your father doesn't pester you about marriage?"

"Heavens, no, especially not now that he has Con's heir. I am free of harassment. At least on that front. What of you and your father?"

"He directed his focus regarding marriage entirely on my brother," Gregory said. "Except for the part where he encouraged me—most vociferously—to remain celibate until

I wed. He insisted it was best considering that I was to be ordained."

Lord Lucien stared at him. "You weren't planning to be a *monk*, were you?"

Gregory chuckled. "No, but then I wasn't really planning to be a vicar or a bishop or anything in between. I considered it, but I've known for a couple of years that I didn't really wish to pursue it."

"But you didn't want to disappoint your father." Lord Lucien lifted his glass, but at Gregory's nod, he arrested his movement. "Don't tell me you've remained celibate for the same reason?"

It would be easy to lie. Or prevaricate. But for whatever reason, Gregory decided to share the truth. He liked Lord Lucien. "I did for some time, in fact. I have only recently abandoned my celibacy. And now, I think you must call me Gregory as well as refill my glass. What are you drinking?"

Lord Lucien had continued to gape at him. "Christ, I think I need that story." He made a face. "Forgive me. I didn't mean to curse like that in front of you. I notice you don't swear."

"Another habit to please my father. *Bollocks.*"

"What?" Lucien asked in surprise.

"Nothing. I just thought I'd try it out."

Laughing, Lord Lucien stood. "You must call me Lucien then too. I'm pouring you a divine Irish whiskey that arrived just yesterday. That's what I'm drinking. I stashed a few bottles in here to hide them from my brother-in-law. Wexford is terribly greedy with the Irish."

"That makes sense, I suppose." Because he was Irish. That was about the extent of what Gregory knew about him. And that he had married Lucien's younger sister last Season.

Lucien returned a moment later with a glass of Irish whiskey for Gregory. He took the empty wineglass and deposited it on a table before retaking his seat. "Now, tell me how you finally managed to get shagged. Did you consult a professional?"

"Er, no. Though my brother has invited me to brothels for years. He's long tried to convince me to take a mistress." Gregory sipped the whiskey and decided it was what curse words were made for—in the complimentary sense. "This is spectacular."

"Don't tell Wexford. They're due back from Gloucestershire any day. Then it will likely disappear." Lucien took another drink. "I recall seeing your brother at a brothel or two. I used to frequent them, but it's been several years."

"And did you find mistresses there?"

"Typically, I was just looking for a companion for the night. However, I did find my favorite mistress at one of them." A soft, nostalgic smile flitted over his mouth.

"That was quite an expression," Gregory noted. "She must have meant a great deal to you."

Lucien nodded. "I was quite fond of her. Some men fall in love with their mistresses. Indeed, that happened to this woman's sister."

Gregory thought of what Susan had told him about the Creightons. "That sounds like my brother's neighbors. Or so the rumor goes. I'm not sure I believe it since I heard it from my sister-in-law."

A look of horror passed over Lucien's features. "Oh hell, yes of course, the Creightons. They are a lovely couple."

"That was true, then?" Gregory flinched. "Never mind. I am not one to gossip. They are charming, genuine people, and I enjoyed meeting them." Because that was how he'd met Evie. If not for her visiting them, he never would have encountered her at the hedgerow.

Lucien rose to refill his glass. "I'm still waiting to hear about the loss of your innocence. If you didn't hire someone for the deed, whom did you engage?" He grinned as he sat back down. "Are you still shagging her?"

Gregory readjusted his weight in the chair. "Isn't there some saying about gentlemen not telling?"

"I haven't heard it, but it's probably a good maxim. In any case, I hope you are enjoying yourself and that it was worth the wait. I, for one, can't imagine."

Most men struggled to comprehend why Gregory had remained celibate. "It cost me a friend or two over the years, but then I don't think they were probably going to be anyone I wanted to call friend anyway."

"I would agree. Boys and young men can be cruel and stupid. I ought to know."

"I can't see you as cruel," Gregory said.

"No, but I was plenty stupid, getting into scrapes and generally infuriating my father." A wicked smile curled Lucien's mouth. "It was great fun."

"Did you go out of your way to annoy him?"

Lucien's dark eyes glinted with mischief. "Oh yes."

"And do you still?"

"Not entirely. Though, I do wear a brightly colored cravat when I pay him a call. He hates that."

Gregory had taken a sip of whiskey and now sputtered. "Why do you do it? Annoy him, I mean."

Lucien shrugged. "Because it's expected? Isn't that why you behaved in the way you did? Because your father expected it?"

"I suppose," Gregory murmured. "Though I am beginning to think it's perhaps better to do the unexpected." That was what had prompted him to pursue Evie. And he had no regrets. "I doubt your father expected this club."

"Perhaps not the club, but he certainly expected me to champion what he would call outcasts and miscreants. Present company excluded."

"Damn, that sounds exciting. I might like to become one or both."

Lucien let out a hollow laugh. "Trust me, you don't. It sounds captivating until you're on the outside. Much easier to stay within the realm of polite acceptance." He took a drink of whiskey. "Now, back to your meeting yesterday—and your brother and sister-in-law. They aren't going to receive invitations, I'm afraid. The membership committee will not be intimidated. Is that going to cause problems for you?"

"Not personally, no. It's no difference to me if they're invited or not." That wasn't precisely true. Gregory would actually prefer they weren't, but he wasn't going to tell Lucien that.

"What about the appointment to the Office of the Lord High Chancellor?" Lucien asked. "I don't think Hargrove would allow that sort of nonsense to determine a man's future, but his wife is, to borrow the word you used for Lady Witney, tenacious. She may have worn him down."

"I've explained to my brother that I have no influence with you or anyone else. He didn't care. I told him I'd speak to you. I've done that. If he sabotages my career for something I can't control... Well, I want to say I'd be surprised, but the truth is, I almost expect it. Clifford can be rather devious —and for apparently no reason."

"Damn. My brother and I have had a strained relationship —we've overcome that now, I'm glad to say—but we would never harm each other in that way. I'm sorry to hear it."

"I'm used to his spite. My hope is that Hargrove will judge me for who I am."

"I expect he will," Lucien said, frowning slightly. "Still, perhaps I'll speak with him."

"It isn't necessary, but do what you will." Gregory took

another drink and realized his glass was rapidly reaching empty once more. "This is exceptionally good."

"I told you. Another glass?"

Gregory thought about it for only a moment. He wasn't seeing Evie later, so why not? "I think so." He held his glass out and Lucien leapt up with a grin.

It was nice to have a new friend.

CHAPTER 15

The week had dragged, probably because Evie had only seen Gregory twice—one of which was a meeting in Green Park, where she'd also spent time with Ash. That had been the best day and made her smile now even as a mild anxiety swirled in her belly due to the imminent patroness meeting.

Her smile faded as she realized she didn't know when she would see Ash again. She missed him terribly, and her heartache only increased with each encounter. She ought to stop seeing him—and Gregory—now, rather than draw out the inevitable.

She was still hopeful that she'd tire of Gregory. But she knew she'd never grow weary of Ash. He had stolen a piece of her heart forevermore. And therein lay the problem: *none* of it was supposed to be forever.

Harriet strolled in with several minutes to spare. "Are we ready for today?" she asked weightily, one eyebrow arching.

Evie took a deep breath. "I think so. Thank you for coming early. That helps to steel my nerves."

"And mine," Harriet said, moving to pour herself a glass of sherry.

"I really ought to just have four glasses filled." Evie clucked her tongue.

"This gives me something to do instead of pluck at invisible threads." Harriet sipped her sherry. "I am actually rather anxious."

"Did I hear someone say anxious?" Emma sailed into the room with a grim expression. "Pour one for me too, and don't be stingy."

Harriet filled a second glass, which she handed to Emma, then a third. "I assume you want one, Evie?"

"At least one." She accepted the wineglass and lifted it. "To friendship and support."

"To a united front," Emma added.

"To the best damn sherry in London," Harriet said.

They all grinned, then drank.

"Better," Emma said with a nod before walking to her chair. "Any idea whom Millie is going to propose?"

Evie shook her head. "None."

Harriet took her seat. "I haven't a clue. I tried to think of members who are her close friends, and honestly, I couldn't." She looked at both Evie and Emma.

"You're right," Emma said. "I can't think of anyone either. I can think of ladies I've seen her with or heard her speak of, and none of them are members."

"Well, this doesn't bode well," Evie murmured before taking another sip of the delicious, and absolutely necessary today, sherry. "Let's discuss the first themed ball in case she arrives early."

There was a moment of silence followed by laughter— none of them expected her to be early. In fact, she ended up arriving almost ten minutes late. Her cheeks were flushed as she closed the door. There was no mention of her tardiness.

She simply went to the table, poured her sherry, then took her seat with a rather prim look.

Evie set her sherry on the table next to her chair and summoned a bright smile. "Good afternoon, fellow patronesses." She decided not to waste any time. Why delay the discomfort? "Millie, are you prepared to suggest a potential patroness?"

"I am," she said, lifting her chin. She took a long drink of sherry and seemed to take extra time in swallowing, as if she were trying to draw out their anticipation. She likely didn't realize they felt more dread than excitement. "I think Lady Corby would make an excellent patroness."

Had she not listened to what Evie had said? Resisting the urge to smack her forehead, Evie pulled her mouth into a tight smile. "Unfortunately, Lady Corby is ineligible as she is not a member."

"She should be. I've recommended her several times. I've recommended her again. Just this morning, in fact. I sent a note to Lord Lucien."

He either hadn't read it yet or he'd been too busy to tell Evie. They'd certainly discuss it later.

"Well, seeing as she is not currently a member, we can't vote on her today." Against her better judgment, Evie offered her another chance. "Is there anyone else you'd like to propose?"

Millie sputtered, her face redder now than when she'd arrived. "Not anyone who has been granted membership."

"All right, we'll go ahead and vote on the ladies proposed last week. All those in favor of—"

"It isn't fair!" Millie shot to her feet, spilling her sherry. Muttering a curse, she set the glass on the table between her and Emma's chairs. She shook her hand out, and sherry droplets went flying.

"No, it isn't. Such a waste of good sherry," Harriet murmured.

Evie had to bite her cheek to keep from laughing, and she purposely didn't look at Harriet or Emma lest she not be able to contain herself.

Millie sent Harriet a furious glance. "None of my closest friends are members, and they are the ladies I would propose."

"You know membership is not up to us," Evie said quietly, bracing herself for the coming storm.

"You can deny being a part of the committee all you like, Evie Renshaw, but I know the truth."

Evie said nothing. She clasped her hands in her lap and sat placidly.

"Let us vote," Emma said. "Who is in favor of inviting Lady Edgemont and Lady Warfield to join us as patronesses?" She, Harriet, and Evie raised their hands and said, "I am."

"I am *not*," Millie said angrily. "But you will all do as you please." Letting out an enraged growl, she spun on her heel and quit the room, slamming the door behind her.

The remaining trio sipped their sherry in silence. It was a long moment before Evie spoke. "The majority has voted in favor of inviting Ladies Edgemont and Warfield to join us as patronesses."

Harriet smiled broadly. "Splendid."

"How shall we inform them?" Emma asked.

"Lady Warfield is in her office. We could invite her to join us," Evie suggested. She could hardly wait to tell Ada that she was now a patroness of the Phoenix Club. Though Ada knew her name was being proposed, she didn't expect it would happen. She'd just never imagined herself in such a position. But then she'd never thought of herself as a bookkeeper of a large, impressive London membership club, nor as a viscountess. Yet, she'd carried off both with grace, integrity, and irrefutable success.

"Oh, let's!" Harriet said. "She'll be delighted, don't you think, Evie?"

"I do. What about Lady Edgemont?"

"How about we invite her for tea here tomorrow?" Emma suggested.

Harriet nodded enthusiastically. "That's an excellent idea. She'll be thrilled too, I think."

"Then we are agreed." Evie didn't really want to talk about Millie anymore, but they must. "What are we to do about Millie? She is not going to simply accept this and go along her merry way."

"When has she ever been merry?" Harriet curled her lip and rolled her eyes. "I don't suppose we can ignore her."

Evie shook her head. "We've tried that, at least with regard to her membership recommendation complaints. However, this is something different."

"Are you hinting we should ask her to resign as patroness?" Emma asked. She grimaced. "I don't think that will go well."

"I don't disagree, but I'm not sure the situation can be repaired," Evie said. "I'll speak with Lucien."

"Perhaps with the new patronesses, she'll hold her tongue," Harriet mused. As they had before Millie had arrived, they fell silent just before bursting into laughter. Although, this episode lasted much longer than the last.

Evie wiped her eye. "She is already in the minority with the four of us and will only become more isolated in her opinions and complaints after Ladies Edgemont and Warfield join us. I still hold out a fraction—however small— of hope that she'll resign."

"As patroness or her entire membership?" Emma asked.

"As patroness, but both would be welcome. I can't see her

doing the latter when her husband is still a member." Evie blew out a frustrated breath. "In truth, I can't see her doing either."

"I should like it very much if she would just go." Harriet sipped her sherry. "Pity, because Hargrove is quite pleasant."

"Yes," Emma agreed. "Perhaps he could be prevailed upon to calm Millie." She looked to Evie. "Could Lord Lucien speak with him?"

It wasn't a bad idea. It might be all they had left to try. "I will ask him. I'll go and fetch Ada from her office."

Smiling, Evie stood and went to the door. Ada's office was on this floor. It was part of her living quarters. Or had been, until she'd become Lady Warfield. On occasion, she and Max still used her room when they were in London, but for the most part, they stayed in a hotel. However, Max had apparently leased a house for the upcoming Season, and Ada said they planned to purchase one this year or next.

It was a short walk to Ada's office. The door stood half open, which typically indicated she was inside working but could be interrupted.

Evie pushed the door open wider and stepped to the threshold. "Ada?"

Ada looked up from her desk. "Done with the patroness meeting already?"

"Not quite. We wanted to invite you to join us." Evie was fairly brimming with excitement.

"To discuss the Frost Fair Ball?" Their first themed ball of the Season was a celebration of the frost fairs held on the Thames when it froze over.

Evie leapt on that excuse. "Yes." While Ada knew she was being considered as a patroness, she didn't know today was the day they'd voted to make it official.

"Let me just bring something to make notations." Ada

picked up a small book where she kept lists and information that she consulted regularly along with a pencil.

Gesturing for Ada to precede her, Evie followed her from the office, closing the door behind them. It wasn't unusual for Ada to join in their meetings, particularly when it came to organizing the details of the balls.

As soon as she stepped inside, Ada stopped short. "Is someone missing?"

"I suppose you could say that," Emma responded with a mischievous glint in her eye.

Evie moved around Ada. "Millie left. She was disgruntled about...things."

"Can I tell her?" Harriet asked eagerly. At Evie's nod, she continued, "Lady Warfield, we would be honored and delighted if you would agree to join us as a patroness of the Phoenix Club."

Ada sucked in her breath and darted a look at Evie. "This isn't about the Frost Fair Ball."

Evie shrugged. "Not entirely. But we do need to discuss that."

"I'm...humbled," Ada murmured. "I'm just... Well, never mind. It is *my* honor to serve with you." She looked among all three of them. "Are you certain you want me?"

"Of course!" Emma laughed. "Pour yourself some sherry and sit. We'll be inviting Lady Edgemont tomorrow."

"How wonderful," Ada said, smiling. She looked toward Millie's empty chair. "Should I sit there? I understand Millie has left the meeting."

"No, don't sit in her space. You and Lady Edgemont need your own places."

"Here, I'll fetch your usual chair," Evie said, moving to the other side of the room where there were a few chairs in a seating area. She pulled the one Ada normally used when she attended their meetings and situated it between her chair and Emma's. "There. This can now be your official spot."

Ada went to sit down, moving slowly, almost reverently. Harriet rushed to pour a glass of sherry and brought it to Ada. "You forgot this."

"Thank you." Ada accepted the glass with a grateful smile.

Emma raised her glass. "To our newest patroness."

Evie hastened back to her chair to join in the toast. "Huzzah!"

After the meeting concluded and Emma and Harriet had left, Ada turned to Evie. "Thank you."

"What did I do?"

"You plucked me from loneliness and despair and gave me the chance for a life I never imagined."

"A life you wholly deserve." Evie had known so many young women who didn't think they deserved comfort or happiness. They believed themselves to be unworthy. Evie had feared she was one of them but refused to accept that. Which was why she'd fought so hard to be precisely where she was now.

"I know. Sometimes I just need reminding." Ada cocked her head at Evie. "Is something amiss? You've seemed a trifle tense this week."

"I was dreading this meeting today. Because of Millie. She's proving to be more difficult than ever. She was supposed to come today with a name to propose as patroness because she was outraged that she didn't know to suggest someone last week."

Ada's brow pleated. "She needed a week to think of someone?"

"Apparently, and even that wasn't enough. None of her close friends are members, it turns out, a fact she finds outrageous."

"Let me guess. She launched into another diatribe against

the membership committee regarding her recommendations being ignored." Ada pressed her lips together. "The irony is that we don't ignore them. We simply dismiss them."

"Well, I wouldn't tell her that even if I could." Evie laughed softly. "I'm going to speak with Lucien and see if he can talk sensibly with Hargrove. I think we'd all be happy if she just resigned from the club, but I doubt she'd do that without Hargrove leaving too."

Ada shook her head. "I can't see him doing that. He enjoys the gaming room far too much."

"Indeed. We'll see what happens next Friday when we gather with our new patronesses."

"Perhaps Millie won't come," Ada said, lifting a shoulder. "She could decide to be a patroness in name only."

"I hadn't considered that," Evie said, immediately warming to the idea. "I'll propose that to Lucien too. He can suggest it to Hargrove. Ada, you are brilliant!"

"Sometimes. Other times, I don't always get things right. For instance, when I first came back to town, I could have sworn there was something different about you."

"Different how?"

"You always sparkle, but you were somehow even more dazzling." Ada smiled. "Honestly, I wondered if you'd finally decided to take a lover. I would understand if you decided not to tell me. I hid my liaison with Max from you for a time." Her smile faded. "I wish I hadn't."

"Don't feel badly about that. Sometimes there are things we need to keep close—for a variety of reasons. I consider you my dearest friend." Evie couldn't help thinking she was making her own plea for secrecy since there was so much Ada didn't know. Her liaison with Gregory was only a fraction of what she could—and probably should—share.

Should she tell Ada about her past? Ada would never tell anyone, and she'd be another support, even more than she already was. But Evie had locked that part of her life away. She didn't even like thinking about it, let alone discussing it. Seeing Arbuthnot at that Yuletide party at Witney Court had dredged up her fears that she'd be discovered. Then there would be no hiding herself.

For now, she decided to share a fraction with Ada, at least. Allowing a small smile, Evie whispered, "I have been conducting an affair. It's been diverting, but I don't expect it will last much longer."

Ada gasped, her eyes igniting with excitement. "I'm so happy for you! I'm sorry it's ending, but if that's what you want…"

"It is." It was what Evie needed. "I still have no desire for anything permanent. Indeed, I wasn't sure I was even ready for an affair. I've kept it simple and temporary."

"Sounds perfect for you." Ada gave her a hug, surprising Evie. "You're such a wonderful friend, Evie."

Evie hugged her back. "So are you."

They parted, and Evie returned to her office. A small stack of correspondence sat on the corner of her desk. She picked up the letters and flipped through them, noting there was one from her sister and one from…Gregory?

Sitting down, she opened the one from Gregory.

Dearest Evie,

I know you are worried right now, and I don't want to add to your concerns. I just want you to know that I'm here when you need me—and even when you don't. I'm waiting and will continue to wait, for there is nothing and no one worth more to me than you.

Yours,

Gregory

P. S. Ash misses you, but like me, he is content to wait.

Joy bloomed through Evie. She needed to end the affair, but how could she when he wrote such thoughtful, charming words? And when he brought Ash into it?

They were being careful and would continue to do so. She'd told Ada she deserved the happiness she'd earned and won. Couldn't Evie do the same?

It suddenly occurred to her that they didn't have to meet at her house. They could meet here at the club. There were several bedchambers on this floor—more on the men's side— and an easy, though hidden, access between the two sides. Evie couldn't believe she hadn't thought of it before. She'd ask him to come to the club tonight and tell him how to get to one of the chambers so they could meet.

A delicious thrill raced up her spine. Yes, she deserved this, and she was going to enjoy every moment while it lasted.

~

Gregory walked into Westminster the following Tuesday afternoon feeling confident and content. Hargrove had sent word that morning summoning him for a meeting this afternoon. He'd given no indication as to the outcome, but Gregory hoped it would be to tell him the appointment was confirmed.

His confidence and contentment came entirely from Evie and the time they'd spent together over the past few days. Her idea to have them meet at the Phoenix Club had been absolutely inspired. They'd met there each of the past three nights. The only thing missing was Ash, but they'd decided they could manage "chance" meetings at the park. It wasn't ideal, but Gregory still hoped things between them would change and progress, that they would become permanent.

He hoped, deep in his heart, that she'd change her mind

about marriage. He wanted her to be his wife. Then they and Ash would be a happy family. And perhaps one of Ash's puppies, if he ended up being the father to Bess's brood. They still didn't know if Bess was carrying.

Gregory went to the same room where he'd met Hargrove before. However, this time, Hargrove was already waiting for him.

"Afternoon, Lord Gregory. Thank you for meeting with me on such short notice."

"I'm pleased to do so," Gregory said. "I trust you have good news today."

Hargrove frowned, and Gregory's pulse quickened. That Hargrove didn't suggest they sit also signaled an alarm. "I'm afraid I've run into some difficulty. Your appointment is in jeopardy."

Gregory tamped down his anger. "Why?"

"This is…indelicate, and I do apologize. However, it's not entirely up to me. I have *some* influence, but… Well, I don't have the final say."

His agitation was evident, but Gregory couldn't tell if he was upset by the position that he found himself in or if he was upset by Gregory. "Have I done something wrong?"

"It seems you haven't done something that's been requested."

Gregory clenched his teeth. "I'm going to need you to speak plainly."

Hargrove exhaled, and his gaze drifted to the left as if he couldn't bring himself to look Gregory in the eye. "If you can ensure your brother and his wife are invited to the club, that would help your appointment to be confirmed. Furthermore, my wife is a patroness of the club and recently suggested a new patroness and was refused because this person is not a member. I'd like you to ask Lord Lucien to invite Lord and Lady Corby to be members, and it would be especially wonderful if Lady Corby could be made a patroness."

Never in his life had Gregory lost control of his temper, but in this moment, he was simply unable to harness the ability to keep himself in check. "Hargrove, you must understand, I have absolutely *no* influence in these matters. I've only recently become acquainted with Lord Lucien. You seem to think we have a deeper connection and we *do not*."

"Then perhaps you can use your considerable influence with one of the patronesses—Mrs. Renshaw?"

Gregory's blood turned to ice. He chose his words carefully. "She, like Lucien, is a friend, and I have no influence over anything to do with the Phoenix Club."

"I see." Hargrove dipped his chin, frowning. Then his gaze met Gregory's and his eyes were inscrutable. "It would be unfortunate if her true identity were to become known."

What the hell was he talking about? Gregory's heart was racing. Sweat beaded along his neck and lower back. "I am not that close to Mrs. Renshaw, so I surely have no idea what you mean by these threats. Really, Hargrove, I'm horrified by this…behavior." Perhaps he could shame the man into ceasing these awful tactics.

"Do you really not know?" Hargrove sounded a bit weary. "Mrs. Renshaw was once known as Mirabelle Renault. For a time, she and her sister were two of London's most sought-after courtesans."

Gregory didn't think he could feel more shocked or confused. "I'm not sure I can believe you," he said quietly, his mind spinning at how badly this was all going. He'd only tried to secure a bloody job, and not a particularly important one at that.

Hargrove shrugged. "Then ask Lord Lucien. He was once her protector."

It was unfortunate that Gregory wasn't sitting down. His

legs felt suddenly light, as if they couldn't support him. However, he maintained his composure. "I am extremely disappointed that you would try to manipulate me in this way. Even if what you say is true, why would you go to such despicable lengths to achieve your goals? No, these aren't even your goals. You're trying to appease my selfish brother and apparently your wife." Gregory refrained from referring to her as a harpy, despite the stories Evie had told him.

Evie.

Had she really been a courtesan?

"This is the way of things," Hargrove said coldly. "We help each other and those of us with the most power achieve our ends. You have the power to achieve what you desire. You have only to exercise it."

"You are mistaken. I have no influence with these people."

"Not even with your lover?" Hargrove made a tsking noise. "I simply cannot believe that. If you explain to her that her life will not continue as she now enjoys it once her past is made public, she'll do what's necessary to reestablish peace and harmony. Furthermore, I highly doubt Lord Lucien would want people knowing one of his patronesses used to be his whore. I should think his father, The Duke, would be particularly upset by that."

Gregory's hands fisted. He'd never considered violence toward anyone before in his life, not even his brother in his worst moments of teasing and belittlement. Now, however, he had to fight the overwhelming urge to knock Hargrove on his arse. "You're despicable," he spat, his lip curling in disgust.

Striding past Hargrove, Gregory quit the room before he did something he would regret. He was fairly certain there was no future for him working in the office of the Lord High Chancellor. Gregory wondered if the man knew what happened among those working for him.

Once he was in his coach, he swore softly but violently.

He didn't want to believe what Hargrove had said about Evie —not because he was upset if it were really true but because he would be upset that she hadn't told him.

It didn't bear consideration until he discovered the truth once and for all.

CHAPTER 16

*E*vie's step was light Tuesday evening, their busiest yet as many people had returned to Town in the past week. The past few nights with Gregory—meeting him here at the club—had been wonderful. They wouldn't meet tonight as the club was just too busy, even into the early morning hours, but she looked forward to seeing him.

Ada met her in the library for a glass of madeira. Fortified for the evening, they went into the members' den, where they immediately noted Millie seated near one of the front windows. She saw them too, for she practically leapt up and stalked toward them.

"Oh dear," Ada murmured.

"Brace yourself," Evie whispered before pasting a placid smile on her face. "Good evening, Millie," she said, trying to inject warmth into her tone and probably failing.

"You're a patroness now," Millie said flatly, her gaze fixed on Ada. "Did Evie tell you my thoughts on your employment?"

"She did not," Ada said evenly.

Evie hadn't bothered to repeat Millie's nonsense about

Ada's position as bookkeeper. She was far too valuable, but she also didn't want to leave her job. Indeed, they'd worked out a way for her to still be the bookkeeper even though she didn't live in London throughout the year.

"I find it inappropriate for you to be employed by the club in addition to being a patroness. It's unseemly."

Ada appeared to take her criticism seriously, her brow creasing. "I'm afraid I disagree. Isn't it helpful? I already spent time with the patronesses with the planning of events, and now I—and my knowledge—will always be there." She smiled brightly as she finished.

"I agree," Evie said, proud of her friend, who was always consistently brilliant.

Millie's nose wrinkled. "It's a disgrace. No *respectable* viscountess would retain employment."

"Then perhaps I'm not a respectable viscountess," Ada said with a shrug.

Evie wanted to hug her. "It's good that she's a patroness here since the Phoenix Club is not concerned with such things."

"It should be!" Millie's voice rose, and people around them took notice.

"Please don't shout," Evie said softly. "Perhaps we should take this—"

"You'd like it if these things weren't aired. You'd prefer the members weren't aware that the club's bookkeeper, a viscountess, is now a patroness and how horrid that looks for the club and for all of us who are members. You'd also prefer they weren't aware of the countless people who are denied membership—dukes and earls and people of import in our government. People who are welcome at Almack's and belong to White's. But they are shunned by the Phoenix Club." She scoffed, cutting her hand through the air. "It's a mockery as this club purports to be inclusive and not leave anyone behind. Balderdash!"

"Millie, you need to stop," Evie whispered urgently. The members' den had gone nearly silent in the face of the woman's tirade.

"I do not." Millie lifted her chin haughtily. "I am a *respectable* viscountess, my husband is a very important nobleman, and *I am a patroness.*"

At "respectable viscountess," Evie clenched her jaw and moved toward the woman. She was not going to be allowed to insult Ada.

Grabbing her forearm, Ada pulled her back. "Don't," she murmured. "Lucien is coming."

Evie turned her head to see Lucien stalking toward them, his eyes darker and angrier than she'd ever seen them.

"Lady Hargrove, if you will accompany me?" he requested politely, but with a sharp edge.

Millie looked him in the eye, fearless in the face of his ire —likely because she didn't realize just how furious he was. "Say what you have to say here."

"I will not. You may choose to accompany me, or you can leave. There is no third option for you."

She stared at him another moment, her mind clearly churning. In the end, she strode past him without a word. Evie wondered if she was leaving.

Lucien followed Millie and inclined his head toward Evie indicating that she should come too. Outside the members' den, they had their answer as Millie paused and looked at Lucien.

"In my office," he said crisply, moving around her and opening the door to his suite. He waited for Evie to come inside, then closed the door.

"I will not apologize," Millie declared, taking the offensive.

Lucien glowered at her. "I had hoped you would. You insulted Lady Warfield—a valued employee and patroness of the club. She is also your peer, whether you like it or not, and she deserves your respect, even if it's manufactured."

"How could you possibly have heard what I said?" Millie demanded, now taking a defensive posture as she folded her arms over her chest.

"I was on the other side of the members' den. Perhaps you don't realize how loudly you were speaking." His eyes narrowed, and he added, "I find you are often incredibly unaware of yourself."

Evie willed herself not to smirk.

"I could have said much worse," Millie said, using a much softer but somehow more malicious tone than in the members' den.

Lucien exhaled. "You give me no choice, Lady Hargrove. That sounded like a threat, and the truth is that I fear you may say worse or continue to cause problems. You seem very unhappy here at the Phoenix Club, both as a member and a patroness. I wonder why you even bother with either. Wouldn't you be much happier clinging to Almack's?"

"Almack's is not a club like this, and you know there is really nothing like the Phoenix Club when it comes to ladies." There was a flicker of unease in her eyes as if she were contemplating not coming to the club anymore and realizing she didn't like that.

"No, there is nothing like it," Evie said. "Which is why it's successful."

"Is it? You ignore so many of the most important people in Society."

Lucien's features were hard, his posture stiff. He was still quite angry. "Many of those people look down their noses at this club and wouldn't want to be members. You seem not to understand that. You also seem to look down your nose at aspects of this club, and yet you want to be a member, which tells me you seek to change the club to suit whatever you imagine it to be. That is not going to happen. This is *my* club, and I like it just the way it is. Except for one thing: I don't want you in it anymore."

Evie held her breath. Was he going to expel her from the club? He'd done that only once before—to his now brother-in-law, Wexford, upon learning that he was behaving inappropriately with his sister. Wexford was, of course, now back on the membership roll.

Millie's face lost a shade of color. "What are you saying?"

Lucien's eyes were like black ice. "You're banished from the Phoenix Club."

Nostrils flaring, Millie's cheeks flushed. "You can't do that."

"I can and you are, effective immediately. I'll have a footman escort you out, and your name will be struck from the membership list."

Millie looked to Evie. "Aren't you going to say something?"

"I've told you, Millie, membership issues are beyond me."

"That's a lie. I know you're on the committee with him." Millie glared at Lucien. "And with Overton and probably Fallin." She referred to two of Lucien's closest friends, and yes, they were members of the membership committee. How did she know that? Or was she merely guessing?

Millie turned her glower toward Evie with such menace that Evie nearly flinched. "You're going to be sorry that you didn't help me." She sneered at Lucien. "This club is going up in flames, and I can't wait to see it burn."

Spinning on her heel, Millie hurried out of the office. Lucien trailed behind her.

Evie paced to the fireplace and back. Why was she going

to be sorry? What was Millie going to do? Trepidation churned Evie's stomach.

He returned a few moments later. "I asked Arthur to make sure she left and told him she was no longer a member." Arthur was the head footman and would spread the information to employees throughout the club.

Nodding, Evie tried to relax. It was futile, however, as she couldn't forget the threat in Millie's eyes.

"What do you think she meant?" Evie asked. "About me being sorry."

"Who knows? We need a drink." Lucien went to pour two glasses of whisky, which Evie only rarely drank. She supposed this was a whisky occasion if there ever was one.

Except she didn't want to drink anything, not with her insides in their current state. "None for me," she said.

Lucien stopped what he was doing and turned toward her. "You sound worried."

"I am. You saw her. You heard her. She's never been this awful. And now you've cast her out."

"'Heaven has no rage like love to hatred turned, nor hell a fury like a woman scorned.'" Lucien quoted *The Mourning Bride*.

"She certainly never loved me," Evie said.

"I don't think she's capable of that." Lucien grunted, clearly still frustrated. "I share your concern."

"You don't think she knows about me?" Evie hated that her voice sounded low and vulnerable. She glanced toward the door and noted it was slightly ajar. She didn't want anyone to overhear this conversation.

"That is highly unlikely. We've done an excellent job of keeping your secrets safe for two years."

Because of the encounter with Arbuthnot, Evie was more nervous now than she'd been in the past two years. Or perhaps it was because in the time she'd spent with Gregory, she realized she'd only been living the life of a shadow, hiding herself and her past. She loved who she was now, the life she led, but Gregory had showed her what she was missing.

What she'd always been missing.

She thought she'd been protecting herself from judgment and disdain, and she had, but she'd also been shielding herself from living her full life, of embracing all she'd been. If not for her past, how could she have found her way here? But to reveal her secrets meant the greatest risk.

She looked at Lucien, fear clogging her throat. "Lucien, I'm afraid I'm going to lose everything."

He swiftly took her in his arms, holding her close. "I will *never* let that happen."

Closing her eyes, Evie let herself sink into his embrace. She'd never loved Lucien romantically, but she loved him as a devoted friend. "Thank you for always protecting me. I love you, Lucien," she whispered.

"I love you too."

The sound of a man clearing his throat broke them apart. While they no longer hugged, they still stood side by side as they turned toward the door.

Standing just inside the threshold, his face a shade paler than normal, stood Gregory. Evie didn't feel a sense of joy upon seeing him. Something was very wrong—she was certain of it.

He avoided looking at her, instead fixing his gaze on Lucien. "I'm afraid I've come with some distressing news." He flicked a look toward Evie. She saw sorrow, concern, and worst of all, pain.

She knew in that moment that she was indeed going to lose everything.

~

*S*he loved Lucien.

Gregory felt as if the world around him had stopped and he was trapped in a horrible nightmare. He hadn't wanted to believe Hargrove, but hearing Evie say she feared she was going to lose everything seemed to validate what Gregory had been told. He'd already put together that Mrs. Creighton was, in fact, Evie's sister. She and Evie had been the popular courtesans to whom Hargrove had referred.

Why had she kept that from him?

It seemed she still loved Lucien, but even worse, he was the man she went to for comfort. Because he was the man who truly knew her—in ways Gregory did not since she'd chosen not to reveal herself completely. He'd watched as Lucien and Evie embraced until he hadn't been able to suffer another moment, then he'd cleared his throat to signal that he was there.

"What news?" Lucien asked. He looked strained, his features tense, his spine stiff.

Gregory closed the door behind him and took one further step into the room. That was far enough. "I had a meeting with Hargrove today. He tried to extort me in exchange for my appointment to the office of the Lord High Chancellor."

Lucien swore rather viciously. "Did he again demand for your brother to become a member of the club?"

"That and something else. He wanted his wife to be allowed to choose a patroness and for that patroness to become a member. I tried to tell him I have no influence, but he didn't believe me. Or he didn't care."

"And what did he threaten?" Evie asked, her expression anxious, as if she knew it was something about her.

He swallowed and looked toward the fireplace, unable to

look at Evie. "To expose your past as a courtesan. Specifically, that Lucien was your protector." He shifted his gaze to meet hers. "He also knows about us."

"You?" Lucien broke in. "The two of you are…ah. Well, that's lovely."

Was it? Gregory couldn't tell if Lucien was being sarcastic. It would make sense if he was still in love with Evie. He suddenly knew the truth about her. He looked at Lucien. "She was your favorite mistress."

Lucien pressed his lips together. "Yes, she *was*."

Was. Past tense. But that didn't mean their feelings had faded—they certainly seemed strong and mutual. Neither had Gregory's. He couldn't just watch Evie be humiliated and ruined.

"What are you going to do?" he asked Lucien.

"Now we know what Lady Hargrove was threatening," Evie murmured. She looked to Gregory. "Lucien just expelled Lady Hargrove from the club."

"What?" Gregory took another step toward Lucien. "You have to fix it. Give her what she wants."

Lucien stared at him, his brow furrowing. "Why, so you can have your appointment?"

"I don't give a damn about that. You can't let Evie be exposed. Lady Hargrove may be going to the papers this very moment."

"I appreciate you saying that," Evie said softly. She'd moved away from Lucien. Away from both of them, as if she were preparing to isolate herself from those around her. "I can't let her win. She would change the entire character of the Phoenix Club, and I won't let her. Lucien has built something wonderful, something special."

"I won't let her harm the club *or* Evie." Lucien turned toward Evie. "Give me a chance to fix this. I'm going to find Hargrove and stop this. I have to go." He shot a quick but inscrutable glance at Gregory, then left, closing the door hard behind him.

Gregory waited for her to say something, but she didn't. Neither did she look at him. Her shoulders drooped in defeat, and he ignored the urge to go to her, to hold her.

"Why didn't you tell me the truth?"

Her gaze snapped to his. "Honestly, I didn't think it mattered. That was the past. I am not that person anymore."

"Who you were is part of who you are. I wanted to know everything about you." He still did, but he hated that she'd kept something so important from him.

"Did you really want to know I'd been a courtesan?" she asked derisively. "I can see from your expression that it disgusts you. That *I* disgust you."

"I don't know how you can tell that because it isn't true. I am angry you lied to me. I'm also upset that you and Lucien seem to still share a bond. Perhaps that is why you wish to never wed—the man you truly want isn't available to you." Gregory knew that Lucien didn't want to marry.

"Don't be jealous, Gregory. Lucien and I share a close friendship, but there is nothing romantic between us." Her words soothed Gregory's agitation and filled him with relief. "I choose to remain unwed because I have spent my life fighting for comfort and stability. I have those things through *my* hard work. I don't want to be beholden to anyone. I didn't even want to accept this job from Lucien when he first offered it. But he convinced me that he needed my skill and talent. And now I'm going to doom his dream." She took a halting breath.

Gregory moved slowly toward her, hating to see her hurting. "It isn't your fault."

She laughed suddenly, a broken, hollow sound that carved into Gregory's heart. "The irony is that my father was a chevalier. During the Terror, he sent us here for safety. He was supposed to follow as soon as he ensured some others were safe. He never came. It was years before we confirmed he had died."

"Evie, I'm so sorry."

One of her beautiful, elegant shoulders lifted. "I don't remember him at all. I was very young when we came from France. Just me, my sister, our mother, and her maid, Nadine." Her eyes met his. "You met my sister—Heloise. Rather, Mrs. Creighton."

"I did think you bore a resemblance to one another," he confessed.

She exhaled. "That has been a problem since I became Evangeline Renshaw. It's why she doesn't come to town. That, and she's a pariah because she married above her station." She gave him a sad look. "I'm sorry your name will be sullied with mine. You don't deserve that. I should have been honest with you so you could decide if you wanted to sully yourself with someone like me."

Gregory couldn't stand another moment without touching her. Yes, he was angry, but he was also outraged for her. In agony—for *her*. He went to her and gently clasped her upper arms. "I would never think that, not even knowing the truth. You are a remarkable woman, Evie. To have lifted yourself from an unimaginable devastation is incredible."

"Do you say that because my father was a chevalier? What if we—Heloise and I—were simply poor girls from the East End? Would you still think me remarkable?"

He understood her point, and the truth was he didn't know, because that wasn't the situation. "I'd like to think so. Evie, I was—and am—drawn to *you*, whoever that is."

"And what if I don't know?" she asked brokenly.

Gregory tried to pull her to him, but she broke away and put distance between them, positioning herself closer to the door. He couldn't help feeling wounded that she'd allowed Lucien to comfort her, but not him.

"You don't need to have all the answers." Gregory had often told his students that. "Life is an endless query and exploration." Hell, he'd only recently decided what he wanted to do. And it appeared he was going to have to shift his goal again since that way was now closed to him.

Evie folded her arms over her chest. "How did they find out about us?"

"I don't know." Gregory thought about what Hargrove had said, but couldn't discern any clues as to how he might have learned about their affair. He knew his brother was involved somehow. Had he somehow discovered there was something between them? He suddenly realized what it could be. "At Witney Court, when you came upstairs to see Ash—"

Her eyes rounded. "Someone knows what we did in your bedchamber?"

"There's no way anyone would have seen what we were doing, but when I left, I saw a maid. If she saw you too and told my brother, or worse, if she told Susan…" Gregory shook his head. "I don't know."

"Your sister-in-law noticed we were both absent," Evie said flatly.

"It's also possible Susan noticed my frequent absences at Witney Court and that you and I spent time together on outings and drew her own—accurate—conclusions. But that is just a supposition."

"There's also my neighbors. Mr. Kirby saw Ash on the street with a gentleman—you. If he somehow identified you…and he knew that same dog spent the night with me, he may have reasoned that you and I were at least friends. Then, if he or someone in his household happened to see you coming to or leaving my house..." She put a hand to her cheek. "We were so foolish."

"We were also rather happy," he added softly, unable to summon even a small amount of regret. Though it sounded as if she had enough for both of them. "Do you have any idea how they learned of your past?"

She exhaled, sounding frustrated. "It has been a risk since the beginning. I've always chosen my invitations carefully, and there were certain people Lucien wouldn't allow to become members for fear they would recognize me. At first, I changed the color of my hair, and I permanently stopped wearing many cosmetics. I also altered my wardrobe, which was frankly necessary after no longer being a courtesan. Over the past two years, I've let my hair gradually go back to its normal color."

"You made a concerted effort not to be recognized."

"Of course I did," she said sharply. "Mirabelle Renault was never going to be accepted anywhere polite. She certainly couldn't be a patroness of the Phoenix Club."

"But Mrs. Renshaw could."

"She was Lucien's idea—a respectable widow. I left town for several months and came back as someone entirely new." Her lip curled. "I should have realized this harmony could never last. Someone was bound to put it all together. I suspect it was Philip Arbuthnot. I encountered him at Witney Court. He found me familiar, but couldn't place our connection. I met him at a courtesan ball."

Gregory knew Arbuthnot fairly well. The man could be a bit arrogant, but was mostly harmless. "Did you and he...?"

"No, and don't ask me that ever again. You can't have unhindered access to my past. I locked it all away for a reason. I don't wish to summon it again. Ever." She spoke with a shocking vehemence. Was she ashamed despite being proud of what she'd been able to accomplish on her own?

"That's fair. My apologies."

What a bloody mess. He didn't know what to say to her. She was upset and hurting and rightfully so.

"You should go," she said. "I don't know if anyone saw you come in here, but I'm fairly certain everyone in the club knows I came in here with Lucien."

She didn't continue, but he knew she was concerned people might deduce they were in here together. And since their affair was soon to become public knowledge, it was probably best if they didn't feed the gossip. Perhaps there was something he could do to prevent that happening. He would at least try.

Gregory went to the door and paused. "I'd like to help, if I can."

"There is nothing you can do. The truth will come out, I suppose. I always knew it was possible. I was a fool to think it could remain buried." She squared her shoulders. "I did try, and I'll find my way. *Alone.*"

He didn't doubt that she would. "Like a phoenix," he said, smiling faintly. He realized this was the end, that she wouldn't invite him to meet her here tomorrow or any other day. "I'll be cheering you on."

Opening the door, he left the office and made his way from the club. He didn't look back.

CHAPTER 17

*E*vie wasn't sure how long she stood in Lucien's office. A numbness had settled over her, and she didn't particularly want to move, not even to sit down. But she must. And she wasn't going to walk out the door.

Going to the bookcase in the corner, she reached up and pulled a book that worked as a lever for the secret door. The bookcase swung open, and Evie went to light a candle before she stepped into the dark passageway.

It was a short walk to the other end, but she couldn't do it without illumination. Candle in hand, she closed the bookcase and moved forward along the passage, which included a brief flight of stairs down, until she met the other door, which opened into the mezzanine. From there, she made her way to the ladies' side.

A narrow door tucked into a corner led to another flight of stairs up to a doorway just outside her office. Lucien had installed this passageway so they could easily access each other's offices, particularly on busy club nights.

A wave of nostalgia and sadness washed over her. She and Lucien had worked so closely on the success of the club. It was mostly him, but she'd been an intrinsic part. She was going to miss it more than she could say.

She particularly loved her office, from the flower-shaped pulls on her desk drawers to the daffodil-colored chairs to the small landscape painting hanging behind her desk between the windows that looked down to the garden. The painting had belonged to her mother and was one of the few things that had survived their journey from France.

Evie went to the painting and gently touched the frame, which she'd had redone before hanging it here. When she was younger and they lived in their two-room lodging in Soho, the frame had been broken. Evie didn't remember much about her mother, but she recalled her staring at that painting and crying. Later, Nadine had explained that her mother-in-law—Evie's grandmother—had painted the landscape, and it depicted the estate her father's family had owned. This and a simple cross necklace made of coral were the only items they had of any importance. Heloise had the necklace, and Evie had kept the painting. To think that their once-grand family had been reduced to those things and just the two of them made her sad. Which was probably why Evie rarely contemplated it.

She supposed they might have family, particularly in France if they'd survived the Terror. Or perhaps they'd escaped—either to England or America. Evie wouldn't know how or where to begin searching for people whose names she didn't even know. Her past was of no use or worth, so she typically left it where it belonged: behind her.

Turning from the painting, Evie looked around at what she might take with her from the office. Most of these things belonged to the Phoenix Club, not to her. There were books she would take, and she decided the small statue of Venus near the fireplace belonged to her. Lucien had gifted it to her when the club had opened. Again, a part of her life was being reduced to things.

Knowing Lucien, he wouldn't mind if she took every last item in the room. Indeed, he might even insist on it. But, he would say, she wouldn't have to because he was going to make sure she was able to stay. Evie didn't believe for a single moment that he would be able to stop what was happening, not without giving Millie what she demanded.

Evie pounded her fist on the desktop. She braced her hands on the wood and hung her head in defeat. She'd vastly underestimated Millie. A woman with her measure of entitlement was never going to simply allow Evie or the Phoenix Club to deny her what she thought she deserved.

And Evie had been a fool for thinking she deserved any of this. She pushed up from the desk and fell into her chair, which was positioned so that she could easily look out the window at the garden, lit with dozens of torches, below. She stared at the reflecting pool for some time.

She thought of Nadine, who'd been the only parent she'd really known. As she lay sick and dying, she'd apologized repeatedly for how things had turned out after they'd come to England. Their father had wanted them to find someone who would help them, but that hadn't happened, perhaps because their mother had been too despondent and couldn't recall everything he'd told her. She'd been absolutely brokenhearted after leaving her husband in France. Then, about two years later, when she'd seen his name on a list of people who'd died, she'd become a shell of a person until she'd followed him into death.

Nadine had done her best to raise them, working hard as a seamstress to provide for them. Still, they'd lived in poverty, so far beneath where they belonged, or so Nadine had always said. When you heard that all the time, Evie realized, you began to believe it. She and Heloise had hoped and dreamed of a better life. Going to work in a fancy brothel had given them that opportunity. They'd been young, pretty, and they both spoke French. That had made them desirable, and, as a result, successful. It had seemed they *did* deserve a better life.

But who really deserved anything? There were plenty of girls in their neighborhood who were just as deserving, but who hadn't escaped poverty or hard work. Why was Evie any better than them? She wasn't.

She didn't *deserve* any of this, and she'd be fine without it. There would be plenty to miss, primarily her friends who had become her family. But she couldn't stay here in London, even though leaving would break her heart. It was the only home she'd ever known.

What if she left, and perhaps went to Cornwall again, then returned to Soho to open her own business? She'd saved enough as a courtesan and over the past two years working at the club that she could reinvent herself again and start anew. She thought of the Siren's Call, a gaming hell run by a brilliant woman, Jewel Harker, who'd opened its doors some fifteen or twenty years ago. It employed only women, and they lured men to come drink and gamble. They did not, however, offer sex, and any man overstepping with any of the women there was quickly and soundly thrown out on his arse—by women.

Evie didn't want to duplicate the Siren's Call, but she could speak with Jewel and ask her advice on what to do. Yes, she'd do that soon.

A soft knock on the door drew Evie to turn her head. She didn't really want to see anyone.

"Evie, are you in there?" It was Ada.

Exhaling, Evie didn't want to ignore her friend. "Yes. Come in."

Ada slipped inside, closing the door behind her. She

walked slowly toward the desk, her features tight, her hands clasped as if she'd been wringing them. "I was waiting for you to come back to the members' den. When you didn't, I determined something must be wrong. Or you were just incredibly fatigued after having to speak with Millie."

Evie actually cracked a smile. "That is certainly possible, but no. Fatigued is not the right word. You may as well sit. This is a rather horrible story with a not very happy ending, I'm afraid."

Blanching, Ada went to move a chair toward the desk. Evie stood and waved her to stop. "We'll sit here." She gestured to the central seating area with a wide settee and the daffodil-colored chairs Evie loved so much.

Perching on one of the chairs while Ada sat on the settee, Evie told her what had happened with Millie, that she'd tried to force Lucien to do her will, and when he refused, she'd said Evie would be sorry. "Then Lucien expelled her from the club."

Ada gasped. "He's only tried that once before, and it didn't stick."

"He did that to Wex out of anger," Evie said, referring to when he'd banished his now brother-in-law. "He doesn't want to let Millie come back."

"Nor should he." Ada sniffed in disgust. "He'll fix this."

"I don't know that he can," Evie said softly. "There is more, and please don't be angry with me for keeping it from you. It was important to me—and to my livelihood—that I kept it secret. Very few people knew the truth." Now all of London and beyond would know. Ada should know before any of them.

Ada's eyes were wide and dark. "Now, you're making me quite anxious."

"Before I left London for Cornwall, where I met you, I was a courtesan named Mirabelle Renault. My last protector was Lucien." She paused as Ada's jaw dropped and waited until she'd snapped it closed. "He offered me a job managing the club and then later decided he needed patronesses and wanted me to be one of them. I didn't see how any of that would be possible since I'd been a courtesan. He came up with the plan for me to leave London for a period of months and return as a widow."

"You were undergoing that change when I met you," Ada whispered. She stared at Evie's hair. "I noticed recently that your hair is darker now. Did you change it at first?"

Evie nodded. "I used a powder to lighten it. I wore almost no cosmetics when I became Mrs. Renshaw, and of course, I changed my entire wardrobe."

"I remember you wore nothing but gray and lavender for many months after we met." Ada stared at her. "I'm just... I hope you didn't think *I* would judge you."

"I would never think that." Evie moved to sit beside her on the settee. "And that's not because you also engaged in trade, if only for a short time. I would have trusted you—I *do* trust you—because you are the best friend I have ever had. I knew from the moment we met that we were kindred spirits. You understood what it meant to have to fight for yourself, to do whatever it takes to survive."

Cast out by her family before she was grown, Ada had struggled for years, ultimately becoming a governess, which had also turned out poorly. When she'd met Evie, she'd needed help as much as she'd needed a friend. "We found each other at the exact right time," Ada said, a tear leaking from her eye. She wiped at her cheek.

"Yes, and the only reason I didn't tell you the truth was because I had to keep myself safe from exposure. I also, foolishly, believed if I didn't tell anyone about it, didn't even think about it, I could more easily pretend it had never happened, that I had always been Evangeline Renshaw. I only recently began to understand how it was in fact hurting me to keep everything hidden, particularly from those closest to me. In hindsight, I wish I'd told you. Not just about being a courtesan, but my entire story. I was born in France, actually."

"I look forward to hearing *everything*." Ada took Evie's hands and squeezed them. "Please don't feel bad about not telling me before. It doesn't matter. I'm here for you now, and it sounds as though you need a friend."

"I do, thank you."

Ada released Evie. "I won't be as effective as Lucien in actually helping you with this, but I'll be at your side providing all the support you need."

Evie almost smiled at Ada's misplaced certainty. Lucien was a wonder, but he couldn't work miracles. "Lucien can't fix this. Not even he can keep the Hargroves from ensuring my secrets are exposed. If he doesn't give in to Millie's demands, the club will suffer."

"But he can't!" Ada's voice rose. "*You* will suffer. And the club will suffer if she's allowed to stay."

Evie appreciated her friend's outrage, but it wouldn't solve anything. "We are all in agreement, not that it matters. Lucien has built a wonderful place here, and he can't let it falter. I don't see any outcome that doesn't include my exposure." She was surprised to find that the numbness she'd felt earlier persisted. Good, she didn't have the energy to despair.

"I wish that weren't true," Ada whispered. "This is so unfair."

"Perhaps, but we both know that fairness rarely enters into anything. I've had a lovely run the past two years here. Now, it's time to move on."

"Must you really? Surely, no one will resign their membership if you stay. And people will still come. The population of the Phoenix Club is made up of people who have either been maligned or ignored by Society or are so far removed from it to not give a damn."

"Mostly, yes. However, there are some who will see the expulsion of a patroness and the well-respected Lord Hargrove as unjust. They may not resign their membership, but they may very well stop coming to the club, at least for a while or perhaps the entire Season. Or they may never return." Evie could see the calculations going on in Ada's head.

"That would be devastating," Ada said quietly.

"Yes." Evie wouldn't let that happen.

Ada shook her head rather vehemently. "No, this isn't going to be how it plays out. The anonymous pair on the membership committee will protect you and the club. There may be a scandal, but it will be minimized, and it will be brief."

A kernel of hope nestled in Evie's chest. It was hard not to be persuaded by Ada's optimism. And now Evie was thinking of Gregory. Perhaps he'd rubbed off on her more than she wanted to admit. In fact, she wondered what he was doing now. Was he working to protect Evie? She had to think he might be, but she was better off not thinking about it—or him—at all.

Evie smiled faintly at Ada. "You speak as if you know who those anonymous members are."

"I don't." Ada blinked. "Do you?"

"I do not." Though Evie had long suspected the esteemed Lady Pickering was one of them. She was always very friendly with Lucien, and the fact that she'd avoided accepting her now-two-year-old invitation to join the club had always struck Evie as odd.

Evie was also fairly certain the other was a man, someone to whom Lucien was incredibly loyal. He'd slipped up a time or two when talking to Evie over the years. She hadn't drawn attention to it, but had tucked the information away.

She recalled what she'd considered recently, that those two anonymous people might have invited the Hargroves and others like them to join the club. Perhaps they had more control over the club's membership than she or anyone else realized. "Whoever they are, if they tell Lucien to go along with Millie's demands, he will have to. Society will insist upon it."

Ada frowned. "I don't understand Society, and I hope I never do. I may be a viscountess in name, but I am just a girl from Devon who happened to fall in love far above my station."

Evie looked at her intently. "You are a brilliant woman who works very hard. That a viscount was smart enough to see how wonderful you are and make you his own is his good fortune."

"What about your good fortune?" Ada asked. "You shouldn't have to leave the club."

Evie didn't want to discuss it anymore. "I think I'm going home." She stood, suddenly eager to be on her way from the club.

Ada jumped up, her face creasing with worry. "Am I driving you away?"

"Of course not." Evie gave her a brief, reassuring smile. "I just don't wish to see anyone else."

"I understand. I'll walk out with you."

Nodding, Evie left the office with her and went down-stairs. One of the footwomen quickly fetched Evie's things from the cloakroom—they were not busy since it was Tuesday and most of the ladies who might have been here were instead next door.

Ada bid her good evening, and Evie stepped out into the cold February night. Sparse snowflakes drifted in the air as

Evie made her way toward St. James's Square. She made this walk nearly every day and night, though at night, she was often in the company of a footman from the club, whose duty it was to see her home.

Tonight, however, she preferred to be alone to contemplate the storm that was coming. She only wished she knew if it would decimate everything or if she'd find a way to survive.

～

"*L*ord Gregory, what a pleasure to see you." Lightner, the butler at Witney House, greeted Gregory despite the lateness of the hour. Nearing sixty, Lightner had been at Witney House as long as Gregory could remember. He was one of many people Gregory would miss seeing regularly now that his brother was the marquess.

"I'm surprised you're still at the door," Gregory said, handing the man his hat and gloves.

"Lady Witney prefers I am on duty until midnight." The man didn't reflect his thoughts about that, but Gregory could imagine he didn't like it. For heaven's sake, the man ran a large household and would need to be up early to manage things.

Gregory tried not to frown and failed. "That's far too late. Or have they let all the footmen go?" Of course they hadn't. If anything, Susan had probably insisted they hire more.

"No. There is even an underbutler."

"Then there is really no need for this," Gregory said, growing angrier than he already was. He'd come here to read his brother the riot act. "I'll speak to Clifford."

"That isn't necessary, my lord, but you are considerate to think of me. You always have been." His gaze was warm and kind, and Gregory was sorry the man had to work in this household. Perhaps if Gregory ever found himself with a household large enough to support a butler, he'd hire him away.

When would that happen when Gregory couldn't even launch the career he wanted?

"If you're here to see Lord Witney, I'm afraid he's not returned home yet," Lightner said. "Lady Witney is in the Greek room." He referred to Gregory's father's favorite room on the ground floor, which was decorated with Greek sculpture. A large, fanciful painting of Greek gods and goddesses held a focal point in the center of one wall. "Though, they aren't calling it that anymore. It's now the Gold Room."

Gregory's stomach knotted. What had she done? He found he had to see for himself. He could also vent some of his spleen at her since she was the primary source behind their ridiculous demands. "I'll just go and say good evening," Gregory said, his tone sounding sharp even to his own ears.

If Lightner noticed Gregory's agitation, he didn't indicate so. He merely inclined his head.

Walking swiftly as he allowed his anger to flow through him. Gregory made his way to the Greek Room. He wasn't ever going to call it the Gold Room. As soon as he reached the threshold, his jaw dropped. Gold didn't begin to describe the amount of…gold on display. Everything was either made of gold or gilded or colored gold. There were brief accents of cream. There wasn't a Greek sculpture to be seen, and his father's favorite painting was gone. In its place was some massive gilt-framed Rococo nightmare.

"You've made some changes," Gregory said tightly.

Susan sat in a chair near the fire, a magazine in her lap. "Gregory, what a surprise."

"I came to see Clifford, but Lightner said he was out."

"Yes, he's so busy since we returned to town. Everyone wants to spend time with the new marquess." She laughed lightly, and it only further grated on Gregory's nerves. "I've only just returned home a short while ago."

Gregory noted she was still dressed in her evening finery. "Do you expect him back soon?"

"Yes. Are you hoping to speak with him? I have to assume you've finally come to your senses and are here to tell us that our Phoenix Club invitations will arrive tomorrow." She smiled sweetly, but there was nothing sweet about the superiority in her gaze.

"I am not here for that reason, actually. As I've told you and Clifford *many* times, I have absolutely no influence when it comes to who is invited—or not—to the Phoenix Club."

Susan gripped the magazine and stood. Her brows dipped as her eyes narrowed at him. "I don't understand why your paramour can't just fix this problem. From everything I've been told, she makes some of the most important decisions at the club. You're being willfully nasty."

He was being nasty? For the second time that day and perhaps in his entire life, he lost his temper. "Do not speak to me as if we are friendly or as if I would do you any favors when you have been nothing but entitled and awful since you wed my brother. Just who do you think my 'paramour' is?" He wasn't going to admit anything regarding Evie.

Susan rolled her eyes. "It is no secret to us that you've been meeting with Mrs. Renshaw, at least when she was in Oxfordshire over the holidays and probably since you both returned to London. Don't bother denying it. One of the maids at Witney Court saw both of you enter and leave your bedchamber during the party. And you disappeared for long periods of time, often with your filthy dog. It makes sense that you were meeting her, especially since you became inordinately...happy. Clifford said you hadn't been remotely cheerful since your father died. Then, after we learned she used to be a courtesan, there was simply no longer any question."

Gregory considered defending Evie by saying they couldn't prove any of it, but what would be the point? They believed it, this narrative suited their needs, and the damage would be done if it wasn't already when they exposed Evie to the world.

He did, however, want the full story. "How did you learn she was a courtesan?" The question was so low as to be almost a growl, and Gregory was certainly feeling feral.

"Oh, Arbuthnot remembered her from that time. She seemed familiar to him when they met at the party at Witney Court, but he didn't realize why until later. One night at White's, he asked Clifford if he realized he'd invited a courtesan to his party." Susan cocked her head to the side. "Well, aside from Mrs. Creighton. It makes perfect sense now that that they'd be such close friends!" She smiled, no *gloated*, and Gregory wanted to say something that would permanently wipe the smug expression from her face.

"You know you're being purposely horrible. You like to be horrible. It gives you pleasure. You are the most abhorrent person I've ever met."

"Gregory!" Clifford strode into the room and made his way to Susan's side. "I must insist you not speak to my wife in that manner!"

Gregory pinned him with an icy stare. "But I suppose it's completely acceptable for you and her to manipulate me so you can receive invitations to join the Phoenix Club? Or to use extortion to achieve your goals? You have no qualms about ruining someone for the sake of your own petty desires."

"Well, look at you," Clifford said, his eyes narrowing. "I suppose taking a mistress has finally loosened you up."

Gregory took a step toward his brother, but stopped

himself. He realized his hands were fisted and his arms taut with fury. "You've always been mean spirited, but this extortion attempt is as low as I've ever seen you go. I'm glad Father isn't here to see it." Gregory found satisfaction in the hardening of his brother's gaze, but he kept himself from saying anything more that he'd likely regret.

"You've no move to make, Gregory."

"Neither do you. Your invitations will not be forthcoming."

"How do you know that?" Susan asked, her voice high and breathy.

Gregory reveled in giving her a haughty look. "Because I do."

"I thought you said you weren't that close to the people in charge."

"I said I didn't have influence. I consider Lucien a friend, and it seems you're well aware of how close I am to Mrs. Renshaw." Gregory glared at them both.

"I refuse to believe you about the invitations," Clifford said, but there was a shadow of uncertainty in his tone and in his expression. "Hargrove assured me our efforts would force the club's hand."

"Have you no shame at all?" Gregory felt suddenly defeated. He began to understand why his father had, after a point, heaped all his attention on Gregory.

Neither of them answered his question. They just stared at him, indignant, as if he were in the wrong.

Gregory curled his lip. "Know this: even if I could have helped you, I wouldn't have."

"You'll have no future in government now," Clifford said, his eyes glittering with anger.

"So you say, but I'll wait and see what happens. You typically prove to be ineffectual, and I expect this will be no different. The smarter gentlemen in the Lords will soon realize you don't take after Father, that you barely under-stand the duties of a marquess, let alone a member of the upper house of Parliament."

Clifford squared his shoulders. "Get out."

"Gladly. It's rather irritating to see what you've done to Father's Greek Room. I'm glad he isn't here to see it." He gestured toward the wall where his father's favorite painting once hung. "If you aren't going to use the god and goddess painting, I'll take it."

"I think it was burned," Susan said snidely.

"Or will be," Clifford added. "I wouldn't give it—or anything else—to you. Don't come crying to me when you need funds."

Gregory had pivoted toward the door, but now he looked back over his shoulder at his brother, triumph surging through him. "You aren't aware that Father settled a rather large sum on me several years ago. I believe he anticipated this very behavior and wanted to make sure I could make my own way. You see, Clifford, I don't need you at all."

Striding from the ghastly room before Clifford or Susan could respond, Gregory encountered Lightner in the entrance hall. "It was very good to see you, my lord," the butler said as he handed Gregory his hat and gloves.

"It was excellent to see you too, Lightner. Indeed, it was the best part of this visit. I regret I wasn't able to speak with Witney on your behalf, and I won't be returning." He lowered his voice to just above a whisper. "I do hope you'll contact me if things become untenable here. I will do my best to see you situated in a more pleasant household."

Lightner's pale blue eyes widened slightly. "I do appre-ciate that, my lord. Thank you." He opened the door, and Clifford left Witney House for what was probably the last time.

He felt a rush of sadness, but it was all to do with his

father and the memories Gregory had of growing up here. His only emotion at turning his back on his brother was relief.

Suddenly exhausted, which was unsurprising, Gregory climbed into his coach. He looked forward to getting home and snuggling with Ash. He adored the pup and their nightly routine. He also loved that Ash reminded him of Evie.

Gregory leaned his head back against the squab. In his mind, he saw her frigid stare and felt her despair. He didn't blame her for not telling him about her past. He understood why she'd wanted to keep it secret, even from him. Still, it hurt. He'd wanted to share everything with her.

He'd wanted to marry her.

But she'd been clear from the start, and now he knew why. She'd been beholden to men and didn't want to be ever again, even to a husband. For even if she had an equal marriage—as she would have had with Gregory—everything she owned would become her husband's property.

Letting her go was the hardest thing he'd ever done, and yet he knew it was the right thing to do.

Is it?

A voice in the back of his mind questioned that decision.

You should fight for her.

Except, Evie wouldn't want that. He couldn't will her to change her mind with the power of his own optimism. He couldn't want or love her enough for both of them. Neither of them would be happy with that.

And that just left…heartache.

CHAPTER 18

$\mathcal{E}$vie watched from her drawing room window as Lucien approached her door. She'd told Foster she wasn't receiving, but suspected Lucien might insist on seeing her.

Sure enough, a few moments later, Foster came in to tell her that Lucien said he wouldn't take much of her time, but that he urgently needed to see her. He'd added that he hoped she was all right.

Resigned, Evie told Foster to send him up. She rose from her chair at the table and smoothed her plain gray morning gown. When she'd first returned to London after becoming Mrs. Renshaw, she'd worn nothing but grays and lavenders. This gown was from that time.

Lucien came in, and Evie was instantly alarmed. She moved toward him in concern. "You look as if you haven't slept."

"I haven't." He threw himself onto the settee, slumping so that he was practically lying down with his legs extended. "Have you?"

"A little." She nearly smiled in response to the concern in

his eyes. Whatever they had been, he was a dear friend. "I assume you have news? Otherwise, you would have let me wallow." She sat in a chair next to the other end of the settee from where he was sprawled.

"You don't wallow. Stew, perhaps, but not wallow. If you did, I'd be disappointed."

She had, in fact, wallowed, but he was right. That wasn't like her, and she'd resolved to stop it, which was why she'd bothered getting dressed that morning. "Just tell me."

He exhaled, straightening himself a bit, but not entirely. "I am, unfortunately, in an impossible position. I refuse to allow Lady Hargrove—or her husband—to remain in the club. However, the club will be affected by their expulsion."

"In what way?" Evie could already guess, as she'd told Ada the night before, but she wanted to hear what Lucien would say.

"Members will resign, and fewer people will come, at least for a while. Perhaps for the entire Season." His shoulders twitched, and he glowered at the hearth.

"Will they really? You've been very careful about membership."

"Yes, but as I repeatedly tell everyone—the final decisions aren't up to me. There are members, such as Lady Hargrove, who don't necessarily share our vision. But, they wanted to be part of something new and exciting."

She heard the agitation in his voice and sought to ease his mind. "The club will be better for their departure, won't it?"

"In the end, yes, but the club's reputation could be impaired in the short term."

It seemed he wasn't revealing everything. "What aren't you saying?" He glanced at her, and she sensed his hesitation. She decided to alleviate his worry. "I have to think you met with the anonymous pair on the membership committee last night. I have thought for some time that Lady Pickering is one of them. She is a very powerful voice in Society, and if she is not in favor of you expelling the Hargroves, that will almost ensure the club is negatively affected. I don't know who the other person is, but I believe it's a gentleman and that he has considerable influence over you."

Lucien snapped his gaze to hers, surprise etched into his features.

"Am I wrong about any of that?" she asked, folding her hands in her lap.

"No. You are far too smart for my good." He scrubbed a hand over his face and straightened himself entirely, pulling his legs up. "I don't own the club outright. I can't tell you more than that, but suffice it to say that while you—and others—think I have the final say in all matters, I do not."

"Are they the reason the Hargroves were invited?"

The subtle lift of one brow was the only answer he gave.

"So, Lady Hargrove must stay," Evie said, her extremities feeling suddenly lighter.

His gaze met hers with regret. "No, they're allowing me to expel the Hargroves, but—"

"*I* have to go," Evie whispered. "It's all right. I expected as much."

He scooted down the settee toward her, his face a mask of anguish. "I don't want you to."

"I know that. If you recall, I didn't want this job in the first place. You convinced me to take it."

"Please don't do that." He looked down at her hands for a moment before he spoke again. "You love what you do. We both know it, so please don't try to tell me otherwise."

He wasn't wrong.

Evie took a breath and was surprised to find she could produce a smile. "It's been a good two years." The best of her life. So far. Perhaps the best was still yet to come. "I always knew it could be temporary. I reinvented myself once—

twice, really." She counted her decision to work in the brothel as a new beginning. "I'll just do it again."

He smiled faintly, his dark eyes glimmering with admiration. "You know I'll help however I can."

"Not this time, Lucien. I mean it. I'll be fine on my own—financially and in every other way."

"What about Lord Gregory?"

The question momentarily upset her equilibrium. She'd been trying very hard not to think about him. Everything else was quite enough at the moment. "What about him? I don't blame him, if that's what you mean."

"I don't either. He was a pawn—who refused to be manipulated. I hope this won't affect what you share."

She looked at him sharply. "Please just leave it." Flattening her palms against her lap, she gently shook the tension from her shoulders. "Now, let us determine next steps. I will formally resign as patroness and as a member of the Phoenix Club, then I will move my things out of my office. Will tomorrow be soon enough?"

The anguish returned to his features, and Evie wondered if Lucien was perhaps taking this harder than she was. No, of course not. He was just reacting differently. This was a situation he despised—one in which there was nothing he could do to change the outcome to be what he wanted. He likely felt defeated.

Lucien swore. "I hate this."

"I do not enjoy it either, but we must carry on."

"You are awfully British for a Frenchwoman," he said wryly.

"I am far more British than French, as you know." She didn't even remember her homeland, and had no plans to return. "The most important thing is for the Phoenix Club to go on. I shall be heartbroken if all my—and your—hard work has been for naught."

"Bloody hell, Evie, you are taking this far better than I am."

Evie nearly smiled. Apparently, she'd been right. "You'll get there. Things will continue to run smoothly, particularly with Ada as a patroness now. She's basically the new me."

He pinned her with a serious stare. "No one could ever be you." He rose from the settee. "I'm going to check on you again tomorrow."

"No need. I'll be at the club to fetch my things. Do you need a written resignation from me? I can write it now, if you like."

He held up his hand. "No. I refuse to accept anything in writing. That makes it too…real. Allow me at least a day to live in denial." Moving to her chair, he leaned down and kissed her cheek. "You really are a marvel."

She laughed softly. "Now leave me alone."

Lucien left, and Evie let herself sag back against the chair. She wasn't as strong as Lucien believed. She was simply good at pretending to be. It had been an integral part of her childhood.

Standing, she went to ring for Foster. When he arrived, she informed him that she wouldn't be receiving visitors for the rest of the day.

Then she retreated to her chamber, where she clutched the drawing of Ash that Gregory had made for her.

∽

The morning after his awful encounter with his brother, Gregory sat, pensive, in the sitting room adjacent to his bedchamber. Ash trotted up to him, his rope dangling from his mouth. His appearance immediately alleviated some of Gregory's agitation.

"Shall I take this away?" Gregory said, initiating Ash's favorite game.

Gregory pulled at the rope, and Ash clamped down, growling. He planted his back feet on the carpet and gave no quarter as Gregory pretended to try to wrest the rope free. After some minutes of this play, Gregory released the rope in mock defeat. "I'm afraid you've bested me."

Ash barked happily and settled down, his front paws extended. He dropped the rope onto his paws and grinned at Gregory. It was almost as if he could tell Gregory was maudlin. But of course he could. "You are a very smart dog," Gregory said, ruffling the white fur on his head.

Harris entered, and Gregory asked the valet where the morning's newspapers were. He typically set them on the table for Gregory to read while he ate breakfast.

"I don't know that any arrived, my lord." Harris's tone carried a higher pitch than normal. Add that to the fact that he wasn't meeting Gregory's gaze, and it seemed clear he was hiding something.

Gregory could surmise why he would wish to do so. "Harris, do the papers contain something about me, perchance?"

"I couldn't say." Harris tried to continue on his way into Gregory's chamber.

"You know I'll just go purchase one—or more," Gregory called after him.

Pivoting, Harris came back exhaling a sigh. "There may have been…something."

"Fetch them, please." Gregory looked down at Ash and shook his head.

A few minutes later, Harris returned with the newspapers, wearing an apologetic expression. "We only wanted to spare you any discomfort so early in the day."

"I appreciate your consideration." Gregory browsed through the first paper until he found the "something."

There were big changes afoot at the "controversial" Phoenix Club. The Hargroves had been expelled, and one of the patronesses was revealed to be a courtesan. Furthermore, she was conducting an affair with Lord Gregory Blakemore.

"*Former* courtesan," Gregory muttered, not that it mattered. But they could at least get their facts straight. Leave it to his brother to leave that detail out. Gregory had no doubt Clifford was behind this information being made public. He wanted to smear Gregory as much as Evie. No, he didn't care about Evie at all—she was simply the damage he left in the wake of his destructive selfishness.

Gregory didn't give a damn about himself, but this had to be incredibly painful for Evie. She'd been respected by so many, and hopefully she still would be. But there were many who would now cut her. That truth filled him with anguish.

He longed to go to her, to comfort her. She likely wouldn't allow that, especially from him.

Ash nuzzled his leg with a soft whimper, prompting Gregory to pick him up and set him in his lap. He fed the pup a small piece of kipper from his plate. "You know there's something wrong, don't you, lad?" Gregory knew Ash missed her, just as he did.

Perhaps there was something Gregory could do to cheer at least two of them—well, three, for doing this would make him feel better too. He called for Harris.

The valet, who'd gone into Gregory's chamber to prepare his clothing for the day, returned. "Yes, my lord?"

"I've an errand for you to run," Gregory replied. "With Ash."

"He prefers to visit the park with you." While Harris was now quite fond of Ash, taking him to the park was his least favorite activity.

"You aren't going to the park," Gregory said. "You're going somewhere far better." He stroked Ash's head and smiled, wishing he could see the expression on her face when the dog arrived.

~

a day of not wallowing but stewing was precisely what Evie had needed. She felt much better today, ready to move forward as she'd said she was doing yesterday when Lucien had visited. The news in the papers hadn't upset her. She'd known it was coming, and the moment she'd seen it in print, she tossed the paper into the fire. Then she'd directed Delilah to burn the rest.

After breakfast, she carried out her usual toilet, ready, if not eager, to meet the day. Once she fetched her things from the Phoenix Club, she would feel even better. Then she could close the book on that chapter of her life.

As if it would be that easy.

Foster came into her sitting room. "Mrs. Kirby is here."

Oh dear. Had the woman come to query her about what she'd read in the papers that morning? Evie had no desire to suffer anyone's interrogation or commentary.

"She said she's here to ask after your dog."

"Oh?" That was surprising. They couldn't know if Bess was increasing yet. "I'll meet her in the drawing room."

"Very good." Foster departed, and Evie took herself to the drawing room to await Mrs. Kirby.

A few moments later, the round-faced woman entered, her dark eyes warm and her smile bright. "Good morning, Mrs. Renshaw, please forgive my early call. I wanted to let you know that the hole in our wall is being repaired today. At last."

That required a visit? Evie decided not to offer tea, since

it was so early. She perched on a chair and gestured for Mrs. Kirby to take the settee. "Splendid."

Mrs. Kirby sat and clasped her hands in her lap. "I must thank you for your visit, which finally prompted Mr. Kirby to have the work done. He was distressed to think that Bess might be having a litter of pups with your Ash and wanted to prevent any further occurrences. It was his fault she was out there in the first place. He took her out before going to bed and left her in the garden." Mrs. Kirby shook her head. "He does that sometimes and always tries to blame it on someone else."

Evie didn't know what to say to that, so she said nothing. Mrs. Kirby went on, "How is Ash?"

"He's fine." That Evie didn't really know pained her.

"Oh, good. I'm glad to hear it." Mrs. Kirby smiled widely. "And now you won't need to worry about the hole in our wall."

They fell silent, and Evie became certain Mrs. Kirby hadn't just come to talk about dogs or the repair in her wall. The woman was fidgety, adjusting her weight and glancing about the room.

"Is there something else, Mrs. Kirby?"

"Well, I hope you won't think me too forward." Mrs. Kirby gave Evie a sheepish look. "I read the papers this morning and thought you could use a friend to check on you."

A friend… Evie didn't think of the woman that way and was surprised, and perhaps a bit charmed, that Mrs. Kirby would think of her in that manner. "You're brave to come here. It's quite a scandal," Evie said wryly.

Mrs. Kirby waved her hand. "Bah, I don't care about that nonsense. Besides, it's not as if I'm concerned about my lofty position in Society." She'd adopted a faux haughty tone, her eyes glittering with mirth. "You were very good with Bess—

she liked you. Dogs are far better at identifying good people than people are."

Evie couldn't help smiling. "I suspect you're right."

"About that anyway." She tipped her head slightly, her gaze searching. "You're truly all right?"

"For the most part," Evie said. Even if that wasn't true, she wanted it to be, so she'd make sure it was. "How is your Bess?"

"She is well, thank you. We can't know if she's expecting puppies yet, but Mr. Kirby has kept two appointments with our friends to accomplish the deed. Time will tell."

"If you'd like to bring her over to visit next time, I'd be delighted to see her." Evie shocked herself by saying so, but didn't regret it. She missed Ash so very much. Spending time with Bess might help ease her heartache.

"I'll do that." Mrs. Kirby stood, and Evie rose with her. "I'll be keeping you in my thoughts. Do let me know if you need anything."

"Your husband won't mind us being friends?" Evie had the sense he was far stodgier than his wife.

"I won't mention it, but he won't be aware of this gossip anyway. He doesn't read that part of the paper, says it's silly." So perhaps he hadn't told anyone that he'd seen Gregory—if he'd ultimately recognized him—in the neighborhood with Ash or that Ash had spent the night with Evie. "I hope you won't let this quash your spirit," Mrs. Kirby added, her brow drawn. "If you were a man, reactions would be quite different. It's bloody unfair, if you'll pardon my saying so."

Evie suppressed a smile. "It is indeed. I will endeavor not to let this affect me in an adverse manner." Somehow, Mrs. Kirby's unexpected visit had made her feel even better.

Foster came in to say that Ada had arrived.

"I was just leaving," Mrs. Kirby said. She patted Evie's hand. "Take care, dear."

Evie was surprised to feel as though her throat were clogging. Mrs. Kirby was of an age to be her mother. It was incredibly heartening to think she might have a friend like that. "I will, thank you. Foster, send Lady Warfield up."

Mrs. Kirby left, and a moment later, Ada hastened into the drawing room. "Who was that?"

"My neighbor, and new friend, Mrs. Kirby. Ash may have impregnated her dog."

Ada blinked. "Ash is the dog you found with Lord Gregory?"

"Yes, and when I had him overnight, he got out of the garden—the gate was left open—and found his way through a hole in a wall into the Kirbys' garden where their very sweet Bess had been left out by mistake."

"An affair by moonlight." Ada wiggled her brows and smiled.

"An affair by opportunity is more like it."

"Moonlight is far more romantic," Ada said, sitting on the settee Mrs. Kirby had just vacated. "I came yesterday, but Foster said you weren't receiving."

Evie retook her chair. "He told me you came. I just needed a day to myself."

"I understand. I hope I'm not intruding, but I would guess not given Mrs. Kirby."

"As I said, I just needed a day to…adjust."

"And how are you today?" Ada asked tentatively.

"Better, despite the papers."

Ada grimaced. "So you read them."

"I started to, but then I chucked it into the fire. Why torture myself?"

"Precisely. I'm so pleased to hear you're in such fine spirits." Ada's sunny expression dimmed. "I'm sorry you had to resign from the club. Honestly, I want to resign too."

"Please don't. Lucien needs all the help he can get right

now. He is concerned many people will resign or that they'll simply stop coming. I suppose you'll see if attendance is down tonight since everything was made public today."

"We have so many members who don't pay attention to that. For instance, the gentleman who used to train Bennet." Ada referred to a pugilist who coached their friend Prudence's husband, the Viscount Glastonbury.

"Perhaps I should visit Prudence," Evie mused. She'd given birth to a son just a few weeks ago.

"You're thinking of leaving town?" Ada asked.

"I was considering it. But I won't go to my sister." Never mind that they lived next door to Witney Court—the officious marquess and his wife weren't in residence. How was Evie ever going to visit Heloise again when they were? "I don't want to trouble her with my presence when this scandal is so new."

"From what you've told me, it seems she wouldn't mind. And she dealt with her own scandal after she wed Alfred."

"Which is why I shan't burden her with mine." Furthermore, going back there would only remind Evie of Gregory. She'd recall how they met and the glorious time they'd spent together at the cottage. Forget his brother and sister-in-law, how was Evie going to visit Witney without wondering if Gregory was so close by?

"I think Prudence would be thrilled to have you visit. But you'll have to write first. With Bennet's family, I think they have to make certain preparations for guests." His great-aunts were eccentric—at least that was the word they mostly used—and could be off-putting. They could also be disrupted, and Bennet sought to keep them comfortable.

"That's true," Evie said.

"You could always go to Stonehill," Ada suggested, referring to her country home. "And you'd be completely unbothered since Max and I are in town."

That wasn't a terrible idea either, but Evie couldn't help feeling as though she were running away. When she'd left before, she'd done so with the purpose of reinventing herself. If she was going to leave London, she needed a plan other than trying to evade scandal. She couldn't simply come back as a new person as she'd done before. If she wanted to do that, she needed to find a new place to live.

But the thought of leaving London, the only home she'd ever known, made her queasy.

"You seem indecisive," Ada said quietly.

"Because I am. I probably should leave London for good, but I don't really want to. However, if I stay, my life will be completely different than it has been the past two years."

"I don't want it to be." Ada frowned. "I want everything to go back to the way it was."

"That is, unfortunately, impossible."

The sound of barking carried upstairs, driving Evie to her feet. She recognized that bark. Rushing from the drawing room, she went to the stairs and immediately made eye contact with Ash at the base.

"Ash!" she called. "Come here, my sweet boy."

The dog was already halfway up the stairs before she finished speaking. Evie crouched down and hugged him, grinning as he licked her face. "How are you?" she asked, as if he could respond. And she supposed he did, for he was clearly as happy to see her as she was to see him, his tail wagging and his face nuzzling hers.

Evie looked down the stairs, her breath snagging as she expected to see Gregory. But he wasn't there. Just a gentleman she didn't recognize.

"Mrs. Renshaw, I am Harris, Lord Gregory's valet. He bade me bring Ash for a visit and hopes that is acceptable."

It was far more than acceptable. "Please thank him. How long will you stay?"

"How long would you like, ma'am?"

Forever.

The answer came to her mind so fast and with such absolute certainty that she nearly fell onto her backside. "If you'd like to make yourself comfortable downstairs—Foster will take you—I'd be delighted to have Ash for a while." The thought of sending him back to Gregory was an ache she pushed aside. Though, it would only increase when the time came.

Harris inclined his head, and Foster led him away.

Evie scooped Ash up and carried him toward her sitting room, where she still had one of his rope toys. Ada stood watching her from the entrance to the drawing room. Blinking, Evie realized she'd forgotten that Ada was even there.

Ada's blue -gray eyes were soft with care. "I don't think I've ever seen you so full of joy. Over a dog, no less." She laughed warmly.

"It's shocking to me too," Evie admitted. "Come and meet him." She carried Ash into the drawing room and set him down. After introducing him to Ada, she went to fetch his rope. He jumped around giddily when he saw her with it and took it greedily between his teeth when she offered it. She tugged it gently, and he growled as he worked to pull it free of her grasp.

"Is he angry?" Ada asked, sounding concerned.

"No, he's playing." Evie let go of the rope, and Ash bounded off with it. She watched him adoringly as he settled near the hearth.

"He's very cute," Ada said.

"Isn't he?"

"You're very attached to him."

Evie shot her friend a glance. "Yes. Surely you can see why."

"I suppose so. You must miss him a great deal since he lives with Lord Gregory. You've never mentioned it."

"That I miss him?" Evie shrugged, smiling at Ash playing with his rope. "I do."

"Just him or Lord Gregory too?"

Evie swung her attention back to Ada. "We aren't making this conversation about Gregory."

"You can't ignore him." Ada's voice was low. "I tried to do that when I left Max at Stonehill to return to London, and I failed miserably."

"I am not you, and Gregory is certainly not Max."

"Thank goodness, for I am not at all certain there needs to be two of Max. One is plenty." Her smile faded. "He's the first man you've been with since...Lucien?"

"Yes. I didn't think I'd want to be with anyone again. Gregory was just so charming and attentive. He seemed to be genuinely interested in *me*. And he was incredibly invested in saving a puppy." She looked lovingly at Ash. Yes, she loved this little dog in a way that she hadn't loved anyone besides her sister.

Was there any chance she also loved the man who'd saved him?

Evie hadn't wanted to consider it, and she still didn't. But she couldn't deny the longing she felt or the sadness that their affair was over.

"So why is Ash here without him?" Ada asked.

Evie pondered that question. Gregory had consistently followed her demands, even when he didn't like them. He'd left her alone when she'd ended their affair. Until he hadn't been able to. She'd told him she would carry on from this alone. She hadn't heard from him. Except he'd sent Ash and wasn't that a message of sorts? Was he simply reiterating that he was there for her, even if it was just to share a dog?

She suddenly felt awful for sending him away. And she

hadn't even explained to him about her past, about why she'd become a courtesan in the first place. She didn't owe him an explanation, but she realized she wanted to share it with him. To share *herself* with him. In ways she'd never done with anyone before.

Evie finally answered Ada's query. "Because I told him not to come." Implicitly, but it had been enough. "He's the most considerate person I've ever known. He puts everyone above himself."

"He sounds rather wonderful," Ada said, smiling. "Why are you still here?"

Blinking, Evie shook her head. "You think I should go...to him?"

"Why not? You'll need to take his dog back anyway."

"He's actually *our* dog." Why had they ever thought they could share Ash without living together? Wait, was she actually considering *living* with him? That would mean marriage. Or something truly scandalous.

Neither of those choices appealed to her. Still, she couldn't do nothing. She missed Gregory—his cheerfulness, his care, his touch, even his optimism. Most of all, his optimism. She needed more of that in her life.

"Well, then you *must* go to him," Ada said as if it were obvious. "And what will you say?"

"I don't know." The emotions were too new.

No, the realization was new. The emotions were not. She'd been growing more and more fond of him since the moment they'd met at the hedgerow. He'd already broken through barriers no one else had. That alone made him special.

Ada put her hand on Evie's arm. "I'm so happy for you."

Ash came over and dropped the rope at Evie's feet. She stroked his head as joy unfurled inside her. "I think I might be happy for me too."

CHAPTER 19

*G*regory tapped his foot as anxious energy coursed through him. He hated leaving Evie alone. Sending Ash to her was the only thing he dared to do. He realized he'd used the dog to get to her before—when he'd finally gone to see her after she'd broken things off.

Would she see through him again? Probably. She was exceedingly clever. And she knew him too well.

The coach drew to a stop in front of Lucien's terrace. Gregory hadn't been able to sit at home and do nothing. Perhaps Lucien could give him advice. Not because he'd been Evie's lover, but because he was her friend and knew her perhaps better than Gregory did.

Gregory hated that too.

He wanted Evie to open herself to him, to trust him. While he understood why she hadn't told him the truth about her past, he was still hurt. But then he'd gone into their affair with complete investment, his heart bared. He'd fallen in love with her swiftly. Wholly. Irreversibly.

Jumping from the coach, Gregory strode to Lucien's door,

where the butler, at least Gregory hoped it was the butler, greeted him.

So tall that Gregory had to look up at him, the man sported a horrible red scar across his cheek. He was, in a word, menacing.

Gregory handed the man his card. "I'm here to see Lord Lucien."

One of the butler's brows twitched very slightly. It was his only reaction. "I'll find out if he's receiving. You may wait in the entrance hall." He opened the door wide for Gregory to come inside.

Removing his hat and gloves, Gregory waited, his anxiety increasing. What if Lucien wouldn't see him? Or wasn't home? Of course he was home; otherwise, the terrifying butler would have told him he was out.

It wasn't the butler who returned to the hall, but Lucien himself. He wasn't fully dressed—he was missing his cravat and his coat. There were faint purplish circles under his eyes and lines etched into his forehead. Frankly, he looked exhausted.

"Afternoon, Greg, come in."

"I don't wish to disturb you," Gregory said measuredly.

Lucien glanced down at himself and lifted a shoulder. "Don't mind my state of undress. Unless it bothers you?"

Gregory waved his hand. "It's your house."

"Come to my library." Lucien led him to the back of the narrow house, where a compact room boasted bookshelves, comfortable though sparse seating, and a dazzling array of art on the walls, particularly of animals. Horses seemed to be the most abundant, but there were also dogs, sheep, goats, and even a cat.

"You like animals?"

"I like paintings of animals," he said. "Whisky?"

"Why not?" Gregory lowered himself into a chair.

Lucien poured two glasses and delivered one to Gregory before sitting opposite him in what appeared to be the most well-worn chair. Gregory had presumed that was Lucien's favorite.

"To what do I owe the pleasure of your call?" Lucien asked, as if they were being judged on polite manners.

Gregory didn't care to play along with that. He preferred to cut right to the heart of things. "How is Evie?"

After swallowing a sip of whisky, Lucien shook his head. "I don't know. I should call on her since that rubbish appeared in the newspaper today. Is that why you're concerned?"

"I'm concerned because her life has been completely upended."

"Right." Lucien grimaced, deepening the grooves on his forehead. "How are you? I can't imagine you enjoy seeing your name in the papers."

"I don't really care, to be honest. What harm will it do to me? I won't get a voucher to Almack's this Season? The horror." Gregory took a drink.

Lucien cracked a smile. "We men are never punished the way women are. I can fuck my way through London, and I'd be congratulated."

The unsettling butler appeared in the doorway. Gregory sat up straight as if he'd been caught doing something wrong.

"My lord, His Grace, the Duke of Evesham is here to see you."

"Bloody hell," Lucien muttered. "That is all today demands." He looked down at himself once more. "Reynolds, I need a cravat and a coat. And the cravat has to be one of the obnoxiously colored ones. No, wait. Never mind. As if my state of undress will make him like me any less." He laughed, and Gregory felt a pang of sympathy. How awful it must be to have such a contentious relationship with one's father. But then he recalled the fact that he had a similar relationship with his brother.

Lucien squinted at Gregory. "Did Reynolds scare you?"

"He's rather intimidating."

"Excellent quality in a butler." Lucien grinned. "He served in my regiment, and I hired him after he returned to England."

"Did he get that scar in battle?" Gregory asked.

"He did. If you can believe it, he had a very boyish face before that."

Gregory shot out of his chair as the duke walked in. He was sure he'd met the man at some point, but they'd had no occasion to converse. He was nearly as tall as Lucien and quite fit for a man who had to be in his sixties. His dark brown eyes and Lucien's were almost exact duplicates of each other, but the duke possessed a far more fearsome glower.

Lucien didn't stand. He gave his father a bored stare. "Afternoon, Father."

The duke's discerning gaze fixed on Lucien's torso. "If I'd known you were in dishabille, I would have left."

"It doesn't trouble me," Lucien said with a careless smile. He gestured to Gregory. "Allow me to present Lord Gregory Blakemore. He isn't troubled by my dress either."

Evesham swept his focus to Gregory. "I admired your father. He was an impeccable gentleman." Something in his expression dimmed, almost as if he were silently saying that Gregory was not. Gregory had to assume he'd seen the newspapers.

"Thank you for saying so," Gregory said.

"Time will tell with your brother," Evesham noted. "I have yet to spend much time with him, but he seems somewhat inconsequential in comparison. I hope he will meet his duty."

That the duke had assessed Clifford so accurately was pleasing, but Gregory didn't show it. "I hope so too."

"It's always a shame when sons don't live up to their potential." Evesham's gaze had gone back to Lucien. "Like this one here. Why would you hire your former paramour to do anything other than clean your chamber pots, let alone be a patroness at your questionable club?"

Gregory had to clamp his jaws together to keep from calling the duke out. How dare he insult Evie like that?

Lucien lifted a shoulder, appearing calm, but Gregory noted the tic in his jaw. "If my club is questionable, I should think a courtesan is surely the right person to cast in a leadership role."

The duke let out a low growl. "Don't be clever. Have you no shame at all?"

"You're standing there judging me about a woman—who is brilliant, by the way—in front of Lord Gregory, and I'm the one without shame? If you know she was a patroness and my former mistress, then you also know Gregory was having an affair with her."

Gregory ought to go, but he couldn't leave, not while they were discussing this.

The duke glanced at Gregory. "Having an affair with a courtesan is perfectly acceptable. Why anyone thought that was newsworthy is beyond me."

Gregory despised the manner in which the duke was speaking of the woman he loved. "My brother thought it should be made public, but then he likes to be nasty and doesn't care whom he hurts. I trust you are not in the same vein," Gregory said coolly. "I should note that I am also deeply in love with Mrs. Renshaw, and if she would accept my proposal of marriage, which she will not, I would be happy for the rest of my days."

The duke turned his hooded gaze on Gregory, his tone frigid. "Your father would not approve."

"He would if he met her." Gregory knew it in his bones. Just as he knew his father wouldn't be disappointed that Gregory had decided to forgo a religious path. His father had raised him to make good, sound choices. He was not his brother, who allowed malice and whim to lead him, and he never would be. "My father loved me, and I am confident he would have loved her too if given the chance. I'm sorry he isn't here to meet her."

Lucien took a sip of whisky and gently smacked his lips, likely to annoy his father. "I wonder if you would think differently about Mrs. Renshaw if you knew she was the daughter of a chevalier. She fled here during the Terror with her mother and sister."

The duke's nostrils flared as his eyes narrowed. "What is her family name?"

"Avenses, but they used her mother's maid's name, Renault, when they arrived in London."

"A pity, but no, I do not think differently." The duke sniffed. "Everyone has choices, and she chose to become a courtesan."

Lucien slammed his glass down on a table near his chair. Shooting to his feet, he pinned a fiery glare on his father. "Not everyone's choices are the same, particularly if you are an orphan in a foreign country with nothing but a maid to care for you and your sister. She should have grown up with love and comfort. Instead, she struggled to eat and lived in near squalor. If you had a chance to better your prospects, even if it meant doing something you would not have chosen, what would *you* do, Father?"

"You have always been too softhearted," the duke said, his voice like a knife's edge. "You can't change the world."

"I do what I can. What I don't understand is why you do

not."

The duke straightened, his features smoothing. "Your club is going to fail, Lucien. I didn't hope for that, but I am not surprised."

"Why did you come here?" Lucien asked, his lip curling.

"Because regardless of what you think, I have always cared what happens to you, and I always will." The duke glanced toward Gregory. "Lord Gregory." Then he departed.

Lucien expressed several colorful phrases before retaking his seat. He swilled the rest of his whisky and smacked the empty glass back on the table. "I'm sorry you had to witness that."

Gregory was too, but he would support Lucien however he could—now more than before. "Families can be disappointing. I had to cut ties with my brother."

"I would have done the same. Still, I'm sorry it came to such an extreme."

"It's for the best." Gregory sipped his whisky, grateful for its smooth heat. "Have you tried to sever your relationship with your father?"

"Not entirely, but we generally keep our distance. He's always been nonplussed by me, and when I opened the Phoenix Club, he was particularly disappointed. He said it would fail and that I couldn't come to him asking for money when I was inevitably insolvent."

"That's awful."

Lucien shrugged. "It is what I expected."

"Will the club really fail?" Gregory hoped not.

"It's hard to say. I expect I'll receive at least a few resignations today due to what's in the newspapers. Time will tell if people stop coming. They may decide to keep their distance for a while."

"I can't think that will be good."

"There is little I can do." Lucien leaned forward. "I'm

sorry for what my father said about Evie. I could see you were distressed."

"Furious is a better word. I hate that she is being discussed and judged like this."

Lucien pressed his lips together and swore softly. "If I could trade the club for her not being exposed, I would." He looked intently toward Gregory. "You told my father you would marry her. Do you love her?"

"Yes. I have for some time."

"Does she know that?"

"No. She was clear from the start that she didn't want anything permanent between us, so I've kept that to myself."

"Smart," Lucien said. "I'm sorry to say that I don't think she'll allow herself to love you."

"Are you saying I should give up?"

"That's entirely up to you. You seem an optimistic sort, which I tend to be as well."

"I *can't* give up. I wanted to give her time and distance to do...whatever she needed to do, but in the end, I can't just walk away from her." He needed to see her now, to tell her, at last, that he loved her. Shouldn't she know that?

Gregory finished his whisky and stood. "Thank you."

Lucien looked up at him in bemusement. "For what?"

"For being a good friend—to me and especially to Evie."

"Just be there for her."

Certainty rushed through Gregory. "I plan to be."

〜

*W*here was Gregory?

Evie had been waiting for him nearly an hour now. She'd already investigated every inch of his drawing room, where his housekeeper had sent her to await his return. Ash had accompanied her on her exploration, happily sniffing and tumbling about and generally being unhelpful.

She'd apparently tired him out because he was currently asleep on a large red velvet cushion near the hearth. Given the smattering of white fur already on the cushion, it was clearly a favorite place.

"It's an excellent spot," Evie murmured from the chair next to him. Because of its proximity to Ash's bed and due to the masculine scent of pine and mint, she deduced this was likely Gregory's favorite seat. Sitting here felt almost as if he were embracing her.

Almost.

The longer she waited, the more she began to doubt her decision to come. But every time she considered leaving, her gaze drifted to Ash, and she couldn't bring herself to leave.

At last, she heard a familiar male voice drift up from downstairs. Evie bolted from the chair, startling Ash. She reached the doorway just as Gregory appeared.

His gaze raked her hungrily, his lips spreading into his most dazzling smile. "Evie."

Before she leapt on him, she made sure his housekeeper hadn't accompanied him. He glanced behind himself. "Are you looking for someone else?"

"Just ensuring you're alone." She put her hand on his chest, flattening her bare palm against his lapel. "I keep wondering if I've made a mistake coming here."

"Never. Not in my estimation, anyway. You are welcome here at any time, always." His eyes sparked with heat. "Indeed, you brighten the place immeasurably."

"You're not angry with me?" She hadn't known what to expect from him. "Actually, do you even get angry?"

"Not often. Indeed, I'm not sure I lost my temper fully until recently. You could ask Hargrove or my brother if you'd really like to know."

Evie smiled as a giddy jolt passed through her. He'd only ever lost his temper for her. Or was that just what she wanted to believe? "Is that because your plans are ruined?"

He frowned. "The government appointment, you mean? No, I lost my temper because of what they threatened and ultimately did to you."

"But you had to have been upset that I didn't tell you."

"I confess I was, but only because I want you to feel you can trust me. However, I do understand why you wouldn't trust anyone."

"Not even my best friend, Ada, knew the truth about my past," Evie said softly. "Telling her or anyone else was too much of a risk."

His gaze softened, and he cupped her face. No one had ever looked at her like that or made her feel more cherished. "Evie, you probably don't want to hear this, but I love you. I've loved you for so long, and I don't want to keep it inside any longer. I would do anything to protect you, to honor you, to show the world how incredible you are, and how very much you mean to me."

With every word he said, her heart expanded, and her throat constricted. "I don't want to love you," she croaked. But she did. "I don't want to hurt or feel lost or—"

He kissed her, and she clutched at his coat, desperate for him. She didn't want to be alone either.

Gregory broke the kiss and swept her into his arms, making her gasp, then he carried her from the drawing room and up another flight of stairs.

"Where are we going?"

"Somewhere more suitable for ravishment."

Evie couldn't find fault with that. She held on to his neck as he opened the door and bore her into his chamber. He didn't set her down until he reached the bed.

She didn't particularly want to waste time disrobing,

but after rushing back to close the door, he was already stripping his coat away, then his boots. Evie worked quickly, removing garments until she was down to her corset. The laces knotted, and she muttered a curse. Suddenly, Gregory was there, plucking the strings free. The garment came loose, and he pulled it from her body.

Though she wasn't yet nude, he was, and that was all she needed. Reaching between his legs, she curled her hand around his cock and stroked his length.

"I need you, Evie," he rasped, his lips against her ear as he tugged the lobe with his teeth.

She clasped his shoulder, digging her fingers into his bare flesh while continuing to work his shaft. "Then take me. Now." She kissed him in a torrid frenzy, her tongue tangling with his.

He pushed her chemise up, breaking their kiss long enough to whisk it over her head. She still wore her stockings, but hoped he wasn't going to take the time to remove them.

He did not.

Instead, he lifted her. "Wrap your legs around me."

She was reminded of the time he'd come to the cottage and been eager for her. Guiding his sex to hers, she lowered her pelvis as he thrust into her. Evie closed her eyes as rapture flooded her. There had never been a more blissful joining—not for her. He drove deep, and she encircled his waist with her legs, locking her feet behind him.

He held her tight against him, rocking his hips and pushing her toward ecstasy. She kissed his neck, licking and sucking as she sought to taste and feel more of him.

"I need—" He didn't finish the thought before he laid her back across the bed and came over her, quickly situating himself between her legs and filling her once more. Then he moved with a relentless, almost punishing pace that was everything she'd ever wanted.

Evie dug her heels into his backside and scored her nails along his back as her orgasm broke over her. She plunged headfirst into darkness and joy, her body stiffening as she clenched around him. Gregory shouted her name as he thrust hard and came, his body twitching over hers.

At some point—and she had no idea how much time passed—the sound of scratching at the door drew them both to look in that direction.

"Ash," they said in unison.

Gregory bounded from the bed and went to the door. Evie admired his long legs and backside, as well as the muscular planes of his back.

Ash darted inside with a bark. He didn't slow as he raced to the foot of the bed. In a trice, he was on the coverlet, making his way to Evie's side. "How did you get up here?" Gregory's bed was rather high.

"I made him a ladder of sorts, rather stairs, I suppose." Gregory climbed back onto the bed next to her. "There's a low stool that helps him get onto a bench, and a large pillow he uses to get up onto the mattress."

Evie patted Ash, who lay down beside her. "Lucky pup."

Gregory gazed at the dog's position snuggled against Evie's side, his head rather near her breast. "I concur." He dipped his head and quickly kissed her other breast before propping his head on his hand with a grin.

Laughing, Evie looked up at him. "This dog—and you—have changed my life."

"I hope for the better, but I can't help thinking that if you'd never met me, you would still be a patroness and a member of the Phoenix Club, and no one would be aware of your secrets." He looked into her eyes. "I'm so sorry, Evie."

"None of this is your fault. Lady Hargrove was going to cause problems sooner or later. She blamed me for her recommendations not finding support at the club and for her choice of patroness also not being supported." She glanced over at Ash as she stroked his ear. "Regardless, I regret nothing."

"Is that true?" He sounded surprised.

She met his disbelieving gaze and saw the hope that was always present in him. "Shockingly, yes. I was happy in my life, but I was missing something and didn't even realize it." Gregory had filled a void she hadn't known was there, not until he filled it. Perfectly.

"What was missing?"

It was difficult to explain because she couldn't quite identify it herself. "You're the first man who saw me for me. Men have always looked twice—or more—at me. Because I'm beautiful. I used that to my advantage when I had to. Now, I somewhat resent it. Sometimes I think about wearing nothing but drab brown and covering my hair in a sad mobcap. Perhaps I'll add a veil."

He stared at her a moment before breaking into laughter. "I'm sorry, I am trying to imagine this, and I have to say that you'd still be the most beautiful woman I've ever seen."

Evie rolled her eyes. "You aren't helping."

Sobering, he took a breath. "My apologies. Truly. I didn't mean to make light of your feelings."

"It *is* absurd, which is why I haven't done it. It pains me to admit that I am also a trifle vain. I'm afraid I love clothing. That was actually one of the reasons I took the job in the brothel. That, and I wanted a comfortable place to live and regular food to eat." Evie thought back on her decision to follow Heloise into trade. "It was a very nice brothel. Heloise and I were pretty enough—and we spoke French—so we were lucky."

"What happened to your parents?" Gregory asked softly. "You said your father was a chevalier."

"So Nadine told us. My mother died when I was four. I don't really remember her, and I don't remember my father at all. We left France when I was a babe to flee the Terror. My father stayed behind to help others. He was supposed to join us in a few months, but he never came. A couple of years later, my mother saw his name on a list of people who had died in France. It broke my mother's heart. Heloise remembers that. And that our mother used to sing lullabies to us in French."

Gregory caressed her arm. "I'm sorry you don't remember her. Nadine was your mother's maid?"

"Yes. She was the only person who accompanied us across the channel. She'd taken care of our mother since before she married our father. After my mother died, she raised Heloise and me as if we were her own daughters. And she worked herself to death sewing for a demanding modiste who passed Nadine's designs off as her own." Evie scowled. "It wasn't fair, especially because of how hard Nadine worked." She paused as long-buried love flooded her chest. She hadn't allowed that emotion to resurface in some time.

"I loved her very much. She became ill when I was fifteen. We couldn't afford the medicine she needed." Evie's hand stilled against Ash, anguish overtaking her. "That was when Heloise went to work at the brothel, but it was too late, and Nadine died. She said it broke her heart that Heloise had become a prostitute." She turned her gaze back to Gregory. "But what were we to do?"

"You did what you thought you had to."

Evie was caught up in the past in a way she hadn't been in a long time. "Heloise sent money to me, but it wasn't enough. I tried to sew, but I am terrible at stitching. I knitted instead, but socks don't earn much. Plus, I was lonely on my own, and men in the neighborhood knew I was alone. I didn't know how long I could keep them at bay, and I determined that if I were going to share my body, it was going to be my choice and for a decent sum. I lasted about eighteen months, then I went to work at the same brothel as Heloise. By then, she'd become the most popular lady in the house and was negotiating her first protector."

Gregory had been stroking her arm while she spoke, but when she'd talked about her choice to work at the brothel, he'd stopped. "I can't imagine what you had to do at such a young age without any parent or guiding force." He shook his head, and she thought she saw the shimmer of a tear in his eye.

"Gregory, please don't pity me."

"I don't. I'm sad for your losses, and I'm angry that you didn't have better choices. It's not right, Evie. I can't believe how you've managed. Look at you now."

"Naked in the bed of a man who is not my husband," she said wryly.

"We could change that."

"I am a little cold, actually, though Ash is quite warm." She smiled at the dog.

"Not that part, though I'll fetch your chemise." He got up from the bed and came back with the garment.

She sat up and drew it over her head.

"I meant I could be your husband, if you'd allow me to. I love you, Evie, now and forever. If you become my wife, I'll spend the rest of our lives showing you how much and making you happy."

He stood next to the bed, his brown eyes warm and earnest—and so full of love. She knew he would take care of her in ways she'd never imagined. She'd never want for anything. And she wouldn't ever be alone again.

She could hide in the shadows, but she didn't have to do

that anymore. Nor did she want to. Thankfully, there were no more secrets to keep. She could be Mirabelle *and* Evie. "I love you too."

His eyes widened and his lips parted. She nearly giggled. "Is it that shocking?" she asked.

"I just… I didn't think you would let yourself love me. Actually, that's what Lucien said, and it seems he knows you rather well."

She arched a brow at him. "You spoke to Lucien?"

"After I sent Ash to your house. I needed advice. I wanted to go to you, to fight for you, but I didn't think you wanted me to. I was going to try to let you alone, as I did when you returned to London, but that was excruciating."

"And in that instance, you also used Ash to get to me." She ruffled Ash's fur as she smiled at Gregory. "You're very clever."

He continued to stare at her in disbelief. "I can't believe you love me."

"How could I not? You make me feel valued and important." She took a breath as joy surged in her chest. "Cherished."

He cupped her face and kissed her, soft and lingering, with so much love she felt she might burst. "You are cherished." He kissed her forehead. "Worshipped." He pressed a kiss to her cheek. "Beloved."

Unable to speak past the lump in her throat, Evie kissed him again. It was several minutes before he backed away, smiling. He picked up his discarded shirt and pulled it over his head. "When shall we wed?"

Evie froze. Loving him was one thing. Marriage was something else entirely. That would be a definitive end to her independence, to the life she had so painstakingly built. "I told you I don't want to get married. That hasn't changed." She saw the joy recede from his expression and rushed to explain. "If I marry you, everything I have will become yours. I'm not wealthy by any means, but I've saved for my future, particularly over the past two years. I don't think I can give up my independence." She plucked nervously at her chemise.

He was quiet a moment, and she could practically hear his mind turning. He sat on the edge of the bed, angling his body with one knee onto the mattress so he faced her. "I also have a tidy sum—my father made sure I wouldn't ever have to rely on my impulsive brother. Shall we see who has more?" He said this with humor, and it helped her relax. A little.

"No, because I'm sure it's you." She couldn't possibly compete with the wealth a marquess bequeathed to a favored son.

He smiled gently as he tucked a hair behind her ear. Her hair must look a mess. She hadn't taken it down, so it was likely in a complete state of disarray due to their activities.

"I promise your money will remain your money. I won't try to control anything you do or anything that our daughters, should we have any, want to do. I'll make provisions to ensure you will always have control."

He was educated in the law, so she believed him. "Daughters? I don't know that I even want to be a mother." Loving him was hard enough because she was afraid. There was so much to lose—and to protect—with children. "You can't want to marry me hearing that."

"That doesn't change my mind one bit. I love you, and with Ash, I'd say we have a nice little family right here."

Emotion overwhelmed her, and a tear tracked from her eye. She quickly wiped it away. "I need to think about it. Marriage, I mean." Did that mean she would consider it? She had to if she wanted to live with him—and with Ash. She realized they *were* a family.

He took her in his arms. "Take all the time you need, my love. I will be here waiting, and I will never lose hope."

CHAPTER 20

Gregory hadn't realized just how vulnerable Evie really was. She was so confident and strong, but didn't everyone fear something? He supposed for him it was fear he'd disappoint his parents. Evie's worries were so much more important—or so it seemed to him.

She'd dozed in his arms and now, as he watched her sleep snuggled with Ash, he felt an overwhelming sense of responsibility. He wanted to do right by her, to be the man she not only needed, but the man she wanted.

Rising from the bed, he pulled on his breeches and stockings and went to stoke the fire. What if she couldn't agree to marriage? Was he prepared to continue as they were? That wasn't what he wanted. He wanted this—her in his bed, with their dog folded into her side.

He turned back to the bed and saw her moving. She sat up. "Where did you go?"

"Just tending the fire," he said, returning to the bed.

She pushed her hair, half of which was tumbling from its pins, back from her forehead. "What would we do after we wed?"

Gregory could think of any number of things, several of which they had already done. "I'm guessing you aren't speaking of bedchamber activities."

"Not entirely, but that is lovely to ponder." She gave him a warm, seductive smile as she slipped from the bed. "I meant, how would our lives change? I've been wondering if I ought to leave London, at least for a while, but… I don't really want to. It's the only place I've called home." She came toward him and warmed herself in front of the fire.

Fetching a blanket from a dresser, he brought it to her and wrapped it around her shoulders. "You don't have to leave. We could live in your house, if you prefer. I'm not particularly attached to this place." He'd leased it for the Season, and it was only sparsely furnished.

She clutched the soft ivory wool around herself. "I'd like that. But aren't you concerned about your reputation? I'm a pariah, and if you marry me, I can't imagine your career prospects will flourish."

There was a note of humor in her voice, but her question was valid. "I've considered that. I intend to set myself up as a barrister. It may be that I don't work for the upper echelons of Society." He waggled a brow at her. "I'm quite satisfied with that."

"You've thought this through," she said softly.

"I've tried to. I'd like to make decisions with you. What about you? Without the Phoenix Club to manage, what do you want to do?"

She blinked at him. "As in a job?"

He nodded. "You seem surprised."

"I am. You wouldn't mind?"

"I know I haven't known you long, but I think I've come to know you well. I could tell in Oxfordshire that you were…bored."

"Not true. You kept me quite busy."

He smiled. "But you were more than ready to return to London—to the Phoenix Club, I suspect."

"While that's true, I'm afraid my urgency to leave was also prompted by my encounter with Arbuthnot at Witney Court."

Gregory grimaced as he recalled his horrid conversation with Clifford and Susan the other night. "I am so sorry about that. I wish he hadn't seen you. If not, your past might still be secret."

Her eyes widened and she clasped his arm. "Do you know something?"

"I called at Witney House the other night to determine what role my brother played. He was at the center of this disaster. I have cut ties with him entirely."

"Oh, Gregory. I don't want to come between you and your brother."

"Susan already did that," he said sardonically. "It wasn't difficult. There has long been a gaping chasm between Clifford and me. We could not be more different, and I've no desire to be in his company, even if he is my blood."

"I have learned that family is not dictated by blood," she said, caressing his arm. "I consider Ada and Lucien my family along with many others."

"I admit to feeling a bit envious about that."

"Don't, for if we wed, my extended family will become yours."

"Does this mean you're actually considering it?" he asked, trying not to sound breathless.

"I told you I would. Right now, however, I'm contemplating what I might do to keep myself busy. I've nearly always worked, and I confess it would be difficult not to have something to occupy my mind. I did have an idea. A friend of mine runs the Siren's Call. Are you familiar with it?"

"Isn't it a gaming hell?"

"Owned and run by women. The proprietor is a friend. She was also a prostitute who made her own way in the world, though that was a long time ago. I doubt anyone remembers that about her. She founded the gaming hell to hire women who wouldn't need to sell their bodies to survive. The men who go there enjoy talking to the women who work there—and ogling them, but that's all they're allowed to do."

"You want to open something like that?" he asked.

"Not a gaming hell. I haven't settled on the right idea yet."

"What about a women's membership club? Like the Phoenix Club, but only for women. There wouldn't be a need for a ballroom, but perhaps you could have a shopping area where modistes and milliners and the like could come in a few times a week to sell their wares."

Her fingers tightened around his arm. "You are brilliant. I love that idea!" Her excitement faded. "I don't have enough saved for that large an endeavor, however."

"Between the two of us, I'll wager we do."

"You'd want to do that?"

"I want to do everything with you. If anyone can make something like that a success, it's you."

She stared at him, her eyes full of wonder. "How can you be so persistently optimistic?"

He pulled her against him. "Because I don't like the alternative. That's just who I am. Now, who do *you* want to be?"

Curling her hands around his neck, she pressed her chest to his. "Your wife."

Now he really was breathless. "Truly? You've decided already?"

"I only needed a little persuasion," she said. "A very small amount, as it happens."

He spun her about, laughing. "What did I say?"

"I don't know if it was you or me. Probably Ash. He is most convincing."

Ash barked from the bed where he stretched before trotting down the makeshift stairs.

Gregory looked down at the dog. "Ash, my boy, you have made all my dreams come true."

After kissing Evie soundly, he set her down. They parted and together bent down to give their dog all manner of affection.

"When do you want to do it?" Evie asked.

"Where is perhaps the better question."

Evie rose from her crouched position. "I'd like my sister to be there, but I don't know if that's possible. We'd have to go to Oxfordshire and wait for the banns to be read."

"Or we could race to Gretna Green and be married much sooner," he suggested, standing straight.

"It's February," she said with a laugh. "That journey could take three weeks."

"Oxfordshire it is, then."

Her brow creased with worry. "I'd wanted to avoid taking this scandal to my sister. She's already suffered so much after marrying Alfred."

"Was it terribly difficult for her?" Gregory hated thinking of the lovely Mrs. Creighton struggling under the weight of people's judgment.

"In London, yes. It didn't help that Alfred's father was in trade. He's seen as an upstart."

"I liked him—and your sister. I look forward to seeing them again, especially now that I know she's your sister. For what it's worth, I don't think you going to Oxfordshire will have a negative impact. At the risk of making myself sound far too important, I believe the fine people of Witney will be thrilled to celebrate our nuptials."

Her eyes lit, and she beamed at him. "You are most

certainly right. I had the sense you are more liked than your brother. This will be a joyful occasion."

He could hardly wait. "When can we leave?"

"Is the day after tomorrow soon enough? I will need to pack. And shop for an item or two since I'm to be wed."

"The day after tomorrow is perfect."

"I used to think nothing could truly be perfect." She leaned toward him. "You have shown me how very wrong I was."

Then her lips met his, and it was indeed, perfect.

∾

*T*wo days later, Gregory's coach stopped in front of Evie's house. Ash looked out the window and barked, his tail wagging excitedly.

"You know where we are, boy, don't you?" Gregory ran his gloved hand over Ash's head and shoulders. "You can't come in, though. We're leaving straightaway. I'll be right back, I promise."

Gregory quickly departed the carriage, shutting Ash inside. The dog's whines followed him to the door, and he vowed to be quick.

Foster answered the door. "Good morning, my lord. I'm afraid Mrs. Renshaw is not at home."

What the devil? Gregory swallowed past the surge of anxiety that washed up his throat. "Where has she gone?" Perhaps she hadn't been able to finish all her shopping the day before. He could go meet her wherever she was. But why would she have gone at all knowing when he would arrive?

"A coach came to pick her up. She was in quite a hurry."

"You've no idea where she went?"

"I believe the coach belonged to the Duke of Evesham."

Lucien's father? Gregory was even more confused. The

duke had been clear about his feelings toward Evie and others like her. "Was the duke here?"

"No. The groomsman came to the door. I did not hear what he discussed with Mrs. Renshaw. She left without even fetching her hat or gloves."

That sounded…alarming. There was only one place he could think to go—straight to the duke.

"Thank you, Foster." Gregory turned back toward his coach.

"Where are you going, my lord?" the butler called after him. "In case Mrs. Renshaw returns."

"I'm going to Evesham House." Gregory hoped he'd find her there. If he didn't, his alarm would turn to fear.

$\sim$

*E*vie stepped into the ornately decorated entry hall at Evesham House. As long as she'd known Lucien, she'd never had occasion to set foot inside his father's house. And why would she? The duke had never extended an invitation.

Until today.

She would have been most suspicious—and she still was —but the simple message had galvanized her into action. There was no way she would have refused.

His Grace invites you to come to his house to meet a Mr. Henry Aviers. He may be of relation to you.

She'd asked the footman to repeat it twice.

Mr. Henry Aviers.

Her father's name had been Henri Avesnes. The surname was written on the back of the painting that had hung in

Evie's office and that now graced the wall in her sitting room.

"This way, ma'am," the butler, a thick fellow in his fifties, intoned. He led her up the stairs with its gleaming balustrade to the large, elegant drawing room. It boasted six seating arrangements and four windows that looked out over Grosvenor Square.

An anxiety Evie had never experienced shook her entire body as she walked slowly into the room. She gravitated toward the windows. Who was this man she was to meet? The name was so similar...could he truly be a relative?

"Mon dieu, you are the image of your mother." The French-accented voice sounded behind her.

Evie swung around. How had she missed the presence of another person? Because he was a slip of a man—average height but thin. Not *too* thin. His cheeks were full and healthy, his blue eyes warm. The hair on his head was sparse and gray, making him look older than he probably was. She estimated he was perhaps sixty.

"You knew my mother?" she asked, sounding as though she'd run up four flights of stairs.

"Of course I did. We made three beautiful children together." Evie. Heloise. Their older brother, who'd died shortly after he was born.

Mon dieu indeed. Evie tried to stop herself from falling, but her legs had turned completely against her, going to water. So down she went.

"Mirabelle, my sweet." The man dove to catch her, but was a trifle too late. He grabbed her arms just as she landed on her knees. He came down with her, kneeling before her. "Are you well?"

"You can't be my father," she whispered as tremors billowed through her. "He died."

"I thought so sometimes," he said with a faint smile. "I was captured, but they did not execute me."

She searched his face, looking for any resemblance. There was the blue of his eyes, the same as hers and Heloise's. And something about the position of his eyes and nose—the way they interacted. It reminded her of Heloise. Could he really be him? "Where have you been?"

"In prison, mostly. Upon my release, I came here to look for you, your sister, and your mother."

"How were you able to do that?"

"I had a great deal of help. There are gentlemen here in London who assist those of us who were imprisoned. They help us find our families and establish new lives."

That sounded like something Lucien would do. But Lucien would have told her. And he wouldn't have involved the duke. The duke! No, it couldn't be him.

"Why are you on the floor?" The Duke of Evesham had come into the drawing room without them noticing.

"Come, ma fille," the man—no, her father—said as he rose and guided her along with him. He released her and started to edge away, but she grabbed his hand and held it between both of hers.

"No, don't go," she said, tears threatening as her throat tried to close.

"This has been a shock for her," Evie's father said to the duke. "You should have prepared her."

Evie stared at Evesham. "How did you find him?"

"I and a few other gentlemen are alerted when noblemen are released from prison. We provide for their transport here and ensure they find any missing family."

Lucien's father did this? "Why?"

"I should think it would be obvious. They were treated quite badly by their homeland. We show them how much more dignified the English are."

Her father chuckled. "The duke is full of bluster. These Englishmen like to reunite families. I have heard stories about them."

Evie had great difficulty reconciling this information with the man Lucien had told her about for years. There was no way Lucien knew anything about this. Which was a shame, because the duke could find no better partner in such work.

"Lucien has no idea what you do," she said softly, but with a slight accusatory edge.

The duke shrugged. "I'm new to this. Someone in the group died last year, and I was merely filling in while they searched for someone new." He cocked his head. "It was Lord Witney, if that interests you."

Evie squeezed her father's hand. She had her father back, which was more than a miracle, and it was due to the work done by the father of the man she loved? She could scarcely believe that was possible. Or that it had happened to her. This had to be a dream.

"It definitely interests me since I am to wed his son, Lord Gregory." She turned to her father and raised one hand to touch his cheek. His skin was dry, and she made a note to provide him with some cream. "Are you real?"

He smiled at her with such love that she nearly lost her legs again. "I am, and I am never letting you leave me again. I'm so sorry, ma fille."

"I'm sorry about Maman," she said, tears slipping from her eyes. "I don't even remember her."

"What a tragedy." He pulled her close and hugged her tightly. Evie had never felt such an embrace. It was protection and compassion, and most of all, unconditional love.

She cried for some time, wetting his cravat. When she finally pulled back, she tried to smile. "I've watered you quite thoroughly, I'm afraid."

"Not to worry," he said in French.

"I want to hear everything," she said, using French in return.

His eyes shone with pride. "You speak our language! And so beautifully. Does your sister too?"

"Yes. You must meet her. In fact, I am leaving today to travel to her house in Oxfordshire."

"What about this man you are to marry? Where is he?"

"I am here." Gregory stood near the duke.

Evie wanted to throw herself into his arms and cry again, but she didn't want to let her father go. "How long have you been here?" she asked.

"Long enough to see a magnificent reunion. This is your father?"

"I can't believe it, but yes. Papa—" Evie turned her head toward her father. "May I call you Papa?"

"Oh yes, please." He wiped a tear from his eye.

"Papa, allow me to present my betrothed, Lord Gregory Blakemore. Gregory, this is my father, Monsieur Henri Avenses. Or perhaps you prefer Henry Aviers," she said, glancing at her father in question. He only waved his hand in response, as if to say it didn't matter.

Gregory came forward and extended his hand. "It is my great honor to meet you, sir."

"I am delighted to meet the man who will make my daughter happy." Papa looked to her. "He makes you happy?"

"More than I've ever been. Will you come with us?"

"I think I must. I can't keep living on the kindness of men like the duke." Papa glanced toward Evesham, who stood with his hands clasped behind his back and his gaze fixed toward the windows, as if the scene in the drawing room bored him. More accurately, it likely made him uncomfortable.

"We are honored to help," the duke said gruffly.

Evie looked to Gregory. "Before you arrived, the duke explained that he works with a group of gentlemen who help Frenchmen find their missing families here in England. He has been filling a space following the death of another member—your father. Did you know anything about that?"

Gregory's eyes widened briefly. "A little. I believe he mentioned it once, but I didn't even think of it when you told me of your family."

"Why would you?" Evie asked. "We thought my father was dead."

Gregory turned to the duke. "You asked Lucien her father's name the other day. You somehow made the connection between this man and her. I don't mind telling you how shocked I am to hear you would do this. Pleasantly so, but still shocked."

"I don't have to explain myself to you," Evesham said with considerable hauteur.

"No, you do not. Whatever your reasons, I am most grateful. You should tell Lucien about this."

The duke wrinkled his nose briefly, which told Evie all she needed to know—he didn't want Lucien to hear of it. "I suppose you will."

"You couldn't stop me," Gregory vowed, and Evie had never loved him more. "One of these days, the two of you are going to have to show each other the best of yourselves."

The duke turned his attention to Evie's father. "I'll have your things taken out to Lord Gregory's coach, which I presume is outside."

"It is," Gregory said. "Thank you. This is the best wedding gift we could have received."

"You're truly getting married?" the duke asked.

"Yes." Gregory offered his hand to the duke. "I trust we have your support?"

Evesham glanced at Evie, then back to Gregory. He

emitted a low growl—a sound Lucien sometimes made—and shook Gregory's hand. Then he took himself off.

"I see he's conflicted about supporting me," Evie said.

"Why is that?" her father asked.

Evie's heart clenched. "I have so much to tell you, Papa. Not all of it is good, I'm afraid. I hope you will still look at me with love when Heloise and I have told you about our lives."

"Of course I will, ma fille. I could never love you any less. You and your sister are my heart. I only wish your mother were here to see how you've grown. You are the fulfillment of the dreams we had together."

Evie was going to cry again, but she suspected she was going to be a watering pot for some time. Between Gregory's love and discovering her father was alive, she was beyond grateful.

She took her father's arm and started toward the door. Gregory moved to walk just behind them. "Papa, I can't wait for you to see Heloise and meet her husband, Alfred. He is so kind and clever. You will also meet their son, Henry."

"I have a grandson?" Now tears fell from his eyes.

Gregory thrust a handkerchief into his hand.

"You do." Evie squeezed his arm as they continued on. "You also have a grand-dog, whom you will meet in the coach."

"A grand-dog?" He sounded perplexed.

Evie laughed. At the top of the stairs, she turned her head to look at Gregory. "Will you mind if we make a quick stop before we leave town?"

"I think we must."

She nodded. There needed to be a conversation with Lucien, and it couldn't wait.

CHAPTER 21

*R*eynolds, Lucien's fearsome butler, narrowed his eyes slightly at Gregory and Evie. "His lordship has not yet risen."

"I realize it's early," Evie said, giving him a smile that should have made him want to do anything she asked. "However, we are on our way out of town, and we have urgent information for Lord Lucien. He won't mind that you wake him."

The butler narrowed his eyes even more, so they were barely more than slits. It seemed clear he was not in agreement. He frowned at Evie. "If anyone else were asking, I'd say no."

"As you should." Evie preceded Gregory into the entry hall. "We'll just wait in Lucien's study. Please tell him we need to be quick."

This made the butler's brows practically fly off his forehead. He closed the door and took himself off.

"I hate leaving Papa in the coach," Evie said.

"It's best for Ash." Gregory laughed. "He was not looking

forward to being left alone again. Besides, I don't think Henri minded."

"He didn't, did he?" she murmured, her eyes glowing with a warmth and happiness that he hoped would always be there.

Once they were in Lucien's study, Gregory took one of the chairs while Evie paced. She glanced at Gregory, her brow puckered. "Perhaps we shouldn't have come."

"Lucien should know what his father did."

She paused in the middle of the room. "I agree, but we could have waited until we returned."

"That will be several weeks from now. It's best if we do it today."

Nodding, she resumed her pacing for a few more minutes before abandoning the endeavor and sitting near Gregory. "Do you think it's possible the duke decided to step in after your father died because he was inspired by Lucien's kindness?"

"I couldn't say. Their relationship seems rather contentious." On the short ride from Evesham House, Gregory had told her about the visit he'd paid to Lucien the other day when his father had interrupted. He had not, however, told her what the duke had said about her.

"Yes." She exhaled. "I doubt it's that, but it would have been nice for Lucien."

Gregory touched her hand. "I think it's still nice for Lucien."

"What's nice for me?" Lucien strolled into the study wearing a banyan, his hair unkempt and his jaw shadowed.

"We're sorry to intrude at such an early hour," Evie said.

"And yet, here you are." Lucien smiled blandly as he flopped into his favorite chair. "You have good news?"

"I think so," Evie said, a smile teasing her mouth. "The most amazing thing has happened. My father is alive."

Lucien bolted upright. "What?"

"He was in a prison in France and was recently released. A group of men here in England help people like him—those who are seeking family here."

"After all this time... How did he manage to find you?"

Evie scooted forward to the edge of her chair. "That's the most astonishing part. This group of men actually included Gregory's father until he died." She glanced toward Gregory. "Someone else stepped into his place, and he arranged for my father to meet me this morning. Lucien, it was your father."

Lucien stared at her in silence. Eventually, his eyes narrowed, and he gripped the arms of his chair. His jaw tightened, and he pressed his lips together.

"Isn't this marvelous?" Evie asked. "I confess I was shocked. I still am, really. We wanted you to know straightaway."

"That sanctimonious ass!" Lucien vaulted from the chair and stalked to the fireplace. He braced his hand on the mantel and looked into the fire. "How dare he?"

Evie looked to Gregory, who wasn't entirely certain how to react. "How dare he...help?" Gregory asked.

Lucien pushed away from the mantel and whipped around, his features taut and angry. "How dare he take me to task for helping others. Then he goes and does *this*."

"Perhaps you inspired him," Evie suggested, repeating what she'd told Gregory in a hopeful tone.

Snorting, Lucien sent her a sarcastic glower. "You know that isn't likely."

"What other reason could there be?" Gregory asked.

"Annoying me," Lucien bit out.

Evie frowned at him. "Except he's been at this for months and you weren't aware. He actually brought my father and me together, Lucien. He's done a wonderful thing."

"There has to be a reason. It wasn't out of the kindness of his nonexistent heart." Lucien looked to Gregory. "You heard him the other day. He chastised me for hiring my former mistress."

"Did he?" Evie looked to Gregory.

"I didn't think that bore mentioning," Gregory murmured.

Lucien continued, "He would no sooner help her cross the street than reunite her with her father. There has to be some nefarious purpose motivating him."

Gregory hadn't imagined the conversation with Lucien going this way. He'd known their relationship was fraught, but he'd hoped this would go toward healing it.

"Where are you going?" Lucien snapped his gaze to Evie's, then to Gregory's. "Reynolds said you were on your way out of town."

"We are going to Oxfordshire, to my sister's," Evie said. "We're getting married."

Lucien's expression changed completely. "Are you?" He smiled broadly. "I'm so happy for you both." He fixed on Evie, adding softly, "Especially you."

"Thank you. Between this decision and the discovery of my father, I am quite overwhelmed with happiness. I'd hoped to share some of it with you by telling you about your father's act. Whatever his motive, he has done me a great and wonderful kindness."

"And you're taking your father with you?" Lucien asked. He glanced around. "Where is he?"

"We left him in the coach with Ash," Gregory responded.

"Bloody hell, that's unacceptable. I need to meet him." He pinned Evie with a dark stare. "But first, I must remind you that my father is cold and callous. He was likely hoping you'd take your father to meet your sister and stay there. He can't help but meddle."

"How is he meddling?" Evie asked.

"By getting you out of town away from the Phoenix Club."

"I'm already away from the Phoenix Club," she said, sounding somewhat exasperated.

"Yes, and that was a mistake," Lucien declared. "I refuse to accept your resignation."

Evie leaned forward. "You can't." She glanced toward Gregory, hesitating. Then she returned her focus to Lucien. "You were told I had to leave. Furthermore, even if I were allowed to stay, the club will falter."

Gregory didn't know who had told Lucien that Evie had to leave, but he had the sense she would tell him. She'd said there would be no more secrets, and he trusted her.

Lucien waved his hand. "I don't care. If I submit to others' demands and shun you, I can't say I uphold the ideals of the club. They're going to have to accept my decision." He shook his head as he looked at her imploringly. "You have to stay. Please."

"I don't know whom you are both referring to, but Lucien is right that you must remain at the club," Gregory said, admiring Lucien's integrity, even if it might be slightly motivated by wanting to tweak his father. Keeping Evie at the club would definitely do that.

Evie turned to Gregory. "You think I should stay at the club?"

"We're going away for a month. When we return, you will be Lady Evangeline Blakemore." He cocked his head. "Or would you prefer to be Lady Mirabelle?"

"I am Evie now. Though Mirabelle will always be a part of me. Hopefully, my father will understand."

"Does he know…about you and Heloise?" Lucien asked.

"Not yet. We've a long journey in which to break the news."

Lucien went to Evie's chair and took her hand. "He'll understand."

"Why, because he's my father? You and your father are an excellent example of blood being of no consequence," she said dryly.

Gregory thought of his brother and couldn't help but agree.

"While that is true, that will not be the case with your father," Lucien said with a note of certainty. "I assume your reunion was wonderful; otherwise, you would not be here telling me all about it and making my father out to be some sort of good Samaritan."

"It was wonderful," Evie said. "I shouldn't leave him any longer." She rose.

Lucien put his hand on her arm. "First, you have to agree to stay at the club—as a member and a patroness."

"If I agree, will you let me fetch my father?"

Grinning, Lucien wrapped her in a hug. Gregory smiled, feeling no jealousy. They really were just the closest of friends, and he was glad they had each other.

Lucien let her go. "I am so happy for you both." He sent Gregory a warm glance.

"Thank you." Evie narrowed her eyes slightly. "Yes, I will stay at the club, but some people still won't like it. And I'm not entirely certain it's because I was a courtesan. I don't think they like that I'm a woman with an important job at a popular membership club. The same probably goes for Ada."

"You may be right, but ultimately, their reasons for being judgmental don't matter. If they're going to have a problem with you—or Ada—then they are not worthy of membership," Lucien said haughtily. "I will gleefully expel them if they don't leave of their own accord."

Evie shook her head with a faint smile as she left the

study. Gregory remained behind. "Are you certain this is what's right for the club?"

"Yes. It can't be a haven for people like Evie if it fails to be a haven for Evie herself. And what good am I doing with the club if I can't wield whatever power it gives me to do what is right and proper?"

Gregory couldn't argue with that. "You are a singular man. I know you don't want to hear this, but you may find you and your father are not that unalike. I hope you'll give yourself—and him—the chance to work that out."

Lucien's eyes glittered with dark promise, and Gregory wondered if there was something else going on. There was an underlying tension to him—an unease that seemed to go beyond the news they'd given him today. "Oh, I intend to get to the bottom of this entire affair," Lucien vowed. "Of that you can be sure."

CHAPTER 22

Three weeks later
Witney, Oxfordshire

*E*vie still couldn't believe she was married or that her father had actually given her away to the groom. The drawing room at Threadbury Hall was nearly overflowing with well-wishers, many of whom worked next door at Witney Court. They were thrilled to see Gregory happily wed, and Evie was so glad Gregory could feel that, especially in the absence of any of his immediate family. Some of his aunts and uncles and cousins were in attendance as well. It was an almost overwhelming number of people.

Gregory had never looked happier, which was saying a great deal since he was perhaps the most amenable person she'd ever met—Sir Cheerful, indeed. He and Ada seemed to have been cut from the same cloth.

Ada and Max had come for the wedding, and he and Gregory had struck up a friendship, primarily over horses.

Since neither Evie nor Ada rode, the two of them went riding together. That had left Ada and Evie to shop in the village, which had allowed them to discuss what was happening in London.

Unfortunately, the club *was* suffering. At least two dozen people had resigned their membership, and many more had simply stopped coming. The last two Tuesdays had been uncharacteristically quiet. Evie had asked how Lucien was doing. Ada said he was tense, but tried not to show it.

Evie felt a pull to return despite their plans to remain another week. She would hate to leave her father, but he absolutely loved Oxfordshire. He stood with Heloise, holding his namesake in his arms. Henry was enthralled with his grandpapa. Evie and Heloise had finally stopped crying about it.

Evie had waited to tell their father about their past work until she and Heloise could do so together. He'd sat silent while Evie and Heloise held hands, worried for his reaction. Tears falling from his eyes, he'd assured them both that he could never love them any less and that he was proud of them for not just surviving but flourishing. He'd gone on to say that he'd learned to leave the past behind. To focus on it brought misery and it was nearly impossible to look forward. They'd hugged one another tightly and vowed to live in the moment and anticipate the future—together.

Her mind returned to the club. Perhaps she oughtn't return at all. She was, after all, the problem.

Ada sailed toward her. "Evie, why are you alone in the corner?"

"I just needed a moment's peace. And this way, I can see what a good time everyone is having. Honestly, Ada, I can't believe there are this many people who would wish us well."

"There are many more back in London. I have quite the celebration planned at the club."

Evie turned toward her, unable to keep her concern buried even though it was her wedding day. "Are you sure that's wise? I've been thinking about everything you told me, how the club has been affected. I wish I could be there to support Lucien, but I'm wondering if I should stay away."

"He wouldn't want you to. In fact, he told me to make sure you came back, at least by April."

That was in a few weeks. It wouldn't be a hardship to remain in Oxfordshire awhile longer with her newly expanded family. And Gregory would do whatever she wished. He was incredibly supportive and almost irritatingly adaptable. Almost nothing ruffled him.

Almost.

They'd visited Witney Court on a few occasions so that he could pack some things he wished to take to London. He truly didn't plan on returning. This upset the retainers, and that, in turn, upset Gregory. It was clear they all preferred Gregory to his brother, particularly since the marquess planned to add a large ostentatious wing to the back of the house. There was simply no need for it, other than extravagance, and the work would cause considerable disruption.

"What do you think I should do?" Evie asked.

"I think you should do whatever makes *you* happy. Who cares what anyone thinks or does? Lucien doesn't. I don't. Gregory doesn't."

"That isn't the issue—I don't want to cause more trouble for the club. Lucien has worked too hard to see it fail."

"I don't think we're anywhere close to that," Ada said.

Evie couldn't tell her what she knew, that Lucien didn't own the club, that he'd gone against the other owners by allowing Evie to stay. What if they forced him out somehow, and the club was no longer his?

"I'll discuss it with Gregory." Evie glanced toward him at the same moment he looked at her. Even from across a large room, she could see the love and heat in his gaze. She hoped it would never fade. She loved him with every part of her being, so totally that it frightened her.

But it seemed love lost could sometimes be found—not that she thought of her father's return as anything other than a miracle. She was so thankful.

"You're happy, aren't you?" Ada asked, sounding concerned.

"Of course. Why wouldn't I be?"

Ada shook her head. "Forget I asked. You're worried about Lucien."

"I am. It's an odd sensation."

This made Ada laugh. "He's always taking care of everything and everyone. He eases worries, but I suppose in doing so, he may carry the largest burden of all."

"I couldn't help feeling he was more affected than he let on by what happened," Evie said, thinking about the day they'd departed London. "When Gregory and I saw him before we left town, he seemed…unsettled. Is that how you saw him?"

Ada was slow to respond. "Yes, I think so." She grimaced. "It pains me to say it."

"We aren't being critical. We just want to help, if we can."

"Yes, it's high time someone helps him for once." Evie pondered how they might do that. "If there are forces in Society who are seeking to ruin the club, we need to find a way to counteract that—if we can." She wasn't sure that would even be possible since those forces might very well hold majority ownership in the club. She wished she'd asked Lucien for specific information.

It seemed she had a reason to return.

"All right," Evie said. "You've convinced me to return as scheduled."

"Brilliant! Now, it's time for you to stop lurking." Ada looped her arm through Evie's.

"I wasn't lurking. I was counting my blessings."

Ada gave her the brightest of smiles. "My dearest friend, I couldn't be happier for anyone. Ever."

Evie laughed. "Thank you. Let's go talk to my father. He likes you immensely."

"Does he? He might turn my head. Don't tell Max."

Laughing again, Evie strolled across the room to her family. To *most* of her family—Gregory was now speaking with some of the people from Witney Court.

"Puppy!" Henry wriggled in his grandpapa's arms as Ash trotted into the room. He wore a bright blue bow around his neck and looked quite dashing. Henry adored Ash, and now Heloise and Alfred were discussing getting a dog of their own.

Evie's father set his grandson down, and Henry immediately went to play with Ash, who was more than happy to oblige.

Turning to Evie, Papa smiled. "There you are, ma fille. Such a lovely day. Your mother is smiling down on all of us."

"I hope so," Evie said, glancing at Heloise, whose expression was bittersweet.

"I know so," Papa said, beaming at his daughters. "Now, when can I make a toast to my beautiful daughter and her new husband?"

Heloise patted his arm. "Right now, Papa. I'll have the footmen bring the champagne."

~

*L*ater that evening, Evie slipped into bed with her new husband, delighted that at last they could officially share a chamber. Ash had taken turns sleeping in their rooms, but more often than not, Evie and Gregory spent at least part of the night in the other's chamber.

Worn out from the celebrations, Ash was currently snoring softly in front of the fire.

"He is so cute," Evie said, watching the dog sleep.

"He was especially so in that bow. Where did you get that?"

"In town when I was shopping with Ada the other day. I'm so glad she and Max could come. You two seem to be getting along well."

"We're concocting a scheme to teach you and Ada how to ride." He held up his hand. "Don't try to dissuade us. Just let us plan, and you can disappoint us later."

Evie giggled as she snuggled up against him. "Ada and I talked about Lucien earlier. I confess I'm worried about the club—and him. There's something I haven't told anyone—because he swore me to secrecy, and I am the *only* person who knows this." She turned her body to look up at him. "Will you keep this secret?"

"Your secrets are my secrets, even if they are Lucien's too. I am honored that you would share it with me—and glad, since I hope we will share everything now that we are married."

"Lucien isn't the sole owner of the Phoenix Club. I told you about the two anonymous members of the membership committee, that they wanted Lucien to expel me in order for the club to maintain its integrity." She'd explained that at one point on the ride to Oxfordshire when her father was napping. "They are part owners of the club. I didn't learn that until just before we left London. Since I am not leaving the club as they demanded, I need to know if they're going to force him out or not. I couldn't bear it if he lost the club. I won't let that happen. I'll leave, and nothing you or he or anyone says will stop me."

Gregory nodded grimly. "I understand. And I'll support whatever you decide is necessary. I'll also do what I can to help you get to the bottom of things."

"Thank you, because I don't know if I want to talk to Lucien about it or not. I know who one of the anonymous members is."

"Do you?" He chuckled. "You're too clever. Let me know how I can help."

"I will—you will be my partner in this."

He swiftly rolled her to her back, provoking a gasp as he settled his weight over her. "I would like to be your partner in everything." He kissed her neck, the hollow of her throat, the rise of her breast over the edge of her night rail.

"Partner, husband, lover, friend. You *are* everything." She cupped his face, drawing his gaze to hers. "I love you so, my darling."

"And my heart beats only for you, my love." He turned his head and kissed her palm.

Then he showed her the very best way to partner.

EPILOGUE

March, London

"Yes, those are definitely Ash's puppies." Gregory sent an amused look toward Evie, who stood beside Mrs. Kirby. Mr. Kirby wasn't with them in the small sitting room where Bess and her puppies were ensconced.

"Do you think he'd like to meet them?" Mrs. Kirby asked.

"Probably. We'll bring him by whenever you say it's convenient."

Mrs. Kirby glanced toward Evie. "I'll send word when Mr. Kirby isn't at home. I think that would be best."

Gregory wasn't surprised to hear it. Kirby was likely disappointed the puppies were not purebred miniature greyhounds.

"They are absolutely adorable," Evie said, crouching down next to the three-sided crate where the mother was currently feeding her brood of four babies. "Gregory and I wondered if you and Mr. Kirby might let us have two of them—one for us and one for our nephew who fell in love with Ash."

"I'm sure Mr. Kirby would like it if you took all four of them, but one of the neighbors down the street did ask to have one. Their young daughters love dogs. Might your nephew want two puppies instead of one?"

"I'm confident he would," Evie said with a laugh. "I'd say we should let my sister and brother-in-law decide, but I think they would also approve. Give your neighbors the first pick, and we'll happily take the rest."

Mrs. Kirby exhaled with relief. "Wonderful. This will please Mr. Kirby. I'll let you know when you can bring Ash over."

They chatted a few more minutes before Gregory escorted Evie from the house for their next appointment. They walked down the street to Evie's house where Gregory's coach awaited them. Gregory had moved in when they'd returned to London a few days earlier.

"Should we fetch Ash before we go?" Evie asked.

"We could, but I confess I was looking forward to having you alone in the coach without him." Ash had been an energetic presence during their journey from Witney to London, requiring frequent stops.

Smiling, Evie said, "All right. Just you and me, then."

Gregory handed her into the coach. "It's not a terribly long ride to Richmond, but it will be pleasant to have the coach to ourselves."

Evie sat on the rear-facing seat, and he snuggled in beside her, reaching for the blanket to drape over their legs. As the coach moved forward, Gregory kissed Evie's cheek.

She turned her head. "What was that for?"

"Do I need a reason?"

She pressed herself against him. "Never. Do you really think it's wise for us to look at this house in Richmond?

Perhaps we should make sure we have enough to found the ladies' club first."

"I know you doubt that we do, but we went over everything with Al, Heloise, and your father at Threadbury Hall. Everyone is in agreement that the ladies' club is an excellent business proposition, and with Al and Heloise's investment, we have plenty of our own funds to purchase a house for respite outside London." They'd discussed their desire to have an escape but didn't want to be too far from the city Evie loved.

"Then I suppose I must tell Lucien about it soon. I fear he'll feel betrayed that I wish to open another club."

"I think he will be wholly supportive. It won't compete with the Phoenix Club."

"He's rather tense just now," Evie said, her tone concerned.

They'd seen him last night, and he'd been guarded about the club. Evie still worried that her staying was a mistake.

"He is optimistic things will improve," Gregory murmured. "He said the night before last was their best attendance in weeks."

Evie frowned. "But it's half of what it was before my past was exposed. What if people only came because they'd heard we were back in town and they hoped to see us?"

Gregory shrugged. "If it gets people into the club, who cares?" He angled his body toward hers. "Unless that upsets you."

"Not particularly. I don't enjoy being a pariah, but I can't worry what other people think or say about me."

He reached to cup her other cheek and turn her head toward his so he could place another kiss on her lips. "I admire you so very much."

"I have everything I want. It seems silly to be bothered by things I can't control." She kissed him back, then pressed her shoulders against the squab and stretched her neck, revealing a small but tantalizing patch of flesh. "Now, tell me again how many rooms this house has?"

Gregory couldn't think of anything but kissing that delectable spot. So he did. "Mmm, I can't remember just now."

"Are you still intent on hiring some of your brother's London retainers away from his household?"

"Most definitely." He continued kissing her neck.

Evie giggled. "Can't you wait until we're on the way back to London?"

He pressed his lips beneath her ear. "Why not now *and* on the way back?"

"I've created an insatiable beast." She arched her neck to give him even more access with his mouth. "And you used to be such an impeccable gentleman."

Lifting his head, he looked into her captivating blue eyes. "You've created nothing. I am the man I've always been, just waiting for an impeccable lady."

She gave him a saucy smile. "I don't know that I've ever been *that*, but I was waiting for you too—I just didn't know it."

"All thanks to a dog," he said with a soft laugh before returning his lips to her neck.

She took his hat off and ran her fingers through his hair. "Ash completely changed my life. I never dreamed of such happiness with you and with my father returned." Her voice caught, and Gregory lifted his gaze to hers once more.

"Don't for a moment think you don't deserve it. I'm going to make sure all your days are filled with joy and laughter."

"You can't guarantee that, Sir Cheerful, but I believe you will do your best, and I trust you more than I've ever trusted anyone in my life." She touched his cheek and looked at him with emotion so deep, it stole his breath. "Thank you."

February, the day Evie and Gregory left London

ucien ignored the surprised look on his father's butler's face as he entered Evesham House. Bender's gaze had dipped to Lucien's *white* cravat. "I know what you're thinking," Lucien said grouchily.

"It's good to see you, my lord," Bender said evenly.

Lucien glanced down at his cravat. "Do you think the duke will notice?"

"He'll never tell you."

No, he would not. Still, it was the best white flag—since it was literally white—that Lucien had for this frustratingly necessary meeting. "Shall I go to his study?"

Bender inclined his head. "Of course."

Sometime after Evie and Gregory had left his house, Lucien had sent a note to the duke requesting a meeting. It galled him to do this, but there was simply no other way.

Lucien walked stiffly, his head high, to the study. As usual, the duke sat behind his desk, reading or scribbling—today it was the latter—until he deigned to register Lucien's presence.

After a few minutes, the duke looked up. His gaze lingered briefly on the cravat, and Lucien was glad he'd gone to the trouble, even if it was supremely annoying.

"This is a surprising meeting. Sit."

Lucien would normally do the opposite, but he needed the man's help, so he sat. He kept his spine rigid away from the back of the chair. "I'll get right to the reason for my visit. As you undoubtedly know, my club has become a bit...notorious of late."

"Your club has always been notorious," the duke said with mild derision. "Isn't that what you wanted?"

Gritting his teeth, Lucien tamped down his irritation. It wouldn't do to lose his temper. "That was not my goal, but I can't say that I care." Damn, this was even harder than he'd anticipated. Perhaps there was another way. There had to be. "On second thought, never mind." Lucien stood and turned toward the door.

"You want money."

Lucien clenched his right hand into a fist and winced as if the words his father had uttered were a knife in his back. How had he known?

Reluctantly, Lucien turned. "Yes," he replied softly. "I need to buy out an investor in the club."

The duke's eyes narrowed. "It isn't that simple, and I think you know that. If you don't, you aren't as smart as I've given you credit for."

Lucien nearly laughed. "You've never given me credit for anything."

"You can't force the Foreign Office out, Lucien. Not with money and not with anything else."

Shock jolted through Lucien, along with a frigid fury. The scheme behind the Phoenix Club, that it was primarily a place for the Foreign Office to conduct necessary business, was known only to a handful of people. "How the hell do you know about that?"

Lifting his shoulders in a gentle shrug, the duke simply said, "I'm a meddler." His eyes, so much like Lucien's own, darkened. "Like you."

The anger pulsing in Lucien grew white hot. First the business with Evie's father, now this? "We are *nothing* alike." Lucien's voice and hands shook.

The duke slammed his fist on his desk and vaulted to his feet. "Dammit, Lucien, stop being such a sullen brat. You knew what you were getting into when you agreed to this deal. You can't change the arrangement now."

The arrangement had been a club that Lucien would style as a haven for all manner of people. This allowed for a variety of characters to frequent the club—individuals doing work for or with the Foreign Office whose presence wouldn't draw notice. *"They* are changing the arrangement." Lucien curled his lip. "They don't get to dictate whom I employ."

The Foreign Office had given Lucien free rein when it came to the club's management, but Lucien had always been aware it wasn't really his club. And dammit, he wanted it to be.

"They get to dictate *everything.*"

The fact that his father knew this much meant he had to know more. "You've always been so disappointed that I was wounded in Spain and had to come home. How long have you known I work for them?"

"That hardly signifies."

He was right. Because regardless of when he'd found out, he hadn't changed his opinion or treatment of his middle child. "Nothing I do will ever matter to you, will it?"

Lucien didn't actually want to hear the answer. He swiftly raised his hand. "Never mind. I haven't needed your support in a long time, and I don't need it now. I don't need it ever." He turned and stalked toward the door.

"You can't buy them out," the duke called after him.

Tearing at the offensive white cravat he'd worn like a bloody sycophant, Lucien strode to the entry hall. He took his hat and gloves from Bender without a word and quit the house.

He bloody well *would* buy them out. The Foreign Office wasn't going to tell him he couldn't have Evie at the club. Her presence wouldn't affect anything they sought to accomplish via the club. It could still host secret meetings and offer shelter to those in need. *Nothing* had to change.

What, then, was really going on?

Lucien vowed to find out.

Don't miss the exciting conclusion to the Phoenix Club series when Lucien must fight for his club and deal with his tenuous relationship with his father, all while trying desperately not to fall for his best friend's sister who wants his help with her research of...mating rituals. What could go wrong?

Preorder INSATIABLE now!

Would you like to know when my next book is available and to hear about sales and deals? **Sign up for my VIP newsletter** which is the only place you can get bonus books and material such as the short prequel to the Phoenix Club series, INVITATION, and the exciting prequel to Legendary Rogues, THE LEGEND OF A ROGUE.

Join me on social media!

Facebook: https://facebook.com/DarcyBurkeFans
Twitter at @darcyburke
Instagram at darcyburkeauthor
Pinterest at darcyburkewrite

And follow me on Bookbub to receive updates on pre-orders, new releases, and deals!

Need more Regency romance? Check out my other historical series:

The Matchmaking Chronicles
The course of true love never runs smooth. Sometimes a little matchmaking is required. When couples meet at a house party, what could go wrong?

Lords in Love
A new six-book series from me and my BFF, NYT Bestseller, Erica Ridley! Coming in 2023!
For those in want of a husband or wife, there is no better time or place to find one's true love than the annual May Day Matchmaking Festival in Marrywell, England. Princes and paupers alike fall head over heels, sometimes with the person they least expect...

The Untouchables
Swoon over twelve of Society's most eligible and elusive bachelor peers and the bluestockings, wallflowers, and outcasts who bring them to their knees!

The Untouchables: The Spitfire Society
Meet the smart, independent women who've decided they don't need Society's rules, their families' expectations, or, most importantly, a husband. But just because they don't need a man doesn't mean they might not *want* one...

The Untouchables: The Pretenders
Set in the captivating world of The Untouchables, follow the saga of a trio of siblings who excel at being something they're not. Can a dauntless Bow Street Runner, a devastated viscount, and a disillusioned Society miss unravel their secrets?

Wicked Dukes Club
Six books written by me and my BFF, NYT Bestselling
Author Erica Ridley. Meet the unforgettable men of
London's most notorious tavern, The Wicked Duke.
Seductively handsome, with charm and wit to spare, one
night with these rakes and rogues will never be enough...

Love is All Around
Heartwarming Regency-set retellings of classic Christmas
stories (written after the Regency!) featuring a cozy village,
three siblings, and the best gift of all: love.

Secrets and Scandals
Six epic stories set in London's glittering ballrooms and
England's lush countryside.

Legendary Rogues
Five intrepid heroines and adventurous heroes embark on
exciting quests across the Georgian Highlands and Regency
England and Wales!

If you like contemporary romance, I hope you'll check out
my **Ribbon Ridge** series available from Avon Impulse, and
the continuation of Ribbon Ridge in **So Hot**.

I hope you'll consider leaving a review at your favorite
online vendor or networking site!

I appreciate my readers so much. Thank you, thank you,
thank you.

ALSO BY DARCY BURKE

Historical Romance

The Phoenix Club

Improper

Impassioned

Intolerable

Indecent

Impossible

Irresistible

Impeccable

Insatiable

The Matchmaking Chronicles

The Rigid Duke

The Bachelor Earl (also prequel to *The Untouchables*)

The Runaway Viscount

Lords in Love

Coming in 2023!

Beguiling the Duke by Darcy Burke

Taming the Rake by Erica Ridley

Romancing the Heiress by Darcy Burke

Defying the Earl by Erica Ridley

Matching the Marquess by Darcy Burke

Chasing the Bride by Erica Ridley

ABOUT THE AUTHOR

Darcy Burke is the USA Today Bestselling Author of sexy, emotional historical and contemporary romance. Darcy wrote her first book at age 11, a happily ever after about a swan addicted to magic and the female swan who loved him, with exceedingly poor illustrations. Join her Reader Club newsletter for the latest updates from Darcy.

A native Oregonian, Darcy lives on the edge of wine country with her guitar-strumming husband, incredibly talented artist daughter, and imaginative son who will almost certainly out-write her one day (that may be tomorrow). They're a crazy cat family with two Bengal cats, a small, fame-seeking cat named after a fruit, an older rescue Maine Coon with attitude to spare, an adorable former stray who wandered onto their deck and into their hearts, and two bonded boys who used to belong to (separate) neighbors but chose them instead. You can find Darcy at a winery, in her comfy writing chair, folding laundry (which she loves), or binge-watching TV with the family. Her happy places are Disneyland, Labor Day weekend at the Gorge, Denmark, and anywhere in the UK—so long as her family is there too. Visit Darcy online at www.darcyburke.com and follow her on social media.

CPSIA information can be obtained
at www.ICGtesting.com
Printed in the USA
LVHW101947271022
731745LV00003B/587